THE BOOK -
LEGEND OF SHIVANI

DR VARSHA GOGTE-DEOPUJARI

To

The Almighty

and

My late parents, Hemant and Dr. Madhuri Gogte

and

My Readers

Dr. Varsha Gogte-Deopujari

TABLE OF CONTENTS

CHAPTER ONE

AN UPROOTED LIFE

"Christina!" Ann bellowed, storming inside her house. There was no reply. She hurled her purse over a nearby table and raced up the stairs. Throwing an agitated glance at the closed door of Christina's room, she halted momentarily in front of it. Loud music spilled out from under the door. Ann knocked but heard no response. Smoldering with anger, she immediately pushed open the door and gasped at what she saw.

It was complete chaos. Papers, books, CDs, clothes, empty Coke cans, and chip crumbs littered the room. Sprawled over the clutter like a queen was her daughter, Christina. Gazing at the ceiling with a vacant expression, she seemed to be lost in her own world. Shaking her head in frustration, Ann stepped inside. Christina simply threw her an indifferent glance and kept staring at the ceiling, angering Ann further.

"Christina! Why aren't you ready yet?" Ann pursed her lips, waiting for a response that never came. "Are you listening to me?" she demanded.

Christina looked at her mom for a moment and suddenly screamed, "Can't you ask me nicely?"

"Do not scream at me like that! I am your mother!" Ann's lips quivered with anger as she kicked the boom box to shut it off. "Don't you remember that Aunt Sheila is coming today? I remember telling you this several times, and you…you agreed to come with me to pick her up at the airport!"

"Yes! I do remember." With her voice full of bitterness, Christina continued, "But now…I…I have decided not to come with you."

Hearing Christina's decision, Ann slowly sat down on the floor. She had really wanted Christina to come to the airport to welcome her sister. After a few moments of silence, Ann moved closer to Christina. Gently running her fingers through Christina's hair, she asked softly, "Hon, can I ask you a question? Why don't you want to come? Don't you like Aunt Sheila?"

Christina didn't answer.

Ann continued, "Chris! You are Aunt Sheila's only niece, and she loves you very much. Do you remember when she visited us last time? You would climb onto her lap as she sat on the sofa, and she would hold you and tell you stories." Christina moved slightly. Taking this as a sign that her persuasion was working, Ann squeezed Christina's hand gently and continued. "All these years, she was working far, far away from us, as a United States Ambassador in India. It wasn't possible for her to visit us for a long time…even after your dad's accident."

Ann's voice wavered slightly. "But I can imagine how desperate she would be all these months just to see us. Chris, she loves us a lot. We are her family...the only family she has. Today, she is coming straight to us after retiring from her job. Your aunt is coming home! I am sure she must be counting down every second, every moment... just to see us again." With a final, pleading look, Ann said, "Christina, please come to the airport."

Without saying anything, Christina got up. Ann beamed with joy.

On their way to the airport, Ann could not control her enthusiasm and kept telling Christina about her own childhood. Sheila was Ann's older sister. The two were best friends, and after their parents passed away, Sheila became Ann's father, mother, sister, and guardian too. Ann was so thrilled with the idea of seeing her again that she was positively bouncing in her seat.

Oblivious to her mom's excited chatter, Christina stared out the window. Buildings, trees, houses, and shops ran backward, their colors blurring together. Looking at them, Christina's mind too receded back in time.

Just a few months earlier, Christina's life had been a picture-perfect fairy tale embellished in gold. Along with her mother and father, she enjoyed her life, living in a big Californian house complete with a marble fountain encompassed by a circular driveway. Being an only child, her each and every wish was eagerly fulfilled. She was the beloved princess of the house. Surprisingly, the extreme love didn't spoil Christina. She remained an obedient, pleasant, kind-hearted girl. At school, too, she was very well received and adored for being a bright, sincere, hard-working student.

Then, out of the blue, the heartbreaking news of her father's death in a fatal car accident engulfed her and her happy life was ruined completely…and her whole world broke apart. Her life was torn to pieces and blown away in a wild whirlwind, never to come back again.

The disaster left Christina and Ann completely devastated. The two struggled to hold their broken lives together. After Ann was offered a small job in a software office by one of her friends, the mother and daughter moved to northern Virginia. It was hard for them to adjust to this dramatically different lifestyle, moving from a grand, luxurious house in California to a cramped old townhouse.

While Ann worked long hours at her office, Christina was left alone at home with her dark, muddled thoughts. Trying to adjust to a new school, friends, teachers, and a whole new life was quite difficult for her, and eventually, the emotional turmoil started to take its toll. Christina, a happy, outgoing, social girl, changed into an introvert, a sad, quiet hollow of the girl she had once been. All these changes were complicated by sporadic mood swings that greeted Ann when she came home every night and were her teachers' worst nightmares.

Ann did notice the changes in her daughter's behavior but was simply helpless about the situation. Her new job was quite demanding and took up most of her time. By the end of the day, she would be too exhausted to provide any emotional support to her daughter.

She tried taking Christina to a counselor, but unfortunately, that hadn't worked out well. At the counselor's office, Christina refused to speak. She had locked up her mind, denying access to anyone— even to her own mother.

Every day, looking at Christina's expressionless face was killing Ann. She wanted someone to help her. She wanted to see the joy once again radiating from Christina's face. And there was only one person who would be able to do that: Sheila, their only living relative. Aunt Sheila was very dear to Christina too. She would love talking to her for hours on the phone or writing her letters. But her father's tragic death had shocked her in such a way that she'd cut all her bonds with her family, as well as with her friends.

As the car came to a halt in the parking lot, Christina jolted back to the present. Ann parked the car hurriedly and soon they were walking toward the arrivals area at Dulles International Airport.

Sheila was waiting outside with only two suitcases, searching for Ann and pausing occasionally to check her watch. Ann saw Sheila from across the road. Waving her hands, she yelled with excitement, "Sheila!" Sheila looked up abruptly and her face broke into a wide grin. Hardly bothering to look both ways, Ann ran across the street.

Standing a bit far from them, Christina observed their reunion. Hugging, crying, and laughing, the two were squealing in delight in their own world. Christina watched her aunt. There was a remarkable difference in Sheila's appearance. Her previously overweight body was trimmed down to a beautifully sculptured figure. She wore an entirely different outfit this time: a sari, a traditional dress from

India. The neatly pleated saffron sari further accentuated her graceful figure. Her long, silky blonde hair flowed gently with the breeze. And her face!

"Wow!" Christina murmured, "Her face looks so gorgeous, so... radiant. It's...it is literally glowing." Just then, Sheila looked at Christina, and soon, she was in her aunt's warm embrace.

Staring at Christina's face, Sheila exclaimed, "Hey, look at you, young lady. You look so pretty! I just can't believe this same girl was nagging to sit in my lap the last time I visited. You have grown so much!" As her voice broke, she once again pulled Christina toward her, holding her tightly to her heart. "Oh....how much I've missed you, honey!"

Slouching on the couch after a hearty meal at Ann's house, Sheila remarked, "Thanks for the wonderful dinner, Ann. Your cooking always turns out fabulously. Between the two of us, you always were a better cook." Christina had eaten her dinner in silence while the two sisters reminisced. After dinner, she quickly disappeared upstairs, leaving Sheila and Ann alone. Ann was about to call her downstairs, but Sheila stopped her, insisting Christina needed some time alone. Flashing Ann a bright smile, Sheila continued. "After that long, tiring flight, this gourmet meal was the best thing anyone could ever dream of."

Drying her hands with the kitchen towel, Ann beamed and walked to the nearby chair. Sitting in it, she admitted, "Sheila! You can't even imagine how relaxed I feel with you being here." After a pause, she added, "After Roger's death, we missed you so much." Letting out a soft sigh, Sheila came to sit next to her.

Caressing her shoulder, Sheila whispered, "Don't worry, honey. I am here now."

"Sheila, I am learning, slowly, how to live this life...forgetting the past. But lately, I have become worried about Christina. The... incident has totally destroyed her. She is like a quiet volcano, ready to erupt at any moment." After a moment's pause, she continued. "It's really, really scary..." Her voice faded as she heard Christina's footsteps coming down the stairs.

"Hi, Christina...do...do you..." Ann was carefully searching for the right words.

Sheila came to her rescue. "Hi, Christina!" Smiling pleasantly, she added, "Please join us." Then turning to Ann, Sheila asked, "So... what were you asking me about my face?"

"Oh, yes!" Ann took the cue. "Sheila, I was wondering about your makeup. Your face looks so radiant. Can you tell us about that?"

"Oh, yes, definitely." Sheila chuckled and moved in closer as if to tell them a big secret. "Listen, I don't use any more makeup on my face now."

"What?" Ann gasped in disbelief.

"Really! While in India I was introduced to a very interesting person by one of my friends. We call him 'Guru.' He taught me the art of meditation, and I started meditating every day. Believe it or not, it has made a magical transformation. My face, my personality, and my attitude...everything has changed completely. This glow on my face is natural. I swear!"

"I don't believe this, Sheila. You used to always paint your face with makeup! Now you've stopped?" Watching Sheila's face intently,

Ann commented, "You don't use any makeup, and still your face is...it seems unreal."

"I know it is hard to believe for someone who is unaware of the magical effects of meditation, but I have experienced them myself and now do believe in them. My Guru says practicing meditation regularly brings a unique glow to our faces. This glow is the reflection of a divine ... a serene mind."

Leaving Ann in surprise, Sheila turned to Christina. "Sweetie, aren't you eager to see your gifts?" Christina gave a nod without speaking. As soon as Sheila pulled her bag out, Ann jumped closer. "No, no, no, Ann. You are not allowed to touch my bag," Sheila teased her, adding, "I will take the gifts out myself."

With a gesture of a magician, one by one, Sheila started taking out the gifts from her bag. The first gift was in a long, silver, cardboard box with a silver bow. "This is for...Ann!"

Ann slowly opened the box. She gasped and let the lid fall to the floor. From inside the box, she lifted up a gorgeous, knee-length, light pink dress. The soft neckline was outlined in off-white pearls.

"Oh...Wow! It's beautiful. Thank you!" Ann chirped. Spinning and holding the dress in front of her, she peeked in the mirror.

"And this necklace is for you too," announced Sheila. Ann looked away from the mirror with surprise. Sheila was holding up a long gold chain from which hung diamonds of various sizes. The smaller ones on the ends of the chain increased in size until there was one large, multi-faceted jewel in the very center of the necklace. The shine of the diamonds glistened over the walls of Ann's tiny room. Ann opened her mouth, but no sound came out. Sheila nodded her head, accepting Ann's silent thanks.

"This jewelry box is...for Miss Christina," Sheila announced, pausing momentarily to notice Christina's reaction. "Honey, I am pretty sure you will love it. Just look at the intricate design."

Christina took the box and murmured with a straight face, "Thanks, Aunt Sheila." She ran her fingers over the hand-carved ivory elephants and peacocks on the face of the box.

Sheila reached back into her bag and exclaimed, "And now, here comes the best gift." She placed a small, red velvet necklace box in Christina's hands. "This one was the hardest to part with," she added.

Christina slowly opened the box. The gold necklace lying on the rich blue velvet winked at her.

"Let me show you its special feature," Sheila said, taking out the necklace and placing it gently in Christina's lap. "Look at this pendant."

"Oh, my..." Ann breathed, coming closer to inspect it. The pendant was carved in the shape of a partially blossomed lotus flower with petals made of many shining rubies arranged in two swirls. The petals from the outer swirl curled outward while the petals from the inner swirl joined together in the center in the shape of a bud.

Sheila asked Christina to gently push on the top of the bud. As Christina did, the bud opened to reveal a dazzling golden frame displaying Christina's picture in the center.

For a few moments, Christina said nothing. Sheila watched her patiently. Finally, Christina whispered in quiet awe, "This is so pretty. Thanks, Aunt Sheila. It must have been quite expensive. Thank you very much."

Looking at her affectionately, Sheila said, "Honey, your joy and happiness are my treasures. I just want you to be happy." Closing the inner petals of the pendant again, Sheila looked at Christina and asked, "Would you like to wear it for me, please?"

"Sheila, where did you get this?" Ann interrupted, unable to hold back her curiosity.

"Mumbai, India! These pendants have become very popular over there recently, thanks to a new book called *The Book: Legend of Shivani.*" Sheila continued, "The hero of the book wears this pendant."

"That's interesting," Ann said.

Helping Christina put on her necklace, Sheila said, "Interestingly enough, my next gift for Christina is the same book." She handed over a book wrapped in a golden cover. "It's said that the book is based on a true story that happened thousands of years ago in ancient India."

"Really?" Ann asked, widening her eyes.

Sheila smiled. "Yes, Ann. I have read this book and really liked it. I'm sure Chris will like it, too."

Thanking Sheila again and wishing her good night, Christina walked slowly upstairs with all her gifts—including, of course, the book. More than her fully loaded arms, her aunt had given her much to think about.

She opened the door and hurriedly dumped the gifts onto her bed. As she turned away, she caught her foot on the boom box that had been lying on the floor. After twisting her ankle, Christina stumbled into the crystal glass unicorn on her dresser. Ignoring the pain in her foot, she reached up quickly to catch the unicorn before it fell, but she was a bit late. The unicorn had smashed into pieces that were now adorning the metal base of her lamp.

It seemed like time stopped for the heartbreaking eternity. Christina stared mutely at the broken beauty of her favorite gift. The crystal unicorn wasn't just any ordinary trinket. It had been presented to her by her father on her fourteenth birthday. While rushing to an important office meeting after celebrating her birthday, her father had gotten into a car crash and died. She remembered her squeals of delight at seeing the rainbow patterns the unicorn threw every day on her plain white bedroom walls. Every night before going to bed, Christina would hold the unicorn near her heart and wish it good night; it had become a ritual for her.

The crystal unicorn, her precious memento, had broken so suddenly that Christina simply stood frozen on the spot. With shock and disbelief, she stared at the broken pieces and fell down like an uprooted tree. Holding each glass piece near her heart in turn, she started sobbing wildly, her whole body rocking violently. Suddenly something poked her in the back. It was the velvet box Sheila had given her. In enormous anguish, she threw it into the farthest corner of her room. Snatching the gold necklace from around her neck, she hurled that too, into another corner. Still crying uncontrollably, she let her body collapse onto the floor in exhaustion.

Engrossed in a movie downstairs, Ann and Sheila were unaware of the drama unfolding upstairs. Lying helplessly on the cluttered floor, Christina suddenly noticed a faint glow emanating from somewhere beneath crumpled papers on the floor. She shoved the papers aside; it was *The Book: Legend of Shivani*. With a wry face, she was ready to throw it away too, but just then, something strange happened.

Golden light, almost like sparkles, began rising from the book. Soon the whole room was engulfed in the enchanting shimmer. In awe, her spellbound eyes locked onto the book, and the great saga of Shivani began unfolding in front of her.

CHAPTER TWO

A RAY IN THE FOREST

In the skies over the forest of Raat-Raan, the full moon was completely shrouded by thick clouds. Without warning, the rain came in great heavy curtains and slapped the whole forest. With it came the deafening sounds of thunder, echoing through every tree and bush. Amidst the dark skies, the streaks of lightning were dazzling, enhancing the eeriness of the forest. The swooshing and sweeping sounds of rain infused fear in every life that existed in the forest. Bracing themselves from the rain, the creatures huddled under any kind of shade, possible for them.

The forest of Raat-Raan stood along the northeastern border of the kingdom of Suvarna Raaj—one of the richest and mightiest kingdoms of ancient India. Raat-Raan meant "night forest," an appropriate name because even on bright, sunny days, there would be complete darkness inside the forest. The densely packed trees were so tall that they formed a solid roof above. Rarely, a few shafts of sunlight would shine through. In addition to being a shelter for deadly cobras, scorpions, and leeches, the forest was notorious for its mammoth-sized green pythons and carnivorous trees.

The cold, rain-filled night seemed as though it would never end. But then, the most unbelievable thing happened. The splashing sounds of heavy rains, the utter darkness, and the eeriness of Raat-Raan were suddenly shattered by the cries of a newly born baby—a human baby. On such a dark, stormy night as this, the dreadful forest witnessed the birth of a human baby for the first time in its life. With each passing moment, the shrill cries grew stronger, reverberating through each and every corner of Raat-Raan.

Upon entering the horrifying world around her, the tiny speck of life was crying desperately. She was lying under the branch of a tree that had, for the most part, sheltered her from the wetness of the rain, but not from the frightful noise. That particular tree was no ordinary tree. Apart from being the tallest in the forest, the tree had thick, gigantic leaves slathered in slimy, silvery juice. In the whole forest, there was no other tree like it. Of course, the baby was neither aware of that fact nor did she care about it. She was crying for help. Her small, pale face was being slapped by the angry raindrops. Trying to avoid the rain, she was wiggling her limbs violently in a fight for her life.

Suddenly a drop of silvery juice from the tree landed right on the baby's forehead, where she had a red, circular birthmark. The silvery dew angered the baby even more. May be because of the silvery juice the birthmark began casting a red glow. Slowly the glow started to get brighter and brighter until it was transformed into a circular, shining red spot in the eerie, dark forest, and another miraculous event happened. A similar red spot glistened in the dark leaves of the overlying strange tree and gradually began moving downward. It landed on the ground and began moving closer to the crying baby. Upon reaching the baby, the red spot halted.

In a flash of lightning, it became clear that the red, glistening spot was the red spot on the hood of a baby cobra. Fanning its hood out and flicking its tiny tongue, it watched the crying baby intently. With its eyes fixed on the baby's red birthmark, it slithered closer. Gradually the two red, glowing specks came very close to each other.

It was indeed a wonderful sight. After wrapping its slender coils around the baby, the cobra held its hood over the baby's face and stood there with poise. A baby cobra was protecting a human baby in a deadly forest. It was simply unbelievable. Now swaddled within the cozy coils with her face sheltered from the rains, the baby stopped crying. A faint smile sparkled on her face, and she began cooing.

Maybe it was simply a coincidence, or magic, but at that very moment, it stopped raining. A gentle breeze began to flow, pushing away the dark, ominous clouds. Soon, the gleaming full moon appeared in the sky with millions of sparkling stars dazzling against the beautiful dark blue skies. The stars were attempting to sneak a peek at the marvelous scene on the earth in Raat-Raan, but the thickly packed leaves hindered them. With great difficulty, a few moon rays landed on the baby. By then, unaware of the countless dangers surrounding her, the baby was fast asleep in her friend's comforting embrace.

Just then, in the dark bushes, a pair of eyes shone. The very next moment, a huge tigress pounced out of the bushes and landed softly in front of the baby. Witnessing the dramatic entry of the powerful predator, the little cobra hissed and threw a defiant glance at the tigress. But soon, after judging her intent, it swiftly retreated. The determined tigress speedily approached the baby. As the cobra moved away, the baby began crying once again.

That night was simply meant to witness the unbelievable, unreal, and magical events happening one after the other. The tigress stared at the crying baby for a moment. The next moment, she picked up the baby and the underlying silk sash in her mouth and started walking away. Carrying the tiny, wiggly bundle very carefully, the tigress moved swiftly with a specific destination in her mind.

CHAPTER THREE

A DANGEROUS RIDE

Even from a distance, the forceful waters of river Mahatejaa could be heard. After running through most of the kingdom of Suvarna Raaj, the river was seen coursing through Raat-Raan. Mahatejaa was known for its dangerous, speedy currents. The continuous heavy rains had further swollen the river to its fullest. With its roaring waters, it was flowing like a monstrous serpent challenging its surroundings.

Answering to the river's challenge, the tigress began heading straight to the river. Glancing one more time at the riotous waters and reasserting her grip on the bundle, she jumped into Mahatejaa. Fighting hard with the currents, she began swimming. In spite of her enormous strength, it was hard for her to stay afloat. Moreover, she had to worry about the safety of the bundle in her mouth. With all her might, she fought with the raging waters and managed to keep the precious bundle above them.

Straight ahead of her stood a huge, stony cliff in the path of the river. The cliff was so tall that it seemed to pierce straight through the skies. Overlooking the ferocious river, it stood quietly. The river, after dashing onto the great cliff, was bouncing backward in defeat, resulting in a sharp bend in its course. The river, retreating back from the cliff, looked very calm and serene, as if she acknowledged the supremacy of the cliff. Losing all her wrath at the bend, the return-ing river flowed with tranquility.

Slowly but steadily, the tigress swam toward the great cliff. But as the cliff got closer, she began facing increasingly turbulent cur-rents. Right before the bend, two distinct currents started forming. The current on the right side of the tigress was much stronger and more violent than the one on her left side. The tigress could have easily chosen the calmer path and would have eventually entered the tranquil part of Mahatejaa, receding back from the cliff.

Surprisingly, she chose the other option and deliberately pushed herself into the fiercer current on the right. The moment she entered the violent waters on the right, she began getting dragged toward the great stony cliff. The water was literally churning her from all sides. The part of the cliff where she was being pushed was completely covered with numerous intertwined vines. Within a few moments, the raging waters pushed the tigress into the curtain of vines, mak-ing her disappear from the world…only to let her reappear in a secret part of Mahatejaa.

This secret stream of Mahatejaa was in fact the main river. After dashing onto the cliff covered with vines, the main river contin-ued flowing through a tunnel under the mountains while its smaller branch bounced back from the cliff. That smaller branch of Mahatejaa was the only river visible to the rest of the world. The whole phenomenon had created an illusion of the river, Mahatejaa bouncing back off of the cliff while keeping the main river well hidden under the mountains. This was one of Mother Nature's exclusive wonders.

Now the tigress, having entered this secret Mahatejaa, pursued her journey further. She continued swimming inside the long, dark tunnel. Eventually, the sight of predawn rays swaying over the river waters delighted her. She eagerly pushed herself out of the tunnel. Glimpsing the open riverbanks, she instantly jumped out of the river onto the bank. After her arduous journey, she placed her precious bundle down on the sparkly sand of the riverbank. Risking her own life, she had successfully brought the treasured bundle into this secret world of hers. Now it was time to relax, at least for a few moments.

Shaking the water off her body, she proudly stared at the heavenly place in front of her. Though the night was almost over, the full moon still lingered over the horizon. Gently removing the veils of darkness layer by layer, each passing moment made the skies brighter and brighter. A few feathery, soft clouds still around were being showered in brightness.

The pastoral landscape was surrounded on all sides by tall mountain ranges. While vigilantly guarding the land, the mountains too were enjoying the beginning of a marvelous morning. Singing sweet tunes, throngs of birds flew around. Apart from their tweeting, the entire space was filled with a unique, enchanting fragrance, infusing each and every particle.

Having entered the picturesque world through the secret tunnel, river Mahatejaa had become calmer, too. Enjoying the divine serenity, it snaked leisurely all across the place, trying to spend some extra time before fading away at the foothills of the faraway mountains. Many different kinds of colorful fish cruised happily in its crystal clear waters. Reflections of stars still shining in the sky dazzled among those jumpy fish. As if carrying the fish in their laps, the stars enjoyed swimming in the river waters.

On both sides, the river was flanked by soft, sparkly sand. On the opposite bank, the river had lazily slouched inland, creating a large lagoon filled with numerous blossoming lotus flowers. The vibrant red lotuses were big enough to easily hold a small animal. The gentle ripples over the water tickled them, making them sway happily. With the arrival of the morning, white swans, fluttering their wings, began swooping elegantly onto the lagoon one by one. Some were busy fishing, but many others, still enjoying their sweet sleep, just glided over the waters among the lotuses. The pure white of the swans against the red lotuses and blue lagoon was indeed a splendid view.

Beyond both banks of the river, endless cascades of lush greenery were whispering serenity. The greenery was present in every shape and size: tall trees, bushes, shrubs, small plants, hedges, and different kinds of grasses. In some places, the plants had literally shrouded the river. Dazzling among them were the bursts of brightly colored flowerbeds. Every single color existing in the world shone in there. The panoramic view of patches after patches of flowerbeds, sparkling against the lush landscape, was absolutely breathtaking. Enjoying their company, many small springs jumped toward the river. Listening to their tunes, the surroundings were slowly waking up with a caressing, soft breeze.

After realizing the divine beauty and sanctity of that place, it was very easy to understand Mother Nature's motive for secretly hiding it from the world. She was successful in treasuring the spot in the heart of the deadly forest, Raat-Raan, and securing its blissful wilderness for her very own getaway spot.

Enjoying the phenomenal beauty of the place, the tigress was suddenly brought back to reality by the newly risen cries of the baby. Her precious package on the sandy bank was wiggling vigorously. Till then, the baby had been completely unaware of countless dangers passed by. During the whole travel inside her cozy, swinging bundle, she enjoyed a sweet sleep. But no sooner had the tigress put the baby down on the bank than the baby's sleep was disturbed.

Hurriedly, the tigress picked up the bundle and resumed her course across the bank. After a while, she entered the luscious greenery. But by then, some alarmed eyes had already spotted her. They were monitoring each and every action of the tigress very carefully. This was the first time they had seen the tigress in their world.

As the tigress continued walking, undeterred, a sense of panic appeared among the spying eyes. Keeping a safe distance from her, they all started following the intruder. Among them were cheetals (spotted deer), snow-white rabbits, and peacocks. With extreme caution, they all inched forward, pursuing the tigress. Flying above them were the flocks of kokils—the singing birds exclusive to that land. Without even glancing at them, the tigress was well aware of her pursuers. Still she continued walking because there was no time for her to entertain anyone but the baby. Each moment was very precious.

Now she had come to a spot where a raised hillock could be seen a little away from her. Over the hillock, a small, makeshift hut peered through the huge trees all around it. It was the first sign of humanity in that utter wilderness. Behind the hut was an area bounded by densely packed mango trees loaded with glistening, juicy-looking mangos. The very sight of the mangos would make anyone instantly hungry.

But the tigress's attention was focused on a small patio in front of the hut, where a human figure sat on a big boulder facing the gold-laden eastern sky. The figure was still...very, very still, as if it were a part of the boulder. Glancing at the figure, the tigress started walking speedily toward it.

By then, the skies were sprinkled with the golden rays of the omnipotent Sun, who had yet to rise from the horizon. To watch its grand arrival, many little flimsy clouds had gathered along its path. Impatiently they were sticking their heads up and trying to locate the source of the golden rays. They too were getting showered with gold, thrown by the yet-hidden emperor of the skies—the Sun.

After approaching from behind, the tigress stood in front of the boulder. Now she was facing the human figure. Gently putting the bundle held in her mouth down on the ground, she began gazing at him expectantly.

Nobody remembers exactly when that particular human first appeared in that divine land and became an inseparable part of it. His name was Yogidev. In the bright sun's rays, his original fair color looked more radiant. With half-closed eyes, he was settled in the lotus position of yoga. His breathing was so slow and deep that it was difficult to detect whether he was breathing at all. His long, silvery hair was tied in a knot atop his head, but still some short hair dangled on his huge forehead. Just like his hair, his beard too, was silver colored and was swaying gently with the breeze. Caressing him frequently, the soft breeze was listening to his message, the message of love and kindness. Rippling away from him, it carried that message and spread it through the surroundings. There was one remarkable feature about that human: Apart from his silvery hair, there was no other sign of his age. His straight posture, muscular body, and wrinkle-free, glowing face were all defying his old age.

Well before dawn, he would bathe in the cold, crystal clear waters of Mahatejaa. Then he would settle on the boulder in front of his hut. Facing the sun, he would start his meditation and soon slip into a serene state of trance. That divine state would carry his soul away from his body, disconnecting him from the surrounding world. Once in a trance, he could stay there for a few hours or a few days.

Yogidev's trance was well known to the animals, birds, and trees around him. They didn't know where he came from. They didn't know his past. They simply knew him. After coming out of his trance, he would first feed the animals and birds gathered around him. Then he would break his own fast by eating some fruits and tubers. As he began humming pleasantly, throngs of birds would swoop down and sit on him. Soon they too would join him by singing their sweet songs. It would feel as if all the bliss in the world had arrived there. That was one landscape on the earth where all the creatures were living lovingly and harmoniously.

Although the tigress was waiting patiently for Yogidev to come out of his trance, the baby inside the bundle wasn't. Thrashing her limbs around, she began crying again. As the tigress moved a bit closer to the baby, a strange sight made her step back. Staring with disbelief, she stood totally astounded.

A tiny black cobra was slithering out of the sack in which the baby was wrapped. Gathering its coils and spreading its tiny hood, it stood by the side of the crying baby. Proudly displaying the red circular spot on its hood, it stared at the tigress. Unfortunately for it, the red spot didn't impress the tigress. On the contrary, she was annoyed by the unexpected and unwanted presence of the cobra. Gazing at it with a perplexed look on her face, she wondered how in the world that little snake had entered the sack. Imagining it tagging along with her baby made her quite upset. She started growling at it with displeasure, but this time the cobra wasn't ready to retreat. Spreading its hood further, it hissed at the tigress. The pursuing crowd of animals and birds had no choice but to witness the strife.

The baby, completely unaware of the tug of war over her, kept crying and crying. Eventually those shrill cries broke Yogidev's trance. The moment his eyes caught a glimpse of the newborn human baby, flanked by a huge tigress and a black cobra, he sprang up from his position at once and rushed forth. Standing speechless by baby's side, he simply kept staring at her. His blue eyes had widened with utter disbelief.

"My goodness!" he whispered softly in a voice as silken as his silvery hair. Instantly, his hands went forth to reach for the baby. In a desperate search for comfort, the baby's tiny fingers grabbed his silvery beard. That gesture of innocent trust and utter helplessness moved him. Swaddling her in his arms, he squeezed the baby to his heart. After listening to Yogidev's kind heart, the baby became comfortable and stopped crying.

"Don't you worry, little one. I am here to take care of you. There is absolutely no reason for you to worry. You are a…tiny, cute, cuddly bundle of mine!" Caressing and kissing and rocking the baby, he whispered with his mellow voice. Still holding the baby near his heart, he lowered his face toward the tigress.

"Thank you very much, O kind one!" he said.

The tigress just purred.

"But where have you brought this baby from?"

In response, the tigress started growling. Just then, the cobra slithered in front of Yogidev and began hissing and flickering its tongue. It too was demanding credit for taking care of the baby. As Yogidev looked at the cobra's hood, he was wonderstruck. In a daze, he kept swiveling his eyes back and forth between the baby's forehead and the cobra's hood. The miraculous coincidence of those two red, circular spots, one on the baby's forehead and the other on the cobra's hood, left him stunned.

The baby resumed her cries again. Now, the cries were quite intense. Holding her closer to himself, Yogidev tried desperately to console the baby by rocking her, singing a lullaby, and so on. But this time, nothing seemed to console the baby. On the contrary, the cries intensified further. A total sense of panic and helplessness was displayed on Yogidev's face. A Guru, the winner of several human emotions was experiencing frustration for the first time in his life.

As if to worsen his frustration, the tigress had started pulling his hands that were busy swaddling the baby. Glancing at her helplessly, Yogidev asked, "What do you want now? Do you want this crying baby? What...what are you going to do with her?"

The tigress stepped back a bit. The puzzled Yogidev, without realizing what he was doing, put the baby down in front of her. Closing his eyes in despair, he also sat down on the ground near the baby. The sudden ceasing of the furious cries compelled him to open his eyes. When he saw the scene before him, he was frozen in surprise. His jaw dropped while he kept staring, dumbfounded.

An unbelievable event was happening in front of him. The tigress was sitting near the baby, trying to feed the baby with her own milk. The hungry baby was gulping the falling drops of milk.

The speechless Yogidev kept gazing at the wild beast exhibiting the most delicate of instincts—the maternal instinct.

"Oh, you are a mother, too! I….I didn't know that," he whispered softly to himself. That great sight moistened his eyes. The spellbound Yogidev moved a bit forward. To make the feeding easier, he moved the baby closer to the tigress. While the mother and baby shared their special love, the whole environment stared at them in amazement. Everyone was moved by the unique pair of mother and baby of two different species. While rising in the sky, even the sun stalled at its spot for a moment, just to witness that unprecedented event. The sight, more dazzling than its own golden rays, overwhelmed it.

"Yes, any mother can understand the language of a hungry baby." Yogidev smiled. "I did forget that." He began caressing the little cobra that by then had climbed on Yogidev and was slithering all over him anxiously.

The tigress was enjoying feeding the baby. She was lost in her own world. Licking the baby lovingly, she was probably consoling herself for her lost cubs. Probably she was seeing them in that tiny human baby.

As soon as her hungry tummy became full, the baby started snoozing. Slowly, the tigress hauled herself away. Gently picking up the baby, Yogidev glanced at his tiny hut. The walls of the hut were made of tree trunks. A tiny frame of tree branches covered with leaves served as its roof. That primitive hut standing there was enough for him to be his shelter from inclement weather. When he'd made the hut, he hadn't had the slightest inkling that one day, a baby might be living there.

Flashing a smile, he addressed his hut. "See! You are getting a baby. Aren't you happy? Until today you were just a shelter for a hermit like me. Now get ready. You have to raise a baby!"

By then an enormous herd of all the native animals was gathered around him, nudging each other to get a glimpse of the human cub sleeping in Yogidev's arms. To ease their excitement, he inched forward toward them. Slightly lowering the baby and spanning them with his eyes, he asked, "Isn't she pretty? I am sure all of you will help me to take care of this little baby girl." After a quick pause, he asked, "By the way, what should we name her?"

At once there was an enormous excitement. Each one of them was trying hard to suggest a name. Watching their enthusiasm, he grinned. "Maybe you will all agree with the name I have come up with." After an anxious pause, he announced, "Her name will be Shivani. I think it is perfect for this pretty baby!" With a content feeling, he looked at the crowd of animals nodding their heads in unison.

While talking to them, Yogidev's eyes were captivated by the wonderful, perfectly circular, vermilion-colored birthmark on the baby's forehead. Sitting exactly in the center of her forehead, that unique birthmark enticed him. It was dazzling, like a red gemstone under the morning sun's rays. He kissed the baby's forehead affectionately and turned toward his hut.

CHAPTER FOUR

NURTURING HOPE

After placing the orphan baby in the hands of Yogidev, Mother Nature was relieved of one big responsibility. She knew the secret land was the most impeccable home for raising that particular child. To her relief, little Shivani was also getting settled into the little paradise, or the little paradise was changing to the rhythm and rhyme of Shivani.

Every morning Shivani would wake up listening to the songs sung by kokils—the native birds of the place. The tiny black kokils were endowed with melodious voices. Their tweeting would sound like some heavenly concert. For Shivani, starting a day listening to that music was indeed a privilege. Soon she would join them by babbling and cooing. Her mama tiger would earnestly address her babbles. She would rush in to feed her baby. Afterward the energetic Shivani would be ready for the day's exciting activities.

It would start with the entry of the black cobra that was also growing up with Shivani. It would slither all around, tickling her. Attempting to capture its wiggly tail, Shivani would try crawling ahead. Soon the two would be crawling across the patio. While chasing the cobra, Shivani's curious eyes would be diverted by ants, bugs, and beetles passing by.

Getting irritated by her distraction, the teacher Cobra would jump back on Shivani and start slithering over her. That tickle would restart giggles and babbles and would draw many more creatures. The flocks of cheetals, rabbits, and peacocks would start racing to the sight. Fanning their vividly colorful feathers, the peacocks would strut around. Shivani's huge eyes would further widen with the charming panorama of colors, and she would start clapping.

Trying to seek her attention, the little cheetal fawns would inch forth through the dancing peacocks. Their beautiful, big, brown eyes would be fixed on Shivani. Sometimes, from among those fawns, a brave one would come forward with a wobbly gait and lick Shivani, its ticklish touch letting out another burst of giggles. Those refreshing giggles would shoo away any remaining fear from the hearts of the ever frightful and shy white rabbits. Like white, furry balls tumbling down a slope, they all would start running toward baby Shivani, resulting in wild giggles and gurgles sweeping the entire place.

Shivani and her friends were growing up fast. Soon she started taking steps by holding the cheetal fawns, now grown up too. In no time, her wobbly, slow steps transformed into a swifter and steadier walk. With her newly found feet, she started chasing butterflies, cheetals, and rabbits. She and her friends would wander all over the place. They would run through trees, bushes, shrubs, brooks, creeks, and almost anything that would come in their way.

They had discovered many favorite spots, but the most favorite among all was the soft, sandy banks of Mahatejaa. Apart from walking, jumping, and hustling with her friends in the soft sand, Shivani would spend hours lying on her tummy, watching the colorful fishes cruising in the crystal clear waters. The beckoning sight of the underwater flashing fish lured her to wade in the waters. Soon, she learned to swim with the help of Mama Tiger. Now, Shivani wasn't constrained by the banks. Instead of simply watching them, she began swimming with the fish. One more exciting activity was added to her list. After a long and tiring day, she would head straight to her mama tiger for snuggling up and sleeping in her lap.

Of course, everything was happening under the vigilant eyes of Yogidev. He had happily accepted the responsibility of raising Shivani. In fact, he himself was enjoying it. The tiny girl had totally changed his life. His hermitage began blooming with the touch of vibrant spring. According to his new routine, Yogidev would finish his morning rituals much faster to leave the rest of the day for Shivani. Bathing, feeding, and dressing her, and making her sleep would take up the majority of his day. He was very particular about Shivani's diet and would spend a lot of time searching for nutritious food. Luckily, the secret place was stuffed with lots of tasty fruits, tubers, roots, and the greens that had miraculous properties. Instantly after eating that, an enormous amount of strength and energy would be infused. Yogidev was aware of this fact, and his strong, youthful-looking body was its proof.

For Shivani's clothing, he really had to think hard. Living in such a place, remote from humanity, he was using tree barks to protect himself from the rough weather. Although he wasn't ready to use the jagged barks for the baby's delicate skin, there was no other option. Unwillingly, he resigned to using tree bark garments for the baby, but he would choose the softest possible barks.

Another challenge was finding a proper bed for her. He decided to use soft grass for that purpose. After tucking her into her grass bed, he would tell her many stories, stories of fairies and their wonderlands, various animals, plants, fishes, stars, the moon, and so on. Sometimes the storytelling period would be frequently interrupted by Shivani's silly questions, funny comments, and bursts of innocent laughter. But most of the time, watching the overhead starry sky and listening to the stories or lullabies in Yogidev's mellow, resonating voice, Shivani would slip into her dreamland. For Yogidev, those were the most blissful moments of his hectic day. Caring for a baby had transformed him from being a hermit to being a caretaker, a father, a mother, and a guardian, and he was enjoying all those roles. Staring at Shivani's innocent face, a wave of content would sweep over him, and soon, he too would be fast asleep.

Once he was suddenly jolted out of his sleep and found himself in the middle of a dark ocean. He was desperately searching for some support, but couldn't find any. He sank deeper and deeper into the ocean. An eerie silence was everywhere around him. Just then his eyes caught a glimpse of a shiny speck floating near him. Instantly he lurched forward and grabbed it tightly in the cusps of his hands. As he peered inside his fist, he was surprised. "Oh! It's a sparkly grain of sand," he whispered.

Suddenly a majestic sound echoed throughout the dark waters. "Yogidev!" He glanced around but couldn't see anyone. "Yogidev!" the imposing voice boomed again. "Keep holding it tightly. Don't let it go!"

The mesmerized Yogidev continued clutching onto the sand grain. After a while he realized that his fist was getting weaker because the sand particle inside his fist was getting larger. When he stared at his fist, he was frozen with the wonderful sight. He opened his cupped hands. Instead of the tiny sand particle, there was a huge, dazzling pearl sitting inside, glowing pleasantly. Its divine glare had wiped out all the darkness of the ocean. The spellbound Yogidev kept staring at the pearl nestled by his cusped hands.

Just then, everything disappeared. Instead, he witnessed the night sky resigning to the arriving rays of dawn. "Hmm!" Sighing deeply, he whispered, "So, it was.......a dream ..... another dream! I wonder for how many years this same dream has been visiting me...over and over again!"

He glanced around him. It was quiet everywhere. The world was enjoying its sweet morning dreams. His thoughts still whirling around the mysterious dream, he slowly got up and began heading to the river for his morning bath.

Days after days, months after months, and years after years passed by speedily. Grabbing the speedy wings of time, Shivani was growing up. Now she had turned into an eight-year-old, active girl. She was an expert in jumping, running, swimming, climbing trees, and so on. She would easily surpass all her friends. She could slither better than the cobra, run faster than the cheetals and bunnies, and climb trees faster than the monkeys. Also, she had created special bonds with each and every flower, plant, animal, and bird, even the fishes in the river.

Among all her activities, swimming remained Shivani's favorite. In the cold waters of Mahatejaa, she could stay forever. Diving without splashing a single drop of water was one of her specialties. After a flawless dive, she would disappear into the water, cruising with colorful fish. Sometimes, one of the white bunnies would get a joy-ride on her back. They would head to the opposite bank, where the lotus lagoon was. There she would put the bunny in one of the huge lotuses, and the fun of hide and seek would begin. Sometimes a good game of hustle in the soft sandy bank with other bunnies and cheetal fawns would keep her engaged for quite a while.

Apart from all these boisterous sports, she would also enjoy artistic activities such as singing, dancing, and creating designs with flowers and leaves. With her sweet voice, she would join the kokils in their concerts. Listening to the inviting tunes, the fascinated peacocks would enter the stage. Fanning and displaying their scintillating feathers, they would start dancing. Soon Shivani and her friends would join them.

With the help of Yogidev, she named each one of her friends. The black cobra, her first friend, was named Naagraaj—the king of snakes. A kokil who would always be with her was called Madhur—sweet. A girl cheetal fawn became Sunetraa—the one with beautiful eyes. Shivani's dance teacher, a peacock, was named Mayur. The pair of white, fluffy rabbits, always jumping and tumbling on Shivani, became Shubhra and Dhawal—two different names for the word white. Shivani's loving mama tiger became known as Jwala—flames of fire. The preciseness of the name would be appreciated when the tigress would start moving, splashing her bright orange fur under the sunlight. Shivani's neighborhood got the name Aashrum—hermitage. That consisted of her tiny hut, the banks of Mahatejaa, the lotus lagoon, the meadow, the forest of mango and other fruit trees, and a tiny waterfall.

But that wasn't enough for Shivani. She named all her plants that she could recognize by their texture, feel, and fragrance. She named all the birds that she could identify by their voices and chirping. She named all fish that she could recognize correctly by their cruising speed and color.

Satisfied with the naming ceremony, turning to Yogidev, Shivani asked, "We have named everyone except for you. It is not fair."

"What do you want to name me? You already know my name!"

"Still, we have to name you!"

"OK. How about...calling me Guru Yogidev!"

"Guru! Means..."

"Guru means 'the one who teaches.'"

"Oh! But...but you don't teach me anything!"

"Do you really think so?" Smiling at her innocent face, he asked, "Who taught you to speak?"

"I learned it all by myself!"

"Really?" Yogidev started laughing. Hanging onto his neck Shivani started giggling, too and fell down in his lap. Getting the cue, all her friends raced and began jumping on Yogidev. The neighborhood was engulfed in the riotous laughter, giggles, and screams.

Shivani would love every single activity, except the studies. With Naagraaj dangling from one of her shoulders, Madhur sitting on the other shoulder, the pair of white rabbits—Dhawal and Shubhra—swaddled in her hands or sometimes tumbling in front of her, Sunetraa walking by her side, and Mayur trailing behind, she would wander all around. From morning until evening, the whole horde would be playing, jumping, or simply hanging around the neighborhood.

Academics were the one and only field untouched by Shivani. Frequently Yogidev would lecture her about the importance of learning in one's life. He wanted her to progress in academics and had tried to teach her reading and writing. Also, he tried introducing yoga to her.

"A disciplined mind and a healthy body are the keys to overcome hurdles and achieve success in life!" was his motto.

Unfortunately the motto was being ignored, and his efforts were going in vain. Instead Shivani would enjoy getting indulged in naughty tricks. And, to Yogidev's despair, that naughtiness was increasing day by day.

Shivani had a long list of pranks, which she would practice frequently. The most beloved was to scare the animals by making scary, weird noises. Watching them running away in panic would make her laugh so hard that she would simply fall down on ground.

One more prank was putting Naagraaj on the backs of peacocks. Here Naagraaj would be her chief helper. After spying carefully, she would select a peacock engrossed in preening its feathers and would put Naagraaj on its back. Then she would swiftly run away to her observation point. After realizing the cobra had been sitting on its back, not only that particular peacock but the whole flock would start screeching and stumbling on each other. Then Shivani would run up to them and pick up Naagraaj. But it would take a long time for the flock to return to normalcy. Holding Naagraaj in her raised hands, she would swirl around, radiating in great triumph.

Yogidev would scold her for teasing the animals and throwing such pranks, but Shivani wouldn't listen. Instead she would run away and climb high up in one of the mango trees, where her pranks would continue. Sitting on a mango tree, she would watch the kokils around her and wait patiently until they disappear in search of food for their babies. Then she would change the positions of their nests.

The return of kokils would spark a great commotion in the forest of mango trees. Her face dazzling with the successful prank Shivani would sneak down the tree. By then her loyal friends would be waiting beneath the tree. From the tree, Shivani would jump straight onto the back of *Sunetraa* and off the whole horde would go galloping. Along with the galloping of hooves, Shivani's riotous giggles would fill the entire place.

But even with her busy schedule, Shivani would make sure to visit her mama tiger, Jwala, at least two times a day. By then, Jwala had begun living in a den on the opposite banks of the river. To be able to meet her, Shivani would swim across the river from her hut. After a tiring day, cuddling with her mama was a rare treat for her.

Recently her attention was diverted away from her mama tiger to something else. Her mama had given birth to two very cute cubs. That made Shivani extremely happy. She would bring all her friends; turn by turn, to show them her prized possession—her brothers. The tiny, soft cubs were cute enough to hook her for hours together. But also, they encouraged her prank-loving mind.

Shivani would love playing with the cubs if they were awake. A game of tag, peek-a-boo, or tussle would keep them all engaged.

Cuddling with their soft, fluffy, tiny bodies was her comfort. But if the brother cubs were in middle of their naps, Shivani wouldn't miss that perfect opportunity to play her naughty tricks on them. Cautiously tying their tails together with a piece of vine, she would wait somewhere, hiding, until the beginning of real fun. The cubs would wake up to find that they were tied together and would start falling on each other. After enjoying some joyful time watching them, Shivani would come forth to their rescue. She would untie the tails and fondle with the cubs. Of course Shivani knew the trick had to be played only while Mama Tiger was asleep.

With each passing day, Shivani's naughtiness was growing. Even Yogidev couldn't escape from her tricks. The moment after the beginning of his mediation, she would start pulling his long beard, tickling his feet or tummy, or sprinkling water on his face. Sometimes she would put Naagraaj around his neck and watch him slither and flicker his forked tongue up Yogidev's nose. From a distance, along with her friends, Shivani would wait impatiently for his trance to break. But she didn't know that nobody in the world could break Yogidev's trance without his willingness. Sometimes, simply to make Shivani happy, he would pretend to be falling for her tricks.

"Aachhoo! Aachhoo !!" Yogidev would start sneezing after his nose had been poked with tiny twigs inserted by Shivani. The delighted and proud Shivani then would giggle and fall into his lap.

"Yogidev! Why do you meditate?" Shivani asked, wrapping her tiny hands around him.

"Meditation is good for your mind." Enjoying the pure joy on her face, Yogidev said, "It makes your mind strong and powerful."

Sunlight showered the hermitage with joy and bliss.

CHAPTER FIVE

"LIFE IS FUN!"

Bursting with renewed life, spring entered Shivani's neighborhood. Pure energy was percolating through every corner. The earth was covered with a downy, green carpet of grass. Carving through it, water springs were jumping jubilantly. The trees displayed their newly gifted, tiny, delicate greens. With the emergence of young blossoms, the bushes shined with vibrant colors. With their sweet fragrance, the flowers enchanted butterflies and birds as they hustled across the pleasantly azure sky, singing songs of happiness. With regained fervor, the sun's rays were infusing virility through every speck of life.

No wonder Shivani was extremely busy in the festive atmosphere. Throughout the day, there would be many projects for her to finish, such as making valances of various flowers and mango leaves for the hut, decorating the patio with designs made with colorful flower petals, and making flower jewelry for herself.

She also had to guard the freshly planted rose bushes around the patio from bunnies. Bunnies would love nibbling on the soft rose petals, very dear to Shivani. Dodging the trees, skipping over roots and brambles, Shivani and her friends would chase after the bunnies. She would do everything possible to keep them away from her flowers. She loved the ruby-red rose petals. Wearing them on her fingernails had recently become one of her favorite hobby.

In guarding her roses, she would get help from her tiger cub brothers, who by then had grown enough to swim by themselves to Shivani. Their mere entry with soft snarls would shoo away all the bunnies, except for Dhawal and Shubhra.

One day, Shivani was pleasantly surprised by the unexpected arrival of her cub brothers. "Welcome, my babies!" Shivani said. Hauling them to a nearby spot, she continued her project—a rose garland for her hair. "Now you two watch me doing this, OK?" After a while the duo began losing their interest. Just then, their tiny ears heard something. They started jumping on Shivani to seek her attention. A throng of monkeys had just entered the forest of mango trees.

"What's the matter with you guys?" Scoffing at them, Shivani looked in the direction of their gaze. As she sighted the monkeys, she raced to the mango forest, leaving all her treasured and fanciful artwork behind. The monkeys were busy eating the delicate mango flowers. The moment they saw Shivani approaching with the cubs, they leapt away frantically. Then the victorious Shivani and her cub brothers started climbing on the mango trees. Numerous tiny blossoms hung from almost every branch, their captivating fragrance capable of embodying any spirit passing by.

After picking a few flowers, Shivani came down and began feeding the gathered peachicks, eagerly waiting to taste the blossoms. The remaining flock of peacocks swooped down and began strutting around her. Very soon the blossoms from Shivani's hands vanished. Once again she raced up another tree to get more food. This time it was her friends' turn to eat. Sunetraa, Dhawal, and Shubhra all began relishing the luscious treat.

After a while the gang headed to another favorite spot—the meadow behind the hut. The spring had covered the meadow with a fresh coat of green grass. Shivani couldn't resist the soft, inviting green carpet. Soon, from the hilly corner of the meadow, the race started—the race of rolling down the hill. With everyone bumping into each other, a wave of enormous commotion of bleating, growling, snarling, screaming, hissing, and screeching erupted, but it was all overshadowed by the riotous laughter of Shivani.

Just then, suddenly everyone except for Shivani became quiet. Still lying on the grass at the end of the slope, she was puzzled by this transformation. But as she turned around, she became rooted too to her spot as a statue. It was Yogidev standing with a very serious face. His serious face reminded Shivani about her forgotten assignment. She was supposed to write her words before going out to play.

"Shivani!" Similar to his face, Yogidev's voice was serious too.

With her head hung low, Shivani stood remorsefully. She couldn't say a word.

"Shivani! My child!" Looking at her long face, Yogidev's tone became a bit softer. "I don't want to snatch the fun away from you. You can play as much as you want, but first, finish your homework. I want you to take some interest in your studies. It is very important and will help you become successful in life." Stroking her hair he asked, "Do you agree?"

"I do agree, Guru Yogidev!"

"OK. Very good! Should we start now?"

Shivani nodded and began following him silently. Pausing for a moment, Yogidev turned to her friends and smiled. "I promise you, I will send your friends back to you as early as possible."

In front of their small hut, Yogidev resumed his teaching session. They began working on the art of writing—calligraphy. From the pile of lotus leaves, he pulled a fresh leaf out and began writing on it with a tiny twig of a plant.

"Shivani, watch me. Every letter you carve should look pretty. Once you master this art, it will be your very own, everlasting treasure." Frequently changing her positions and glancing at her friends, Shivani was sitting near Yogidev. She was counting each and every second, waiting for the lesson to finish.

"Shivani! Please pay attention to me," Yogidev warned her. "Why are you moving so much? Can't you sit still?"

"I...I am having an itch...very...very bad itch...over my legs."

"Let me see." Yogidev knew she was faking. "Your legs look fine to me."

"Guru, Yogidev! Can you teach me...something more interesting?"

"More interesting?...means what?" Yogidev stared into her eyes. "Hmmm. How about...learning yoga exercises?"

"Excellent!" At once Shivani jumped up excitedly and stood by the side of Yogidev.

"Shivani, today I will start teaching you a very important exercise. It is called, Surya-Namaskaar."

"Surya-Namaskaar," Shivani repeated.

"Being a very smart girl, you will learn this in a snap!" Yogidev exclaimed, snapping his fingers.

"Wow! How did you make the snapping sound, Guru Yogidev?" Shivani started copying her Guru but was having a hard time snapping her fingers.

"Shivani, you may practice it later. Right now let's concentrate on Surya-Namaskaar. If done early in the morning, especially in the rays of the rising sun, this exercise infuses enormous energy into your body." He glanced at Shivani, who was still engaged in practicing the snap.

"Shivani!"

The seriousness in Yogidev's tone startled her. "I am sorry," she said meekly.

"Pay attention here!"

"Yes, Guru Yogidev."

"So, we are learning about Surya Namaskaar. Surya means sun and Namaskaar means a respectful greeting. Namaskaar has to be offered by joining both hands together, closer to our body. Like this." Yogidev watched Shivani join her hands together. He continued, "And bend the hands a bit at the elbow."

"Yes, Guru Yogidev."

"There is one..."

"Excuse me, Guru Yogidev?"

"What?"

"I have a request."

"Say it," Yogidev glanced at her with a puzzled face.

"I was thinking that your name is too long. Every time calling you 'Guru Yogidev' wastes a lot of time. So, can I just call you Gurudev?"

"Sure! That's a wonderful name." He smiled. "Now shall we continue? Well, there is another name for namaskaar."

"I know: Namaste!"

"Correct! With Surya-namaskaar, we are offering our respectful greetings to the sun, the source of vibrant energy."

"Isn't this the way we do namaskaar, Gurudev?" Shivani asked with her both hands joined correctly.

"That's right. But after you join the hands, you need to bend them at the elbows so that both your joined palms stay near your heart." Gurudev placed Shivani's hands in the proper namaskaar position.

"Why should our hands be near the heart, Gurudev?"

"This way we offer our respects from the heart, and in return, the sun's blessings are conveyed to the heart."

Yogidev closed his eyes and continued teaching. He had a habit of closing his eyes while talking on some important issues. Surely it was a funny and strange habit.

"Shivani, Surya namaskaar, is not just a simple namaskaar. In fact, it is a special yoga exercise. One single Surya namaskaar consists of eight different exercises. These exercises are designed in a way to activate all the critical and vital points of our body. In addition to making the body strong and healthy, it helps the mind to stay alert and sharp. Believe it or not, the secret behind my strong and healthy body is my regular habit of doing these exercises. I have been doing these since my childhood. See, even at this old age, my body is still strong and flexible. I can still wrestle and defeat anyone." Yogidev smiled. "I am sure you must be excited to try these phenomenal exercises." After taking a deep breath in, he opened his eyes to watch excitement on Shivani's face but was left dazed. With widened eyes, he kept staring at Shivani's empty spot. Just then, from a distance, he heard very familiar giggles.

Shivani and her friends were rolling down the meadows. Displaying her infectious grin, Shivani was singing a song.

Life is fun,
Life is the one,
Life is the friend
With everyone!
Run with the wind,
Swim not to win
Sing, dance, and play
Just for the fun!
We have no worry,
We have no hurry
Watch those clouds,
Fly, one by one!
Life is fine,
Either rain or shine
All the joy is mine
O beautiful one!
Night is so pretty,
Shining stars zesty
Watch the fireflies
Dazzle one after one!

Soon the pretty night gathered all the tired bodies in her loving lap and took them far away to their dreamland.

The aimless wandering of Shivani and her gang continued, and so did Gurudev's attempts at teaching her. With great patience, every day he would come up with a new plan to make learning more interesting.

One morning he woke up with determination. "Today, I am going to be successful in my mission," Yogidev whispered to himself. After finishing his morning prayers, he woke up Shivani. With bleary eyes and a sleepy gait, she began following Gurudev toward the river for morning baths.

"Isn't it refreshing, Shivani?" Gurudev asked after making her bathe in the river and perform some yoga exercises. "Morning air is always magical and magnificent and energetic."

"Not really, Gurudev!" Shivani answered honestly. "I am still feeling sleepy...very sleepy."

Disappointment flashed on Gurudev's face momentarily. "OK. We will take care of it!" Throwing a mischievous glance at her, he asked, "How about a quick swim lap?"

"Oh! Yes...absolutely!" Shivani jumped in her spot. "Gurudev, you are very nice. You are the best teacher in the whole wide world."

She squeezed him tightly and then dashed back to the river immediately.

Summer had already begun. Although the sun had not yet risen high up in the sky, it was quite hot. The breeze was simply a blazing draft of hot air. The clouds had already run away from the angry-looking sun, leaving the unfettered sun alone to rein over the entire sky.

But the hot day had turned out to be a blessing for Shivani. Swimming in the cold waters of Mahatejaa was an enchanting event. Submerged in the lovely waters, she continued swimming.

"Shivani! Stop swimming, now. Please come out," Gurudev reminded her.

"Now I am hungry, Gurudev."

After a snack of fruits and some sweet tubers, finally Gurudev had a chance to begin his teaching session.

"Shivani!"

"Yes, Gurudev." Shivani was trying to be very attentive. But as she witnessed the members of her wandering club nearing her one by one, her restlessness began to increase. Impatiently, she began to rub her fingers on the coils of Naagraaj, sitting by her side quietly.

"Now, we will start our studies. I want you to be a good student."

"Yes, Gurudev."

"Excellent! To become a good student, you should have an alert and focused mind."

"Yes, Gurudev."

"Then it will be easy for you to learn the lessons. Soon you will be a talented and respected person in the world. Now I will…"

"Excuse me, Gurudev?" Shivani interrupted.

"What?"

"I am thirsty now."

Gurudev stared in her eyes to read the authenticity of that request. Those innocent eyes were flashing honesty. He blamed himself for raising the doubt and gave her the permission.

"Shivani, come back quickly. I am waiting for you!"

"Yes, Gurudev!" She ran to the river at once. The friends who followed her earnestly noticed that.

With cupped hands, Shivani drank the cold, fresh water of the river. It was simply heavenly, especially on a hot day. She splashed some cold water on her face too. Just then she happened to get a glimpse of her favorite red fish darting up and down in the water. Instantly she jumped in the river and began chasing it. Those tiny, red fish were a rare find in Mahatejaa.

Watching Shivani chasing the fish, her friends began cheering for her. Unfortunately that red fish vanished from Shivani's sight, which made her a bit sad. But just then, Shubhra and Dhawal jumped on her from one of the shoots of a banyan tree dangling over the river.

That excitement sparked a fabulous idea in her mind. Within a few moments, she raced toward the old banyan tree. There were plenty of shoots growing down toward the ground from its branches. Grabbing one of the shoots, she gave herself a good swing and jumped into the river. Her tiger brothers quickly imitated her actions. After turning back for another round of fun, she noticed Gurudev standing by the banyan tree.

"Gurudev, I am sorry. Are...are you angry at me?" she asked remorsefully.

"No, my child. Not at all. Have you seen me getting angry?"

"Never!"

"Long ago, I drove that nasty emotion away from my mind. So don't worry about my anger." Taking a deep breath he said, "But I am a bit disappointed because you broke the promise. I want to teach you and make you wise. I would like to see you taking interest in studies. I want you to become a great person in your life."

"Gurudev, I also want to become a great and famous person."

"Good! For that you will have to work hard. You will have to live a disciplined life. You will have to stay focused on your goals. Greatness doesn't come easily, my child."

"I understand, Gurudev."

"Now, are you ready for the lesson?"

"Yes, Gurudev."

"OK." Holding a leaf in his hand, he asked, "Remember yesterday, we learned some words. I want you to practice those words on this leaf."

"Gurudev, ummm...I forgot the words."

"OK." Gurudev let a sigh out. "Now I will write, and you will recognize the words. Ready?"

"I am ready, Gurudev. But...can I ask something? Is it good to study with a hungry stomach?"

"No, never. Hunger should be taken care of, first."

"Excellent. Gurudev, I am very hungry right now. Can I go get some snacks? I promise you, I will be back very fast."

Staring into her innocent eyes, Gurudev nodded. He had no choice. "Come back, fast."

His words faded from Shivani's ears.

In a dash Shivani reached the mango forest and climbed one of the trees. Every single tree was loaded with juicy, bright reddish yellow mangoes. Heaving with the enormous weights of mangoes, the branches were drooping. The sweet fragrance of the ripe mangos floated everywhere. After her hungry tummy got filled up with the heavenly mango juice, Shivani realized her friends were waiting for her beneath the tree. To her, all looked very thirsty and hungry. So she began throwing down the mangoes at them. Soon she noticed a problem. Her friends were not good at eating mangoes.

"I need to help them!" With a few mangoes in her hands, Shivani jumped off of the tree and began squeezing the juice out in bowls made of leaves. Watching her friends relishing the tasty juice, she felt content.

"Oh boy! What would you all have done without my help?" By then the mighty emperor of the skies, the sun, had reached its zenith. Its hot rays were scorching the life on Earth. Sheltering under various shades, everyone was seeking solace from the angry king. Even the breeze appeared to have stopped flowing and hidden somewhere. Except for a few bees buzzing around, there was no sign of life anywhere. The entire landscape wore a deserted face.

But defying the supremacy of the wrathful sun, Shivani and her friends were frisking, frolicking, and partying in the mango forest. Suddenly Shivani remembered Gurudev. Leaving everything behind, she slued back just to pause again.

"I must take some juice to Gurudev. He must be hungry too." After climbing on a nearby tree, she began another bout of snacking. After refilling her tummy, she came down with a bunch of mangoes. With two bowls filled up with the juice, she eventually began walking toward Gurudev. Holding one bowl on her head, supported with her left hand, and another bowl in her right hand, she began walking very carefully. Needless to say, by the time she reached Gurudev, her whole body was covered with the sticky juice, leaving both the bowls almost empty.

"Sorry, Gurudev. I know I am a little late, but I got mango juice for you too." Placing the almost empty bowls in front of Gurudev, she continued. "I remembered how much you love this juice. Just the way I can't learn with a hungry stomach, you can't teach with a hungry stomach either...right?"

Flashing the utmost pride on her face, Shivani looked at Gurudev. The overwhelmed Gurudev kept gazing at her. Shivani's whole body was slathered with juice. Her face was stained; her hair had been matted together by the fallen, sticky fluid; and a bunch of leaves were stuck all over her body. "Gurudev, please drink this refreshing mango juice. Drink it *slowly*! I don't want you to rush for the studies."

Gurudev didn't have any words to express his emotions. The wisest of the pundits had become speechless before the gesture of innocence and affection. Finally he rose up from his seat. Squeezing Shivani's head at the bosom of his heart, he whispered, "Thank you very much, my child." Stroking her hair softly, he said, "I am indeed very thirsty."

"You are welcome, Gurudev!" Gurudev began drinking the remaining few drop of the juice. It surely had the heavenly taste.

"Shivani, before we start our studies again, don't you feel like getting a quick wash? You are all covered with the sticky juice."

"Absolutely! I was just thinking about it." Shivani stopped licking the juice from her fingers at once and jumped with excitement. "Should I head to the river now?"

"Yes, you may go." Gurudev smiled. Staring at her tiny image running to the river, he whispered softly, "I wonder when will I be able to channel this immense, endless energy toward its goal." He got up from his seat. "I guess I will have to wait for my turn. Until then, I will have to deal with this whirlwind very...very patiently." From far away, Gurudev could hear the familiar riotous laughter of Shivani.

CHAPTER SIX

THE MONSOON

The long-awaited monsoon finally arrived on Earth. After a harsh summer, the sight of arriving bluish black clouds in the sky made everyone thrilled. Soon, the heavily overcast, dark sky gave way to rains, and the falling rain drops began caressing the scorched earth. The enchanting fragrance steamed up from the parched land and began infusing through every speck. The sparkly pearls and their divine scent engulfed every single life: animals, plants, humans, birds, insects, and more. Even the nonliving things were exhilarated by the soothing sprinkles. An invigorating energy started splashing throughout the world.

The little paradise around Gurudev's Aashrum was also welcoming the monsoon. The exotic scent of the first monsoon rains turned Shivani and her friends further wild. They were dancing and singing crazily under the electrifying raindrops. Even Gurudev joined them in celebrating the grand arrival of the monsoon.

The rains continued for more than two whole days and eventually lost their charm. The mango trees, the berry patch, the bushes, the meadow, the river, the banyan tree, everything got shrouded behind one thick veil of water. Even the ground was covered with sheets of water. Confined by the never-ending rains, Shivani was sitting inside her small hut, looking in despair at the torrential downpour.

"These rains may continue for a few more days," Gurudev said. Glancing at the thick, dark skies, he got up. "I can't wait any longer. There is no more food in the hut."

"Please, can I come with you, Gurudev?" Shivani begged as he began heading to the door in search of food. Usually he would encourage Shivani to accompany him in collecting the food.

"Shivani, I want you to stay inside and be safe." He picked up two wooden containers. "I will quickly fetch some tubers and roots for our lunch."

For Shivani to be imprisoned inside a small hut was not a happy time. Luckily she found some company. Apart from Naagraaj, her forever buddy, the pair of rabbits, Shubhra and Dhawal, were with her. Unfortunately, that day Naagraaj wasn't looking energetic. For the past few days, Shivani had noticed him getting lazier. Probably, she thought, it was time for him to shed his old, thickened skin. Gathering his long body, he lay motionless in a corner.

In contrast, the white bunnies were jumping like bouncing balls, jumping from every single object as Shivani tried to catch them. Suddenly Shubhra stopped jumping. After sniffing something, he began digging in the ground. "Hey, buddy! What are you digging up there?

Don't make any holes in the ground or else Gurudev will scold me," Shivani yelled.

Turning toward her, Shubhra wiggled his nose and began squeaking. He raced to Shivani and started pulling her to his digging spot.

"I am coming, my friend!" Impatiently Shivani ran to the spot and peeked through the partially dug hole. Her eyes began sparkling with surprise. A small piece of saffron-colored cloth was jutting out though the hole.

"Oh, my goodness! It looks like you have found something very interesting!"

In a moment, all the dullness of that rainy day was swept away. She began hustling to widen the hole further. "Wow!" Shivani screamed with excitement as she pulled the mysterious find through the hole. Holding it gingerly with both hands, she stared at the unusual item speechlessly. It was a bundle of soft, silky, saffron-colored cloth pursed together with a string. Flanking her on either side, the bunnies were nudging her to get a closer glimpse of the mystery. To her surprise, even Naagraaj had slithered closer. Sitting down, she started opening the bundle. Suddenly something slipped off her lap and fell to the ground. As she looked at the fallen thing with utter disbelief, the rest of the bundle just slipped from her hands.

"Oh! My...goodness!" the mesmerized Shivani whispered. It was a dazzling pendant threaded over a golden chain. The pendant was uniquely shaped like a partly bloomed lotus flower. "Doesn't it look like one of the red lotus flowers from our lotus lake?" she asked, picking it up in her hands and showing her friends. Just then she sensed Gurudev at the footsteps of the patio.

Forgetting to breathe, Shivani grabbed the pendant and the saffron cloth bundle and stormed outside to share her exhilarating discovery with Gurudev. "Gurudev! Gurudev!" Screaming with excitement, she reached him like a shot. "Gurudev! Look at this, Gurudev! I found something very strange! It was inside the hut, buried under the ground. Shubhra found it." The words were pouring out from her mouth.

The moment Gurudev glanced at Shivani's hands; he jolted with a shock and stood frozen at the very spot. After a moment, closing his eyes, he let out a subtle sigh. Shivani was too flabbergasted to notice his reaction. One hand clutched the surprise find against her chest while the other hand clung onto Gurudev she kept staring at him.

Overcoming the initial shock, Gurudev stared at Shivani's gleaming face with affection. Flashing his usual smile, he said, "Shivani, my child! At least let me come inside." After placing the fruits, tubers, and roots neatly in a corner, Gurudev sat down on the floor. Holding her wonderful possessions, Shivani was following his every step.

"Now, I am ready. Let me see what have you explored." With his blue, misty eyes, he was gazing at the displayed treasure. How could he forget the saffron-colored silk bundle and the lotus pendant... and a lot more? Although he himself had buried those inside his hut many years ago, their pristine condition amazed him. They looked just the same as they had many years ago. The red rubies of the pendant were still dazzling, more or less with the same glow. He looked into Shivani's eyes and whispered, "Either the destiny chooses the time or the time chooses the destiny!"

Shivani looked at him puzzled by his sentence.

"My child, you will always remember this day. It will be the most important day in your life. These things, this silk cloth, this pendant, will connect you with your own past." He paused momentarily. "It may alter your life completely...and forever."

Shivani was further perplexed at those incomprehensible sentences and kept staring at Gurudev.

"Shivani," Gurudev continued in a mellow voice, "see, this is called a pendant." He held Shivani's tiny fingers and moved over the red pendant.

"Isn't it pretty, Gurudev? Doesn't it look like a lotus flower?" Shivani's exuberance was bubbling.

"Yes, Shivani! These petals are made of rubies, a kind of gemstone. This is the outer layer of the petals, partly open. The inner layer is still closed, like a bud."

Shivani, for the very first time in her life, was looking at a fine piece of jewelry. Completely enthralled, she kept caressing it.

"And there is a surprise for you inside this closed layer," Gurudev said.

"For me?"

"Yes, my child. Only for you. Put your finger over the top of these closed petals and press it."

As soon as she put her index finger and pressed over the exact spot shown by Gurudev, the closed part instantly snapped open. Hidden inside was a delicate, tiny golden frame carved as a petal displaying a painted picture of a beautiful lady and a handsome man.

"Wow!" Shivani exclaimed with amazement. "Who are they, Gurudev?"

"They are your parents," Gurudev murmured. "This is your father, and this pretty lady is your mother."

Her eyes hooked onto the picture, Shivani kept staring at it.

"Shivani, this saffron-colored silk cloth belonged to….your mother."

"My...my...mother." It was one more unbelievable surprise for Shivani.

"You were brought to me, here at this place, wrapped up in this lovely sash of saffron silk."

"Really?" Shivani's voice was filled with mere disbelief. Her eyes rolling all over the cloth, she was trying to imagine her tiny body tucked inside.

"Gurudev, why didn't you tell me this before?"

"My child, you never asked me this before." He smiled. "And I was waiting for the right time. Today it brought itself about unexpectedly and accidentally. I wanted to tell you about your parents..."

"Really?" Shivani blurted out, her voice filled with excitement. "Gurudev, I want to see them. Can they come and live with us, Gurudev?"

"They can't come here...now." Gurudev stared at the pendant. "Shivani, they are not living in this world any more. Both of them are...are...dead."

All the brightness from Shivani's face disappeared instantly as Gurudev finished the sentence. In its place, one and only one emotion began creeping—grief. For the first time, Gurudev witnessed that particular emotion in her joyful eyes. He felt his heart being wrenched. He remembered the event that took place after baby Shivani's unexpected arrival in his life.

He still couldn't forget the sight of the baby lying before him, flanked by a tiny cobra and a giant tigress. The sight shook as well as amazed him inside out. His mind was stormed by numerous possibilities and infinite queries regarding the baby's presence. After getting the baby settled inside his hut, on a small grass bed, he noticed Jwala, the tigress, growling and nudging him and pulling his hand. She wanted to convey some message to him. Gurudev could sense a mystery hidden in her eyes and let himself be led by Jwala.

After they swam upstream in Mahatejaa toward the great cliff, the tigress entered the tunnel hidden under the mountains. As they reappeared on the other side of the tunnel, Gurudev kept staring at the sight, completely dumbfounded. It was the same view he had witnessed many, many years ago. After looking from side to side numerous times, there were no more lingering doubts in his mind. It was the same notorious forest of Raat-Raan. Frozen, he was trying to grapple with the unexpected surprise. But the impatient tigress kept pulling him further inside the forest.

It was a day full of bright sunshine, yet the thick forest remained swallowed in the darkness. Soon they came across a horrifying sight. It was the place from where the tigress had picked up Shivani. The scene in front of him shattered Gurudev, the one famous for his stoic mind. His heart was sheared with the pain. He dropped down near the two listless bodies...the bodies of Saritaa-Devi and Himraaj—the parents of Shivani. Their motionless bodies were lying in a pool of blood. The fatal arrows were seen still pierced in them.

To Gurudev's extreme surprise, suddenly the woman's fingers quivered. Gurudev bolted toward her and gathered her in his arms.

"Child!" wiping away water from her face, he whispered, "Don't worry, my child. You are safe in my hands." To her left side was some rain water collected on a huge leaf. He fed a few drops of water to the woman. After drinking the water, the woman found the energy to narrate the tragic events that had occurred around Shivani's birth.

That night, in spite of knowing its viciousness, a couple, Himraaj and Saritaa-Devi, had entered the forest of Raat-Raan. There was no other choice for them. As they entered the forest, the rains started. The drizzles soon turned into full blown rains. There were densely packed, giant trees hovering over them on all sides. Squeezing themselves through, in the utter darkness, the two were desperately trying to find their way. Frequently glancing back, they would pause momentarily, just to sense their pursuers. Then once again, they would resume their course, threading through the forest. Bearing the lashing rains, they kept walking forward.

Suddenly the lightning dazzled the skies, forcing them to hide behind a nearby tree. As soon as the darkness was restored, the two resumed their way. One of the two was Saritaa-Devi, pregnant with their first child. Although longing to sit down and rest a while, she continued walking with her husband, Himraaj. Their predicament was such that she couldn't allow herself to rest. Supported by her husband's hand, sometimes leaning on the trees, she ventured further as fast as she could. In a cautiously low tone, Himraaj was appreciating her for her courage and endurance.

They had crossed quite a distance so far. Himraaj was happy. Just then, Saritaa-Devi sank down. Words were not necessary to inform Himraaj about the initiation of her labor pains.

"Naath!" Saritaa-Devi addressed him, wincing with pains. "I can't walk...any...further!"

Himraaj's fear had become reality. He blurted out in shock, "You ….can't… walk …any ….. further?" Every word was full of disbelief and frustration.

"I am very sorry…" Saritaa-Devi's voice trailed off as she started whimpering. Frustrated with the pains, she just hid her face behind her hands helplessly.

Himraaj got lost in his own thoughts for a few moments, but soon, he sat by his wife's side. "Devi Sarita, please do not feel sad. You have no reason to blame yourself. Only because of your determination could we venture so far away from them. Now, just a tiny bit of the course is remaining. Once we cross this kingdom's limit, we will be safe." Glancing back in the darkness he whispered, "Sarita, we both are aware of the dangers of staying here and getting imprisoned again. I don't want our baby to be born in this cruel kingdom, Suvarna-Raaj. Simply for our baby, we must move on. Or else…" sighing subtly, he continued, "…all our painstaking efforts will go in vain."

"Naath!" Again in an apologetic voice, the lady said, "But…but I cannot take even a step ahead."

"Please do not worry, Devi Saritaa! I am here. In no time, we will be out of the hands of those devils."

Saritaa-Devi kept staring at Himraaj as he swiftly lifted her up with his strong hands. Once again, they started their arduous journey.

The skies continued pouring with heavy rains along with frequent bursts of thunderous flashes of lightning. The tired Himraaj was hauling himself and his wife in search of a safer place. He had no time to recognize Saritaa-Devi's increasing pains. As he paused momentarily to catch his breath, he caught a quick glimpse of her face, which scared him to death. In dismay, he looked once again at the ghastly conditions around them—the streaming rains, the flooded ground, the huge pythons hanging down from the trees, the poisonous cobras slithering around for a drier place, the wild, hungry beasts peeking from behind their hideouts.

"I don't want my child to be born here," he thought, quivering inside.

The lightening struck the skies one more time, and a thunderous laughter left Himraaj dazed with fright. It was Krurvarmaa, the leader of the team pursuing them. He was standing just a few yards away from them. Due to sheer luck, he had spotted the couple in the flash of lightning. That surprise turned Krurvarmaa mad with joy.

After their escape from the prison, the king of Suvarna-raaj had issued an order to search for the couple. As per the royal orders, Krurvarmaa and his team were scouring the forest for Himraaj and Saritaa-Devi. While obeying his orders on that deadly night, he himself had been separated from his team. Wandering blindly in the forest, he was worried about his own safety. Just then, unexpectedly, his eyes caught the glimpse of Himraaj and Saritaa-Devi, and he began envisioning the highest prize offered by the king. He couldn't contain his joy.

"Ha! Ha! Ha!" his victorious roar echoed through the forest.

"Oh, no!" Himraaj whispered, hopelessly covering his wife.

Soon arrows from Krurvarmaa's bow plunged into the bodies of Saritaa-Devi and Himraaj. As Saritaa-Devi collapsed to the ground by Himraaj's side, she could still hear Krurvarmaa's deafening laughter.

"Ha! Ha! Ha!" Krurvarmaa was roaring like a wild beast. He began calling his teammates and announcing his victorious achievement. As he was moving forward to claim his hunt, suddenly a mammoth sized python fell on him. Within a few moments, he became listless inside the strong coils of the python. His approaching friends halted in shock as they witnessed the ghastly sight of Krurvarmaa disappearing inside the python's huge mouth. After glancing around and seeing a few more pythons dangling from nearby branches, they all stepped back instantly and ran away.

Forgetting her excruciating pains, Saritaa-Devi was watching the horrifying scene with utter helplessness. She witnessed Krurvarmaa getting swallowed by a huge python and his soldiers running away. Everything was simply unbelievable. She closed her eyes momentarily. As her child entered the world she passed out.

Saritaa-Devi's withered face dazzled with the utmost satisfaction after hearing that her daughter was safe with Gurudev. She was pleasantly surprised to learn about the wondrous escape of her child from the dreadful scene. Painstakingly, she turned toward her husband, her trembling fingers caressing his mortal remains. After handing over her red ruby pendant to Gurudev, Saritaa-Devi left the mortal world to join her husband.

Shivani was listening to the chilling details about her parents, her clear face reflecting her tumultuous emotions: confusion, anger, frustration, despair, and eventually the heartbreaking grief at the loss of her parents. Unable to contain such an enormous sadness, her thin lips began quivering. Soon her huge eyes, ever spilling with joy and mirth, were flooded with tears—the tears of her weeping heart. Covering her face with her tiny hands, she started whimpering.

Gurudev couldn't bare the look on Shivani's face. Until then, he had only witnessed a naughty, playful, vibrant, and happy Shivani. He glanced around and was startled to see Shivani's friends gathered there, sitting on the ground, motionless and quiet. They could sense their friend's pain. He looked again at Shivani. She was sobbing very hard. He wanted to console her, but he didn't know where to start. He gently kept his hand over her back. Suddenly, Shivani shrugged his hand off and stormed out of the hut, crashing open the door. Gurudev instantly followed her, but she was too fast.

The rains had stopped completely. Everything looked clean, as if it had been bathed. All the plants appeared to have thickened in the soaking. Being heavy with water, the foliage caused the branches to hang down in graceful arcs. The water drops were reflecting daylight. It appeared as if all the foliage was sprinkled with heavenly pearls. All that beauty wasn't able to capture Gurudev's attention. His eyes were simply looking for Shivani. Finally he spotted her. She was entering the roaring river.

"Shivani! Shivani! Shivani!" He screamed desperately, but Shivani continued swimming. Soon she was seen heading to Jwala's den on the opposite bank of the river. Gurudev sighed. Although still worried, he was a bit relieved. Shivani had chosen the best place to seek solace for her broken heart. After all, Jwala was also her mother.

"My dear friends," Gurudev said, staring into the pitiful eyes of Shivani's friends, "Please do not worry. Shivani will be fine." He patted the rabbits. "We should give her some time. She will recover from the shock," he murmured, looking at Jwala's den as though in addition to consoling Shivani's friends, he was consoling himself, too. Everyone returned to their places but Naagraaj, who kept slithering over Gurudev's shoulders very restlessly.

A lot of time had passed. The day turned into dusk and then into night. The partly clouded sky began revealing the bright moon, trying to lighten the darkness of night. Everyone had returned to their nests safely, yet there was no sign of Shivani. With each passing moment, Gurudev was getting more and more restless. Finally he picked up the restless coils of Naagraaj on his shoulders and set out in search of his endearing daughter.

First he went to the den. Finding it empty, his heart sank momentarily, but then a thought flashed in his mind and he was relieved. The empty den suggested that Shivani wasn't alone anymore. For sure, wherever she was, her mama tiger was also with her. He continued his search, combing through all the possible sites such as the lotus lake, the berry patch, the meadow, the hill, and the mango forest. The restless Naagraaj was speedily slithering up and down his shoulders. Finally at one spot, the cobra jumped down and slunk inside the bushes by a mango tree. As Gurudev followed him, he witnessed a pair of glistening eyes. That was Jwala, and beside her was the tiny Shivani. The two were sitting, huddled together.

"Shivani!" Gurudev exclaimed ecstatically. "I am so happy to find you here, all safe."

Shivani was very quiet, but her face was all withered and her eyes swollen.

"Shivani, I can understand your grief. It's a natural reaction." He gently picked up her lowered face. "But instead of hiding here, you should have opened up your mind to me. You should have shared your feelings with me, my child."

Shivani was still maintaining her silence. By then, her best friend, Naagraaj, had well settled on her shoulders.

Staring at her face, Gurudev continued in a humble voice, "Sometimes tragic events, over which we don't have any control, happen in our lives. Those events make us sad, angry, frustrated, and depressed." Gurudev paused to judge Shivani's reaction. "In such situations, if we keep our minds closed and let those nasty emotions whirl inside, the results are always devastating. Our lives get ruined forever." Looking at Shivani's puzzled face, he continued. "So, we must open up our minds; share the bad emotions or feelings with our loved ones. This way our mind gets cleaned. This is the best way to deal with such situations."

Still quiet, Shivani was listening very carefully. Running his fingers through her hair, he said, "Shivani, if you fail to banish those nasty emotions from your mind, they keep lingering for a long time and can inflict an everlasting injury." Squeezing her closer to his heart, Gurudev asked, "Understand?"

Shivani conceded.

"Now...do you want to say something?"

"Gurudev! Gurudev!" Shivani's voice was all choked up. "I just don't know what to say...and where...where to start." Her voice quickly trailed off.

"My child...."

"Gurudev." Clearing her throat, Shivani spoke out. "I feel terrible about the death of my parents, especially after knowing how cruelly they were murdered and the reason behind their murder. I feel sad ....very sad. Also, I feel...angry...and frustrated and hopeless and helpless, all at the same time." Shivani was speaking very intensely. With a renewed bout of sobbing, her tiny body began trembling.

Gurudev made her sit on a nearby rock. Sitting beside her, he wiped the tears streaming continuously from her eyes.

When she began to calm down, Gurudev said softly, "My child, all that crying has left you exhausted. But do you know, this crying has done one good thing?"

Shivani glanced at him blankly. Caressing her head, he said, "This crying has drained all your sadness. It has cleansed your mind."

Shivani again looked at him with disbelief.

"Now, take a deep breath in and push it out forcefully, like this."

By then, Naagraaj had climbed onto Gurudev. Just when Gurudev forced his breath out, Naagraaj hissed, sticking his head forward. That hissing and Gurudev's forceful breath happened at the very same time, and the funny sight compelled Shivani to laugh.

"My child, this laughter made me extremely happy. It feels like I have been showered by the stardust, cold and soft. I think even Naagraaj and Jwala are very happy, too."

Shivani smiled again as she noticed Naagraaj trying to repeat his hissing. Until then, Jwala had stood a little away from them. Listening to Shivani's laughter, she came closer and began licking Shivani's hands.

"Shivani," Gurudev said with a soft sigh, "Although...you have lost your parents, you are not all alone in this world. We are here to help you out." Staring at her, he said, "My child, you are sad for your parents' death because you miss seeing and talking to them, don't you?"

Shivani just nodded.

"How would you feel if I tell you that your parents are still living somewhere...somewhere in this universe? Although not in the same world of yours, but I am sure they are happily living in the other world and are watching you. Now how does it feel?"

With raised eyebrows, Shivani stared with a puzzled face.

"Do you feel a bit happy after thinking like that?"

Shivani conceded, nodding her head in affirmation at the thought.

"Shivani, it is well known that the pious souls like theirs are destined for a heavenly life after their deaths. Now, where do they live, we don't know for sure. It's a secret. We call them 'dead' because their spirits have departed their earthly bodies. The death has ended all their sufferings of this mortal world and freed them to join the divine bliss of their heavenly residence."

Shivani was listening to every word very intently. Every single word was caressing her grieving heart. She was feeling as if a heavy weight was being lifted off her chest, letting her breathe freely.

"Gurudev, I do believe in you. But when I remember the reason for my parents' hunt and how cruelly they were murdered, I get restless and angry and sad."

"Shivani..." Pausing momentarily, Gurudev spoke, "Remember, your parents are not alone. There are tens of thousands of people who are still suffering under the brutal regime of Suvarna-Raaj. Hundreds of innocents are being slaughtered, just like your parents. They have no savior. The atrocities and oppression by this ruthless king are increasing day by day. He is smothering the humanity on this earth."

"Gurudev, after hearing this, I am frustrated and helpless. I can't do anything to help the poor victims..."

"Who says so?"

Shivani threw a surprising glance at him.

"Shivani, you can be their savior."

"Who? Me?" Although Shivani kept gazing at him dumbfoundedly, Gurudev's voice sounded magical to her.

"Yes! Shivani, instead of sitting here and mourning about your parents, you can work hard and become the savior for the thousands of feeble, helpless people. Though you couldn't help your parents, you still can help those people to be freed from the evil clutches of the king. This is the right way of paying respects to your parents."

"Gurudev! How? How can I help them? How will that be possible? You just told me that the king is very powerful. Also, he has a huge army." With a quick pause, she stared straight into Gurudev's eyes and said, "I...I don't even have any weapons. Even if I get one, I don't know how to fight with a king." Her voice was full of despair.

"Shivani, I will teach you how to fight with the king."

"Gurudev, you...you...are going to teach me how to fight?"

Shivani sprang up from her position. It was impossible for her to imagine her mellow, soft Gurudev could have ever fought a war or could teach someone how to fight.

"Yes, indeed! Are you surprised?" He smiled at her.

"Of course. Yes," Shivani replied honestly.

"Shivani, if I tell you that I am a fiery and fierce warrior, will you believe me?"

"Never...ever!" Shivani blurted instantly. With a gentle smile, she whispered, "You are such a nice person." She hugged him.

Gurudev let out a soft laugh. "Shivani, nice people have to learn fighting and become warriors, both to defend themselves as well as to protect the weak."

Shivani's face was still perplexed.

"My child, I will teach you all the necessary fighting skills and make you a great warrior. My teaching will enable you to challenge the king of Suvarna- Raaj. This is my promise to you."

"Gurudev, but how do you know fighting? I mean, who taught you?" The lingering question in Shivani's mind was finally asked.

"I will tell you all about it later." Gurudev smiled. Caressing Shivani's hair, he continued. "Child, now push all the lingering sadness out of your mind. You have no time to entertain any sadness or frustration. Now, there is only one goal for you." Gurudev's voice was imposing. "You have to become a warrior and free the people of Suvarna-Raaj."

Sitting under the moonlight, engulfed in the quietness of the night, Gurudev's majestic words of wisdom made an impact on Shivani's mind. She took a deep breath. Now, there was a newly found meaning to her life. The hope of destroying the evil had started flashing in her mind, invigorating her.

"Focusing the eyes on the future helps in forgetting the mishaps from the past. It motivates us to work hard and achieve the noble goal." Gurudev spoke while gazing at the star-laden sky, "Shivani look at the star above us. It doesn't worry about the surrounding darkness but outshines it. Not only that it guides others ….people like us. I want you to be like this star. Help the needy people; destroy the evil. Are you ready for that?"

"Yes, Gurudev!" Shivani replied promptly and stood up.

Gurudev looked proudly at her tiny figure standing before him with the winning attitude. He was satisfied to see the great resolve on her face.

"Shivani!" Gurudev rose from his position and whispered, "Please come with me. I have something to show you." He began walking toward the mango forest. There were two flowering trees amidst that forest—Prajakta trees, blossoming with an abundance of tiny, delicate white flowers that sparkled like little stars. Their heavenly fragrance filled the air. Pointing toward those trees, he said, "Shivani, I know these are your favorite trees. I have seen you many times around them."

"Gurudev, I love these trees," Shivani said, picking up a Prajakta flower by its red stem and inhaling its magical scent.

"Shivani, these trees rose up from your parents' ashes."

With the utter disbelief, Shivani jerked her face toward Gurudev. "It was quite surprising to me, too." Watching Shivani's surprised face, he said, "With the help of Jwala, I brought your parents bodies from Raat-Raan to this place. This is the place where I performed the last rituals on them."

Mesmerized, Shivani walked closer to the trees. Their flowers were caressing her all over her body. Standing a little away from her along with Jwala and Naagraaj, Gurudev was watching with misty eyes.

The next day, Gurudev woke up at his usual time, the events of the previous day still lingering in his mind. In the light of dawn, he threw a casual glance at Shivani's bed and sprang up in surprise. Her bed was empty.

Suddenly his eyes caught the rarest glimpse. His sight still hooked toward the river, he stood frozen as a statue. Totally dumbfounded, he watched Shivani's tiny figure standing in the river, offering her prayers to the rays of dawn.

"I wonder when she saw me doing that." Flashing a pleasant smile, Gurudev happily picked up Naagraaj slithering nearby. "I think the right moment has arrived, Naagraaj."

CHAPTER SEVEN

FACETING A DIAMOND

It was a blissful morning in the hermitage of Guru Yogidev. The golden rays of the sun were anxiously waiting to enter the world. The cool breeze was flowing, infusing serenity through every corner. The humble voice of Gurudev echoed through the sanctity of morning.

"A strong mind is the key to success." Facing the east, sitting under a huge tree, Gurudev was teaching Shivani. "Shivani, becoming a warrior is a hard task. You may face many hurdles and hardships. They will test your patience and endurance. To overcome them successfully, you will need to have a strong mind."

Shivani was listening very carefully.

Gurudev continued. "Our ancestors developed various ways to strengthen our minds. Today I will teach you the way I have been following for many years, and that is- meditation."

Like a devout student, Shivani was absorbing every single word spoken by her guru.

"The first and the most important step in meditation is the posture. Sitting in a perfect lotus position is necessary to acquire the desired effects."

After trying for a while, Shivani settled into a perfect lotus position. Her back straight, legs folded like lotus petals, Shivani sat with her eyes focused straight ahead at the rising sun.

"Excellent! This is the precise seat for meditation. Now the next step is to concentrate all your attention on your breathing."

According to his old habit, Gurudev closed his eyes. This time, Shivani didn't sneak away. "The breathing should be slow, deep, and rhythmic. Initially, it can be a bit difficult, but with practice, you should be able to succeed. Once you get into slow breathing, try pulling yourself away from the surroundings."

"Why should we do that, Gurudev?"

"There are lots of distractions around us, such as these chirping birds, the flowing river, the animals moving around, and so on. Distractions are the biggest hurdles in meditation. By pulling yourself away, you will help your mind stay focused. It is the hardest step but the most crucial one for meditation."

Gurudev paused momentarily and glanced at Shivani. She was following him very earnestly. Sitting by his side with closed eyes and a serene face, she was breathing calmly. Another nod of appreciation came from the happy Gurudev.

"Good job, Shivani!" he exclaimed. "Now try breathing slower and deeper. Imagine with each breath the power, the energy, and the confidence flowing into your body, permeating through each cell. Every time you release a breath, imagine the sadness, the weakness, the depression, being pushed out of your body. Now your mind has become quiet. There is no more fear or stress or anger or frustration lingering inside you. It is completely engulfed in the pure bliss. With this blissful mind, you are ready to set forth for the spiritual journey. This is the journey which will take you inward, toward the eternal spirit, and grant you the rare and unique spiritual power."

The soft breeze was reverberating Gurudev's magical words around the meditating pair. "Eventually the success will be yours, Shivani. It will be waiting there to embrace you at the end of a daunting path."

The moment Gurudev looked at Shivani to judge her progress; his eyes remained transfixed on the perfectly still figure of Shivani, swept away in meditation.

"Shivani!" he whispered softly.

There was no response from Shivani. She had already pulled herself away from the surrounding conscious world and had set out for the divine path shown by her guru. Her little, perfectly calm statue was displaying pure bliss. The circular, vermilion birthmark on her forehead was shining under the golden rays.

For Shivani, a new life began. It was completely different from her previous one. It was arduous and challenging. She would wake up well before dawn. Shrugging off the remaining sleep in the cold waters of Mahatejaa, she would rush to the exercise area behind the hut. There she would start doing Surya- Namaskaar. Initially it was hard for her, but with perseverance, she was able to do all 108 of those exercises at a time. By the end, she would be covered with sweat.

After a quick snack of fruits, Gurudev and Shivani would sit in mediation until lunch break. For lunch there would be fresh fruits, roots, and of course the bitter-tasting green herbs. The magical powers of those greens would instantly sweep away all her tiredness and make her energetic. Then it would be time to learn scholastics. She would work on writing and reading. Also she had started learning about the world, the civilizations, politics, astronomy, health, and so on. After those lessons, there would be time to relax and play with her friends.

Initially her friends missed their playful and naughty friend. But soon, they got used to the newly transformed Shivani. Now, they were not able to divert this Shivani's attention from her studies. Eventually they learned to wait patiently until the break time. The moment Gurudev would get up from his seat, they would instantly rush toward her and start pouncing upon her.

Shivani was progressing rapidly in every field. Her miraculous ability to absorb knowledge made Gurudev very happy. Her questions would reflect an extraordinary intelligence. Now, she was ready for another new chapter in her learning.

One morning Shivani was practicing her assignment when she heard Gurudev calling for her, his voice full of excitement. She instantly raced to him. "What is it, Gurudev?" she asked, catching her breath.

"Look here!" Gurudev was holding some strange things in his hands that she had never seen before. "This one is called a bow, and this one is called an arrow."

In their remote hermitage, Gurudev had managed to make a bow by bending a flexible, long yet sturdy stick and tying its ends with a tough, slick, leafless vine. Another slender, pointed stick was ready to work as an arrow.

"What are we going to do with this, Gurudev?"

"We are going to learn archery—the technique of using bow and arrow." Looking at her innocent face, Gurudev answered her unspoken question. "My child, you will need to learn and master this weapon to achieve your goal. From now on, this will be your weapon. Let's begin."

With her eyes transfixed on the unique weapon, she began following Gurudev.

Behind their tiny hut was an open meadow. The tall trees were quite far away from there. The ground beneath their feet was remarkably even and smooth. That indeed was the best spot for learning archery. Gurudev walked to the center of the area and placed both the bow and the arrow on the ground. Then he kneeled down in front of them and did namaskaar.

Shivani's eyes were curiously following his every movement.

After paying his respects, Gurudev picked up the bow with his left hand and gave a powerful jerk to the tightly stretched vine of the bow with his right thumb and index finger, resulting in a loud strumming sound that echoed through the whole surroundings.

Although a little startled with the sound, Shivani sensed a unique thrill and fervor electrifying her whole body. Walking toward Gurudev, she asked, "Wow! What was that?"

"It is called a bow twang. This is the sound that challenges the enemy and fills the hearts of warriors with valor and excitement." Gurudev took a deep breath. He held the bow in front of him and placed the makeshift arrow on it with its end sitting on the tightly tied vine of the bow. Aiming at a leaf far away on a tree branch, he pulled the arrow back toward his ears with his right thumb and middle finger and released it. The arrow instantly zoomed through the sky with a great speed and hit the aimed target precisely. Rooted to her spot, Shivani was marveled by this very first demonstration of archery.

"Now, would you like to try?"

"Who? Me?"

"Yes!" Gurudev kept the bow on the ground. Taking her closer to the bow, he said,

"First pay your respects to your weapon. Please namaskaar to the bow and then pick it up."

After doing namaskaar, Shivani hesitantly picked up the bow. Her face reflected her anxiety as well as excitement. Taking a deep breath, she attempted to shoot an arrow. It didn't work. She tried again and again, but it was all futile.

"I can't do it," she said, putting the bow down on the ground.

Flashing an assuring smile, Gurudev said, "Shivani, don't feel discouraged. Learning a new skill is not easy. It tests our patience. But with the help of commitment, perseverance, and a positive attitude, you will be able to master it." Handing the bow to her, he continued. "Believe in yourself, reflect the self-confidence, and now try it again, and again, and again...till you can shoot an arrow."

Soon enough, Shivani's first arrow dazzled the skies. "Gurudev! Gurudev!" Shivani's voice was spilling with exuberance. "I did it, Gurudev!" The feelings regarding the great accomplishment enabled her to ignore her bruised thumb.

A new horizon was now opened for Shivani. She would keep practicing her archery even during her spare time, which enabled her to advance her skills at a dizzying speed. Her animal friends would happily participate in her archery practice. Sunetraa, Dhawal, and Shubhra would fetch the arrows falling on the ground, while Madhur and Mayur were responsible for catching the arrows soaring high in the air. Soon it became difficult for her flying or running friends to catch her arrows, zooming out with great speed. They would keep staring at them in wonder.

After mastering the basics, Shivani turned to the techniques of advanced archery. She would ask Mayur to swing a tree branch and try shooting the swinging branch. Holding fruits in their mouths, the white bunnies and the deer would run in different directions, helping Shivani practice shooting accurately at the fruits. Every day she would set more and more difficult goals for herself. Then she began practicing archery with her eyes blindfolded, aiming and shooting simply by listening to the sound. During all her learning sessions, Naagraaj would stay with her as her cheerleader.

As the days passed by, Shivani's archery intensified. Bathed in sweat, her fingers all scraped and bloodied and her feet bruised, Shivani would keep practicing to master a specific skill. Her determination was admirable. Her friends would scramble to catch the never-ending stream of arrows whooshing harshly through the air and then pouncing to the ground. With great perseverance, she had excelled in many advanced skills. She was able to shoot multiple moving targets precisely at the very same time with lightning speed. Also, she could accurately aim and shoot a distant target in the pitch darkness.

Gurudev was very happy with Shivani's excellence. He was amazed by her magnificent memory and abilities. Whatever he taught her would be readily absorbed. Her diligence in every subject would awe him. Each and every learning event would reflect one more new quality of Shivani. Her commitment, dedication, determination, endurance, methodical planning, and logical thinking were all signaling her ability to become a great archer. With just a single stroke, the impulsive, boisterous, naughty, wanderer Shivani was gone. In her place, the new Shivani had emerged, dazzling gloriously as a multifaceted diamond.

It was nighttime, and Shivani was having difficulty falling asleep. No matter how hard she tried, sleep kept running away from her. The constant tossing and turning in her grass bed was breaking the silence of the night. Gurudev was listening to the rustle. After a while, he got up.

"What's the matter, my child? Is anything hurting?" His voice was full of concern. "I think you are working too hard. Maybe you should take a break tomorrow."

"Gurudev, I...I am fine." Shivani sat up in her bed.

"Is anything bothering you, my child?" he asked, sitting near her.

"Gurudev, I...I don't know why, but I feel scared."

"Scared? Of what?"

"This darkness. This darkness is scaring me."

"The darkness?" Gurudev jolted with surprise. "Shivani, when you were very young you would never get scared by the darkness. Instead, you would like it. You would play hide-and-seek and chase the glowing fireflies. You would happily stare at the moon and the stars. You would love the smell of night blooming jasmine planted around the hut. Do you remember that?"

"Yes, Gurudev! I remember that. But now...now I feel scared about this darkness. It is so huge. I feel like it is going to swallow me."

"Hmmmmm. What should we do now?" Gurudev sighed softly. He stole a quick glance at Shivani and smiled. "How about listening to a nice story?"

"Oh, yes! A story!" Shivani jumped immediately. She always enjoyed Gurudev's stories. For a long time, she hadn't listened to any story. By the end of the day, she would be so exhausted that the moment her back would touch the bed, she would start snoring. Turning onto her belly, supporting her chin with her hands, she looked at Gurudev expectantly. That was her familiar story-listening pose.

Gurudev cleared his voice.

Long, long ago, there was a man. He was living in a big city. He had a beautiful wife and a lovely son, just like you.

"Gurudev, I am not a son..." Shivani said, wrinkling her forehead in a frown.

"But...aren't you lovely and...adorable?"

"Yes, that's true."

So, the son was just like you. The man was very rich and owned a big house. He had plenty of gold coins in his treasure chest. He was living a very nice life." Gurudev changed his position. *"But this man had a very bad habit. He would always whine about one or the other thing. One day he was alone in his house because his wife and their son had gone to her parents' house, in a different city. As usual, he began cursing his bad luck for not having a mansion and three treasure chests like his friend. Eventually he got so upset that he left his home.*

"Really?"

"Yes, Shivani."

Cursing his fate, he started wandering the streets. Soon he realized that he was out of the city. While wandering around, he sighted a shiny thing on the ground. It was a stone. Though very shiny and transparent, it was simply a stone. Kicking it, he screamed, "How unlucky I am! I thought I found a diamond." Just then, magic happened. The stone started speaking.

"Speaking? How is that possible, Gurudev?"

"Shivani, it was a magic stone!"

The stone said to the man, "Hey, gentleman! Please do not throw me away. I am not an ordinary stone. I am the lucky stone."

"The lucky stone?" the man asked in disbelief.

"Yes! Indeed I am. Please trust me and keep me with you."

After thinking for a moment, the man unwillingly slid the stone in his pocket and resumed walking. Now he had entered a jungle. As he walked under a tree, a few thugs sitting on that tree suddenly jumped down and attacked him. They robbed him and ran away after taking all the diamond rings from his fingers and the gold coins from his pockets. Of course they didn't take the stone. It was worthless to them. After the robbers fled the scene, the man started grumbling again. As the lucky stone started consoling him, the man's whole anguish became directed toward that stone.

"Hey! You deceived me. You are not at all a lucky stone. You are just an ugly, bad, cursed stone!"

The stone tried to defend itself. "Hey, my friend, you don't know the truth. Only because of my presence, the thugs left you alive."

"Alive?" The man was puzzled.

"Yes! After looting you, they were about to kill you, but my presence saved you. You have lost only your wealth, but not your life."

"I don't believe you," the man scoffed at the stone and began walking. Some time later, he spotted big, dark clouds gathering in the sky. Soon it started thundering and raining. The winds blew with all their might. Wet and cold, the grumpy man began walking faster toward a tree for shelter. Just then he tripped over a big rock and

landed on nearby thorny bushes. Whining and glancing at the scrapes and cuts on his body, he started cursing his fate and, of course, the stone. "How stupid I am for trusting a silly stone!" Taking the stone out of his pocket, he cried, "You are not lucky at all. You are my misfortune."

The stone spoke pleadingly, "Hey, my friend! Please do not cry. Just look ahead in front of you."

The man was startled, witnessing the scene in front of him. The powerful winds had knocked down the big tree he was going to use as his shelter.

"Had you not tripped over this rock, you would have been crushed under the tree."

The lucky stone's words assured the man, but he didn't say anything. He got up and shrugged the dirt off his body.

Shivani was listening to the story very intently.

Happy to be alive, the man began walking toward his city. He carefully kept the stone in his pocket. By the time he neared the city, the storm had stopped. But after getting a glimpse of the city, he was stunned and stood frozen at his spot. Due to the storm, there was widespread devastation. The streets were flooded, the trees had fallen down, and the houses were collapsed. He waded through the water and reached his house. It had crumpled completely, and all that was left was the rubble. This time, the grumpy man didn't curse his fate. Instead he thanked the stone for saving his wife and son, who were away. The stone smiled.

"Did it really?" Shivani asked, widening her eyes.

"Yes, Shivani! Remember, it was a special stone.

The grumpy man. . .

"Gurudev, I think you made a mistake," Shivani interrupted. "The man wasn't grumpy anymore."

"Shivani, you are absolutely right. Now, he had begun changing into a nice, happy man."

The man entered the ruins of his house. There, under a fallen pillar, was his treasure chest. It was completely broken and empty and submerged in the floodwaters. All the gold coins from the chest had been washed away. When he looked carefully, to his surprise, he found one gold coin still glistening in a corner of the chest. He thanked the luck as well as the stone for saving that gold coin.

While trying to put the gold coin into his pocket, the man accidentally dropped the lucky stone into the floodwaters. The magic stone began drifting away speedily. The man tried hard to catch the stone but was unsuccessful. A little farther from him, another man, weeping over his lost wealth, happened to spot the stone and grabbed it. Watching that, the grumpy man smiled and whispered, "Now, I don't need that stone anymore. Instead the other man needs it." After carefully placing the gold coin in his pocket and admiring his luck for saving the coin from getting washed away, he walked away happily.

"It was a very good story, Gurudev!" Shivani exclaimed.

"Thank you, Shivani." Gurudev smiled. "Do you think the stone really was a lucky stone?"

"No, Gurudev."

"Then what do you think the story was about?"

"I think the essence of the story was about having a positive attitude." Shivani sat up in her bed. Gazing at the darkness, she said further, "After every unhappy event the stone showed the man a different perspective. Viewing the event from that angle the man thought he was lucky and it could have been worse. That very outlook helped him cope with the sadness or loss." After a pause Shivani added, "If we follow this approach, I think we too, would feel luckier and happier."

Hearing such an astonishingly perfect analysis from a naïve young girl, Gurudev was totally surprised. He thought to himself, "It's amazing to believe how easily this young girl can comprehend such a complex story." He looked at her adoringly.

"Gurudev, am I right?"

"Absolutely!" Flashing a nice smile, he asked, "Shivani, are you still scared of the darkness?"

"Nope! I am enjoying the darkness around me." Shivani giggled. "I am happy that due to this darkness, I am able to enjoy the dazzling beauty of the moon and those millions of stars."

"Excellent!" Gurudev exclaimed. "Shivani, look at the moon. It is so tiny as compared to the enormous sky." After a quick pause he continued. "Do you think it is scared of the sky?"

"No, Gurudev." Shivani said, watching the moon intently. "It keeps shining bravely, governing these humongous, dark skies."

Time was flying in Guru Yogidev's hermitage, Aashrum. The days, months, and years were passing by at an immense speed. All the seasons were taking turns witnessing Shivani's unwavering hard work. They all were admiring her tenacity, dedication, and, of course, her ascent toward becoming the best archer the world had ever seen. She didn't pause for the scorching sun, the torrential rains, or the bone-chilling cold. While undergoing her training, Shivani was emerging, glowing with multiple virtues.

Finally, in the premises of the hermitage, a day rose that was filled with fervor and excitement. It was the day of witnessing Shivani's exemplary accomplishments in the field of archery. There was a lot of hustle and bustle around the place. To watch the demonstration of Shivani's archery, all her friends had gathered around the open area behind the hut where Shivani had been practicing archery for the past few years. They were all pouncing, jumping, slithering, and flying. A little away from them, Gurudev sat on a wicker mat eagerly waiting to watch his disciple's performance.

Standing in the center of the arena was everyone's beloved, Shivani. Removing the veil of childhood, she had emerged as a pretty teenage girl. She wore a long dress made of tree bark. Over that skirt, she had wrapped her mother's saffron sash, for she liked to be caressed by it all the time. One end of the sash was tucked inside the dress, while the other end flared freely from her left shoulder so that it looked like she was wearing a sari. Her usually free-flowing, long, silky black hair was neatly gathered together and tied in a bun on her head. She had tied a quiver filled with arrows to her back, and a long bow was tucked up over her right shoulder. Facing the rising sun, her big brown eyes were focused straight ahead. All these years growing along with her, the vermilion-colored, circular birthmark on her forehead was dazzling in the sun's rays. Her whole face was beaming with confidence.

After doing namaskaar to her revered Gurudev, she did namaskaar to the sun. Then the wonderful presentation began. Holding her bow in front of her, she placed an arrow on it. After carefully aiming Shivani shot her arrow at the target, a parrot made of straw and hung high up in a tree. Zooming speedily toward the tree, the arrow precisely hit the target—the eye of the straw parrot. Instantly a wild ruckus was heard from every corner of the arena. Gurudev smiled happily.

Now, Shivani turned to the next event. There were seven fruits kept in a single straight line on the ground. In a blink, a single powerful arrow plunged through all of the fruits and appeared out from the last one. Soon six of her friends headed in different directions, each carrying a tuber in its mouth. As they reached their positions,

Shivani quickly judged them and shot six arrows in quick succession. Without hurting her friends, all her arrows correctly pierced through the tubers at approximately the same time. Gurudev raised his right hand.

"Well done, my child! Well done."

"Dhanyawaad, Gurudev! Thank you," Shivani replied politely. Then, holding a tiny berry in its beak, Madhur, the kokil, flew high up in the sky. At the same time Mayur, the peacock, rose up carrying a mango. From a good height, the two targets, a berry and a mango, were dropped. Instantly, with lightning speed, Shivani's arrows dashed and pricked through the falling berry and mango. Before anyone realized, both the mango and the berry had landed perfectly in front of Gurudev.

"Excellent!" Gurudev whispered and began enjoying the sweet treats presented to him.

For the next event, Shivani put a blindfold over her eyes. Getting a cue from her, two swans entered the arena carrying a rose garland Shivani had made. With immense concentration, Shivani was listening to their moves. The moment they dropped the garland, Shivani's arrow soared toward it and, in a flash, carried it toward Gurudev. While all the spectators stood watching in awe, the garland landed perfectly around Gurudev's neck. The arena filled with the cheers. Even Gurudev couldn't hold himself back.

"You are simply amazing, Shivani!" he exclaimed joyfully. Accepting the appreciation from her guru and taking off her blindfold, Shivani stood at her position with renewed vigor. Next, with tremendous speed, she shot multiple arrows into the air. Her speed of shooting the arrows was such that it was difficult for observers to notice her taking out arrows from the quiver, placing them on her bow, and shooting them. All the phases simply blended together, creating an impression of one continuous stream of arrows arising from Shivani. Soon there appeared a carpet, woven beautifully with arrows, gliding down slowly from the sky.

"Wonderful!" the astonished Gurudev whispered as the carpet landed softly on the grass. He was astounded by the pretty presentation. He had never taught her that art. After settling down on the carpet, he remarked, "Shivani, today you have excelled the basics of archery. Being your teacher, I feel exhilarated at this very moment." He raised his right hand. "Shubham Bhavatu, my child. My blessings will be with you forever."

As soon as he began waving his hands, the numerous birds, sitting on nearby trees, stormed the sky. Within moments, Shivani was showered with countless delicate, colorful petals. The overwhelmed Shivani raced to Gurudev. Wiping her tears, she touched her guru's feet. "Gurudev, I am very fortunate to have you as my Guru." Her voice was all choked up.

Gurudev was moved. Patting her back gently and glancing at her friends, he said, "Shivani, I think your friends are expecting something more to celebrate your success!"

Shivani flashed a naughty smile. Soon many arrows darted toward the mango trees and returned, bringing juicy mangoes with them, all without touching or dropping even a single leaf. All the mangoes landed in a neatly arranged pile. Another of Shivani's arrows plunged deep into the ground, creating a stream of clean, clear water jetting out. Without blinking his eyes, the amazed Gurudev kept staring at the marvelous event. Pointing at the pile of mangos and the water stream, Shivani said, "All the spectators of the show are now requested to enjoy these sumptuous mangos and this cold drink."

Watching her friends dig in to the mangoes, Shivani said, "Gurudev, remember a few years ago, I had to climb on trees to get mangos for them."

Gurudev hustled from his position toward Shivani. "My child, today my eyes are content after witnessing the marvelous, breathtaking show."

CHAPTER EIGHT

THE DIVINE INTRODUCTION

The next day Shivani woke up well before dawn and raced to the archery arena. Gurudev was going to teach her something very special. Shivani had no clue what it would be, but the excitement had kept her awake for the whole night. While cleaning the arena, she heard Gurudev's footsteps.

"Namaskaar, Gurudev!"

"Bless you, my child. Shubha-Prabhatam!" Gurudev smiled as pleasantly as the morning's cool breeze.

"Gurudev, yesterday I didn't sleep at all."

"Why?"

"Because I was so excited about today."

"Shivani, as a good warrior you should be able to control your emotions. Remember, an emotional mind makes you weaker and leads to wrong paths."

"I know that. But I couldn't keep myself away from guessing today's surprise lesson."

"Hmmm!" Throwing a naughty glance at Shivani, Gurudev asked, "Then shall we start the lesson?"

"Yes, Gurudev…right now." Shivani jumped. "Can I bring your quiver?"

"I neither need a quiver nor an arrow. Only my bow is sufficient."

Leaving the puzzled Shivani at the edge of the arena, he walked to the center. The sun was gleaming in the blue skies. After doing namaskaar to that master of energy, he picked up the bow. Holding it in front of him, he closed his eyes and muttered a mantra. The moment he finished chanting the mantra, an arrow magically appeared on his bow. Gurudev shot the arrow into the sky, and it zoomed with a thunderous sound. As the magic arrow pierced through the skies, the dark clouds began swarming. Soon the heavily overcast skies started showering rain paired with thunder and lightning. Just then Gurudev shot another magic arrow. It soared high up and started blowing an enormous breeze that instantly pushed all the clouds away, and the mighty sun once again began dazzling in the clear blue sky.

All those events happened merely within a few moments. Frozen at her spot with widened eyes, Shivani was watching the unreal, stupendous, magical extravaganza. Then, without her knowledge, she raced to Gurudev.

"Gurudev!" Prostrating herself before him, she exclaimed, "Gurudev, you are one of the world's greatest magicians. I bow to you."

"Shivani!" helping her get up; he said smilingly, "Listen to me carefully. I am not a magician. Whatever you have just witnessed was not at all a magic show." Keeping the bow down, he continued. "My child, this is an advanced and intricate branch of archery. These weapons are called Divya-astras, the divine weapons."

"Divya-astra!" Exclaimed Shivani.

"The arrow which made thunderous rains is called Parjanya-astra, and the other, which created the wind and wiped away the clouds, is called Vayavya-astra."

Shivani merely stood in wonder.

"There is a science behind these weapons. Anybody can perform this act."

"Really?"

"Yes!" After a quick pause Gurudev asked, "Can you tell me the five elements existing in nature?"

"Water, fire, wind, earth, and air!" Shivani blurted out.

"Excellent! All these elements are tremendously powerful. With the proper recital of the mantra and the power of concentration, you can request each one of them to work for you. They arrive in a form of arrow and help us with their majestic power." After a quick pause, he said, "These immensely powerful elements of nature help us win over the enemy. In return, we need to pay due respect to them. You should never use their powers just for the sake of entertaining someone."

"Gurudev, I wonder how many people in the world are able to use Divya-astras."

"These weapons are pretty difficult to learn. That's why only a few people are able to use them at present."

"Only a few people! And…and you are one of them. Gurudev, who taught you these weapons?"

"My mother."

"Your mother?"

"Yes, my child." Gurudev whispered. "She was a great archer. She taught me all about warfare. Now I am here to teach you everything that I learned from her."

"Will I be able to learn it?" Shivani asked hesitantly.

"Although it is very hard to invite Divya-astra onto your bow, it is not impossible. You need to have a great concentrating ability." Watching her face, engrossed in thoughts he added, "Shivani that's why I taught you meditation. Now, you have been practicing it for many years. I think you should be able to perform this 'magical' event. You have everything that is necessary to learn this archery, such as intelligence, great concentrating ability, and correct mantras, which you will learn from me. But in addition to that, you need to be confident about yourself."

Shivani stared at him with a puzzled face.

"Shivani, you should always trust yourself. Self-confidence, perseverance, and…"

"And hard work are the keys to success." Shivani said, completing her guru's sentence.

From that moment, Shivani's advancement to acquiring Divya-astras began. Over the period, Gurudev taught her the precise posture for the bow as well as for herself. He stressed the importance of chanting the mantras for different weapons in their unique rhythms.

"I am ready, Gurudev," Shivani said, holding her bow.

"Then start chanting the mantra for Agneya-astra—the weapon of fire," Gurudev ordered.

Shivani stood with her bow and chanted the mantra for Agneya-astra, but nothing happened. She kept staring at the empty bow in front of her. She tried again and again.

Gurudev was watching her carefully. "Shivani, the bow in your hands is quivering. The divine weapon won't appear on a shaky bow," Gurudev said.

"I got it, Gurudev." With renewed vigor, Shivani resumed her lesson. In a few moments, a fiery arrow appeared on her bow, and as it zoomed up, the whole area was engulfed in flames. Instantly, Shivani chanted another mantra and Parjanya-astra appeared on her bow. It extinguished the flames with rain showers.

"Today, I am one lucky Guru, for I have the best student." The content Gurudev blessed Shivani. "Now, you have acquired the most difficult aspect of archery, the Divya-astras!"

In a very short period, Shivani mastered all the Divya-astras known to Gurudev. By using Parvat-astra, she could create humongous boulders to rain on her enemy. Its antidote, Vajra-astra, would appear as a gigantic mace, crushing all the boulders into fine powder. The weapon Dhoomra-astra could give rise to streams of thick, dark, smoke, blinding and suffocating the enemy. The most favorite weapon for Shivani was Mohini-astra—the hypnotizing weapon. Without physically hurting the enemy, it would hypnotize and defeat him.

After assuring himself of Shivani's ability to handle the various weapons, Gurudev started teaching the strongest of the Divya-astras—the Brahma-astra.

"Gurudev, is this the most powerful weapon?"

"Yes, indeed. Its use leads to widespread devastation, far beyond the actual site of its use. It is able to kill any living being in water, in air, or on land. Those who survive are left crippled for the rest of their lives. It destroys not only the living beings, but the water, the earth, and the air, all become affected for a long, long time."

"It seems to be a really powerful weapon."

"The area where this Brahma-astra is used remains hostile to any life for many, many years. This is the most terrible of weapons. That's why...that's why, Shivani, I will never give you my permission to use this weapon."

"Then why should I learn it?" Shivani blurted out.

"Listen! This knowledge will enable you to negate the dreadful effects of Brahma-astra, used by your enemy. You will be able to protect yourself as well as the world around you from the devastation."

Shivani couldn't help but stand there puzzled.

"Except for that specific situation, I prohibit you from using this weapon."

"I will obey your orders, Gurudev." Tucking her bangs behind her ears Shivani said with a smile, "Given a choice, I would like to use Mohini-astra on all my enemies."

"I wish it could work on everyone," Gurudev muttered to himself.

One day, under the basking golden rays of the sun, Shivani started her routine practice of archery. But nothing was working well that day. She was constantly missing her targets and was unable to invite any of the Divya-astras.

"Shivani, what's the matter, my child?" Gurudev's voice was full of concern. "Aren't you feeling well?"

"I miss my parents," she whispered. "Last night, I dreamed of them. They were begging for help, and I couldn't do anything. I kept watching them helplessly." Her voice was all choked up. She let herself drop to the ground. The bow from her hand tumbled down as she tried to push back the tears from her welled up eyes.

Gurudev hustled to her and began patting gently without speaking. The whimpering Shivani continued. "How am I going to fight with the powerful king? How can I win the war against his mighty army?"

Gurudev closed his eyes and sighed subtly.

"Gurudev, I failed today. I wasn't able to shoot a single arrow. What will happen if I fail again in front of the enemy? All your efforts of teaching me have gone in vain. I am not the person who can fulfill your dream of destroying the evil king."

"Shivani, why are you worrying about all these things right now?"

"Gurudev, aren't you teaching me this warfare to enable me to challenge the king one day?"

"Hmmm..."

"What if, surrounded by his army, I start failing in my attempts... just the way it is happening now? Today you have witnessed it. I was unable to shoot even a single arrow, and I forgot some of the mantras for Divya-astras. Gurudev, I am afraid I will not be able to fulfill your dreams. If this happened during the war, I would be killed instantly."

"Shivani…" Gurudev held her hands. He could feel the tremors…the tremors of fear and uncertainty.

"Gurudev … I am not worried about being killed but if that is my destiny then why should I continue to work? ……..what"s the use of all this hard work?" Shivani was inconsolable. "I was responsible for my parents' death. They were hunted down just because of me. In the past I made false promises to you about punishing the evil king and liberating the kingdom. Today, I am ashamed of myself…and my failure…and the faulty promises." Shivani began sobbing. "I am unable to fulfill your dream. Please forgive me, Gurudev." Shivani's frustration, her anger were bursting out.

With his blue, affectionate eyes, Gurudev kept staring at Shivani. He remembered, just a few years ago, when she was a baby, he would make funny faces to stop her crying. He smiled, stroking his fingers through her hair. "Shivani, my child, stop crying now. Look at me."

Shivani raised her withered face up.

"Honestly I don't like your self-pitying attitude. You are targeting and destroying yourself by continuously blaming and making you responsible for events over which you had or have no control. Shivani, today you have become your biggest enemy." He let out a soft sigh and continued. "My child, always remember…this self-pitying brings only sadness and misery in life."

Gurudev's words quieted Shivani a bit.

"I understand, Gurudev. But isn't the possibility of my defeat true? Do you really think I would be able to challenge and defeat the king? I am just an ordinary girl."

"I think you are worrying unnecessarily and that too at a wrong time. You are wasting your valuable time thinking about the future. A wise person always plans for the future but is never preoccupied with it, and thus avoids getting anxious or nervous. Shivani, keep in mind, anxiety prevents you from performing your duty or your Karma." He paused to judge her reaction. His humble voice was booming. "One should choose a particular path which would enable him or her to reach the desired and noble goal of life. Thereafter the person should concentrate only on performing the necessary duties related to the goal and should not worry about the results. Focus on your Karma—your duty—and leave the results to the superior one."

Shivani was looking at him with a stunned face. She had never heard him speaking in such a mystic tone before.

"Shivani, now I will ask you a few questions. Please try to answer me. After your birth, you could have easily died in that hostile forest. Who saved you from dying?"

Shivani had no answer.

"Tell me who brought you here?"

"Mama Tiger! She brought me here."

"Who gave the wisdom to that wild tigress for saving a human child?"

"I don't know."

"Who saved you and her during the dangerous travel through the roaring waters of Mahatejaa? Who asked her to bring you to me?"

Shivani kept staring at him speechlessly. Until then, she hadn't thought about all those questions. Looking at Shivani's perplexed face, Gurudev asked, "Do you have any answer to all these questions? You don't, correct?"

Shivani simply conceded.

"You have seen the seasons—summer, monsoon, winter, and spring—visiting us in one specific sequence. Who asks them to follow that particular sequence? Have you ever seen them changing the sequence?"

"No," Shivani answered.

"Shivani, in the past, I have taught you about our universe. It consists of innumerable stars, galaxies, suns, and moons. They all move in their specific paths. Who governs them? Who maintains this gigantic universe in a proper order?"

"Gurudev," Shivani whispered in frustration, "I don't have any answer to any of your questions."

"My child, I know that, but you are not alone. I myself have no answers to my questions." He started laughing freely. "And I am sure no one else in the world has them. I am aware of the one and only fact. There is some kind of unseen, mysterious force present that maintains this whole universe. Although unperceived, that force nestles every single grain existing here. That supreme power decides our fates and leads us along the preplanned course." Gazing deeply at the skies, Gurudev continued. "Shivani, we should keep ourselves focused on our duty, Karma, and let the Almighty worry about the fate and the results." He paused and looked at Shivani, who was nodding in agreement. "Shivani, right now, what is your duty? Tell me."

"To master the archery and become a competent warrior."

"Very good! You are working toward becoming a mighty warrior. You have a noble intention of helping the innocent people from the clutches of the evil king, right?"

"Yes, Gurudev!"

"During the fight, you may win or you may not. The supreme commander will decide that. Your present duty is to work hard and be able to challenge the king. You should not fall short in performing your duty."

After a long time, finally a dazzling smile flashed on Shivani's face. Her beaming face made Gurudev happy. He continued. "Many times we keep worrying about the future or regretting the past. That makes us deter from the current duty."

"Gurudev, I understand my mistake," Shivani spoke out. "From now on, I will never swerve away from my Karma—my duty—my goal." There was a unique confidence reflecting on her face. "I will work hard to be able to win the war. I may win it or not, but I won't worry about it. I will try my best."

"Excellent!" The satisfied Gurudev exclaimed. There were still a few dried, mud-stained tears on Shivani's radiant face. It looked as if a withered flower had blossomed again under the soothing showers. He softly wiped off those mud stains. After getting up from his place, he ordered, "Shivani, pick up your bow and resume your duty!"

The majestic voice echoed through the neighborhood. The spell-bound Shivani walked to her bow and picked it up. Her face was glistening with great determination, her eyes twinkling with the ultimate resolve. The previous sadness, despair, or anxiety got completely evaporated just as the morning fog gets vanished under the shining sun. With enormous vigor, she twanged her bow. The loud bow twang invaded the surroundings, booming her resolve.

CHAPTER NINE

THE KING

It was the middle of night in the capital of Suvarna-Raaj. The mansions, palaces, majestic streets, and royal gardens were all enveloped in utter quietness. Suddenly Kaalkoot was jolted out of his sleep. Sitting on his luxurious bed, he was breathing heavily. His anxious eyes were swiveling all around, trying to judge the situation. After seeing the armed guards outside his window, he let out a subtle sigh of relief. "It just was a bad dream," he assured himself and gently wiped off the sweat from his forehead.

For a few moments he stared through the darkness at the dimmed lights of the royal palace and got lost in some serious thoughts. Then, springing up from the seat, he whispered, "As a loyal servant, I must inform my king about it."

Moments later, Kaalkoot ordered the charioteer and began heading toward the palace. As the chief adviser to the king, he had permission to enter anywhere, at any time. A few years ago, he had entered the kingdom of Suvarna-Raaj simply as a taantric—a person practicing voodooism and black magic. In the very first meeting, he mesmerized the king with his breathtaking magical acts.

Within a short period of time, he earned the king's trust and was appointed as the royal advisor. He was rewarded with two beautiful mansions, one in the city and the other near the mountains. Kaalkoot, a wanderer, was moved by the king's generosity and fell to his feet. In turn, the king asked his help in acquiring the status of Samraat—the emperor. Becoming Samraat was King Veersen's lifetime goal, and he had rightfully judged Kaalkoot's potential as a great magician able to help him achieve the goal. Until then despite being a mighty warrior and well known for his prowess, King Veersen was not able to win the title of Samraat. After witnessing Kaalkoot's unbelievable magical powers, the hope of acquiring his lifetime ambition was renewed.

The loyal Kaalkoot proved his worth. From the time Kaalkoot entered the king's life, no one had been able to defeat Veersen. Before starting a war, Kaalkoot would perform a special taantric ritual, granting paranormal powers to King Veersen. Endowed with these dark powers, the king could easily win any war. With every win, King Veersen's kingdom began expanding and his power started rising.

As the chariot came to a halt near the palace entrance, Kaalkoot swiftly got out and began walking toward the king's personal chamber. He was the only royal dignitary allowed entrance to the inner courts of Veersen. Shoving off the maids at the door, he walked into the chamber. The stateliness of that chamber was evident from the graceful, tall arched windows, the elegant drapery covering them, the stylish sconces on the walls, the magnificent paintings, the rich carpet spread across the floor, and the delicate canopy above the bed. On either side of the king's bed stood two maids, fanning the sleeping Veersen and his wife—Queen Lalita-Devi.

"Maharaaj!" Kaalkoot whispered in a concerned voice, gently tapping on the king's shoulder. The bleary-eyed Veersen hustled and sat up in his bed.

"What's the matter, Kaalkoot?"

"Please pardon me for interrupting your sleep." Staring at a huge golden lamp nestling a glowing flame at the king's bedside, he continued. "Maharaaj, I would like to talk to you...right now."

Listening to those words, Veersen jolted out of his sleep. Leaning back on his jewel-studded headboard, his face turned serious. "Kaalkoot, what is it in regards to?" Throwing a suspicious glance at the maids and the queen, Kaalkoot hesitantly suggested, "Can we discuss this inside the Gupta-Bhavan, the secret chamber?"

"You are absolutely right."

Leaving the baffled queen behind, Veersen got up and, with a staggering gait, headed toward the secret chamber.

Coming near King Veersen, Kaalkoot glanced around to make sure that, apart from the king and himself, no one else was there inside the secret chamber.

"Maharaaj, I...I happened to witness a bad omen."

Veersen stared at the worried lines on Kaalkoot's old face.

"I saw your death, Maharaaj! Please believe me. It surely is a dreadful omen." Looking at Veersen's face, Kaalkoot added pleadingly, "Maharaaj, I hope you trust me enough regarding my loyalty toward you. Before coming to this kingdom, I was merely a poor magician roaming from place to place in search of a living. You have offered me a respectful life. Now my whole life is yours, and my goal is to work for your success and protection. To enable you to win the wars, I must engage in various rituals, where I have to deal with many vicious spirits. During some of those rituals, I put my life at stake. But I do this happily as my loyal duty toward you. For me, your life is the most precious thing in this world."

As Veersen gazed at his loyal adviser, Kaalkoot continued. "Please trust me, Maharaaj! Your life is in danger."

"Hmmm...so you witnessed my death!" King Veersen's deep voice echoed through the chamber.

"Yes, Maharaaj."

"Now, tell me...how is that possible when I am protected by your powers?"

"Maharaaj, currently, under the umbrella of my protecting powers, you are safe from every single life in this world, except..."

"Except from whom?" Squinting at him, Veersen asked angrily, "Kaalkoot, who is threatening me? Who can kill me?"

"You know the person, Maharaaj. It is the same person, about whom..."

The alarmed Veersen shot up instantly from his chair. "Impossible!" His voice, tinged with fear and disbelief, boomed inside the four walls. "*That person is already dead.*" He was stressing upon each word.

"Maybe...not," the jittery Kaalkoot muttered. "Maybe that person is still alive." He paused to judge the king's reaction. "Or else I wouldn't have had the sinister dream."

Veersen's perplexed face quickly turned pale. He almost sank in the chair, shaking his head in disbelief. He neither wanted to question the truthfulness of Kaalkoot's foretelling nor his loyalty. Kaalkoot was the one foreteller whom he could trust the most. Whenever he would predict a threat, it would be certain to happen.

"What should be done now? Tell me," Veersen said helplessly.

Kaalkoot replied calmly and assertively, "Maharaaj, my powers can't offer you any protection from that person, but they can kill that person." Flashing an assuring smile, he continued. "So, it is my belief that...we should resume the search and imprison the person."

"But where to search?"

"Maharaaj, you know the place. I don't need to speak it out loud."

"Oh, I see." After a few moments of silence, the king said, "I agree with you, Kaalkoot. Tomorrow morning, I will order the chief of Special Forces to..."

"Maharaaj, forgive me for interrupting you," Kaalkoot blurted impatiently. "Please, order him now...at this very moment."

"Alright. I will summon the chief right now."

Kaalkoot looked satisfied with the king's decision.

"Maharaaj, while the chief will be doing his duty, I will perform mine...in my own way."

"Your own way? You mean...?"

"I can't speak about it now. But as soon as I obtain more information about the person, I will immediately share it with you, Maharaaj." Kaalkoot smiled and left the chamber.

"I trust you, Kaalkoot." Veersen relaxed a bit and began waiting for the chief of Special Forces of the kingdom of Suvarna-Raaj.

In his fifties Veersen- a handsome looking king was well known for his ruthless and brutal heart. After the untimely death of his father, King Dharmasen, the reins of the kingdom landed in Veersen's hands. He immediately became a symbol of living terror. The mere utterance of his name would evoke quivers of fear among the people. He was respected, not in the loving sense but rather fearfully across the kingdom. The citizens of the kingdom were well aware of the deadly wrath of their king. They were familiar with the violent punishments he had ordered to the rebels, and they had witnessed the atrocities committed by their cold-blooded ruler and his army.

After each victory in war, there would be a procession welcoming the king and his army's victorious return to the capital, Suvarna-nagari. The king demanded the citizens be present and welcome the victorious army. The throngs of fearful citizens would stand on either side of Raaj-Path—the majestic street leading to the palace. While chanting the victory slogans, they would throw pitiful glances at the defeated king, being dragged and whipped mercilessly behind King Veersen's chariot. Nobody had the courage to oppose that cruelty. The whole kingdom was living under the hovering shadows of terror and death.

The same King Veersen, a symbol of terror amongst the people, now sat slouched in a golden chair in the Gupta-Bhavan, himself being terrorized, his fearful eyes scanning the future nervously. As he sensed the nearing footsteps of the chief, he sat up with borrowed vigor, trying to hide his fear.

CHAPTER TEN

THE NEW MOON

Humming a favorite tune, Shivani was collecting food for dinner. She gathered a few fruits, roots, and some green leaves, just enough for herself. As it was a day of fasting for Gurudev, she didn't get his favorite legumes. His weekly fast would stretch from one sunrise to the next sunrise.

In the past, Shivani had asked him many questions regarding the fast. Each time she would listen to the same answer: "Learning to control hunger is a very effective way of strengthening our own will power. Maybe you too should start fasting."

At that point, Shivani would stop questioning, for she couldn't give up her food even for a day.

Packing her food in a wicker basket, Shivani returned to the hut. Sitting on the patio, Gurudev was busy writing in his book made of lotus leaves.

"Gurudev?" Putting the wicker basket down on the ground, Shivani asked, "What are you writing?"

"Tomorrow we are going to start lessons on Astrology."

Shivani looked at him quizzically. Gurudev explained. "Astrology is a wonderful science, dealing with the effects of various planets and their position on our lives."

Widening her eyes, she exclaimed, "Oh, really?"

"Yes! It is quite fascinating to study this subject."

Gurudev momentarily glanced at the lowering sun and said, "Shivani, while I work on this book, you should start eating. Remember, according to our health science, we should eat our dinner before the sunset."

Flanked by the rabbit duo, Shubhra and Dhawal, Shivani sat on the patio with her dinner plate. After offering some roots to the rabbits, she began eating while gazing at the sun. After having ruled over the sky for the entire day, the master was returning toward the horizon. A plethora of magnificent colors spread all across the sky with various shades of pink, orange, red, and yellow blending into one another. A few wispy clouds, enjoying the sight too, were sprinkled with the same colors. Captivated by the view, Shivani forgot to eat her food. After finishing his work, Gurudev glanced at Shivani's half-empty plate. His adorable child was engrossed by the beauty of the sunset.

Sitting near her, Gurudev asked, "Isn't it a beautiful sight?"

"Indeed it is." Without taking her eyes off the sky, Shivani whispered, "Gurudev, look at those pretty swirls around the sun. It looks like they are trying to hold back their master from going away."

"Yes, it looks like that." Swiveling his eyes to Shivani, he said, "Shivani, by now, you must have witnessed many sunrises and sunsets."

"Yes, Gurudev. During both events, I love watching the sky, changing its colors every moment."

"Yes. Shivani, have you noticed any difference between sunset and sunrise?"

"Nope!" Shivani jerked her head. "To me, they look the same."

"You are absolutely correct. The sun, the emblem of power, displays the same grand show at the time of its rise and set." After a moment of taking in the beauty before him, Gurudev continued. "It is a telltale sign of wisdom and greatness. The wise and the great people display the same, balanced behavior during either victory or defeat. They accept joy and sadness with the same smile."

"Gurudev, I had never thought about it in such a way before."

"Shivani, nature is the best teacher. You simply need to be observant. Look at that gorgeous sun. It is going down with the same grace with which it will rise tomorrow morning."

Lying in her bed gazing at the stars, Shivani was still thinking about the sunset.

"Shivani, can you name that constellation?" Gurudev's question brought Shivani back to the present. Lying in his bed in another corner of the patio, Gurudev was pointing to the overhead cluster of stars.

"I think, its Swati. Am I correct?"

"Correct."

"Gurudev, I was wondering about how these distant stars influence our lives."

"It is very hard to believe, but it is true."

"Nowadays I am fascinated by this gigantic universe. The more I think about it, the more I get mystified."

On Shivani's innocent remark, he laughed. "Now, try sleeping."

In a few moments, he heard snoring from Shivani's bed. "One tired child." Smiling to himself, Gurudev fell asleep shortly after.

Shivani's sleep suddenly broke in the middle of night. This had never happened before. Shivani tried changing her positions, but her sleep seemed to have disappeared completely. Every time she changed position, the rustle of her bed would make Naagraaj, sleeping in a nearby wicker basket, wiggle. Finally she decided to get up. She started walking away from the patio.

Suddenly a breeze of air passed her, and its captivating scent compelled her to rush toward it. It was a musk deer. Carrying the magic scent in its belly, it stood on the hill. The last time she had seen this kind of deer was a few years ago, for they would rarely come to Gurudev's hermitage. Since then, Shivani had been waiting for this fragrant encounter. Now she was enjoying being in the vicinity of it and inhaling the wonderful aroma. But as soon as the musk deer sensed her, off it went. Gazing in its direction, Shivani stood for a while before returning back to the hut.

She glanced around. There was an absolute silence everywhere except for the buzzing night bugs. Just then a gentle breeze brought another burst of fragrance to her. It was of her favorite bushes of night jasmine, Raat-Raani, blooming a little away from the hut. Taking deep breaths, she was greedily pulling in the heavenly fragrance. She caressed its white blossoms. Shivani could have sat there forever, enjoying the beauty of night, but the sudden screeching of a bird broke her reverie. She looked in the direction of Mahatejaa, from where the screeching sound came.

It was a clear night of the new moon. The absence of the moon from the night sky had enabled many stars to dazzle. Crowding heavily in the sky, their twinkles were celebrating the night. Their reflections had turned the river into a shimmering, silvery path. Just then Shivani's eyes caught a glimpse of an unusual sight, and she instantly raced to the river. To her surprise, it was a fish wrapped up in some sort of covering, flapping frantically to get itself freed. Hovering over the fish was a hungry bird, screeching and trying to grab the fish.

Without wasting a moment, Shivani jumped into the river. After freeing the fish and watching it disappear into the water, she returned to the banks. Along with her, she had managed to bring the covering that had trapped the fish. Her eyes carefully screened the soft, silky piece of cloth. The cloth was as soft as her mother's sash.

"What could it be?" She had never ever seen anything like this flowing in the river before. Her imagination started flying from one possibility to the next. Holding the cloth in her hand, she began walking upstream along the riverbank.

After walking for a while, she spotted a few more similar pieces of cloth, bobbing up and down in the water. She reflexively ran to the hut to get her bow and quiver before returning to the river. With the help of a few ricocheting arrows diving silently into the water, she recovered all the pieces.

Now, settling down on the soft, sandy banks, she began to solve the mystery. After joining the pieces together, it appeared that they all were parts of one single structure, maybe a flag. On it was displayed the picture of a king. As she stared at it, something flashed in her mind that left her totally dazed. The mind-boggling discovery had deepened the mystery further.

"Oh, my goodness!" Shaking her head, Shivani whispered in disbelief, looking at the giant, triangular-shaped flag lying in the sand. The joined pieces of the flag displayed King Veersen's picture with his name written on it.

"I am pretty sure...this is the flag of his army," Shivani muttered. "But...if that is a possibility, how and why has it landed here?" Shivani's mind started spinning. She kept staring at the flag and the far away mountains—the entry point of the river to her neighborhood. "Maybe Veersen's army is on the other side of the giant mountains." The very thought swept her with a wild thrill. "Maybe some kind of strife is going on the other side, and that's how the flag landed in the river."

Mystery after mystery, possibilities after possibilities were churning up her mind. "Or just some old flag, lying there for quite some time, happened to fall into the river and was carried over here by it." Her clenched fists were relaxed by the thought. "There is only one way to solve this mystery." Shivani gazed at the mountains. She had never ventured to those mountains before. She was excited at the very thought of seeing the royal army, and even the king about whom she had learned a lot. "I will first tell Gurudev all about it."

She started back toward the hut but stalled the very next moment. "If I tell him now, there is a possibility that he wouldn't let me go there at all. He has always discouraged me from swimming upstream near the mountains."

She glanced at the patio. There was an absolute silence. The teen-aged, adventure-loving mind of Shivani wasn't ready for the possibility. All these years she had been learning the art of warfare, and she was not ready to miss this golden chance. She kept glancing at the flag, the river, and the mountains over and over again. Some fantastic adventure was beckoning her. Eventually she decided to dive into the mystery. Soon, Shivani, along with her bow and a full quiver, began heading toward the mountains, fighting with the upstream currents. "I will solve this mystery well before the dawn," she assured herself. Tucking her bow further up over her shoulder and tightening the knot of her quiver, she was inching forth. Soon she entered the dark tunnel in the mountains.

Deflecting the scary thoughts from her mind Shivani kept going forth. The currents were getting stronger. She was literally fighting with the waters. Leaping along with a surge of courage, she kept pushing herself against the mighty river. Eventually she was successful in threading herself out of the thick vines at the end of the tunnel. She held a vine and paused to catch her breath. At once a welcoming, cool breeze swept over her. She inhaled the fresh air. Now, the upstream of the river was visible in front of her. The waters were churning up the starry reflections within them, hinting about the violent currents ahead. A strong rumbling could be heard, warning her to be more careful on the next part of her journey.

She checked her bow and quiver one more time and began surveying the area in front of her. It was the forest of Raat-raan. The place where she was standing was the same tunnel through which her mama tiger had carried her to Gurudev. Needless to say she was unaware of that. From the end of the tunnel a smaller branch of river Mahatejaa was seen. That smaller river was flowing away from the mountains. In between the main, upstream river and its smaller branch a speck of land was seen wedged. With the help of the vine, Shivani gave herself a wild swing and managed to haul herself up onto the land. Dense forests on either side had flanked the river.

To her amazement, on the opposite banks, there were flickers of lights glowing though the darkness. Also, she could hear some human voices. The enthralled Shivani gathered herself and lurched forward with a renewed vigor. Sneaking through the dense trees, she began trying to get closer to the human voices. While inching forth, she frequently paused and reassessed her safety. Now, she had come to a spot from where she could see the opposite bank very well. Her eyes widened with wonder as she watched many human figures moving along the banks. It was her first time ever seeing other humans, apart from Gurudev.

"Oh...my...goodness!" Shivani exclaimed cautiously and thrashed herself forward. The people on the opposite bank were talking among themselves. Some of them were riding animals fitting the description of horses, as per Gurudev's lessons. Shivani was witnessing many wonders for the first time in her life.

"I wonder how they brought the animals, horses, into this thick jungle." Watching the men closely, she became almost certain that they were Veersen's soldiers. She gasped for breath.

"I can see the flags similar to my find, tied to the backs of those horses. Maybe I can find Veersen too!" She held one of the tree branches tightly in her grip.

They surely were the soldiers of Veersen's Special Forces, searching the forest for something. Crouching low by a tree, Shivani was enjoying spying on the soldiers. At that moment, she felt a strong grip on her shoulders...and in the blink of an eye, before she could move; both her hands were seized tightly from behind.

"Ha! Ha! Ha!" the riotous laughter tore through the forest. After throwing away her bow and the quiver, Shivani's most trusted means for self-defense, the monstrous voice thundered again. "I found a little spy here," he announced while still standing behind her and tightening his grip further on Shivani. In a flash a flock of lighted torches crossed the river and came toward them.

With that unexpected attack, Shivani was literally frozen with fear. The most disheartening fact for her was the loss of her bow and quiver, as if she had been stripped of all her powers. Her whole body was splinted so tightly that it was impossible for her to sneak a glance at her captor. Blaming herself, she kept trying to get freed, but all her efforts were in vain.

Soon she was surrounded by a group of armed soldiers of King Veersen's royal army. The man who had captured her was the chief. For the past few days, they had all been combing through the forest, obeying their king's orders. During the hunt, many of his soldiers had succumbed to the dangers of the horrifying forest. Unfortunately they had no option of returning back without fulfilling the royal order. They were aware that if they returned with empty hands, they would be killed instantly. Needless to say, that kind of death would be more painful than the one hovering over them amidst the Raat-Raan. No wonder the chief was ecstatic after seizing Shivani.

After his soldiers took over the responsibility of holding the captive securely, he came in front of Shivani for the first time. Observing her face in the light, he screamed with joy. "Ah ha! My fate has opened a treasure trove for me, it seems. I think we found what we were ordered to find."

Celebrating the triumph, he raised the spear in his hand and addressed the jubilant crowd gathered around. "I think we should wrap up the camp and start marching back to the capital to celebrate the victory."

Though silent, the fearful Shivani kept gazing at the reveling crowd. Blaming herself from time to time for her foolishness, Shivani was being dragged by the soldiers. Still, with all her might, she continued trying to escape from the nightmare. Suddenly, to her surprise, a very familiar sound was heard in the neighboring bushes. Even while being nudged and pulled, she recognized the rustle, and instantly her eyes twinkled with hope. Soon a fierce-looking, huge tigress pounced out of the bushes like a lightning bolt. By the side of her head was the fanned hood of a black cobra, hissing furiously while keeping its body coiled around the tigress's neck.

The dramatic appearance of Jwala and Naagraaj shocked the joyous crowd. They were witnessing an unprecedented danger with two vicious heads. The next moment, the circumstances were swept with a wave of panic and chaos. The forest was shattered by the frightful screams, shouts, and yells, and, of course, the majestic roars of the furious tigress. Taken totally off guard, the soldiers ran away in panic, forgetting their weapons and leaving behind their prized catch. A few of them, with their trembling hands, were trying to fight the violent tigress but without any success. The angry Jwala was pouncing amidst them like a streak of lightening, dazzling in the sky.

Taking advantage of the situation, Shivani leapt away. Freeing herself, she reached for her bow and quiver. After seizing her trusted weapon, Shivani's face beamed with awe. Immediately a horrifying bow twang echoed through the forest. The sound percolated a new wave of fear, forcing the remaining soldiers to run in disarray. But

Jwala and Naagraaj heartily welcomed that sound. It instantly calmed them. Standing at a nearby spot, Jwala, Mama Tiger, and Naagraaj were ready to witness the breathtaking archery of their dear Shivani.

By then a few soldiers had successfully returned to the opposite banks after crossing the river and joined the rest of the troop They began shooting their arrows at the site of chaos, but it was too late for them. Shivani was all fired up with her mighty weapon. She began answering their attacks precisely with her arrows. Her amazing dexterity for archery literally stunned the veteran warriors from Veersen's royal army. The shots fired at them were surely echoing the warrior's excellent skills. After witnessing a single arrow bursting into a barrage of arrows, the soldiers were convinced of their fatal defeat and decided to turn back.

Watching them run frantically, Shivani couldn't hold her laughter back. Laughing freely, she went near Mama Tiger. "Jwala!" Hugging her hard, Shivani kissed her and whispered, "Thanks for your help, Mama. This is the second time you have saved my life."

Jwala was very happy to see Shivani safe. While being kissed and hugged, she began licking the multiple wounds covering Shivani's body.

Just then, Naagraaj entered the scene by slithering up Shivani's legs. "Oh, Naagraaj!" Picking him up, Shivani said, "I am thankful to you, too. You are my best friend." Removing some dried leaves stuck around his body, she kissed his fanned hood.

Climbing up to her face, he began staring at the vermilion-colored, circular birthmark on Shivani's forehead, which was glowing brightly ever since Shivani got captured. It was the same glow that he had sensed from Aashrum, alarming him of life-threatening dangers around Shivani. The same glow had enabled Naagraaj and

Jwala to track down Shivani's location. Once again, the glowing vermilion birthmark did its job of fetching Naagraaj and Jwala to rescue Shivani. It was a secret known only to the two of them. Shivani was not aware of this fact.

"Hey, Naagraaj! What are you looking at?" Shivani at last asked him. She gingerly moved her fingers toward her forehead, where the mesmerized Naagraaj was staring. At once the intense heat from that area shocked her fingers. It was hot as a fire. Suddenly Jwala stood still, sensing an alarming new danger.

As Shivani jerked her head in the direction, she noticed surging flames of fire approaching them from all sides. The fire had erupted from the torches dropped by the soldiers, running away in panic. Now, it had spread over almost the whole land wedged between the two streams of the river. Shivani watched those bellowing flames creeping toward them. The intense heat could easily be felt from her spot. In an instant, a dazzling arrow from her bow soared into the sky. It was Parjanya-astra. The next moment, thundering clouds engulfed the area. Soon the drenching rains encased the fire, extinguishing it completely.

The soldiers from Veersen's army, running away, stalled momentarily at the sight of the sudden and mysterious development of the thunderstorm. But very soon, they resumed running—now more speedily than before.

At the first sight of dying flames, Shivani, after gathering Naagraaj's coils around herself, jumped into the river with Jwala and began pursuing her way back home. The trio once again was riding the same route to safety, just the way they had done many years ago.

Gurudev woke up with a very strange feeling. Sitting on his bed, he threw a casual glance at Shivani's bed and froze. Her bed was empty. A premonition replayed in his mind. He sprang off his bed and began searching for Shivani. To his surprise, the basket of Naagraaj was also empty.

"Where can they be at this time?" he muttered to himself, glancing at the still dark sky. "I hope she is alright." His face revealed his worry. He came down from the patio. Looking everywhere, he started calling for Shivani. There was no sign of her anywhere. Stretching his sight as far as he could, Gurudev kept scanning the surroundings.

Just then, his eyes picked up an unfamiliar object in the sandy banks of the river. He raced to the banks immediately. There were Shivani's arrows, lying near the pieces of Veersen's royal flag, fitted together by Shivani. Although the pieces had been moved a bit by the breeze, the king's face could still be recognized. The sight of the flag whitened his face with the ultimate fear—the fear for Shivani's life. Each beat of his heart was now worried for Shivani.

"Shivani is in danger…serious danger," the engrossed Gurudev muttered, crumbling the pieces of the flag and glancing at the far away mountains. Letting the pieces fly loosely with the wind, he whispered, "I need to go…urgently." Gazing momentarily at the worried faces of Shivani's friends who had gathered around him, he stormed back to fetch his bow and quiver from the hut.

Just when he was all ready to jump into the river, Gurudev sensed a wave of frenzy among the gathered animals and birds. After looking in the direction of the running horde, he held his breath in surprise. Against the darkness, two figures were seen gliding over the river waters emerging out of the mountain tunnel. He sighed with great relief after recognizing one of the figures as Shivani. Balancing Naagraaj on her shoulders, Shivani jumped out of the river and raced to her friends and embraced them. The sight was filled with extreme commotion, and Gurudev also got swallowed in that frenzy.

"Gurudev! Gurudev!" Shivani called, bursting with excitement. "I was...I did...I mean..." The tumultuous exhilaration of winning her first-ever battle had made Shivani unable to relate the incident in proper words.

"Yes, my child," Gurudev said in an assuring voice, hiding his emotions and maintaining his usual calm. He was staring at her wet, matted hair dangling over her sand-covered face.

"Gurudev, you just can't even imagine where I have been."

"Where have you been, Shivani?" He didn't want to disappoint her.

"Gurudev, I fought a real, live battle with King Veersen's army. It happened there, on the other side of the mountains."

"Oh, my goodness!"

"And, Gurudev, I won that fight. I single-handedly defeated all of them. They ran away from me in panic. Can you believe?" Shivani was giggling. "Aren't you proud of me, Gurudev?" she asked him innocently. Her big eyes were looking at him, expectantly.

"Well done, my child. I am extremely proud of you, Shivani," he said with a quiet face.

Looking at that face, Shivani's heart skipped a beat. "Gurudev!" In an apologetic tone, Shivani said, "I should have told you before... but after retrieving the pieces of the royal flag, I couldn't hold myself back. I am extremely sorry, Gurudev." Hanging her head down, she said in a lowered voice, "Gurudev, are you...angry at me?" Breathing deeply, she uttered further, "You have every right to be angry at me."

Her remorseful gesture melted Gurudev's mind. Flashing a pleasant smile, he said, "Shivani, I am always proud of you, my child. You are my daughter, my disciple, my friend, and everything." Moving his fingers through her matted hair, he said, "But...but I was extremely worried for you, Shivani."

"Gurudev, we don't have to worry now. All the soldiers are gone. They ran away."

Shivani was trying to comfort him. Suddenly she gasped and began moaning. Gurudev instantly noticed it. There were multiple cuts and abrasions all over her body. After being pounced on by her friends, a few cuts had started bleeding again. Holding her whole body stiff in anticipation of pain, Shivani was trying to stop the bleeding from a deep wound on her left wrist by pressing upon it.

Witnessing that Gurudev leapt forth. "Shivani, let me first tend to your wounds." The two, along with the whole herd of friends, began walking toward the hut. After fetching some herbs, Gurudev crushed and ground them into a thick paste. Very gingerly he began applying the paste over her wounds.

"Ahhhh...Gurudev, that stings...a lot," Shivani whimpered, wrenching her face in pain.

"Shivani." Gurudev smiled. "These herbs are a little naughty. First they sting, but then they help to heal the wounds."

"It is burning...a lot!" she screamed again.

"I know, dear, but this is necessary. We want the wounds to get healed fast." Gurudev continued covering the wounds with the paste. "While I am doing this, why don't you tell me about the whole incident?"

"OK!" Slouching on the bed amidst her friends, Shivani began narrating the story of her adventurous triumph. That helped to divert her attention away from the burning wounds. "Gurudev, now I have enough confidence to challenge the king. We can easily...Ah..."

"I am extremely sorry, Shivani," Gurudev whispered softly. "This wound on your left wrist is quite deep."

"Oh, no...no more, Gurudev, please." She was trying to muffle her screams by pressing her mouth with her right hand.

"Honey, I am all done. See, the paste is gone now." Throwing away the empty bowl, Gurudev stood up. As the herbs began working on Shivani, she became very sleepy. Within the next few moments, she was fast asleep. Staring at her satisfactorily, Gurudev thanked the herbs. Glancing at the sky, he began walking toward the patio. There was still some time before daybreak.

When Shivani woke up, she was feeling rather energetic. The sky was glowing with a divine, blue hue. Seeing her awake, Madhur, the kokil, fluttered his wings and flew toward her. As the previous night's incident flashed in her mind, she glanced at her wounds but couldn't believe her eyes. All the wounds were gone...completely. There was no trace of them, not even one.

"This is magical!" She jumped from her bed and moved her hands and legs vigorously. "Nope, no pain at all!" She shook her head in disbelief. "I have to tell this to Gurudev."

Gurudev was in his meditative trance. That was a little unusual, as he would always wait for her to start the meditation. As she walked toward him, he happened to open his eyes.

"Suprabhatam! Good morning, Shivani," he said, flashing a pleasant smile.

"Suprabhatam, Gurudev!" she replied.

"How are you feeling, my child?"

"I am feeling great, Gurudev. See, all my wounds are disappeared."

"That's great news." Gurudev paused and looked at the sky. "Shivani, I want to discuss with you something very important. Now, get ready as quickly as possible and come back."

Shivani sensed the calmness in his voice was surely different. That alarmed her. "Definitely it is related to yesterday's incident," she thought. "I should get myself prepared for a good scolding. After all, it was my fault. I will listen to him and confess."

After bathing in the river Shivani returned. "Gurudev, Namaste."

"Shubham bhavatu. Bless you, my child." Closing his eyes, he started speaking in a humble voice. "Shivani, I still remember the time when you entered this place. With your arrival, my life was infused with joy and happiness. After I started teaching you, I noticed many of your wonderful virtues. Now, I am proud to say that you are the most ideal student I have ever seen. You have learned almost everything that I know. Currently you are the best archer in the world."

Shivani was listening very quietly. It was hard for her to predict when the scolding would begin. That was increasing her anxiety.

Gurudev continued. "Shivani, there are still a few things necessary for defeating Veersen that I wanted to teach you."

"Gurudev," the perplexed Shivani blurted out, "I am sorry for interrupting you, but what do you mean by 'wanted to teach you'? You...you still are my Gurudev, and I am still your disciple. If you want to teach me, I am ready to learn...even right now."

"Shivani, last night's incident has suddenly changed my plans, and the directions of our lives, too."

With her head hung low, Shivani gulped.

"After yesterday's event, I can't teach you anything, now." Gurudev suddenly stopped speaking.

"I...I am extremely sorry, Gurudev. I disobeyed you. I won't do it again. I promise you. Please forgive me." Shivani was speaking remorsefully. "But please, don't say that you can't teach me anymore. Gurudev, please don't get angry at me." Shivani's voice trailed off. She was pleading pathetically. With welled-up eyes and a reddened face, she broke down.

Gurudev instantly rose up from his seat. "Shivani, my child, who says I am angry? I am not at all angry," he said, wiping her tears. As Shivani looked up, he smiled. "I mean it. I am not angry at you. "

"Then why can't you teach me?"

"Obviously you disobeyed me! But that wasn't your fault. It was your immature, adolescent, adventure-loving mind that forced you to jump into the unknown territory without informing me." He paused momentarily and added, "Anyway, that's not the reason. Last night's incidence compelled me to make some harsh decisions."

Shivani was having a hard time comprehending his speech.

"Shivani, after thinking quite hard, I came to a decision."

Holding her breath and bracing herself, Shivani continued listening.

"You need to leave this place at once."

The sentence sheared into her as a spear. She kept staring at him with an empty stare.

"Shivani, do you understand?" Gurudev asked calmly. "My child, this is not a safe place for you now. You have to depart from this place as soon as possible. Veersen's men will be here any time, and most probably Veersen, too."

Shivani was speechless.

"Shivani..."

"*Gurudev!*" She was scrambling for words. "Where should I go?"

The utter helplessness in her voice tore Gurudev's heart. Controlling his emotions, he said,

"Anywhere...away from this place."

"Should I run away from this place...from my home?"

"Yes, my child."

"Like a coward? Why should I run like that?"

Gurudev became quiet as her anguish started springing out.

"Gurudev, you always call me 'the best archer in this world.' Last night my win has proved your remarks, I suppose. I defeated the most elite platoon of Veersen's royal army." Shivani's face became enlightened. "Gurudev, do you still think I should run away from this place...just to save my life? Should I leave this place simply because there is a possibility of Veersen coming to this place?"

With a quick pause, she added confidently, "Sorry, Gurudev, but I don't agree with you. Let that cruel Veersen come here. I am scared of neither him nor his big army. I am confident enough to deal with all of them and defeat them. After all, you have taught me the techniques to be able to duel with him and banish his evil face from the earth. For the past few years, I have been waiting for this moment, and now, I am not going to miss this chance. Also, you will be here with me. Together we are capable of wiping out Veersen's whole army. In that case, why should I run away? I would rather be dead fighting with him than running away."

Gurudev was looking at his disciple with pride, admiring the spirit of a fiery warrior. His tireless efforts were successful in imbibing the proper teachings. He smiled with satisfaction.

"Shivani, I have no doubt about your archery skills. You indeed are the best archer, much better than Veersen." Sighing heavily, he continued. "Unfortunately, in spite of having so many qualities, you will not be able to kill Veersen or even injure him. That's why I have advised you to run away from here."

Glancing at the far away mountains, he said, "Shivani, listen to me carefully. Veersen is no match for your superb archery skills. You can readily defeat him. I am not worried about that. What worries me most is the presence of ghastly powers hovering over Veersen. These powers, emerging out from Kaalkoot's taantric rituals, can be quite harmful to you. Also, as long as Veersen remains shielded within these dark swirls, not a single weapon existing currently in the world can harm him. These powers not only protect him but increase his strength too. That's why he keeps winning each war."

Glancing at Shivani, lost in serious thoughts, he added, "If Veersen gets stripped of those powers, he can be easily defeated. But no one in the whole world knows how to destroy the shield of the evil powers. I have been working for many years, trying to find a way to vanquish them. Recently, I had become quite hopeful to destroy them with the help of…"

"With the help of what, Gurudev?"

"With the help of you, Shivani."

"Me?" Shivani jerked with surprise.

"Yes, my child. Believe me, you are not an ordinary girl. There are some extraordinary things going around you. Hoping to get help from them I started working on a plan to destroy Veersen. I was quite happy with the progress until the recent event." Nodding his head in despair, he whispered, "Last night, your fight with Veersen's forces aborted my plans."

"I am sorry, Gurudev. I acknowledge my fault. I am guilty."

"Shivani, I know you are well aware of your fault and are remorseful about it. But some mistakes can't be corrected. They change your life forever. In that case, you have to take responsibility for your actions. That's why .... you need to listen to me, now."

"Gurudev," She asked desperately, "How in the world would my action be responsible if I run away from here? What are we going to achieve with that? After listening about the evil shield around Veersen, I have lost all my hope. If a great warrior and wizard like you can't fight with the evil Veersen, then who else can? Let him come here. I am ready to die fighting with him. At least it would satisfy me for trying to accomplish my goal. I will not run away." Shivani was speaking calmly and sadly but fearlessly.

"Shivani, I want to keep my hopes alive in the form of you. This is only possible if you can run away from here and go to a safer place. I said, 'nobody in the world knows how to destroy the dark powers around Veersen.' This doesn't mean they can't be destroyed at all. Certainly there are ways to demolish the evil darkness around him. Unfortunately I wasn't able to find one, yet. But something is telling me that you will be successful in this quest."

"Me?"

"Yes, you, Shivani. I can sense your astonishing qualities. This is why I am asking you to run away from here. With you staying alive, my hopes of killing Veersen too, will stay alive." Glancing at the fading skies, Gurudev sprang up from his position. "Come on, Shivani; hurry up." Rushing to make her stand up, he continued. "Each moment is precious. Please follow me, now."

The very idea of leaving her lovely home was killing Shivani. She began following Gurudev's footsteps. Suddenly stalling at her spot, she exclaimed with excitement, "Gurudev! I have a wonderful idea. Why can't you also come with me? We will go far away from here and you will continue working on your plan."

"I can't come with you, Shivani," he said, staring into her happy, expectant eyes. He was feeling guilty for disappointing her but had no choice.

"Why?"

"You will notice that shortly. Now please follow me." Soon they came to their meditation site. The east was wearing a beautiful golden hue, which was spreading across the sky. Some dew drops on the grass were glistening with the same shine. Following Gurudev's instructions, Shivani settled down into the lotus position on the ground facing the east. Her eyes were focused on the sun rising in the sky.

"Shivani, until today, I have taught whatever was known to me." Sitting down by her side, Gurudev said, "My child, I tried to give as much knowledge or wisdom as was possible for me. Now, before you leave, I have to give you one last thing." His eyes lingered for a few moments on the circular birthmark on Shivani's forehead. He closed his eyes blissfully. Soon his humble yet majestic voice began reverberating through that serene environment. "Now, close your eyes and let your mind be clear of all thoughts. This will help it to enter a receptive state."

A few moments passed by silently. When Gurudev opened his eyes he watched the desired reflection of serenity on Shivani's face. Smiling satisfactorily he again closed his eyes and gently placed his right hand on Shivani's head. At once an enormous amount of energy leapt into Shivani's body, jolting her backward. She experienced a mysterious current plunging deep into her body, igniting every single cell. It felt like she was engulfed in an intense heat. That strange incident lasted only for a moment.

Reflexively she opened her eyes. She was feeling extremely energetic, but as she glanced at Gurudev, she couldn't believe the sight. He was looking very old, extremely fatigued, and totally worn out. His whole body was trembling, but his face looked content. He was able to endow his hard-earned spiritual energy, acquired by many years of meditation, to his favorite disciple, Shivani. But Shivani wasn't aware of that. She was devastated to witness such a pitiful sight of her beloved Gurudev.

"Gurudev! What has happened to you?" Shivani tried to control herself from crying, still a few tears rolled down her cheeks.

"Shivani, please do not worry," Gurudev said, flashing his usual smile. His voice was trembling too. "Believe me, this is a temporary phase. I will be all right in a few days. Now you will understand why it's not possible for me to come with you." Gathering himself with much difficulty, he slowly stood up. He had made the ultimate sacrifice for humanity. He had made his wise and noble disciple immensely powerful, enabling her to proceed further on her mission and become successful in saving the world from evil.

Watching his plight, Shivani started crying.

Smiling softly, he said, "Shivani, please calm down. Don't be a baby. Be mature and responsible." His calm but assertive voice resonated. "Look forward. Always maintain your identity; be confident and be successful. My blessings are always with you, my child."

"Yes, Gurudev. I guess I need to pay for my foolish actions," Shivani muttered. After wiping her eyes with determination, she bowed down and did namaskaar to Gurudev. By then, all her animal and bird friends had gathered around her. They had sensed the situation. Naagraaj was slithering around her feet, and Jwala was standing as close to Shivani as she could be. The surprising silence, spread all over, had infused a somber feeling. Their long faces were ripping Shivani's heart apart. Saying good-bye to all of them and to her home was very hard for her. But the next moment, she turned around and, fighting the urge to glance back, began walking away from her home.

Shivani was walking very fast. After having reached the desired place, she decided to use Pratismruti, as suggested by Gurudev. The literal meaning of Pratismruti was "as fast as the mind." It was an advanced method for traveling to a distant place with extreme speed. After revising the steps quickly, she was ready to use Pratismruti for the first time in her life. Keeping both hands crossed across her chest, she stood up straight facing the north.

The moment she chanted the mantra for Pratismruti a unique feeling dawned on her. She felt as if she was being blown away by the whirling winds. The dizzying speed compelled her to close her eyes. Within a few moments, everything became calm again. "I guess I have reached the correct place," she whispered to herself after feeling the lovely touch of land. Gingerly opening her eyes, she squinted. The sight of picturesque mountain ranges spread all across the landscape hooked her attention instantly. The divine beauty of those mountains was indeed doubtless.

"Grand! Awesome! Magnificent! Splendid!" As her sight was gliding over the scenic beauty of the Himalayas, Shivani was blurting out the words. She was dazed by the sight. The countless snowy peaks, covered with many rivers coursing downward, had surrounded her from all sides. The bouncy rivers had carved gorgeous designs over the peaks. Some of the peaks, streamed with the bright sunlight, looked as though they wore golden crowns. The whole view of the lush green grounds and bold blue skies was simply divine. The beauty and brightness of that place was overwhelming.

Deeply inhaling the fresh, cold air, Shivani whispered, "So, these are the Himalayas. I heard Gurudev describing the beauty of these mountains before, but witnessing it personally is simply divine and breathtaking. Their splendor can't be conveyed in words." For a few moments, the enchanted Shivani stood at her spot, as if she was experiencing a beautiful dream. Eventually she succeeded in refocusing herself on her topmost goal.

As per Gurudev's advice and intuition, she had arrived at the Himalayas. The question "Now what?" appeared before her as gigantic as the mountains. There was no answer in sight to the lingering question. "What should be the next step for me? What should I do now?" Lost in thought, the restless Shivani began pacing the landscape.

CHAPTER ELEVEN

CRASHING THE WILDERNESS

The forest of Raat-Raan was packed with hundreds of soldiers of Veersen's royal army. It was being scoured in search of the girl who defeated Veersen's elite platoon. King Veersen himself was heading the special hunt. He was livid over the fact that the girl had escaped after attacking and killing his soldiers. The description of the girl given by his soldiers matched exactly with that of Kaalkoot's vision.

Vowing to capture the girl, the determined Veersen wasn't ready to wait until daybreak. As soon as he got the news, he entered Raat-Raan with all his might. Riding his horse, hoisting a gorgeous, diamond-studded umbrella atop, he was ordering the soldiers. To clear the path quickly for himself, he was frequently using the whip on the soldiers and demanding they work faster. Numerous trees were being cut down, and many soldiers were being trapped under the falling trees or being attacked by cobras, pythons, and giant ants from the trees.

Veersen had no time to worry about those miserable soldiers. Their lives were not precious to him. He kept moving forward, leaving them to die. The animals were running amok from the place, which once was their peaceful home. The forest was frequently being shattered by dreadful screams. The poor soldiers were struggling hard to carry out the royal orders. They were praying for their lives. But unfortunately, according to their king, they were not working fast enough.

"Hey, you morons! Speed up your work. You are moving like snails, or like...these pythons in this forest." Throwing a scornful glance around and raising his right hand, holding the hilt of the whip, Veersen roared at his troops.

By daybreak the whole troop had arrived at the desired spot, the banks of river Mahatejaa. Nonetheless, Veersen was a bit disappointed, for there was no trace of the girl. Yet he was feeling happy that Kaalkoot had agreed to join him for the hunt. Swirling around, he looked at Kaalkoot, who was riding behind him on another horse. For Veersen, Kalkoot was the everlasting source of fabulous solutions. In Kaalkoot's presence, Veersen always felt safe.

"Kaalkoot, now what?"

Kaalkoot didn't acknowledge the question because he was lost in some serious thoughts.

"Kaalkoot." Veersen galloped near him. "What are you thinking about so seriously? Are you scared of this forest?" He loved teasing Kaalkoot.

"Maharaaj!" The king's question brought Kaalkoot out of his trance. Very politely he continued. "Maharaaj, you are correct. This is really a dreadful forest. A person like me, who can't even hold a sword properly, needs to be worried." After pausing momentarily, he whispered in a more serious tone, "But right now, I am thinking about that girl. I mean...how could she stay alive in this dangerous forest after her birth? Not only that, for the past so many years, she has managed to be alive and has become a warrior with the ability to shoot Divya-astras."

"Kalkoot, you are absolutely right. These...these questions didn't strike me before," Veersen said, gazing at the thick forest. Sighing subtly, he added, "Anyway, why should we waste time thinking about that? Right now we are prepared to kill her instantly. Just advise us on how to find her. Use your knowledge, magic, anything to inform us of her whereabouts." The desperate Veersen looked at his adviser in chief, Kaalkoot, expectantly.

"Maharaaj, according to my calculations and foresight, the girl has to be somewhere here." After thinking for a moment, Kaalkoot's face sparkled as a fabulous idea struck him. He instantly took out a long bone from the sack tied to his horse's back. While everyone was watching his actions, he ran to the river with the bone and the sack.

"Kaalkoot." Veersen couldn't keep himself quiet.

"Yes, Maharaaj!" Kaalkoot hustled forth, balancing his heavy sack in one hand and the bone—apparently of a human—in the other.

"What are you doing?"

"I am trying to find the girl."

"Where will you find her? Will she be here...in this river, or on the top of that humongous cliff?" Veersen scoffed at him haughtily.

Kaalkoot was too engrossed in his work to notice Veersen's satire. Holding the bone in his left hand, Kaalkoot swirled it through the waters of Mahatejaa. Muttering the spell, he took out some dark powder from his sack and sprinkled it into the water. Again he swirled the bone through that powder...and the overjoyed Kaalkoot jumped with excitement.

"Maharaaj!" he screamed happily.

"What?" Veersen ran to the banks. He had never seen Kalkoot so happy before.

"Kaalkoot, what's the matter?"

"Maharaaj, please, look here, in the river." Kaalkoot's face was gleaming with pride. His magic had clearly demarcated the two streams of Mahatejaa. The stream, entering the secret tunnel under the mountains and used by Shivani, had turned darker than the other stream. After witnessing his magician's fabulous work, the enraptured King Veersen couldn't contain himself. The embrace of that powerful king almost lifted the old, frail body of Kalkoot high up in the air.

A few moments later, the throngs of soldiers stormed the river, heading toward the great cliff. The shrouds of vines hiding the secret entrance to Shivani's home were torn down. Nature's beautiful paradise was about to be ripped apart.

CHAPTER TWELVE

PEERING INTO THE PAST

The rapidly disappearing figure of his adorable daughter wrenched Gurudev's heart. The past memories of that lovely child—her innocent demands, her naive pranks, and her flawless laughter—flashed in his mind. With her presence, his hermitage had been sprinkled with joy. The emotional Gurudev returned to his hut with great difficulty. There was a feeling of emptiness everywhere. Unable to keep standing, he let himself drop down onto the patio. Glancing at the mountains, he was envisioning Veersen's army hustling on the other side.

"Veersen, along with Kaalkoot will storm in here at any moment," he muttered to himself.

Guru Yogidev had known Veersen for many years, even before he became the king of Suvarna-Raaj. Yogidev had a special relationship to Suvarna-nagari—the capital of Suvarna-Raaj. It was the most endearing and sacred place for him in the whole world. It was his birthplace. It was his home. The mere sound of the name Suvarna-nagari would fill his heart with the utmost respect.

Apart from being his birthplace, there were many special features for which the capital was famous. It was one of the most beautifully built cities in ancient India. Its majestic, tall edifices; well-planned, broad roads; glorious gardens; numerous lakes and rivers all were well known. Dharmasen, the ruling king, was known for his bravery and kindness. Under his reign, Suvarna-nagari enjoyed stability and prosperity.

Yogidev still remembered the day when, holding his mother's hand, he had first entered the magnificent golden palace of King Dharmasen. His mother, a great scholar, was honoring the respect-ful seat of royal preacher RaajGuru. King Dharmasen would always respect her. After her death, that seat was offered to Yogidev, and he became Guru Yogidev.

In a very short period, Guru Yogidev became known for his prodigious skills in warfare. King Dharmasen was impressed by the breathtaking demonstrations given by Guru Yogidev. According to him, Guru Yogidev was the best archer he had ever seen. Along with his son, Prince Veersen, he began learning many wonderful skills from that young, fiery warrior.

Besides warfare, Guru Yogidev was greatly acknowledged for his wisdom and wit. His mastery over many academic subjects was reflected in his speech. The king was highly impressed by his Raa-jGuru. He found Yogidev a unique blend of prowess and wisdom.

Guru Yogidev was well respected all across the kingdom of Suvarna-Raaj. Apart from his great wisdom and marvelous archery, his pious nature and unmatched love for the truth were well revered by the citizens. They had started addressing him as Mahatma—the great soul.

The untimely death of King Dharmasen let the kingdom fall into the hands of immature Prince Veersen. Unlike his father, Veersen was notorious for his ruthless and arrogant nature. Moments after stepping on the throne, Veersen began abusing the infinite powers that fell suddenly into his hands. Guru Yogidev couldn't tolerate the injustice by the king. Without caring about the king's fury, he would object to the injustice done by Veersen. No wonder he became the focus of King Veersen's wrath.

Kalkoot's entry further widened the cliff between Yogidev and Veersen. Yogidev strongly opposed Kalkoot's interference in the court, for voodooism and witchcraft were always discouraged in the noble kingdom of Suvarna Raaj. That triggered the long-held anger of Veersen to burst out. He ordered Yogidev into exile. While the whole court was stunned by the order, Guru Yogidev maintained his calm even after hearing it. Raising his right hand, halting the guards swarming at him, Yogidev spoke fearlessly. "King Veersen! You don't need to bother your guards to force me out of your kingdom. Save their energy for some other work. I, myself, can walk out of this place. At this very moment, I am leaving this court, this city, and this kingdom."

Leaving everyone shocked, Yogidev began walking away stoically, calmly. The whole court kept staring at the door, even after Guru Yogidev's figure receded from their vision.

Lost in a blur of thoughts, Yogidev kept walking away from his favorite city, Suvarna-nagari. Soon he realized he was amidst the notorious forest, Raat-Raan. Ignoring the numerous dangers dangling from and peering behind the trees, he continued walking. As he reached the river Mahatejaa, he became aware of his long-forgotten thirst. Standing on the banks of the river in an attempt to drink water, he lowered himself down and found himself tumbling helplessly into the forceful currents. In spite of being a good swimmer, he couldn't keep himself afloat. Within a few moments, his unconscious body was being churned and carried along toward the great cliff standing in the course of the river. It was a wonder that instead of floating along the river bend at the cliff; his body was threaded through the tightly tangled vines and entered the secret tunnel of Mahatejaa.

After regaining consciousness, Guru Yogidev found himself on the sparkly banks of a river, in a heavenly part of the world. He didn't know he was lying on the banks of the same river Mahatejaa, but on the other side of the mountains. After entering the secret mountain tunnel, Mahatejaa had now changed into the most serene river. Sitting under the crystal clear skies, surrounded by the divine beauty, he was busy thinking of the mysterious dream he just had woken from.

In his dream he was floating in a dark ocean. In his fist he was holding a sparkly sand particle that got magically turned into a glorious pearl. The pearl with its marvelous sparkle had enlightened the dark ocean. The divine voice, heard in the dream was still booming in his ears. Everything in that dream was puzzling and mysterious. Was it a message or just a dream? That dream became his friend and kept visiting him over and over again.

Isolated from humanity, he started living in that picturesque land as a hermit. The humongous mountain ranges had separated his new home from Suvarna-Raaj—a fact he never knew until Shivani was brought by Jwala to his neighborhood. That day, when Jwala dragged him through the secret tunnel in the mountains toward Shivani's wounded parents; he was surprised to discover how close the border of Suvarna-Raaj was to his new home. The mountain ranges had divided the river Mahatejaa into two parts—the serene and the turbulent. He was living on the serene side of the river, in the world of bliss, secluded from the outside world by the guardian mountains, the great cliff, and the secrete tunnel, harbored within. That awareness left him amazed. When he reached Shivani's parents in the forest of Raat-Raan, there was another shocking surprise waiting for him. He instantly recognized his friend's son, Himraaj, lying dead in a pool of blood with his wife, Saritaa-Devi, who was still holding onto her life by a thread. The scene tore him apart from inside. Himraaj and Saritaa-Devi were the parents of the newborn baby Shivani.

While the past flashed in his mind, Gurudev sat quietly on the ground. Suddenly a very familiar voice boomed in his ears.

"Guru Yogidev!" After entering that sacred place with his army, Veersen was astonished to find his past RaajGuru sitting there.

Gurudev looked ahead. Veersen and his army stood before him. Kaalkoot was also there. All his predictions had turned out to be true. He smiled because by then he knew that Shivani had gone far away and reached a safer place. He sighed contently.

"Guru Yogidev!" Veersen again roared, staring at him. "Hey, old man, get up. You were able to hide away from me all these years, but now I have found you. Get up and bow to me. This area is also a part of my kingdom, and I am your king, the most powerful Maharaaj Veersen!"

The blissful smile on Gurudev's face did not fall, not even for a second.

That further fueled Veersen's anger. He roared again. "Why are you smiling like that? Aren't you surprised to see me here?"

"King Veersen! You haven't changed a bit." Getting up slowly from his place, Gurudev started speaking in a humble voice. "I am not at all surprised. In fact, I was expecting you."

Suddenly coming forward, Kalkoot whispered, "Guru Yogidev, it's not respectful to stare into the king's eyes."

Gurudev reflexively turned to him. As Gurudev gazed at him, Kaalkoot swiftly turned back and hid behind Veersen. He couldn't tolerate the intense glare of those two pious, bright eyes.

"Kaalkoot, don't worry about teaching the etiquettes to this old person," Veersen blurted with a scornful glance at Gurudev. "After having lived in this wild for so many years, this beast has forgotten all the royal etiquettes."

"Veersen, sometimes wild beasts are better than the humans like you." Gurudev's voice had become quite serious. "In this richly embellished body of yours lies the heart of a ruthless, wild beast. That heart doesn't have the pricey moral values of humans."

Such harsh comments ignited Veersen's fury. Clenching his fists, he stormed forth and kicked Gurudev. The frail Gurudev fell to the ground.

Ignoring his fear, Kaalkoot ran toward Gurudev. He was very much aware of Gurudev's power—the power of truth. Gurudev's curse would not have physically harmed Veersen, but it definitely would have halted his progress toward the Emperor's seat, and Kaalkoot wasn't ready for that.

Bowing in front of Gurudev, he said pleadingly, "Guru Yogidev, please forgive Maharaaj Veersen. We are not here to bother you. In fact, we are looking for a girl supposedly hiding here. As soon as we find her, we will leave the place at once."

After a moment's silence, Guru Yogidev opened his mouth. "Why are you searching for that girl? Has she committed any crime?"

"Yogidev..." Shoving Kaalkoot aside, Veersen said, "Don't you dare ask any more questions. Simply answer. This is my order. I am the king. I can arrest anybody, anywhere, without any reason."

"Maharaaj, please calm down!" Kalkoot was pathetically trying to protect Veersen from Gurudev's wrath. Again turning to Yogidev, he said, "Guru Yogidev, the girl we are looking for is ominous, not only to the king but to the entire kingdom of Suvarna Raaj. So in the interest of our beloved king and the kingdom, we are seeking her arrest."

"Who says the girl is ominous?" Gurudev asked.

"It is my prediction. My predictions always come true," Kalkoot said with pride. "I had predicted this even before the girl was born."

"That's why you had advised the king to hunt down her mother?" Gurudev's sentence stunned Kalkoot.

Turning to Veersen, the fearless Gurudev said, "And Veersen, you followed his advice. You ordered the death of Saritaa-Devi, a pregnant, helpless woman. You are the most disgusting human being living on this earth. You are a monster."

"Hey, you old man, control your tongue." Grabbing Yogidev's long, silvery beard, Veersen, maddened with anger, pulled his face closer to him. "Yogidev, listen very carefully. Until now, I have tolerated you because once upon a time, you were my Guru. But now you are testing my patience." Pushing Gurudev back, he roared, "I am quite confident that the girl lives here." Staring at Gurudev's face, Veersen continued. "The moment my soldiers told me about a girl, living in the forest and capable of using Divya astra, your name instantly flashed in my mind. Now, after having found you here, I have no doubts that she is your disciple."

"Veersen," Gurudev said, smiling subtly, "I think for the first time in your life, you have used your brain to draw a correct conclusion. Yes, I know the girl. I raised her here, and she is my disciple."

"Where is she now?"

"I can't tell you."

"Why?"

"Because, I don't want to tell you that." Gurudev's fearlessness was as staunch as the surrounding mountains.

"Gurudev!" the furious Veersen screamed, clenching Gurudev's neck and lifting him up. Then turning to his soldiers, he ordered, "Comb the entire area, and find the girl at once."

Immediately the soldiers swarmed the neighborhood. Releasing Gurudev from his clinch, Veersen slued back to his bodyguards. Watching Gurudev fall to the ground with a thud, he ordered the bodyguards, "Start lashing this old man who has disobeyed the royal order."

As the guards began whipping Gurudev's bare back, Veersen's voice boomed again, "Keep lashing until he opens his mouth and gives us some information."

The sound of whipping shattered the bliss of the entire region. The bewildered flocks of birds and animals left the area where once serenity and sanctity reigned. The terrified Kaalkoot was staring at the scene aghast. With jitters, he was bracing for the curse to emerge at any moment from Gurudev's mouth. But surprisingly, Gurudev, without any resistance, was enduring all the whipping. He wasn't even wincing. While his body was completely covered with blood, his face was quite tranquil.

Not only Kaalkoot but even Veersen was baffled by the sight. He ordered the soldiers to pause. "Kaalkoot, go and see if he is alive at all."

Veersen's order was immediately followed. To Kaalkoot's surprise, Gurudev was still alive, although his breathing and heart beat were extremely slow.

"Maharaaj, I think he is just unconscious." Still holding Gurudev's hand in his, Kaalkoot said, "Please don't get angry at me. Can I request something?"

"Speak!"

"Please revoke your orders. Although Gurudev is still alive, I am sure after a few more whippings; his frail body will not withstand it. If he dies, our hope of finding the girl will die with him."

"What is your advice?"

"I can suggest one alternative. We can take him back to the capital as a hostage. He is the only one who knows the girl very well. After reaching there, I will try and convince him to provide us with the girl's location. That is one possibility." Staring at the soldiers returning, empty handed, from Gurudev's neighborhood hermitage, the desperate Veersen was beginning to consider Kaalkoot's suggestion.

"What is the other possibility?"

"Maharaaj, after hearing the news about Gurudev's capture, the girl will turn herself in to save her guru." Watching Veersen lost in serious thoughts, Kaalkoot resumed talking. "According to me..."

"Don't speak anymore," Veersen scoffed as he kicked the ground in despair. He was frustrated for having lost the girl again. "I agree with you. There is no alternative in sight." Then turning to his chief, Veersen ordered him to imprison Gurudev. Leaving the chief busy to restrain Gurudev and tie him to a horse, Veersen began walking back to the river. But after walking for a while, he suddenly stopped and thundered, "Kaalkoot, cast your spell and destroy this place at once. At least that will make me a bit happy." His vengeful laughter echoed through every corner even after he stormed out as a raging whirlwind.

CHAPTER THIRTEEN

AMIDST
THE SILVERY STREAKS

Pacing anxiously across the hilly terrain of the Himalayas, Shivani was lost in serious thoughts.

"What should I do now?" The haunting question had become gigantic ever since she had landed amidst the silvery streaks of the Himalayas. In fact, it dwarfed those majestic mountains. There was complete darkness on the path ahead of her. Except for herself and the speechless beauty of the mountains, there was no one else to advise her. Glancing around, Shivani sighed subtly. On the humongous background of the Himalayas she was simply a negligible dot.

The pretty mountain ranges spanned all across this place, obliterating the seam between the earth and the sky completely. Those lofty, snow-bathed peaks were soaring into the sky, as if competing among themselves. It looked like they were trying to peer through the skies to discover the mysteries hidden beyond. During their course, they were frequently being bumped into by white, fluffy clouds. Wrapping the peaks momentarily within their soft fur, the clouds would then hustle away with wild giggles.

Those clouds instantly reminded Shivani of her white, fluffy friends, the bunnies, Shubhra and Dhawal, tumbling on Gurudev. Staring at the mountains, the emotional Shivani sat down on the ground.

The Himalayas! The mighty, humble, revered Himalayas were looking exactly like her Gurudev. The only difference was they were unable to advise or guide her. The emptiness of the majestic mountains was revealed to her. For Shivani, that further accentuated the tremendous absence of Gurudev. While she kept staring at the mountains, all of a sudden Gurudev's words flashed in her mind.

"Shivani, we are never alone. There is one entity always accompanying us, at every step, at each moment. That is our innate energy. It is this energy that helps us at difficult times. It is this energy that guides us out of darkness. We simply need to awaken this mysterious power lying within ourselves."

With renewed vigor, Shivani jumped to her feet. Now, the path ahead had become very clear to her. "I am going to invoke my internal energy," the determined Shivani whispered to herself. "However difficult it may be, I will make it happen." She placed her bow and quiver aside on the ground. After facing the tallest peak of the Himalayas, she settled down in the lotus position. By then, the sun had painted the whole landscape with its golden brush. The icy peaks were reflecting the golden light after multiplying it by many folds. The molten gold was everywhere in sight. Gazing at that, Shivani took a deep breath. Closing her eyes, she recalled Gurudev's image and asked for his blessings. It was her habit. Before starting any work, she would always seek her revered Guru's blessings.

Now, Shivani was about to head for the goal no human had ever achieved before—invoking the internal energy. As she began breathing slowly, the cold, fresh air bouncing off the stately mountains dashed into her body. That magical air recreated the same grandiose feeling in her mind. The air, scented with the divineness, sparked a unique, vibrant energy inside her body. Content with that, the blissful Shivani slowly glided into herself in search of the ultimate guide. Very soon, her body became motionless, making her an inseparable part of that serene landscape. With each passing moment, she was plunging deeper within herself. Time had stopped for her, or she had frozen for the time.

The outside world was moving on. The sun, the moon, and the stars were taking turns showering her tiny body with their divine rays. The majestic Himalayas, with their array of peaks, were vigilantly guarding her body, submerged in complete trance. The earth, the sky, the stars, and the wind were enjoying witnessing the ultimate resolve on the face of Shivani. A fascinating event was about to happen in front of them. Slowly a reddish hue began radiating from Shivani's motionless body, creating the most magnificent sight. With each passing moment, that red glow started getting brighter. Against the vast background of the great Himalayas, her luminous body became quite noticeable. It looked like a tiny red ruby, dazzling against the bright, snowy landscape. At every moment its glow got brighter.

Then, that starry night, an unprecedented event occurred. It was the strangest thing the world had ever witnessed. Shivani's radiant body had become so bright that it resembled a fiery flame amidst the moonlit, snowy land. The red, circular birthmark on her forehead flashed intensely for a moment, and the next moment, an enormously powerful beam of light darted out from that spot. It was so powerful that her tiny body jolted back at once. The light beam that emerged out of her body was the concentrated and awakened internal energy of Shivani. It had blinded the moon and the stars with its shimmer while illuminating the whole Himalayas. That powerful outburst of unified and intensified energy knocked Shivani out of her trance.

With wide eyes, Shivani kept gazing in front of her, where a pretty girl, clad in a red, shimmering sari, was standing with her bright eyes focused directly on Shivani. Her golden crown, waistband, bangles, anklets, and necklaces all were amply studded with bright rubies and dazzling diamonds. Her long hair was flowing with the gentle wind. Her radiant body had changed the night into an utterly vibrant entity. Captivated by the enchanting beauty of the girl, Shivani sprang to her seat. The most surprising thing was the girl's face! It was identical to Shivani's.

"Oh, my goodness!" Shivani gasped breathlessly.

Enjoying Shivani's baffled reaction; the girl came forth, smiling at Shivani. As the girl did namaskaar, her bangles made a melodious tinkling sound.

"Namaskaar, Shivani!" the girl said in a pleasant voice. Shivani had become speechless. "I am here for you," the girl said.

"Who…who are you?" The words spilled out of Shivani's mouth without her knowledge.

"I am your innate energy. I was lying inside you until now. By the intense meditation, you have awakened me to guide you in your mission. So, I am here in front of you."

Watching Shivani's frozen face, the energy continued. "I am sure you are very well aware of this fact."

"Yes, Gurudev...had told me before. But it's still hard to believe that you...you were inside me, and now..." Shivani wasn't ready to believe that she had successfully invoked her internal energy. It was the most unprecedented achievement for her.

"I understand your feelings. It sounds quite unreal because you are the first one to be successful in awakening the innate power. Your ultimate determination, the intense meditation, and the contribution of Gurudev's energy endowed to you made it happen."

Watching Shivani's serious face, the energy continued. "Congratulations, Shivani, for invoking me! I am in fact a small part of the infinite and invincible energy that exists in the universe. Every particle, living or nonliving, embodies a part of that energy, called innate or internal energy. It doesn't matter how tiny that part is, it shares the bond with the universal energy. Hence the innate energy is as powerful as the universal energy. Unfortunately this fact is rarely recognized. That's why this innate energy, lying within all the elements, living or nonliving, stays dormant. But unlike others, you have revived your innate energy in the form of me." Smiling at Shivani, she said, "Now, I am at your service. Please let me know what should be done for you."

"First of all, I would like to welcome you," Gathering herself back to the reality Shivani said and flashed a smile.

"It's my pleasure."

"Miss Energy, I am in dire need of your guidance."

"I can sense that, Shivani."

That stunned Shivani. Staring at the red, circular glow on the energy's forehead, identical to hers, Shivani thought for a moment and then smiled. "I should have already known that. You are my energy and hence can easily read my mind. Right?"

"You are absolutely correct." Laughing freely at Shivani's remark, the energy continued. "I know your past, your present, and your future. What else can you expect from me? I am a part of the power that governs the universe." Then suddenly turning serious, she continued. "Currently people are endangered by the atrocities happening in the capital, Suvarna-nagari, and you need my guidance regarding that."

"You are absolutely right. Veersen is terrorizing the whole king-dom. Unfortunately he is protected by the dark powers that can't be defeated. So, please help me find the solution to this monstrous problem."

"Shivani." Closing her eyes momentarily, the energy said, "The problem is more serious than you think. There is no known solution to destroy the dark powers protecting Veersen."

"So he will live forever, with unrepentant cruelty?"

"Who says that? The dark powers sheltering him can be destroyed, and he will be defeated if you..."

"If what?" the anxious Shivani blurted.

"If you go beyond the earth."

"Beyond the earth? Impossible." The perplexed Shivani sighed with frustration.

"It's actually very much possible, Shivani." The energy was spill-ing the information. "Shivani, listen to me carefully. Within your solar system itself, there is a planet called Shreelok. For the earth, it is the nearest and only planet that harbors life. Although its residents are similar to humans in physical appearance, their civilization is far, far more advanced than humans."

Shivani was listening as if listening to a fairy tale. It sounded extremely fantastic but totally unreal. The energy continued, "The Shreeyans, the residents of Shreelok, have a magnificent weapon called Shree-chakra. It's very powerful. It can be used to destroy the dark powers and kill Veersen. There are other aliens who possess such weapons, but they live quite far away from the earth. For you, Shreelok is the closest one."

The energy was providing a series of information, each item sounding more fascinating and unbelievable than the previous one. Gazing at the energy, the wonderstruck Shivani whispered, "How do you know all this?"

"Remember, I am a part of the invincible, infinite, celestial energy that…"

"That exists in the universe!" Shivani blurted. "So, you know all about the universe. Wow! Fascinating!"

"That's right. We share the same bond. I can tell you many more fabulous stories from all over the universe. I can tell you about various civilizations existing in the world and their secrets and so on." Staring at Shivani's puzzled face, the energy said, "Shivani, nature cannot be constrained by the lack of your imagination. Look at the sky. Do you think there are just these many stars, visible to your eyes, present in the sky? No. There are innumerable stars present up there, hidden from you."

"So, according to you, I should go to Shreelok, get the weapon—Shree-chakra—come back here, and then destroy Veersen." Shivani's every word was filled with disbelief.

"Shivani, please trust me, just the way you trusted about the existence of 'innate energy.'"

Although stunned, Shivani had faith in the energy. Glancing at the sky, she sighed. Somewhere out there was her next target, Shreelok. Suddenly she turned to the energy. "So, where is this planet? Can I see it?"

"No. It is not visible to ordinary sight." Staring at Shivani's perplexed face, the energy continued. "Shreelok harbors an advanced and modern civilization. To conceal their planet from intruders, the residents of Shreelok have created a special shell around it that has turned Shreelok invisible."

"Wow!"

"Yes! To be able to see the planet, you must have the divine sight, which I am going to grant you now."

Having said this, the energy came close to Shivani and placed her right hand on Shivani's eyes. The unique sensation felt by Shivani was beyond any description. A blend of intense warmth and a soothing sensation electrified her entire body. She blinked her eyes and again stared at the sky.

"Wow!" Shivani exclaimed, glancing at an extremely dazzling spot. There was a peculiar hue encircling it. "So that is Shreelok." Suddenly one important question flashed in Shivani's mind, and she swirled back to the energy. "Now I know where the target is, but how do I get there?"

"Shivani, you are a great archer and a disciple of Gurudev. I am certain you don't need my guidance regarding this."

"What does she mean? Does she think that I can shoot myself up there…up to Shreelok?" Shivani muttered with displeasure. But the next moment, she knew she had answered her own query.

"Shivani, I hope I helped you. Now your goal and the path, everything is clear, isn't it?"

"Yes, Miss Energy. I am very thankful to you."

"Shivani, I see a lot of hurdles in your way. But don't get discouraged." After a moment's pause, she continued. "Before I leave, I need to do one more important thing." The energy flickered toward Shivani's bow and quiver that were lying on the ground. As she swiped her fingers over them, they were transformed into solid gold, shinning magnificently. Handing them over to Shivani, the energy said, "This bow is unbreakable now, and this quiver will remain filled with arrows. It will never be empty."

After wishing her success in the mission, the energy zoomed back into Shivani's body through the same point—the circular birthmark on her forehead. Wrapped up again in the surrounding darkness and the mighty Himalayas, Shivani stood, realizing her newly discovered power.

Staring at the planet Shreelok, Shivani remembered Gurudev's words from the past.

"*For your mission, you might have to cross the horizons.*" This mystic sentence now came alive with its true meaning. "No wonder he had an intuition about sending me here to this auspicious spot," she whispered to herself.

CHAPTER FOURTEEN

CROSSING OVER
THE HORIZON

Engulfed by the silence of the night, Shivani stood at her spot for a while. Over that massive landscape of the Himalayas, she was standing all alone, invigorated by the omnipotent energy residing in her. Now, she was feeling much more confident and much stronger. Taking in a deep breath, she smiled back at the gleaming moon, the stars, and the Himalayas—all applauding her achievement. The silvery silhouette of the peaks of the Himalayas against the dark sky was encouraging her to shine with divine sparkles against all odds.

Slowly her eyes turned toward her target—the planet Shreelok. Its wonderful glare was calling her. Keeping her eyes still and focused on that planet, she tied her never-emptying quiver to her back. Tucking the golden bow onto her shoulders, she closed her eyes and did namaskaar to Gurudev. Then, joining both heels together at a particular angle and stretching her spine as well as her hands up toward the sky, her body took on a streamline posture. Lifting her face up, her sight was now focused on Shreelok. Then, after closing her eyes, she began chanting the mantra for Agni-baan—the fiery arrow. Agni-baan was a kind of Divya astra that, with lightening speed, would take a person to the desired destination anywhere beyond the earth.

The moment Shivani finished chanting the mantra, her body was engulfed in a red, fiery sheath. From a distance, it looked as if a red, hot arrow, pointing toward the sky, was standing straight on the ground. The tremendous heat generated by the Agni-baan began melting the nearby icy ground. Just then, in a flash, the Agni-baan, the fiery arrow, soared high up into the sky. Encased safely within the fiery sheath, Shivani began surging up toward Shreelok.

Soon she landed safely and softly on the alien planet. As she stepped forward, the protective Agni-baan sheath disappeared completely, as if got absorbed into the air. Now, she was standing on an unknown planet all alone. Her vigilant eyes started scanning the surroundings.

The place where she landed was the top of a mountain flanked by two contrasting views. On her right was an ocean that spanned the view all the way up to the horizon. For the first time in her life, Shivani was looking at an ocean. The grandness and beauty of the ocean captivated her. Watching the enormous waves dashing on the shore and bringing the pearly, sparkly froth, dispersed gracefully along the shoreline, she forgot about herself. The low, rumbling sound of waves at once enlightened her heart. Tracing the waves back, her sight reached the horizon, where the two gorgeous blues, one from the ocean and the other from the sky, seemed to have blended together without any obvious seam. The two great entities had become one endless, divine blue. Each one was accentuating the other's grandness. Unknowingly, Shivani did namaskaar to the heavenly blue.

On her left was a stunningly panoramic view of the land of Shreelok. The beautiful landscape was packed with trees, bushes, plants, and shrubs displaying an array of vivid colors. Unlike the trees on the earth, the trees of Shreelok were shaded with a variety of colors such as red, blue, violet, pink, and orange. Not only that, the grass was also beaming with bright colors. From a distance, the colorful grass, sprawling over the ground, looked like a pretty carpet with all the colors of the world trapped in it.

"It is dazzling, too!" the wonderstruck Shivani muttered, picking up a shaft of grass from the ground and gazing at it.

Repeatedly Shivani was turning her head from side to side, gazing and comparing the views of a beautifully colored land and a gorgeously blue ocean divided by a tall mountain where she stood. Suddenly she caught a glimpse of a flock of birds heading toward her and was alarmed. It was the first sign of life she had witnessed since her landing. With her arrow vigilantly sitting on the bow she continued scanning the sky.

"They surely look different than my birds on the earth," Shivani whispered with a frowned forehead. "They...they are humongous." The flock was approaching very fast. She tightened her grip on the arrow while keeping her sight focused on the flock. Her arrow, at the slightest hint of danger, was ready to dart ahead. In addition to tracking the flock, her eyes were prowling the surroundings, tuned to spot any danger. Although ready to deal with any attack from anywhere, she didn't want to start attacking without confirming the nature of the flock. Soon she realized the flock consisted of gigantic sized eagles.

While she was busy admiring the majestic wings of the birds, the flock swooped down and landed on the ground in unison, a little away from her. Her eyes were cautiously recording their each and every action. Soon, after realizing the similarity of those eagles to the ones described in the past by Gurudev she was astounded.

"Impossible!" Shivani whispered under her breath. "I can't believe I am watching such birds fly." The mystery of the unusual-looking eagles was revealed before her widened eyes. She had correctly judged them. They were Vimaanas—flying machines used by advanced civilizations. With her eyes glued to the sight, her jaw dropped. Shivani stood frozen at her spot as the bellies of the Vimaanas opened and a few figures climbed down from inside. They looked like humans. They were Shreeyans, the residents of Shreelok.

"Oh, my goodness!" While the words spilled from her mouth, tumults of thoughts began soaring inside her mind. "Will they attack me? Should I start attacking them now? Or should I reveal my intentions first? Maybe I should tell them I have come here for the Shree-chakra and not to harm them. Will they listen to me? Will they trust me?" The armed Shreeyans were getting closer. Shivani had to choose one of the options quickly.

"Saavdhaan! Attention!" Revealing herself from behind a tree, Shivani warned the Shreeyans. They all halted instantly. "Please do not move forward. I mean no harm to you. Please trust me. Let me explain the reason for landing on your planet." Taking her bow down, Shivani continued. "First, I would like to apologize for landing on your planet without your permission. Please believe me; I am..."

Her sentence remained incomplete as she spotted one of the Shreeyans still walking toward her. That puzzled Shivani. She couldn't decide whether to shoot or wait and watch cautiously. After noticing that the Shreeyan was unarmed, Shivani kept observing her. Soon it became clear, the approaching Shreeyan was a girl .... a beautiful, young girl. A little older than Shivani, the girl was wearing a lavender-colored sari embroidered with gorgeous pearls. With each elegant step, her crown and the rest of her jewelry were dazzling pleasantly. The most noticeable feature was her hair. The brownish gold hairs were so long that they were almost touching the ground.

"Namaskaar, Shivani."

The girl's sentence stunned Shivani. "Who are you, and how do you know my name?" Shivani asked, staring at the girl with a puzzled face.

"Hmmm." The girl ignored the question and smiled, looking at Shivani. She was observing Shivani from head to toe. "You seem to be very brave."

Was that an appreciation or a scornful comment? Shivani couldn't recognize the tone. "Now, answering your first question, I am Princess Aryaa, a princess of this planet and daughter of the king of Shreelok----Maharaaj Aaditya-Raaj." After a quick pause, the girl continued. "The answer to your second question: I know your name, where you are from, and your intentions. Not only that, but we were expecting you here."

Shivani was staring at her dumbfoundedly. The girl laughed at the bewildered Shivani. "Shivani, just remember, we Shreeyans are one of the most advanced civilizations in the universe. We are aware of the events occurring all over the universe. Since we knew your good intentions, we didn't prevent you from landing here, although we were watching your every step." The princess smiled again at Shivani. "Are you satisfied now?" Then, spreading both her hands, she said, "We Shreeyans welcome you here." After gazing for a moment into the two gorgeous blue eyes, Shivani read the princess's honest mind. Keeping the bow and arrow on the ground, she jumped into the assured and warm embrace of the princess.

Shivani was quite thrilled to have a window seat inside the belly of one of the Vimaanas. For the first time in her life, she was sitting on such a soft seat. It felt as if she was sitting on one of her fluffy bunnies. A little away from her, Princess Aryaa was seen sitting and instructing her guards. As the Vimaan, disguised as an eagle, took off, Shivani was excited. The very thought of flying through the clouds toward the royal court of Maharaaj Aaditya-Raaj thrilled her. As she peered out the window, the magnificent view of the ocean enticed her. But within a few moments, it vanished behind the veil of clouds as the Vimaan soared high up in the sky.

Having landed on the steps of the court, Shivani was overwhelmed by its loftiness. The edifice of the royal court was standing, or rather floating, in midair, several thousand feet up from the ground, without being supported by even a single pillar. As the

166

mesmerized Shivani was nodding her head in disbelief, a few wispy clouds nudged her lovingly as if to welcome her.

"Come on, Shivani!" Princess Aryaa's words brought her out of her daze, and she began climbing the steps. Now they were at the entrance to the royal court. There were huge arches almost reaching the sky. Those golden arches were intricately carved and ornately decorated. Standing under one of the arches, Shivani glanced inside the royal court.

The richness of the palace couldn't be conveyed by words, she thought. The royal court was uniquely designed as a dome. Its towering ceiling was made of a transparent material, tinted with a pleasant blue shimmer, making it quite dramatic. The view of surrounding clouds caressing it further enhanced its marvel. Tucked snugly in the blue ceiling were multiple, star-shaped lights dazzling vividly. Those gold and silver lights were placed alternating with each other. The sunlight streaming through them was being reflected back, illuminating the entire dome in an awesome glow.

As Shivani turned her eyes toward the floor of the court, she was amazed by the phenomenal view. It was covered with a sumptuously rich, plush white carpet, tinted blue by the blue ceiling. It looked like the whole court was standing on thick sheets of clouds. There was a huge runner made of the regal red with beautiful highlights of blue and ornate gold on the ground. It stretched from the main entrance all across the court up to the lofty dais in the center. Embellished with splashing emeralds and rubies, that one-of-a-kind runner was surely captivating. The Shreeyans had earned another nod from Shivani for their magnificent creativity.

On either side of the runner were hundreds of richly upholstered golden chairs situated in a semicircular fashion around the dais. Sitting on those chairs were the honorable members of the royal court, their eyes curiously focused on Shivani.

Straight ahead of her, in the center of the dais, was a mammoth sized golden throne carved as a chariot. Sculptures of seven elegant horses with their golden leashes were attached to the throne. The back of the throne displayed the rising sun, gilded on all sides by the lively rays. At the top of the chariot was a beautiful umbrella trimmed with glistening tassels, dangling low. Countless diamonds, rubies, sapphires, and emeralds studded throughout the throne were radiating a magical glare. That exclusively divine throne was stealing the whole show, Shivani thought.

Sitting on the sun-throne was Maharaaj Aaditya Raaj, the ultimate ruler of the planet Shreelok. To his left was another gorgeous throne where the queen, Maharani Ushadevi, was seated. Both of them were looking at Shivani standing at the entrance with their daughter, Princess Aryaa.

Coming forward, Shivani did namaskaar to them and quickly snatched out two arrows from her quiver. Leaving the whole court puzzled she shot the arrows high up in the air. They zoomed up toward the lofty ceiling and began gliding down after been magically transformed into beautiful garlands of flowers. Before anyone realized it, the flower garlands landed softly around the necks of Maharaaj Aditya Raaj and Maharaani Ushadevi. Then in quick succession, Shivani shot another bout of arrows, which were transformed into pretty roses, landing in the hands of the royal court. The rich fragrance of those roses filled up the entire space

Forgetting themselves, the Shreeyans were witnessing the splendid performance with astonishment. Even princess Aryaa, standing beside Shivani, was taken aback by the event. She was so stunned that she missed her own gift, a rose gliding down to her. Slowly, as the Shreeyans began regaining their senses, they all, including Maharaaj and Maharaani, stood to honor the prodigious archer, Shivani. Forgetting their supremacy, they were applauding a human. Shivani had won the heart of the royal court—before entering it. Even after Shivani and the princess began walking toward the dais, the flabbergasted crowd continued clapping.

Glancing at Shivani, sitting on a golden chair by the side of the princess, Maharaaj Aaditya Raaj rose up from his throne and began addressing his court. "My honorable fellow members, even before Shivani's arrival, we were aware of the situation on the earth. But I am sure after listening to Shivani, you all feel compelled to help the humans." Letting out a subtle sigh, he continued. "We Shreeyans have a special place for the earth in our hearts for our ancestors lived there once. Although they lived there for a very brief period, a special bond was formed between the Shreeyans and the humans. That's why it is our duty to help the humans and punish Veersen."

Pausing momentarily to judge the reactions of the others, he continued. "My friends, for many years, we, the Shreeyans have been helping to restore justice in this universe. According to the same noble tradition, I feel it is our duty to help Shivani. We should assist her in punishing the evil from the earth and restoring the rule of truth and justice." Glancing once again at his courtiers, he asked with a booming voice, "Do you all agree with me?"

At once the whole court agreed in unison. Their acceptance reverberated through the humongous dome, infusing hope in Shivani's heart.

Turning to Shivani, Maharaaj smiled. "Shivani, are you listening? We all are with you on this mission."

Rising at once from her seat, Shivani went forth. In a very humble voice, she spoke. "Maharaaj, it is difficult for me to explain my gratitude. I...I am really overwhelmed by the love and support shown by the Shreeyans. I am grateful for the generosity of lending the divine Shree-chakra." Once again doing namaskaar to the royal members, she said, "On behalf of all humans, I am very thankful to you all for this help. We will always feel obliged to you."

"Shivani, please don't feel obliged. Restoring peace and harmony in the universe is every Shreeyan's foremost duty. Also, it is your right to ask for our help in that regard." After a pause, Maharaaj added, "The Shree-chakra, whose desire drove you up here, will be presented to you in this court tomorrow."

"Tomorrow!" Shivani whispered with profound disbelief. It was hard for her to hide her extreme disappointment. "Maharaaj...I...I mean, why can't I get it now? It's extremely urgent for me to get back to the earth. My Gurudev is all alone down there. Currently he is too weak to protect himself from Veersen. That's why I need to return back as soon as possible."

"Shivani," Maharaaj's voice was consoling. "I am sorry to disappoint you. Although I realize the urgency of you getting back home, I am helpless. There are certain constraints on me." Glancing at his fellow Shreeyans, he continued. "Shivani, the Shree-chakra is very revered to all of us. Hence there are certain rules regarding handling it. It can be touched only at the most auspicious time of the day, the time of sunrise." Looking at Shivani's long face, he sighed. "This is the reason I can't present it to you right now. Shivani, I am sorry for the delay."

Hearing the apology from Maharaaj, Shivani hustled forth, shrugging off her disappointment. "Maharaaj, please don't apologize. I feel embarrassed for rushing you. I understand your limitations. I will wait until tomorrow to receive the divine weapon."

Maharaaj was impressed by Shivani's polite and sweet speech. He turned to the princess. After exchanging glances with her, he started in an energetic tone. "Shivani, I want your wait to be pleasurable." He stared at Shivani's perplexed face. "I would request Princess Aryaa to take you on a tour of our planet. We have numerous interesting places here. I am quite certain you will enjoy the tour."

Shivani smiled at the princess, and the two walked out of the court after doing namaskaar to Maharaaj and Maharani.

As the two disappeared behind an ornate door to the right, the Maharaaj turned to the chief of royal court, Pradhaan Mantri.

"Pradhaan Mantri, have you obtained the information I asked for?" His voice was serious.

"Yes, Maharaaj!" Coming forth promptly, Pradhaan Mantri said, "I have also brought our astrologer."

An old person came forward and stood beside Pradhaan Mantri. After accepting the greetings from the astrologer, Maharaaj addressed him. "Please start speaking."

"Maharaaj, I am happy to present this information." The astrologer glanced at the court members listening to him intently. "According to my calculations, there will be no more intruders from the earth in the near future."

Although letting out a sigh of relief, Maharaaj asked in a concerned voice, "Are you really confident about it?"

"Yes, Maharaaj. I am absolutely confident about it. To come here, Shivani used the Agni Baan technology. This particular technology is only known to Gurudev and hence to Shivani. All other humans are unaware of it." Flashing a smile, he continued. "Further, my astrological calculations show that eventually, not only Agni-baan but the whole knowledge of Divya astras will be lost in time."

His words relaxed everyone gathered there. Shivani's dramatic entry had made many Shreeyans jittery. They had begun doubting the efficacy of the security shell around their planet, preventing the intruders. Although they honestly wanted to help Shivani, the Shreeyans didn't want another human to land on their planet again.

Looking at their relieved faces, the astrologer said, "The shell protecting our planet is completely reliable and effective. Shivani could locate our planet because she was successful in invoking the innate energy. My fellow Shreeyans, please, do not worry about another human succeeding in this regard. For thousands and thousands of years, humans will not be able to cross over their horizons. But after that..."

Maharaaj couldn't wait for the astrologer to resume his talk. Impatiently he blurted, "Don't pause at a wrong time. After that what?"

"Maharaaj." Hustling to resume his speech, the astrologer said, "After that, a whole new technology will emerge. That technology will be much slower than the one used by Shivani. Even after improvisation of its speed, humans may not reach here for thousands of years."

"And by then, we would be gone to an entirely different location," Maharaaj said flashing an energetic smile.

While walking out of the royal court, Shivani glanced at the princess, who was bursting energetically. After watching the overjoyed princess, Shivani's lingering displeasure was instantly blown away. "Maybe this is a blessing in disguise for me," she said to herself. "It is my once in a lifetime chance to explore this wonderful planet. Maybe something good happens out of this tour." She consoled herself the way Gurudev would have done.

The Princess and Shivani were standing at the top of the stairs. From there, she could watch the city below. The tiny Shreeyans, clad in rich garments, were walking on roads or riding in fancy chariots. Suddenly, to her right side, she caught a glimpse of an unusual thing. It was a flock of golden swans flying toward her.

"Oh, my goodness!" Squinting further, she began watching them. She had never seen such beautiful swans before. "Probably they too are Vimaanas, flying machines," she whispered to herself. Just then the flock along with the attached chariot swooped down and halted near them. To her surprise, they were real, live swans. They looked as if they'd been bathed in the molten gold. As they fluttered their wings, glistening golden dust swarmed up in the air. Shivani was engrossed, observing the beautiful birds. Just then she heard the princess calling, "Come on, Shivani. Our chariot is here."

The mesmerized Shivani began following the princess.

Washed in sunshine, Princess Aryaa's face was glowing with radiance. Her pink cheeks were trying to compete with the pink, gorgeous roses tucked in her long, flowing, silky, golden hair. A diamond stud stuck on red bindi on her broad forehead was dazzling—it looked like a Tilak. Her cute pointy nose further enhanced her beauty. The red, thin lips, parted gently, were flashing a pleasant smile. But the most gorgeous were her eyes, thought Shivani. The gentle, blue eyes were sparking under her pretty eyelids, trimmed with the sumptuous eyelashes. "I wish I had such a beautiful sister," Shivani thought.

CHAPTER FIFTEEN

THE MAGICAL WORLD

"Shivani, hop in here." The princess was calling her from inside the chariot.

The interior of the chariot was upholstered with a soft, turquoise-colored fabric. The subtle hints of ivory and gold throughout the fabric had created delicate designs all over it. The floor was carpeted with a fluffy, thick rug displaying gorgeous flowers painted with gold and silver shine. That carpet was so soft that after stepping on it, Shivani's feet almost vanished inside it, as if she was stepping on a layer of soft clouds. Two oval-shaped windows on either side of the chariot held two elegant chairs. Both the windows were trimmed with a frame studded with diamonds while the door of the chariot was covered with golden sheers, embellished with valances of sapphires.

As the two settled in, the charioteer tapped the swans gently, and in a flash, the chariot soared high up in the air, leaving behind a trail of golden dust snaking through the clouds.

Sitting inside the flying chariot, Shivani felt as if she was having a pretty dream. From her seat, the planet Shreelok looked spectacular. Except for a few mountains, it was quite smoothly surfaced. They were passing by numerous buildings floating in midair, their magnificent architectural details easily visible. Down on the ground, the wide roads were shimmering with a pinkish hue. They looked like sparkly, pink swirls, punctuated frequently by giant, bursting fountains. Around the fountains were lovely decorations of plants blossoming with vibrant flowers. Accompanying them were numerous rivers and springs, jumping jubilantly. The rest of the landscape was filled with the colorful trees, bushes, shrubs, and grass.

Peering out through the window, Shivani was staring at every single thing until it disappeared. Just then, she heard the princess telling something to the charioteer as she pointed her fingers toward a floating object. Shivani pulled her eyes toward it. It was a lofty chamber floating atop a sheet of clouds.

"Finally, here it is. It surely made us wait for quite a while." The princess sprang up from her seat the moment their chariot came to a halt near the chamber. Following Princess Aryaa Shivani went inside the floating chamber. The floating chamber was in fact a huge wardrobe filled with countless dresses.

"Shivani, all of these dresses are for you. Choose any one," the princess said, pointing at the dresses. Shivani's widened eyes were jumping from one dress to another. Each one was prettier than the previous one. She stood flabbergasted by the sight of numerous colorful dresses dazzling with precious stones. Each dress was coordinated with appropriate jewelry, hair accessories, and shoes. Oversized mirrors, placed on the walls of the chamber, were further accentuating the fanciful glow.

"Shivani, there is no rush," the princess remarked, glancing at the perplexed face of Shivani. "Take as much time as you need to choose the right dress for you."

"Princess," Shivani started hesitantly, "I am really pleased with your generosity. But..." While strolling slowly along the wardrobe, Shivani continued, "But I may not be able to accept your gift at this time. Currently I am on a mission. My first and foremost duty is to get the Shree-chakra. Then, as quickly as possible, I need to return back to the earth and defeat Veersen. My morals don't allow me to wear these luxurious fabrics and jewelry at this moment." Glancing at her own rags, she said further, "Until I accomplish my mission, I will continue wearing this attire. It reminds me of my objectives. I hope I haven't hurt your feelings."

The princess was trying to comprehend Shivani's noble words. She was surprised by Shivani's ability to restrain herself from the lure. Walking slowly up to Shivani, the princess held her hand. "Shivani, I am impressed by your thoughts. Your life values would dwarf even a great sage. Such great self-control is rarely seen." Patting her back gently, the princess said, "You will definitely succeed in your mission."

Shivani's cheeks turned red after listening to all the appreciation.

Soon they resumed the magical chariot ride. They were gliding, swooping, and soaring over a picturesque landscape, being showered with refreshing sunshine. As Shivani looked up into the sky, she was surprised to notice the pleasant sight of the sun. There was absolutely no glare. On the contrary, the magnetic sight of the sun was soothing her eyes. She felt as if she was watching the moon. She kept staring at that gorgeous circle of light, engraved in the azure blue skies. Her eyes, until then devoid of the sun's charming sight, were greedily hooked onto it now.

"Shivani," the puzzled princess commented. "You have been staring at the sun in such a way as if seeing it for the first time in your life."

"You are absolutely correct, princess," Shivani replied without looking away. "Although we share the same sun, from the earth, its sight is not as soothing. Because of its bright glare, you can just glance at it momentarily. "

"Hmmm." Thinking for a moment, the princess answered, "I think the shell around our planet might be responsible for the soothing sight of the sun. The shell, designed to make our planet invisible from the rest of the universe, obstructs the sun's glare. This enables us to stare at the sun without hurting the eyes."

"Yes. That must be the reason for such a comforting sight."

"Shivani, there is one more interesting thing about the sun here." Staring at the sun, the princess said, "We Shreeyans have a daily ritual of watching the sun for a certain time early in the morning. This helps us to be healthy and energetic for the rest of the day."

"That's great!"

Just then the sun disappeared completely from their sight as the chariot plunged into a thick swarm of clouds.

"Oh, no!" Shivani started giggling. "Something is tickling me."

"Me, too." Both were laughing very hard. "My charioteer is very naughty. Whenever she sees the courier clouds, she steers through them."

"Courier clouds?" Shivani exclaimed with disbelief.

"Yes. They aren't real clouds, Shivani." As the chariot emerged out of one massive ball of clouds, the princess said, glancing back at it, "These are all artificially prepared clouds. They are used for the fast conveyance."

"Fast conveyance...of what?"

"Shivani, do you remember the huge chamber filled with the dresses? That chamber was delivered to us on one of these clouds."

"That's awesome," Shivani said. Soon she started giggling as one smaller cloud sneaked through the chariot's window.

"This gives me a great idea, Shivani." Watching her, the princess said, "I will take you to a special place." Instantly she ordered the charioteer and their chariot soared high up. As they approached a humongous sheet of clouds, the princess, without waiting for the chariot to stop, jumped onto it. Following her, Shivani too let herself fall on the sheet. The two kept bouncing and, of course, laughing for a long time.

"Isn't it fun, Shivani? The princess asked. "This is called Megh-land. It means the land of clouds. It is one of our recreational parks." Along with the princess, Shivani began strolling in that wonderland. The huge land of clouds was swaying gently with the breeze. Soon they walked over a strip of clouds moving slowly around the area. From there it was easier to catch the glimpse of Megh-land. The clouds were shaped as swings, towers, arches, globes, slides, stairs, circles, and so on. Suddenly from the moving strip, the princess together with Shivani jumped near a massive tower of clouds.

"What is it, princess?"

"Just watch." As the princess clapped once, many strings of clouds came down. All those strings were joined to the central tall beam of clouds. To Shivani, it looked like the banyan tree in Aashrum. As

Shivani held one of the strings, the princess clapped three times. Instantly Shivani went up and started circling around speedily.

"Fantastic!" Laughing riotously, Shivani screamed. After coming down, Shivani was still feeling dizzy from the spinning ride. The two again walked to the moving cloud strip and resumed the stroll. From the strip, they frequently kept getting off at various rides and getting back on again after the ride. Shivani enjoyed all the rides, especially the one that sent her over a gigantic slide. After landing over the soft clouds at the end of the slide, she almost disappeared in the thick, fluffy clouds. Along with the princess, she started laughing very hard. She felt as if she had changed back to the old, naughty, playful Shivani from the past.

"This surely is fun-land," Shivani remarked, controlling her laughter.

"Shivani, whenever I come here, I feel like a small child again. I scream, shriek, and laugh crazily on these rides."

"That's absolutely right, princess. But...wait a minute." Shivani suddenly halted at her spot. "Apart from just the two of us, why isn't anyone else here at such a lovely place?"

"Because this park is reserved for the royal family only." The princess pointed her finger in a faraway direction. "For the commoners, there is a similar park...over there. All Shreeyans love these parks. I am really thankful to its architect," the princess said with pride.

As the golden swans swooped in fluttering their wings, Shivani and the princess had to leave Megh-land. Even after going away from Megh-land, the two were bursting with laughter from time to time.

"Now where are we going, princess?"

"Shivani, first we will feed the swans. They are very hungry, the charioteer was telling me. Is it OK?"

"Absolutely!" Shivani said. Soon they reached a mountainous ridge bordering a big lake. The magical blue of the sky was being reflected from the lake water. All around the lake were numerous tall trees. After glancing at the trees, Shivani dashed toward them.

"Oh, my goodness! This is unbelievable," she exclaimed, staring intently at one of the trees. For the first time in her life, she was watching a tree blossoming with dazzling, golden-colored berries. She was further astonished as the charioteer took the swans to one of the trees. After she waved a stick from her hand, the gold berries began falling down. As the swans started feasting on them, with her jaw dropped, Shivani kept looking at the unbelievable sight.

"Shivani, come on; let's feed the swans."

Still a bit dazed, Shivani ran with the princess, gathering the nearby fallen berries in her hands. As she stood, a swan glided down near her and began eating the berries.

"I still can't believe these swans are eating real gold," Shivani whispered softly.

"Shivani, these gold berries help maintain the golden shine of these swans. Also, this is their favorite food. Look at them how much they are enjoying it." Sighing, she said, "Unfortunately this is the only location where these trees grow."

While feeding the swan, Shivani remembered her dear deer friend, Sunetraa, who would always love eating from Shivani's hands. Just then a sheet of clouds approached them. Grabbing the two plates floating over it, the charioteer walked to them. The plates were filled up with berries that looked similar to the swans' food.

"Our snack is here, Shivani!" Picking up one of the plates, the princess started eating.

"Princess, do you eat gold, too?" Shivani was stunned.

"Shivani, these berries look like gold but are not real gold. Please try some. These are very tasty."

Hesitantly Shivani put a berry in her mouth. After tasting its heavenly juice, she finished the remaining berries in a gulp. "They are sweet with an appropriate tinge of sourness. I love these." By then, the swans had already finished their meals and were ready for their next flight.

"Wait a minute." The princess addressed the charioteer and ran to the lake. Wading through the water, she picked up something and returned back to Shivani.

"What's this?"

"These are pearls." The princess showed Shivani the glistening pearls held in her hands. "These pearls grow inside that lake."

Till then Shivani had only heard about the pearls growing in the ocean. "This surely is a different world," she whispered. While she was still wondering about the pearls, the princess obtained a cloud sheet floating nearby and gave it a gentle push after placing the pearls on it. The mesmerized Shivani kept staring at the sheet until it disappeared from her sight.

"Princess, where are the pearls going?"

"They are going...somewhere. That's a surprise," the princess said, flashing a naughty smile. "Shivani, I come to this lake very often because of two reasons: the food for my swans and the pearls for me. I love these pearls. Almost the whole lake is packed with them. Such marvelous pearls are a rare find. Let's go to the Sangeet arena." As the two settled inside the chariot, the princess ordered their charioteer, and in a flash they flew up. Soon they reached a large edifice, floating in midair. It was shaped like a star painted with sparkling silver.

The silvery star, standing up among the surrounding clouds, surely was the captivating structure. As the chariot touched the top of the star, it began opening slowly. The spellbound Shivani kept watching as the corners of the star curled outward, revealing a majestic, red carpeted arena inside. As the chariot landed, the princess began walking to the center of the arena. Shivani followed the princess's steps. She realized that ever since she had landed on this planet, she had been following the princess everywhere, like a younger sister.

In the center was a huge, transparent beam, reflecting the surrounding silvery shine. The top of the beam was attached to the periphery of the arena by seven delicate strings. Encircling the beam were elegant chairs for the guests. The princess, after reaching the central beam, started strumming the strings. The seven musical sounds—Sa, Re, Ga, Ma, Pa, Dha, Ni—echoed through the entire arena. Its melody was simply unparalleled. The divine notes electrified Shivani. But the real wonder was still ahead.

Paired with each echoed note, there appeared a heavenly beautiful girl out of the transparent beam, clad in extravagant attire. Each one was dressed up in a distinctly vibrant-colored costume representing the specific note. Glancing at the seven girls, Shivani felt as if a rainbow had appeared in front of her. With elegant steps, the girls began coming toward them. The sweet tinkling sounds of their dangling anklets and bangles filled the space.

"These are the famous nymphs arising from the seven notes---*Saptak*. We call them Apsaras," the princess was explaining. "They arise from this beam at our command and entertain us." The Apsaras stopped a bit away from them and did namaskaar.

"Princess! Please accept our greetings." Their voices were very sweet. "How can we entertain you today?"

"Apsaras, this is my friend, Shivani. She has come from the earth."
After a pause, she said, "Please present her with some exciting show."

"Your wish is our command, princess." All the Apsaras chimed
in unison. The performance presented by them was an astonishing
blend of divine music and glamorous dancing. It was breathtaking.
Absolutely nothing in the whole universe could have matched the
performance, Shivani thought. At the climax, the Apsaras exhibited
bursts of colorful petals in the air and disappeared one by one into
the central beam. The princess threw a gentle glance at Shivani, who
kept clapping even after the Apsaras had disappeared completely.

"I hope you enjoyed the show."

"Enjoyed?" Shivani whispered. "Princess, I don't...don't have the
words to describe my feelings. It was such a charming event that I felt
like I was living a pretty dream."

"Your pleasure is our pleasure," The princess said. "I have been
brought up hearing a phrase, 'Guests are gods.' You are my guest,
and my duty is to make you happy." As the chariot lifted up from
the arena, the silvery star began gathering together again. After a few
moments, the star was completely shrouded in the blur of clouds.

The next stop in the tour was a sandy ocean shore. After reaching the shore, the princess began swirling her fingers in the soft
sand and drew a picture of a winged horse. The moment she finished the drawing, the winged horse appeared alive. Shivani couldn't
believe her eyes while staring at the horse, flapping its wings gracefully. Soon she did the same thing and obtained another winged
horse for herself.

"Shivani, these horses read the rider's mind and follow accordingly." Jumping on her horse, the princess said, "...and you know... they travel with the speed of mind."

"Speed of mind!" Shivani exclaimed, settling on her horse. There were no reins for the horses.

"Now close your eyes and order the horse to start," the princess suggested. "Before you finish counting to ten, we will return back here after circling our whole planet."

"Wow!"

Soon the two girls, atop their horses, sprang into the sky with dizzying speed. Shivani felt as if she was traveling, sitting on a shooting star. Before she realized it, they were back at their original spot on the ocean shore.

"Unbelievable," Shivani whispered. "Your planet is full of marvels. Each spot is more fascinating than the previous one. I think you Shreeyans are great magicians."

"Shivani, that's not true. I can give you a scientific explanation for each and every event which seemed magical to you. Do you want to listen?"

That flashed Gurudev's sentence in Shivani's mind from when she was having her lessons on Divya- astra.

"*Everything which looks magical may not be magic.*"

Gurudev's words made her smile. Then, turning to the princess, she said, "I believe you, princess. At present, I don't want to listen to the scientific theory. Let me just enjoy the magic." Looking out of the gliding chariot, Shivani remarked, "From the earth, I would have never, ever imagined about your planet."

"Shivani, you would be surprised to know that there are many other planets in the universe which nestle the civilizations. Many of them are far superior to ours."

"Really?"

"Yes! Although in our solar system, there are only two planets harboring life; one is the earth and the other is our planet, Shreelok." Whispering softly, the princess asked, "Do you know about the civilization that existed once on the planet Mars?"

"No. What happened to it?"

"Mars' residents were quite similar to humans and Shreeyans in their appearance. Unfortunately some monstrous aliens from a remote galaxy destroyed the whole civilization."

"Oh, no!"

"Then my great grandfather, then Maharaaj of Shreelok, began securing our planet. Soon he became successful in building the safety shell around Shreelok that has turned our planet invisible."

"That's what the energy told me. I located your planet only after acquiring the divine sight."

"I know that." Letting out a sigh of relief, the princess whispered, "Luckily for us, obtaining that divine sight is extremely hard."

Shivani, who was lost in her thoughts, didn't hear that. After a moment, she asked, "Princess, have you ever visited other galaxies?"

"Yes, I have been to a couple of places." The princess spoke excitedly. "Once I went with Maharaaj to a planet. There the oceans are filled with milk instead of water."

"Oh, really?"

"Its residents travel in gigantic flying ships all across the universe."

"Do they travel with speed greater than the flying horses?" Shivani widened her eyes.

"Yes." The princess was blurting the details, and Shivani was listening as though listening to a fairy tale. "On another planet where I visited, the residents had multiple limbs, and multiple heads."

"Unbelievable!"

"Shivani, we Shreeyans are quite similar in appearance to humans, except for a few differences."

"Such as?"

"Such as, we can transform ourselves, into varied sizes. We can change our sizes over a wide range, from humongous to minute!"

"Oh, my goodness! Is...is this your..."

"Shivani, this is my original form." Looking at the relaxed face of Shivani, the princess smiled. Glancing at the sun gliding down to the horizon, the princess said, "I think we should start heading back to my palace. Tomorrow will be a big day for you, Shivani. You should have enough rest."

"Yes, you are correct," Shivani replied.

"Shivani, my palace is not far from here. Instead of riding the chariot, should we walk there?"

"Sure. That sounds interesting."

"Until now you have flown through the clouds. Now, I would like to take you along a special trail in the clouds."

"Oh, I can't wait." Shivani jumped down from the chariot. By then she had identified her sister in the princess Aryaa. Just like an elder sibling, the princess was guiding, suggesting, and teaching her. As the chariot zoomed away, Shivani asked, "Princess, I have a question. Till now, I haven't seen any other flying vehicle in the sky apart from ours. Why is it so, princess?"

"Today, during our tour, the Shreeyans were not allowed to fly. Otherwise the sky is always filled with chariots."

Now, the two began walking on a trail snaking through the clouds. The sight was surely a timeless treasure for Shivani. Her eyes were spanning the ground below, up to the towering sky, enjoying every bit of the view. The overhead evening sky was simply a massive canvas of changing shades of enchanting colors.

"Your planet is beautiful," Shivani whispered.

"Thanks, Shivani." The princess smiled. "I heard your planet is very pretty too. My grandfather had gone there many times. During each of his visits, he built magnificent edifices. Not only that, but he educated the locals, too."

"Really?" Shivani smiled. As she stared up into the sky, she was frozen at her spot with surprise. "Wow!" With her mouth wide open, she kept gazing at the four moons, shining in the skies of the planet Shreelok. "How is that possible?"

"Shivani, in fact our planet has five moons. The fifth one is not visible from here." Smiling at Shivani, the princess picked up a star-shaped cloud from the side of the trail. As she blew it up softly, it lighted up and began floating in the sky. Marveled by the incident, Shivani copied the princess's actions. Soon the whole trail began glittering in the floating, star-shaped lanterns.

"Stupendous!" Shivani was pleased with her creation.

"Shivani." Pointing in the sky, the princess asked, "Can you see the star near the second moon, over there?"

"Oh, that tiny one? Yes!"

"I have heard an interesting fact about it. I have heard that the great spirits from the earth are resting there after departing their earthly bodies."

Shivani gasped softly, and without her knowledge, her hands grabbed the lotus pendant on her neck.

"What's the matter, Shivani?" The princess asked in a concerned voice. Just then, she noticed Shivani's hands holding the lotus pendant.

"Shivani, what is it?" she asked, moving closer to her. With a blank face, Shivani loosened her grip on her pendant. "Wow! How pretty this is!" she exclaimed, staring at pendant. "I wonder how it stayed hidden from my sight till now." After a few moments of silence, the princess continued, "Shivani, can I ask you one question?"

After getting a quiet nod from Shivani, she spoke while gazing at the pendant again. "I remember…when you refused to accept my gift of expensive dresses and the jewelry. Undoubtedly, this pendant seems to be quite expensive."

Shivani understood the unspoken query. "Princess." Clearing her voice, Shivani continued. "This pendant has a very special place in my heart." And Shivani began telling her life story. Wearing a quiet face, the princess was listening to the story, although her heart was being ripped apart.

"It's so unreal." She shook her head in disbelief. "How could a king, based on some foolish prediction of a possible threat to his life by Shivani, order to kill Shivani's parents? How could someone be so cruel to kill a pregnant woman? It is unbelievable."

Both the girls were lost in the whirl of their own emotions. Eventually they came to reality. As the darkness was growing around them, they began walking speedily.

After a while, a starry silhouette of charming edifices began to appear in view. They were the residences of the royal family. Standing on clouds, each building was displaying its unique architectural design. Just then Shivani's eyes happened to see a very familiar design. It was a charming palace built in the shape of a peacock. Its multicolored sculpture was dazzling with all the marvelous colors of the world. Standing on its feet, fanning out the charming train of feathers studded with jewels, that lofty peacock palace had indeed trapped all the glamour and stateliness of a live peacock.

"Shivani, this is my palace, Peacock Palace!"

"Wow!" Still watching the palace with her widened eyes, Shivani whispered, "It reminds me of Mayur!"

"It reminds you of whom?" the surprised princess asked, turning to Shivani.

"Mayur, my friend...my peacock friend."

"You...you have seen this bird? A real...live bird?" the princess asked.

"Yes, princess." Shivani smiled at the confounded princess. "Not only seen, but I have played, run, danced with this bird, and I..." Before Shivani could finish her sentence, the crazy princess grabbed Shivani's hands and pulled her inside the palace.

"Where are we going? Why...why are you pulling me like this?" the perplexed Shivani asked while being dragged by the princess. There was no answer. After having crossed many richly decorated chambers, finally they reached the grand suite of the princess. It was a world of sparkles. The lavish gold furniture embellished with precious stones and rich drapery, an elegant bed with a huge canopy exhibiting pearls, numerous glittering chandeliers dangling from the ceiling, and tall, diamond-studded floor lamps all reflected the various shades of peacock feathers. However, the most beautiful item was the headboard of the bed. It was carved like the fanned-out train of peacocks' feathers. The multicolored jewels were engraved to replicate the marvelous plethora of a real peacock feather. The mirrors hung at various places accentuated its charm.

While Shivani was enjoying the beauty of the chamber, the princess swiftly went to a drawer and grabbed a velvety box. After opening it gingerly, she picked up a peacock feather kept inside.

"Shivani, have you seen a bird with this kind of feather? Does your Mayur have one of these feathers?" the princess asked, catching her breath.

"Yes, princess." Caressing the feather, Shivani said, "My Mayur has the same kind of feather, not just one or two, but numerous." Glancing at the headboard, she said further, "His fanned-out feathers look similar to this headboard. Standing here, in this chamber, reminds me of standing among the whole flock of peacocks, with their fanned-out, sumptuous trains." The princess was listening as if listening to a fairy tale. Shivani asked, "By the way, how did you get this feather?"

Glancing at the feather in her hand, the princess answered. "A long time back, some Shreeyans found this feather while visiting the earth. Unfortunately they couldn't bring the bird here." Sighing, she continued. "On one of my birthdays, I got this feather as a gift. Since then, I have been crazy about it. So my father, Maharaaj Aditya-Raaj, built this palace for me." Moving the feather softly along her cheeks and putting it back in the box, the princess whispered, "And he has promised me that one day, he will present me with this bird."

"A peacock is really an elegant bird." Picking up the peacock feather, Shivani said, "Princess, look at this feather carefully. Gurudev says, 'This single feather reflects the earth and the life on it.' See, this central, dark blue color? It represents the ocean. The surrounding lighter blue represents the sky. The gold color extending outward from this light blue stands for the golden sun rays gleaming around. The rest of this feather displays various shades of green. They remind us of different traces of greenery covering the earth." Gently moving the feather at an angle, she continued. "Now just watch the feather carefully as I twirl it. Do you see a lot more colors shining through?"

Enthralled with the wonderful analogy, the princess gazed intently at the feather. "Yes, I sure do," she exclaimed excitedly.

"Similar to this feather, our life too is a colorful plethora of various emotions. Now look at this subtle shine...flickering through. It depicts the happiness of life. Although subtle, this shine brightens our whole life."

The princess was overwhelmed. Apart from its bright colors and the softness, the princess had never imagined a peacock feather could hold so many meanings within it.

From inside the guest suite of the peacock palace, Shivani was looking at the moon rays entering through the window. "Tomorrow will be a big day for me." Muttering to herself, she sat on her grass bed made of Shreelok's shiny, multicolored grass. After hearing about Shivani sleeping on a grass bed at home, the princess had ordered her maid to make a similar grass bed for Shivani. Caressing the soft grass, Shivani was wondering about her new friend, Princess Aryaa. She looked at the friendship bracelet made of pearls offered to her by the princess. They were the pearls from the lake where the trees were blossoming with gold cherries. Under the moonlight, the pearls were gleaming.

Although tired, it was hard for Shivani to fall asleep. Thinking about the princess, she turned onto her other side. Just within a few hours of acquaintance, she had developed a special bond with the princess. Princess Aryaa would be an ideal sister, she thought. The beautiful, charming, understanding and affectionate princess would make a great sister as well as a friend. She couldn't stop dreaming about herself as a younger sister, going with the princess for a long walk, chatting on silly things, screaming with joy, laughing riotously, and so on. Now, for the first time, Shivani was feeling sad to leave the princess's company.

"Tomorrow after getting the Shree-chakra, I will be heading back to my earth!" Lying on her bed, she took a deep breath. "But definitely I will miss this planet and my sister, Princess Aryaa."

CHAPTER SIXTEEN

THE GOLDEN BLESSINGS

In middle of her sleep, Shivani heard some whispers. Her tired body ignored them, and she turned onto her other side. Now the whispers got paired with gentle nudging. Shivani opened her eyes and saw a figure standing beside her.

Springing up from her bed, Shivani exclaimed, "Princess... you..."

"Shivani," the Princess whispered again, "please follow me."

"Where?"

"You have to go."

"Where am I going?" the puzzled Shivani asked with still bleary eyes,.

"Please hurry up. You can't afford to be late." Pulling Shivani out of her bed, the princess began walking. She was clearly stressed.

"Princess…" Halting at her spot, Shivani asked again, "Please tell me what the matter is. Where am I going?"

At her demanding request, the princess paused momentarily and whispered in her ears. That jolted Shivani out of her sleep completely, but at the same time froze her with surprise.

Pulling the stunned Shivani further, the princess added, "Please walk fast. Every moment is precious." There was an extreme sense of urgency. Soon the two came out of the palace. Glancing at a chariot waiting at the door, the princess smiled satisfactorily. Turning to Shivani, she said, "Please rush in," and the princess literally pushed her inside the chariot. After talking to the charioteer, the princess turned to Shivani. "I hope it works out well. I shed a lot of sweat for this." Patting her gently, she uttered, "Good Luck, Shivani."

"Thanks," the still dazed Shivani whispered as the chariot took off and disappeared into the clouds.

At the top of the mountain Mahameru, Shivani got down as the chariot landed. Mount Mahameru was the tallest mountain on the planet Shreelok, and Shivani was standing on one of the tallest peaks of the mountain. Taking a glimpse of her surroundings, she began walking in the direction of a tall, impressive figure. He was around ten feet tall and clad in an orange-colored dhoti and shirt.

"Welcome, Shivani!" The Shreeyan said in a deep voice.

"Namaskaar," Shivani responded while wondering about him.

"I am the royal priest. Also, I am the oldest Shreeyan living on this planet. Can you guess my age?"

"Maybe…a hundred years?"

"I am about three hundred years old." The man smiled.

"Three hundred years old," Shivani muttered to herself.

"Princess Aryaa has told me about you." Staring at the sky, the priest added, "Shivani, you should feel yourself to be very fortunate for this wonderful opportunity. You have arrived at the right spot and at the right moment."

Then the priest began walking toward the center of the peak. Silently, Shivani followed him. Soon they came to a square area bounded by four gold columns at each corner. The columns were decorated with garlands of colorful flowers and leaves. After getting closer, she noticed a huge pit in the ground. It was a fire pit. Although the fire was not yet started, the pit was filled up with pieces of specially scented wood. Around the pit were various golden urns containing flowers, water, milk, fruits, and incense.

The priest began chanting mantras. As he sprinkled holy water from the nearby golden urn, fire instantly erupted in the pit. Very quickly the flames billowed up. Sitting near the pit, Shivani's anxious eyes watched every action of the priest. The priest continued chanting mantras while frequently feeding the fire with flowers, milk, incense, and wood pieces. Surprisingly, with each passing moment, he himself was growing in height. By the time the flames rose high up in the sky, the priest's head was shrouded by the clouds.

Within no time, the area spanning above the fire pit filled with flashing sparkles. A glorious amber-colored hue was imparted to every single object present there, including Shivani. The intense heat from the fire encased the entire area, but Shivani wasn't aware of it. She was dealing with a storm of emotions whirling inside. Although looking quiet from outside, she was jittery inside. She could sense every beat of her heart.

Then a wonderful incident happened on the land of Shreelok. The embers from the fire suddenly transformed into tiny, delicate red flowers and began falling on the ground. That massive rain of flowers extinguished the fire and wiped away the intense heat. Instead a cool, pleasant breeze carrying the magnetic fragrance of the flowers began infusing the area. The wonderstruck Shivani was witnessing the event with utter disbelief. The whole area was blanketed with a beautiful carpet made of red flowers. She stole a quick glance up at the priest, who was flashing a prideful smile. He was gesturing for her to glance upward in the sky to her right. The moment she gazed at the spot, her eyes got widened with wonder. With her sight transfixed, she stood up, stumbling with astonishment.

The jet dark blue of the night sky had given a way to a faint glow. Soon a bright star was seen approaching them. Within no time, it got brighter. Now the gorgeous swirls around it were clearly visible. Standing at her spot, Shivani looked at the star, which was coming closer and closer to her. Without her knowledge, she kept her right hand on her racing heart. The extremes of excitement, eagerness, thrill, and anxiety were surging inside her.

Eventually the wait was over. After coming closer, it revealed that the scintillating star was itself a special Vimaan—a flying aircraft. It landed softly over the red flower carpet just in front of the fire pit. The Vimaan was uniquely shaped like a flame of fire. While Shivani was watching in awe, the cusps of the flame-shaped Vimaan slowly curled out. Two glowing figures were sitting inside it. At once they both got up and began climbing down. They were gleaming with a very peculiar awe—a divine one!

After watching them approach her, Shivani couldn't believe it. They were her parents. She recognized them instantly. They looked similar to their pictures in her pendant. They were the ones who risked their lives to save their unborn child from Veersen's wrath.

Princess Aryaa's crucial efforts had worked successfully. With the permission of Maharaaj Aditya-Raaj and the emperor of Pitrulok—current residence of Shivani's parents—the meeting was arranged for Shivani and her parents.

Planet Shreelok had become the unprecedented spot where the dead and alive from the earth were meeting each other. Time was witnessing the emotional meeting, involving three different planets.

After coming out of the initial shock, sobbing with happiness, Shivani instantly ran toward her parents. For the moment, she had forgotten the rest of the world around her. Soon she got lost in the velvety, warm embrace of her parents. It was the unique experience of affectionate touch she had always dreamed of. Tears of joy were streaming from her eyes. Time had stopped for the three. Huddled together, they were standing speechlessly, for words had no place there. They were enjoying the mere presence of each other. The whole cosmos was watching the unprecedented reunion, relishing the golden moment. Shivani wished she could freeze those moments forever. If possible, she would never, ever let those moments slip off her hands.

"Bless you, Shivani." Her mother finally broke the silence. Her voice was very soft and content.

"Let me do namaskaar to you," Shivani whispered, freeing her from their embrace. After touching their feet, she stood staring at them with respectful eyes. They were not only her parents but great heroes.

"Shivani." Pulling her again in her embrace, her mother, Sari-taa-Devi, exclaimed after flashing a pretty smile, "My tiny baby…" caressing and kissing her head, she said, "…is all grown up now. I am exhilarated to see you, all mature and wise. I am quite fortunate to be your mother."

"Mother." Clearing her choked up voice, Shivani said, "But I consider myself to be the worst child anyone could ever have. I was the reason for your gruesome death. I feel guilty for being the reason for your brutal killing." Her eyes began welling up. "Ever since I came to know about the incident, I have been dying to talk to you and seek your forgiveness. I am...so...sorry." Shivani burst into tears.

Gently wiping Shivani's tears, her father, Himraaj, said, "My child, it wasn't your fault at all." That lovely, assuring voice was quite comforting to Shivani. "Our lives were destined for that kind of death. But the death has wiped out all our earthly sufferings and lifted up our spirits with the divine bliss. Please don't feel sad about our death. With the help of our good deeds on the earth, we are able to live happily on the planet Pitrulok."

Moving her fingers through Shivani's hair, her mother spoke. "Shivani, we were quite worried for having to leave you, our new-born baby, all alone in the midst of a gruesome forest. But Jwala rescued you, and Mahatma Guru Yogidev raised you." After a moment's pause, she added, "Remember....that night, every single event was destined to happen. None of us either had any control over it or were responsible for it." Once again gathering Shivani in her arms, Saritaa-Devi said, "Now we two are the happiest parents in this universe. Your dazzling success has showered all the happiness upon us. Shivani, you made us very proud."

"Shivani, all these years we have been hearing a lot of wonderful news about you on Pitrulok." Himraaj, Shivani's father spoke proudly.

"You were hearing news about me there...on Pitrulok? How?" the stunned Shivani blurted.

"Yes, my child." Glancing at her, Himraaj added, "We are well aware of the current events happening on the earth." After pausing momentarily, he continued. "We also know the reason for which you have come to this planet."

"Really?" Shivani was surprised again.

"Yes. Our advice for you is to keep walking on the right path, and do not let yourself falter away from it. Our blessings will always be with you."

"Mother and Father, thank you for your blessings." The overwhelmed Shivani again did namaskaar to both of them. Soon the couple began walking toward their Vimaan. After a few steps, her mother swirled back.

"Shivani." Gently kissing her on her forehead, she whispered, "Always believe in yourself." She gazed at the vermilion birthmark on Shivani's forehead, which had begun glowing after the kiss. Smiling satisfactorily, she resumed her course. Shivani kept watching them walking away. She wanted to stop them and ask them to stay longer. She wanted to embrace them one more time. She wanted to cry, but she didn't do any of those things. While her parents were bound by the rules of their world, she too was constrained by the rules of her own world. After her parents' Vimaan soared up and zoomed toward Pitrulok, she let her held-back tears flow down freely over her cheeks.

The jet dark blue skies returned, and she slowly turned her eyes toward the ground where her parents had been standing. To her surprise, she saw two white flowers resting on the carpet of red flowers. Those were the Prajakta flowers, blossoming on the trees at her home, near the site of her parents' cremation. Picking them gingerly by their red stems, she kissed the glorious white petals. Holding them close to her heart, she began walking to her chariot.

CHAPTER SEVENTEEN

CONQUERING THE SANCTITY

The royal court was packed with Shreeyans. In addition to the royal courtiers, a lot of Shreeyans were seen hustling in and around the court after having been granted permission to witness the historical event of granting the Shree-chakra to a human. Their faces were reflecting curiosity, their enthusiastic whispers filling every corner of the court. With each passing moment, the restlessness of the crowd was increasing. Their anxious eyes were repeatedly turning toward Shivani, sitting by the princess. On the contrary, Shivani seemed to be calm and composed.

As soon as the announcement about the arrival of Maharaaj and Maharaani was heard, at once, silence spread all across the court.

Everyone stood in their honor. After the two settled down on their thrones, the court resumed its position. Glancing at Shivani, Maharaaj smiled and ordered his Pradhaan-mantri—the chief of the court—to bring the Shree-chakra. Soon, the guards at the right side entrance began blowing huge, ornate horns and conch shells. Their divine and energizing sounds engulfed the whole court instantly. They were announcing the arrival of the Shree-chakra. With their eyes hooked onto the entrance door, the whole house, including Maharaaj and Maharaani, stood to honor the revered Shree-chakra.

As a decorated golden trolley appeared at the entrance of the court, cheerful sounds began emerging from every mouth. The sight created a surge of respect in every heart. The golden trolley was covered with a rich, red-colored fabric. On that was placed an ornate seat upholstered with pearly white fabric lightly embroidered with gold. Sitting regally atop that was the Shree-chakra.

The divine Shree-chakra was shaped as a perfect circle. It was about the size of an orange, with a finger-width hole in the center. The central hole was surrounded by a row of dazzling diamonds. Next to it were the shimmering sapphires, engraved circularly, while the outermost rim was glistening with emeralds. From the outermost rim, there were twenty-one sharp spikes projecting outward. At the end of each of those spikes was a ruby. There was a unique, rich hue encasing the Shee-chakra. Entering through the roof, the sun's rays were caressing the divine Shree-chakra and were being reflected, multiplying their own golden awe. The reflections of the precious stones of the Chakra were shining on every object present inside the court. The simple sighting of the Shree-chakra infused a feeling of splendor and energy in every heart, compelling a respectful namaskaar to it.

The trolley was being pulled further inside the court. About ten well-built Shreeyans were trying their best to advance it. Witnessing their frantic efforts, it was easy to guess about the enormous weight of the Shree-chakra. With each pull, they were wearing themselves out. Witnessing the plight of those Shreeyans, a renewed bout of whispers emerged. Doubts about Shivani's ability to bear the Shree-chakra were reflected on the faces of the attendees. They were worried for her. Glancing at her tiny figure, some were sighing. Even the princess was rubbing her hands nervously on the hand rests of her throne.

Although informed beforehand about the undue weight of the Shree-chakra, Shivani was witnessing the reality for the first time. But that didn't worry her. She had managed to maintain her calm. With a blissful face, she was watching the slow arrival of the Shree-chakra. While her eyes were focused on the Shree-chakra, her mind was reverberating again and again with her mother's sentence: *"Shivani, believe in yourself."*

Eventually the trolley reached the front of the throne of Maharaaj Aditya-Raaj. With numerous eyes glued to it, the Shree-chakra was gleaming with the ultimate grace and style.

Glancing all around, Maharaaj Aditya-Raaj walked near the trolley and did namaskaar. Then looking up at the fully packed court, he started speaking. "My fellow Shreeyans, today is one of the rare occasions when the Shree-chakra has arrived in our court. I am sure all of us feel delighted and honored to get this glimpse of our sacred Shree-chakra!" His rich yet humble voice was booming inside the huge dome. "We are familiar with its glorious history. In the past, the great warriors, wanting to fight and destroy the evil, have used this. Those warriors were not only from our planet but from many different planets as well. On all those occasions, the Shree-chakra has helped to deliver victory over the dark powers." Pausing for a moment, Maharaaj added, "Each victory has infused mystical powers inside this grandiose weapon, accentuating its sanctity further. This has resulted in its mightiness." Pacing to his right side, he continued, "According to its noble tradition, today the Shree-chakra is once again present in our court, ready to accomplish one more goal. Now, respecting the dignified legacy of our great ancestors, on behalf of all my Shreeyans, I request Shivani to come forward and receive the Shree-chakra."

"Dhanyawaad, Maharaaj." Shivani got up and slowly started walking toward the trolley. She politely bowed to Maharaaj and stood by his side. Staring at her, the Maharaaj said further, "Shivani, I am offering this powerful weapon to you. You may proceed forward to lift it up." He raised his right hand and added, "Our wishes are with you."

"Maharaaj." Once again bowing to Maharaaj and to the crowd, Shivani said, "I feel extremely obliged to get this opportunity. Thank you very much." As she started approaching the Shree-chakra, an utter silence swept over the entire court. All eyes were watching her, forgetting to blink even once. Shivani's majestic and confident gait amazed the audience. Soon she reached near the trolley and did namaskaar to it. After climbing up swiftly, she stood in front of the ornate seat of Shree-chakra. Taking a deep breath in, she closed her eyes and remembered her revered Gurudev as well as her parents. An anxious silence had wrapped the court up as the crowd was watching with their hearts paused for the moment. Glancing around quickly, Shivani once again closed her eyes and focused her mind onto the

Shree-chakra. By joining together her hands, she did namaskaar to it and lowered her head near it.

Just then, an unbelievable thing happened. A ruby from one of the spikes on the Shree-chakra touched the vermilion birthmark on Shivani's forehead. In a flash, an extremely bright, blinding beam of light sparked at the very same point, jolting the whole court back with a startle. Shivani herself was completely unaware of the event, for all her senses were unified together on her target. Her face was gleaming with a great resolve.

The next moment, her confident fingers reached the goal and picked up the Shree-chakra as easily as if it were a feather. She hoisted it by wearing it on her index finger. The Shree-chakra, hauled with a great effort by many strong Shreeyans now, had settled onto a delicate finger of a tiny girl. The Shreeyans, who had marveled Shivani with their fanciful planet, were themselves mesmerized by the wonderful event. But Shivani wasn't done yet. The Shreeyans were about to watch another astonishing incident. The Shree-chakra sitting on Shivani's finger began spinning slowly. Soon the royal court of Maharaaj Aditya- Raaj was flooded with the divine sparkles from the shimmering rubies, sapphires, and diamonds, blended with the rich, golden hue.

The whole court, from end to end, came alive with cheers paired with clapping, which reverberated through its mighty dome. The frenzy was beyond imagination. Her tremendous success catapulted Shivani into instant celebrity. Shivani was still standing atop the trolley with her face radiating the ultimate happiness of triumph. Her eyes were gleaming with the utmost satisfaction for accomplishing the daunting goal. Gingerly she took the Shree-chakra from her finger. After holding it close to her heart, she began walking toward Maharaaj's throne.

Seeing the dazzling success in the form of Shivani approaching him, the Maharaaj himself rose up from the throne. Along with him, Maharaani and the princess too climbed down from the lofty dais and rushed forth to congratulate her.

"Shivani, congratulations!" The exhilarated princess hugged her hard. "You changed the impossible to possible."

"Congratulations, my child!" Maharaaj said, flashing a pleasant smile.

"You are great!" Maharaani said in a choked voice, gathering her in her arms,. "Dhanyawaad!"

Shivani was quite embarrassed by listening to so much of her praise.

"You have carved history with pure gold." Maharaaj continued, "You have matched the mightiness of the Shree-chakra with the greatness of your own virtues and noble soul. You are one amazing girl. Today, in this royal court, you have proved your worth for this grandiose Shree-chakra."

"Thanks again, Maharaaj," Shivani replied very politely. "This was all possible because of yours, my parents', and Gurudev's blessings."

Looking at her adoringly, the Maharaaj said, "Shivani, you are one great blend of smartness, bravery, courage, and determination. But your most impressive attribute is your humble nature. "The Maharaaj's sentence was instantly followed by a grand applause. Keeping his hand on the top of the Shree-chakra held by Shivani, Maharaaj whispered emotionally, "The noble legacy of our planet is now in your hands. Please treasure it."

"I promise you, Maharaaj." Shivani replied, still holding the Shree-chakra near her heart,.

"This Shree-chakra, although mighty, has its own limitations." Maharaaj continued talking, looking at the puzzled Shivani. "It can only be used once. After the use of this weapon, it will immediately return back here. So choose its use wisely."

"Thanks for the suggestion. I will keep this in mind." Pausing momentarily, she added, "Maharaaj, apart from lending me this divine Shree-chakra, I will remain obliged to you for one more thing. Your permission made it possible for me to cherish the golden moments with my parents." Her huge eyes became misty. "I will never be able to repay your actions," the emotional Shivani said.

"My child," Maharaaj said softly, "Don't you ever mention about repaying. Your happiness is enough for us. Always treasure those moments and maintain this joy on your face!"

Shivani conceded.

"Now, our special Vimaan is ready to take you back to the earth." Staring at Shivani's confounded face, he smiled and said, "I know you are an expert at using Agni-baan, but now, being an honorable royal guest of Shreelok, you deserve a formal farewell. Don't you think so?"

Shivani just smiled.

Very carefully, Shivani wore the saffron sash on her back, tying its free ends in her front. Within this sash was the precious Shree-chakra, wrapped up. From time to time, she groped it and reassured herself about its presence. Standing near a huge Vimaan, she waved to the crowd gathered around her, including Maharaaj and Maha-raani, but the princess wasn't seen anywhere.

"It would be hard for me to say good-bye to her," Shivani whis-pered, staring at the pearl bracelet presented by the princess. Her eyes were desperately searching the princess. Within a short time, a special bond had been established between the two. When she had landed, this planet was totally alien to her. But fortunately, she met the princess and found a friend as well as a sister in her. She could never forget the wonderful tour of Shreelok hosted by Princess Aryaa. And how could she ever forget the precious meeting with her parents arranged by the princess? Her thoughtfulness, compassion, and affection for Shivani were absolutely unparalleled.

"No! I can't leave this planet without saying good-bye to the princess. I wonder where she has gone." Shivani's mind was busy thinking about various possibilities. Just then the Maharaaj's words brought her out of the thoughts.

"Shivani, I can see many dangers and hardships waiting for you once you reach the earth." His voice was serious. "But my blessings and, more than that, the revered Shree-chakra, is with you. I wish you all the success."

"Maharaaj, I am very grateful to you."

"Shivani, please take care of yourself." Maharaani's worried voice reminded her of her own mother.

They all began walking toward the Vimaan ready for flight. Within a short time, she would be back to her mother planet—Earth. Once again she would be among her dear friends and Gurudev, whom she had been missing intently. She was thrilled with the mere thought of it. Immediately after saying good-bye to the princess, she would be ready to hop in the Vimaan. But Princess Aryaa wasn't anywhere in the sight. Shivani was getting restless. Just then, from a distance, she sighted the princess. Wearing her same, captivating smile, Princess Aryaa was coming. In her hands was a bag filled with the dazzling fruits adored by Shivani. Instantly Shivani raced toward her.

"I was waiting for you, princess." Hugging her crazily, Shivani said, "I didn't want to leave without saying good-bye to you." Shivani had become emotional. "Princess, I have heard how hard you tried to find the location of my parents. Once confirming their presence on the planet Pitrulok, you convinced Maharaaj and the others for the arrangement of their arrival here." With her voice trailing off, Shivani whispered, "Your permission made it possible for me to spend golden moments with my parents." She pushed back her tears. "I will never be able to repay these obligations. I...I am very much thankful to you, princess."

"Shivani, you are not only my friend but also my sister. I will do anything for you." The princess softly patted her back.

"Princess, I am leaving now. I...I am having a hard time saying you 'good-bye'." With still misty eyes, Shivani was looking at the princess. Spreading her hands apart, she asked, "Wouldn't you like to hug me one more time and say good-bye?"

"No!" the princess answered with a very serious face.

Shivani with a dumbfounded face kept staring at the princess. Even Maharaaj and Maharaani were startled with the reply.

"Did you just say no?" Shivani asked her with disbelief.

"You have heard correctly," The princess said. "I don't want to say good-bye to you." Looking at the stunned faces of Shivani and her parents, she couldn't maintain her serious face. She began laughing. "I don't want to say good-bye to you because..."

"Because what?"

"Because...I am coming with you."

"You are coming with me?" Shivani got a wild jolt. The very idea completely floored her with surprise. "Wow!"

"Princess!" the Maharaaj and Maharaani both exclaimed in shock. Maharaani grabbing the princess's shoulders and shrugging her crazily, asking, "You are kidding, aren't you?"

"No, Mother. I am serious," the princess said calmly. "I have decided to go with Shivani."

After hearing the determined answer from her favorite daughter, Maharaani glanced at Maharaaj helplessly. What would Maharaaj do? He himself was shocked. After overcoming the initial shock, Maharaaj began speaking calmly, "Princess, my child, as compared to our planet, the earth is quite dangerous and hostile. How are you going to sustain yourself there?" After a pause, he chided further, "Princess Aryaa, you are not a child. Such a crazy and unreasonable decision doesn't suit you. Princess, come to your senses please."

"Mother and father." Holding her parents hands, the princess said, "I am fully aware of the dangers hovering on Earth. That's why I have decided to go there." Staring at her parents' whitened faces, she continued. "The life here is getting a bit boring. On this planet, everything is too good and too safe. I want to enjoy some thrill in my life. I love adventures." Looking at the Maharaaj, she added pleadingly, "Father, haven't you said many times that I have excelled in all kinds of warfare? I am no lesser than an army in regard to my prowess. I can protect myself. That's why I am confident about surviving on the earth, just the way our ancestors did in the past."

"Princess, Aryaa!" Maharani's voice was quivering. "We are worried ..."

"Mother." Gently holding Maharani's hand, the princess said softly, "I know you both love me very much. It is this love that is making you anxious about my trip to the earth. But you know one fact very well, that no powers on the earth can cause any harm to me." After staring at her parents' thoughtful faces, she said further, "Apart from having some thrill, another reason for my trip to the earth is...I want to help Shivani."

The princess was trying hard to convince her parents. "Please believe me. I will stay with Shivani and help her out. Soon after the accomplishment of her mission, I will return here. I promise you." Gazing at them expectantly, she continued. "Please give me your blessings, as we are getting late for the departure."

Finally the Maharaaj as well as the Maharaani, although reluctantly, gave their permission to the princess for her maiden voyage to the earth. The excited princess hugged her parents very hard. Until then, Shivani was witnessing the family dispute from a distance. She liked the idea of being accompanied by the princess but never expected it to happen. So, after the decision, she too, was overjoyed.

"Shivani," Maharaaj whispered softly, "Please take care of my daughter." The startled Shivani glanced at him. At that very moment, he wasn't Maharaaj Aditya-Raaj but simply a father. After assuring him, she began climbing up the Vimaan with princess Aryaa.

Just then, Maharaani called, "Princess Aryaa." Maharaani whispered, coming closer to the princess, "Let this necklace be with you." Placing her own necklace around the princess's neck, Maharaani added, "This pendant contains the holy water from the Golden River. It's quite powerful. Please keep wearing it, my child, for you may need it."

"I will, Mother." Promising her worried mother, the princess hugged her again and stepped inside the Vimaan.

CHAPTER EIGHTEEN

BACK HOME

The eagle-shaped Vimaan streaked brightly through the skies precisely above the Aashrum area—Shivani's neighborhood. Without making any sound, it plunged to earth, stirring the air slightly, and landed softly on the ground, causing a soft whisper.

"I love you, flowers! I love you, grass! I...I love you, trees!" As the Vimaan touched the ground on the hilltop near the hut, Shivani jumped out and began hugging and kissing everything along her way. Rolling down on the grass, picking up the dirt, she exclaimed, "I love you dirt! I missed you so...much!" Smacking her lips on the bare ground, she picked up the dirt with her fingers and placed it onto her forehead. "I namaskaar you, Earth!" she whispered.

Standing nearby, Princess Aryaa was joyfully watching Shivani's reunion ceremony with her beloved Earth. Just then, Shivani ran toward the princess. Grabbing the princess's hand, she dashed downhill toward her home. She was eager to show her sister to her friends and Gurudev. But suddenly she halted as an eerie feeling dawned on her. After glancing ahead, she sensed a frightful silence engulfing her neighborhood. Princess Aryaa's hand slipped from hers as she stared at the scene before her.

The joyful greenery of her home had vanished. Instead every tree, shrub, and bush was withered and parched. The vibrantly colorful flowers had turned lifeless, adding a more dismal look to the neighborhood. The bursting runs, streams, and brooks had dried out completely. The crystal clear waters of Mahatejaa had turned murky. The exuberant fish, instead of darting up from the river, were floating over the muddied waters lifelessly. The gloominess of the river water was further accentuated by the overcast sky. The absence of chirping birds from the sky could easily be seen.

The blossoming lotuses in the lake had shriveled and transformed into carcasses floating along with the dead and decaying swans. On the ground, there wasn't a single animal in sight. The place, once a haven for the bountiful wildlife, was filled with dead animals scattered all across. Because of the ghastly spell cast by Kaalkoot, the life from Shivani's neighborhood had deserted the air, ground, and water. Even the breeze was unwilling to flow through the area.

Shivani was witnessing everything with frozen eyes. Her beautiful home was ruined. She wished it was a bad dream and wanted to wake up from it to enjoy the enchanting Aashrum once again. But unfortunately, it was the reality, the harsh reality. From every corner, a ghastly feeling was reflected. The horrifying devastation was beyond any comparison. The heartbroken Shivani started calling out for her friends and Gurudev. There was no reply from anywhere.

Frantically she circled all around the hut, looking for any signs of her dear ones. She dashed into the empty hut, raced through the forest of mangoes, the meadow, the hillock behind the hut, and the archery arena. She scoured each and every corner of her Aashrum. Her pitiful calls kept echoing through the area over and over again, without any answers. Eventually her hope dwindled down and she let herself drop down to the ground. Soon she began whimpering helplessly.

Standing near a withered bush, Princess Aryaa was witnessing her friend's ordeal. She was watching the scene as predicted by the advisor to Maharaaj Aditya-Raaj. Luckily for the princess, when the advisor was informing Maharaaj, she happened to be standing near the door to the secret chamber. After hearing about Shivani's neighborhood, she managed to sneak inside and listen to the whole conversation. That particular event made her worried for Shivani and she decided to accompany her on her return journey to Earth.

Although expected, the ruins of Shivani's home were beyond any comprehension. With a perplexed face, she stood there for some time, but eventually it became unbearable for her to just watch the pains of her friend. Slowly she moved forward to console Shivani. Her hand, resting over Shivani's shoulder, could easily sense her suppressed sobs. Just then, a rustle was heard in the nearby bushes.

"Shivani," The princess whispered softly, "look over there." The alarm in her voice made Shivani turn her head in the direction. It was Shivani's mama tiger, Jwala, limping forth.

In the aftermath of Gurudev's capture, Jwala was seriously hurt. The injuries from her fight with Veersen's forces were minor for her, but the injuries from Kalkoot's deadly spell were quite serious. After sensing Shivani's presence, she managed to haul herself with great difficulty toward her.

"Jwala," Shivani sprang up from her spot and dashed into her mother's lap. "Jwala," Shivani whispered, hugging her hard. "Where were you?" Just then she became aware of the extensive injuries on Jwala's entire body. There were serious burns, exposing her bones. "Oh, my goodness! What happened to you? Who hurt you?" Shivani's voice was filled with anguish. Suddenly a heavy thing from an overhead tree fell down on Shivani. It was Naagraaj. He too was badly hurt. She kept looking at them helplessly.

"Oh, Naagraaj!" Tears started streaming from her eyes, witnessing the sufferings of her loved ones. Soon her eyes stretched beyond Jwala and Naagraaj. There were a few more pairs of anxious eyes staring at her from behind the far away, burnt bushes. After sensing the presence of their dear friend Shivani, they slowly revealed themselves and began hustling forth with their wounded bodies. Soon they all landed in the reassuring lap of Shivani. She was the solace to their still fearful minds.

While caressing and comforting them, Shivani's expectant eyes kept spanning the surroundings over and over again for one more figure to emerge—Gurudev. Unfortunately that didn't happen.

Amidst the herd of wounded animal friends, Shivani was sitting vacantly. It was hard for her to watch the misery of her loved ones. Also, she was restless because of Gurudev's persistent absence. Various ominous possibilities were storming her mind. She was worried for him. From time to time, she kept blaming herself for leaving him in a vulnerable state.

"That night, I shouldn't have crossed the mountains without informing Gurudev. I put him as well as the whole neighborhood in a grave danger by exposing the secret place. To make it worse, I ran away, leaving him and these friends to face the evil Veersen. I am the only one responsible for their pitiful conditions and the devastation of this paradise." Shivani couldn't stop repenting for the past. "Gurudev might have been killed." As this possibility sparked in her mind, she shuddered and blurted out loudly, "No! No…this can't happen! Gurudev is still alive…I hope."

She began whimpering again. Turning to the princess, she said, "Princess, I am not a good friend. I can't even welcome you here at my home. Can you ever believe, this once was a charming place?" Sighing softly, she said, "Now it is just a grief-stricken and rotten place. My dreamland is destroyed forever."

"Please don't say that, Shivani. If you allow me, I would like to try something."

Shivani turned her puzzled face to the princess.

"I want to use…"

"Princess, please do whatever you need to bring the life back to my lovely home," Shivani blurted.

The princess sat near Shivani and began singing a raag Sanjeevan—literally meaning a new life. With her eyes closed, Shivani began enjoying the lovely voice of the princess paired with a marvelous, enchanting tune of raag Sanjeevan. She felt as if the exuberance was streaming through her entire body. The enthralled Shivani sat there, forgetting herself and her surroundings. The magical music lifted her spirits. She began swaying over the waves of divine bliss. But she wasn't the only one there. The mesmerizing raag swept the whole surrounding, including animals, plants, and trees, with its magical tunes. Every little nook and each little corner of that place became electrified, and a miracle happened in the neighborhood of Shivani.

A lovely breeze, along with its heavenly fragrance, started flowing once again, pushing the evil away from Shivani's neighborhood. The pleasant blue of the sky invited the chattering birds, and their melodious tweeting filled up the air. Along with them, the white swans swooped down over the sparkly blue lagoon displaying its blossoming lotuses. The transparent waters of Mahatejaa revealed arriving schools of vibrant fish. The green treasure, along with vividly colorful flowers, began dazzling from every corner of the ground. The flocks of bountiful animals resumed leaping across the area. The whole landscape, scorched previously by the evil, was endowed with a new life by raag Sanjeevan.

As the cool, scented breeze touched Shivani, lost in the musical spell, she opened her eyes and glanced at the wonderful transformation. With her jaw dropped in awe, she sprang up from her position and kept staring with her eyes widened in disbelief.

"Unbelievable! Unreal!" she whispered in shock. Just then, Naagraaj, after regaining his swiftness, slithered over her feet.

"Oh, Naagraaj! All your wounds are gone. You are glistening again!" She picked him up gently. Just then, Jwala, with all her renewed vigor, jumped on Shivani and began licking her lovingly. Seeing her mama tiger completely cured of her injuries, Shivani couldn't constrain her joy. Her hard embrace around Jwala was loosened as her Sunetraa, Dhawal, Shubhra and Mayur pounced on her. There erupted a great commotion.

"My friends." Spreading both her hands apart, Shivani was crazily hugging each one, turn by turn, until she got tired and dropped down. Seeing her lying down on the ground, the friends again jumped on her, and once again, the neighborhood began breathing energetically.

The princess was watching the rebirth of happiness contently. After getting freed from her raucous friends, Shivani walked to her. "You have obliged me one more time, now." Squeezing her hand tightly, she continued. "Princess, your gifts are always priceless."

"Shivani, this rejoicing is in my self-interest, too." Flashing a charming smile and looking around, the princess said, "I wanted to witness the divine beauty of this place. Really...this place is far prettier than you described."

"It is still hard for me to believe...this dramatic transformation was brought simply by music."

"Music is a lot more powerful than you think, Shivani."

"You proved to be the goddess for all of us, princess. I can't thank you enough."

"So...do you want to return my favor?" There was a naughty twinkle in the princess's eyes. "How about handing that peacock over to me?" She glanced at Mayur, standing beside Shivani and preening his feathers.

"Mayur." As Shivani called, Mayur instantly hopped onto her right shoulder. "Mayur, this is princess Aryaa." He acknowledged the guest by nodding his head. Looking at the shining crown on his head, the Princess accepted the greeting. "She wants to see your fan." As Shivani smiled at him, he knew exactly what was expected of him. Fanning out his marvelous train of feathers, he began strutting around. With each step, splashes of wonderful colors were reflected from the feathers. The sight captivated the princess in astonishment. Without taking her eyes away from the magnetic sight, she whispered, "My peacock palace is no match to this charm."

CHAPTER NINETEEN

A LOTUS IN THE SWAMP

In middle of Lake Pushkar, in the capital of Suvarna-nagari, a lavish palace was seen floating elegantly. The palace, uniquely shaped as a sphere, was glistening with a soft, bluish hue. The shots of gold among the blue were enhancing its shine further. It was resting over a leaf-shaped platform, completely covered with luscious lawns. The lawns were bordered with a bluish-white railing. From a distance, the floating edifice would resemble a drop of fresh dew over a green leaf, swaying leisurely on the lake.

At the main entrance, there were two beautiful statues of mermaids, carved in soft, white stone. Joining their hands together from either side, the mermaids had formed a graceful arch in the center. From their other hands, curled away from their bodies, cheerful fountains were springing out. The sight was surely a luring symbol of beauty. A few swan-shaped canoes, tied a little away from the main entrance, were used to ferry the people to and from the mainland.

From the inviting main entrance, one's sight would fall on the gorgeously decorated interior of the palace. The furniture, the sconces, the hanging art pieces, the drapery, everything was echoing the theme of underwater life. Artistically designed swans, cranes, fishes, and turtles were peeking from every nook of every chamber. The oversized transparent windows, draped with unique fabric, were enhancing the feeling of living underwater.

Leaning against the railing, a young, handsome prince was gazing at the rippling waters of the lake. He, the Crown Prince of Suvarna-Raaj, Prince Amar, was the owner of the extravagant floating palace. He was the only child to King Veersen and queen Lalita-Devi.

The rain had just stopped letting the sun come out of the clouds. The charming reflection of the palace was spread all across the lake waters. Spanning over it was the beautiful reflection of the rain-bow in the sky. The flocks of swans and ducks were happily glid-ing across the lake. Frequently inserting their beaks in the water, they were nudging the passing fish. Following them were their little babies, proudly imitating acts of their parents. The birds flying in the sky would frequently plunge deep down into the water for a fish, but that couldn't stop some bold fish from darting up from the water and enjoying a cold breeze.

Unfortunately the enchanting sight of the lake wasn't able to lighten the prince's mood. Something was bothering him, surely. His handsome face looked serious. From time to time, he was rubbing his hands over the railings and nodding his head nervously. Although as brave and adventurous as his father, the prince was calm, polite, kind, and compassionate. He inherited those noble virtues from his mother, Lalita-Devi.

As a grown man, he had become aware of his father's mistakes. Helplessly, he had witnessed Veersen's atrocities and injustice rampaging throughout the kingdom. The more he would watch his father's misdeeds, the more he felt isolated from him. He started feeling ashamed of himself after being addressed as Veersen's son. Recently he began opposing and challenging the king regarding his unjust decisions and cruel orders.

Instead of listening to his son's opinions, Veersen would insult him. He wouldn't hesitate to call Prince Amar a defiant and a rebel in front of the courtiers. That would result in bitter arguments. Each day, the rift between the father and son was growing.

That day, while staring at the rippling waters, one such argument was being flashed in the prince's mind. The topic was Gurudev. The news of Gurudev's capture came as a shock to the prince. He personally didn't know him but had heard wonderful stories about his archery, bravery, and pious nature from his mother, Lalita-Devi. Those stories impressed him so much that Gurudev became his hero.

So when the king's army returned with the imprisoned Gurudev, the prince desperately wanted to visit him. Unfortunately he wasn't allowed because the sight of Gurudev's prison was kept extremely secret. Apart from Kalkoot and King Veersen, no one else was allowed to visit him. Although the prince couldn't visit Gurudev, he could listen to the news about him in the court. According to the news, since the time of his capture, Gurudev had remained unconscious in spite of the king's efforts.

In reality, Gurudev wasn't unconscious at all. At the Aashrum, shortly before Veersen ordered his men to lash him, Gurudev had

225

entered a state of deep trance. He had withdrawn himself away from the world. The duration of his trance would be decided entirely by him, and there was no power existing in the world that could interfere with his decision. This fact wasn't known to the world, and the prince wasn't an exception. Just like the others, he was under the impression that Gurudev was unconscious. For him it was torture to hear of the unconscious Gurudev being pinned to the ground with iron chains. So, he had been frequently requesting the release of Gurudev.

That day in the court, after Prince Amar's repeated requests, King Veersen became very angry. He was already frustrated over the fact that he couldn't obtain more information about Shivani from Gurudev, even after his capture. To his dismay, all the voodoo rituals performed by Kalkoot failed to locate Shivani. That had puzzled Kaalkoot himself, but it wasn't his fault. During the rituals, Shivani was not on the earth but was on Shreelok. That's why he couldn't locate her. Of course, Kalkoot didn't know that.

Now, for the king, Gurudev was the only hope to find Shivani. When he heard the prince's request, Veersen became literally mad with anger and a fierce argument sparked. As a result, the king banished the prince from the court for a week.

Standing by the railing of his palace, the whole episode revisited the prince. After thinking for a while, he decided to go visit his mother, Lalita-Devi, the queen. Her wise and sensible words would always make him feel relaxed. As the chariot halted near the gate, he started walking to his parents' chamber.

Queen Lalita-Devi and King Veersen's grand chamber was located amidst a huge, luxurious garden named Madhuban. Heading to the chamber was a trail, snaking leisurely through the garden. The gorgeous trail, paved by colorful marbles, was flanked on either side by tall trees heaving with leaves. Numerous graceful arches, built along the trail, were further anchoring its charm. Fluttering their wings, flocks of parrots atop those arches were basking in the sun. Their sweet chirps reverberated through the whole garden. The meticulously maintained flowerbeds were shining against the green lawn, and the fountains were bursting from the countless ponds situated throughout the garden. Caressing the surroundings with pleasant mist, the fountains had become the sites for white doves immersed in love.

To match the splendor of joyful fountains, spectacular canopies stood nearby. Under each canopy was placed a delicately carved golden swing with rich upholstery. Trapping the grace and majesty inside them, the canopies, sheltered by the elegantly tangled nets of fruit and flowering vines, were surely the sites for lovely retreats from the harsh sunlight as well as the daily bustle of life. No wonder the glorious garden was very dear to King Veersen.

As Prince Amar was walking along the trail, the heavenly beauty of Madhuban had eased his restless mind. Humming a favorite tune, he was heading to meet his mother. Suddenly, tearing the bliss, a whooshing sound was heard, and the next moment, an injured bunny, from behind a neighboring bush, stumbled in front of him. Instantly the prince lurched forward and picked up the bunny. It was trembling violently. Blood was spurting out from an arrow plunged into its leg. Prince Amar pulled the arrow out and wrapped up the wound with his own sash.

Caressing the frightened bunny close to his heart, he whispered softly, "O, little one! There is no need to be frightened. I am here for you, my friend. I will take care of you." The bunny's pitiful condition made him angry at the shooter. Just then a guard, huffing heavily, approached him. He was happy to see the bunny resting in the prince's arms.

"Namaskaar, Prince Amar."

"Namaskaar."

"Prince Amar, I would be obliged if you can hand me the bunny."

"So...you were the hunter?" The prince blurted angrily. "You have injured this innocent life. You will be punished!"

"Forgive me, prince. I am not the hunter." The guard was pleading. "This is Maharaaj Veersen's hunt. Maharaaj has ordered me to bring it back. Please hand it quickly or else the Maharaaj will kill me."

"Oh, so...this is Maharaaj Veersen's hunt!" Swaddling the bunny in his hands, the prince whispered sarcastically, "Doesn't your Maharaaj remember that hunting is prohibited here in this garden?"

The poor guard couldn't answer back.

Just then, stomping his feet on the ground, King Veersen arrived. Ignoring the presence of the prince, he addressed the guard. "You... moron.... Why are you just standing here like a statue? Bring me my hunt, or I will punish you."

The guard was frozen with fear. To his rescue, the prince came forward. "Maharaaj, please don't punish the guard. He has rightly conveyed your message."

"Oh, I see!" Throwing a scornful glance at the prince, Veersen spotted the bunny in the prince's arms. He asked, "So, what has prevented you from returning my hunt?"

Staring at the bunny enjoying his assuring embrace, the prince said calmly, "Maharaaj, don't you know it is illegal to hunt in this park?"

"You...you are teaching me rules and ethics?" Veersen's rage surged.

"When we make the rules, we are supposed to follow them too. Aren't we?"

"I make the rules for others. I can do whatever I want to do. This is my kingdom. I am the king."

"I...I don't agree with you." The fearless prince continued, "I will not return this bunny to you. He has come to my refuge, and it is my duty to protect him."

"Prince Amar!" the king roared loudly. "You are disrespecting me...your father...the almighty King Veersen."

All the nearby guards were dazed with fear by Veersen's thundering, but the prince remained unaffected. With a determined voice, he said, "Maharaaj, does killing helpless and innocent life prove your strength? To me, it is a cowardly act."

"You are calling me a coward? I am the most powerful king on the earth!"

"Maharaaj, if you happen to call yourself the most powerful king, then it is your duty to protect the weak in your kingdom."

With his clenched fists and reddened eyes, the furious king stared at the prince. Holding the bunny tightly, the prince continued. "Maharaaj, I am too young to advise you. But still I would like to mention an important thing. Please listen to me carefully." Staring into the eyes of King Veersen, he said, "Power and wisdom should always go together. If power is disconnected from wisdom, the results are catastrophic for the society. The uncontrolled and unleashed power eventually destroys the world."

Without even waiting for the king's reaction or response, the prince, holding the white rabbit near his heart, resumed walking, fearlessly and with determination.

CHAPTER TWENTY

THE CLUE

Near the river Mahatejaa, gathering herself together with her chin resting on her knees, Shivani was sitting on a rock. While her eyes were fixed on the ripples in the river, her mind was lost in deep thoughts. And the thoughts were of course about Gurudev. Although her home had come back to life, it was incomplete without Gurudev. Suddenly something cold slithered over her legs.

"Naagraaj!" With a refreshing smile, she picked him up. Ever since Shivani had returned, Naagraaj wasn't ready to leave her alone. He was following her everywhere. Resting his body in Shivani's lap, he raised his head closer to Shivani's face and hissed.

Shivani smiled again at him. "I am sorry, Naagraaj. Next time I won't leave you alone in the hut. I promise you. Are you happy now?"

He flickered his forked tongue for "yes." Shivani smiled again. Holding him closer to her, as she happened to glance over his head, she saw a strange sight. A little away from them, Princess Aryaa was trying desperately to catch Mayur. She had left her pretty shoes behind and was walking barefoot through the ragged terrain.

"I can't believe my eyes, Naagraaj!" Shaking her head in disbelief, Shivani exclaimed, "Lured by a peacock, a princess of an advanced civilization is wandering barefoot on the earth!" Naagraaj conceded with her by hissing. Just then, Mayur spotted Shivani and at once raced to her. The princess followed.

"Shivani!" Sitting near Shivani, the princess asked, "What are you doing here?"

"I was relaxing here with Naagraaj. But...what are you doing? I saw you running after Mayur."

"Oh!" The Princess was a little embarrassed. "We were looking for you, right Mayur?"

"Really?" Shivani's eyes sparkled with naughtiness.

"OK!" Glancing at Mayur for a moment, the princess said, "Shivani, the truth is, I was following the whole flock of peacocks. When I get surrounded by them, I feel like...like I'm living my dream."

"Princess Aryaa, I am quite happy to see you enjoying it here."

"Shivani!" Staring right into Shivani's eyes, the princess said, "Now it is your turn to tell me the truth. Tell me why are you sitting with such a serious face?"

"Princess, I am thinking about Gurudev. Definitely he has been imprisoned by Veersen. There is no doubt about it." Taking a deep breath, Shivani continued. "The real problem is how to find him. I...I hope he is still alive." Although calm from outside, she was scared inside with the mere thought of that possibility. The princess kept her assuring hand on Shivani's shoulder.

Just then, they heard a strange voice. "Shivani! Shivani!" It was a shrill sound. The two, with their puzzled faces, began looking up in a tree where the sound was coming from.

"Shivani! Shivani!" As the sound came again, this time Shivani recognized it instantly. "Ravaa!" Spreading both her hands apart, she ran in the direction of the sound. Soon a green parrot swooped down onto her shoulder.

"Princess Aryaa! This is my pet parrot, Ravaa."

"Was he the one calling your name?" the perplexed Princess Aryaa asked.

"Yes! He speaks. Whatever words you speak, he repeats." Settling Ravaa on her forearm, Shivani added, "He sings too. I remember teaching him a few tunes. He is a quick learner. Whatever you say, he picks up those words and repeats immediately."

"Oh, then we have to be careful." The Princess's remark made both of them laugh. But after hearing Ravaa say a few more words, their laughter was suddenly torn. With her jaw dropped in shock, Shivani kept staring at him with her widened eyes fixed on him. Ravaa was saying "Kaalkoot! Veersen! Shivani! Shivani! Prison!" Princess Aryaa too was stunned. Unaware of the shocking words uttered by him, Ravaa continued spilling more words, "Gurudev, Shivani, buddy, prison, Kaalkoot, Veersen."

"Oh, my!" Coming to her senses, Shivani whispered to Ravaa, "When and where in the world did you hear these words?" But she already knew the answer to her own question.

On the patio in front of the hut, everyone was gathered. Shivani was pacing on the patio. Each step was reflecting her restless mind. Although Ravaa's discordant words had revealed important information for her, they also had made her more worried for Gurudev. One word in particular uttered by Ravaa had made her extremely uneasy. That word was—lash.

"Shivani!" Princess Aryaa, standing by the door, broke the silence. "So...when should we attack Veersen?"

"Attack?" Shivani exclaimed, swirling to Princess Aryaa.

"Of course." The princess threw a casual glance at Shivani. "What else would be the next step for us? Use the Shree-chakra and kill the monster at once." After glancing at Shivani's quiet face, Princess Aryaa lowered her tone. "Shivani, is something else going on in your mind?"

"Princess, I don't feel right to attack Veersen without warning him."

"What? Shivani!" the princess exclaimed in utter disbelief. "Do you need to warn a monster? That cruel king has committed countless crimes. He has lost his right to live on the earth. He should be punished at this very moment."

"Princess, I absolutely agree with you. Still I would like to make him aware of his crimes and give him a chance to explain his side before attacking him."

Shivani's words left the princess totally astounded. She kept staring at Shivani speechlessly. Then shrugging her head briskly, she spoke, stressing upon each word, "*Shivani, what did you say just now?*"

Reiterating her words, Shivani said, "Princess, I would like to offer Veersen a fair chance to explain his side. If he accepts his crimes,

I would ask him to correct his misdeeds and do penance. This is the first step for me. Until then, I will not attack him."

Shivani's words completely faded the princess's face. With her vacant eyes fixed on Shivani, she let herself drop to the ground. But soon she regained control over herself, and the words began spilling from her mouth. "What about the ruthless slaying of your parents? What about Gurudev's torture? What about the numerous innocent lives crushed by him? What about their justice? Did they get any chances to explain their innocence?"

"Princess, undoubtedly Veersen is a criminal. But if a criminal accepts his crimes and honestly feels remorseful, then that person deserves a chance to correct himself. He should be forgiven and asked to do penance for his misdeeds."

"Stop it, Shivani! Shut your mouth!" The Princess spoke out angrily. The tone of her scream at once startled Shivani. Until then she had only heard the soft and lovely voice of princess Aryaa. Shivani quickly stole a glance at her. Princess Aryaa's face became red with anger. Her furious eyes were fixed on Shivani. Her fists were clenched. It was totally a different form of Princess Aryaa she was looking at.

"Shivani, I am unable to understand you." The princess erupted again. "How can you think about warning and forgiving Veersen? The person you are thinking about pardoning brutally killed your parents and left you as an orphan for the rest of your life. He has tortured your revered Gurudev by lashing him. He destroyed your beautiful home. He wiped out many people mercilessly at his whim." Breathing heavily with unbearable rage, the princess continued spilling out her anger. "He is a cold-blooded criminal. He is a wild beast. Even if he accepts the crimes and is remorseful about them, he doesn't deserve any consideration. Instead this beast should be immediately hunted. It wouldn't be wrong at all."

Shivani, maintaining her calm, looked again at the furious and wrathful princess. Moving slowly forward, she gently kept her hand on the princess's shoulder. But at once Princess Aryaa shrugged it off and lurched away. With a scornful glance, she exclaimed, "Please do not touch me. I don't like to be touched by a coward."

"Coward? Who? Me?" Shivani whispered and reflexively moved back.

"Yes! I think you are scared of Veersen. Otherwise how can you think of words like redemption and forgiveness for Veersen, who brought only miseries to your life?" With frowns on her forehead, she asked, "If you wanted to forgive Veersen, why did you venture to our planet? Why did you obtain the Shree-chakra? I think with your cowardly thoughts, the divine Shree-chakra has lost its shine." Suddenly staring into Shivani's eyes, she asked, "Shivani, what are you going to tell your parents? Are you going to tell them that you were scared of Veersen and instead of taking revenge for their slaying, you pardoned Veersen? How are you going to tell Gurudev that you couldn't challenge Veersen? Tell me Shivani...tell me!!"

Shivani was very quietly listening to the princess. As Princess Aryaa slowed, Shivani started speaking softly. "Princess, I am very lucky to have you as my friend." The princess hadn't expected this kind of reaction from Shivani. With a sweet voice, Shivani continued. "Your anger toward Veersen has told me how much you love me and how much you care about me." After pausing momentarily, she added, "Princess Aryaa, Veersen has ruined my life in many ways. To take revenge for that, I can kill him at any moment...even right now. But will that satisfy me or my parents or my Gurudev? I don't think so."

Taking a deep breath in she said, "Princess, the revengeful killing doesn't look appropriate for the cultured society. A revengeful attitude is appropriate for the world of beasts and animals. Hit for a hit, slap for a slap, or murder for a murder are the actions of uncivilized society." Shivani glanced at the princess momentarily. Watching her listen quietly, Shivani continued. "I want to punish Veersen, but not for the sake of my own revenge but to rescue the numerous innocent people from his cruel clutches. For his vicious crimes, he needs to be punished, and that is my life's goal. In order to achieve that, I worked hard, made myself a fierce warrior, and obtained Shree-chakra from your planet. Now, I am able to kill him, but it should not be the first step for me. First, I would like to offer him my help in pulling himself out of the evil maelstrom in which he is currently standing.

"Also, I want him to get him on the path of righteousness. If he accepts his crimes, surrenders himself, and does a proper penance for his misdeeds, I would let him live. Instead of killing him, if I can change his heart and make him a good man, the success achieved by me would be far greater than simply killing him. I am confident that my parents, as well as Gurudev, would be overjoyed if I can turn an evil man into a righteous one."

By then the princess had become much calmer. Shivani's humble words had begun to touch her. Glancing around, Shivani added, "Princess, I am not a coward. I am not scared of being killed in battle with Veersen. But it is my conscience that doesn't allow me killing Veersen before offering him a chance to surrender and correct himself. Although the possibility of Veersen surrendering himself is quite bleak, I will try."

The princess was impressed by Shivani's reasoning. It was very mature and calm, she thought. Honestly, she had never thought in such a way before Shivani had explained her perspective. After thinking for a while, she asked softly, "If Veersen surrenders and pleads guilty, what would be his penance? Would he still maintain the title of king?"

"No, absolutely not!" Shivani blurted firmly. "A criminal like him has no right to rule a kingdom. If he pleads guilty, his life will be pardoned just to make him able to do the penance and purify himself. He will have to live in exile. He will not be allowed to enjoy the royal, comfortable life."

Shivani's determined speech satisfied Princess Aryaa. Another marvelous quality of Shivani had revealed itself before her. Looking respectfully at Shivani, she whispered, "Shivani, my anger toward Veersen didn't let me think the way you thought. Revenge was the only way visible to me. You are younger than me in age, but your thinking is great. I am fascinated by this noble thinking." After a moment's pause, she continued in a remorseful tone. "I am really sorry. In a blur of rage, I called you a coward."

"Princess!" Shivani smiled. "I have already told you that your angry words reflected your extreme love and care for me. They didn't hurt me."

"Really?"

"Yes! I mean it."

"Then can I ask you one thing?" The Princess glanced at Shivani with a naughty stare. "Can I get to be your messenger and go to Veersen?"

"What?" Shivani almost jumped with the shock.

"I will warn him and ask him to surrender."

"But…it is very dangerous. You will be…"

"Don't worry! I am safe on the earth." The princess showed her the necklace, given to her by her mother. "Shivani, please...please, say 'yes.'"

Shivani had no words. She was speechless.

CHAPTER TWENTY-ONE

THE MESSAGE OF PEACE

Even from a distance, the extreme bustle could be noticed at the main entrance to the royal court of King Veersen. Riding their chariots, the members were seen rushing to the court to attend an urgent meeting announced by the king. The guards at the entrance were juggling to receive the royal invitees. Not only that, they were trying to keep the subjects of Suvarna-nagari, gathered at the entrance, from sneaking through the gates.

The reason for the commoners huddling near the entrance was to get a glimpse of their beloved Prince Amar. Today, after being banished from the court for a week, the prince would be returning back to the royal court. Among the crowd were old, young, men, women, and children. The gentle and compassionate prince was very dear to them. As a sign of their devotion, they were waiting to welcome his chariot.

Gradually the restlessness of the crowd was increasing. They were anxious to at least see their prince. The initial gentle nudging for a better spot to watch the prince had changed into a violent hustle. The people started pushing and elbowing each other. As a result, suddenly an old woman landed on the ground with a big thud. Whimpering with pain, she was trying to haul herself up but was unable to do so. The guards in front of whom she fell started shouting at her.

"Hey, you old moron." Throwing a scornful look at the woman wearing filthy rags, one of them scoffed, "Get up fast. Don't you know you are lying in the path of the royal invitees? Stand up and get lost from here before getting crumpled by the chariots." The old woman kept looking at them with her weak and helpless sight.

Just then a chariot was spotted at a distance, racing towards them. In a blur of panic, the guards shoved the old woman aside and hurried forth to receive the guest. Her frail body couldn't withstand the force. Pleading for help, she tumbled down the road. The scared crowd began moving away from the guards. The old woman was wailing in pain. Ignoring her cries, the guards stood flanking the gate to pay their respects to the arriving chariot. But the chariot, instead of passing through the gate, screeched to a halt near the entrance. While everyone was watching in a daze, Prince Amar climbed down from the chariot. Instantly cheers erupted from the surroundings. After a quick acknowledgement to the people hailing his arrival, the prince dashed straight to the old woman. He helped her get up and gave an angry stare to the nearby guards. The guards began pleading for forgiveness. Ignoring them, he turned to the woman and did namaskaar to her.

"Hey, noble lady. On behalf of the guards I, prince Amar, would like to apologize to you. Please forgive them for the mistreatment."

"O, kind hearted one; I bless you with a long life!" the woman said, overwhelmed by the prince's gesture. Compensating for her diminished vision, she squinted to get a better look at the face of her savior and whispered, "Prince Amar, God bless you."

"Thank you for the blessings." Helping her to stand up, the prince asked, "May I know what else can I do for you?" His kind voice assured her.

"I have come here from my village far, far away from here." Sighing softly, the woman said, "I have heard a lot about the magnificent royal court. Can I get a chance to visit it?"

The prince became serious. He was worried about the king's reaction. It would certainly not be pleasant. He wanted to avoid another humiliating experience for the old woman.

"Prince Amar, before I die, I would like to see the grand court with my old eyes. After witnessing its majestic architecture, I would be ready to leave this world at any time." With her trembling but energetic voice, she asked, "Will it be possible for you to take me to the grand court? You are the prince. You can certainly fulfill my wish." Watching the prince's face expectantly, she requested again, "I will be highly obliged, for the rest of my life."

After thinking for a while, Prince Amar smiled at her pleasantly.

"Your wish is granted." As he ordered, the charioteer steered the chariot closer to the old woman. Helping her to climb up into it, Prince Amar exclaimed, "Welcome aboard!"

Soon after settling down on his throne, Veersen's face reflected utter disgust as his eyes stalled at the old woman. With her filthy rags covered with dust, she was happily sitting on a chair near the prince. Marveling at the stateliness of the court, she was looking around and enjoying her lifetime dream.

"Who dared to bring this shabby beggar to my court?" Veersen's thundering echoed throughout the massive court. Immediately a wave of horror arose, engulfing the whole court in a frightful silence. All the scared eyes were focused on the prince. "Maharaaj," the prince, getting up from his place, politely greeted the king. "I have invited this old lady to the court."

"Prince!" Wrenching his face in disgust, Veersen shouted, "I am sure these poor characteristics in you are not inherited from me. I am ashamed of calling you my son." Veersen screamed again, "Why did you bring her here?"

"Maharaaj, she was desperate to see our grand court. She requested me to visit the court, and I granted it." Maintaining his calm, the prince continued. More than the king's anger, he was worried about the old woman's feelings. He didn't want her to feel insulted.

"Desperate...to see the *court?*" Veersen bounced off his seat and ordered, "Guards!" After hearing that angry scream, the guards rushed in from all the doors of the court. Addressing them, Veersen pointed at the old woman. "Hurl this dirt out of my court, at once. I am sure by now she has enjoyed watching the court and has fulfilled her last wish."

Watching the guards swarming toward the old woman, the prince swiftly came forth. Shielding the woman, he pleaded to the king, "Maharaaj, please forgive her. She is just an old, innocent woman who wanted to see our court. If you want, I myself will escort her out of the court. But please don't use any force. She is too old and weak to withstand even the slightest force and may die at the hands of these guards."

"Let her die, then," Veersen said very coldly. "I don't need such old and useless people in my kingdom." Giving an angry stare to the guards, he screamed again, "What are you waiting for? Throw her out, immediately." Raising their swords, the guards began pushing the prince aside. That didn't scare the prince. Holding the old woman's hand and shielding her behind him, the prince stood staunchly, raising the sword in his other hand high up in the air.

But suddenly the charging guards began receding backward after halting momentarily at their spots. Their faces were dazed in awe, while the eyes were hooked onto the site past the prince. As the prince turned to look, he too was taken aback with a surprising sight.

In place of the old, dusty, ugly woman was standing a beautiful, heavenly, charming young girl. Clad in richly attire and bedecked with pricey, sumptuous jewelry, she was gazing at the stunned prince. After a few moments, she whispered softly, "Prince, thanks for protecting me. Thank you for standing by an innocent."

"You...who...are?" The mesmerized prince was struggling to find the words. The girl's hand, which he had been holding tightly until then, slipped out of his grip.

"I am Princess Aryaa, the princess of..." She smiled. "Well...I will tell you all about me a little later. First I have some important work to finish." Then she turned to Veersen, who was also stunned with the magical transformation of the old lady.

"Maharaaj Veersen," Princess Aryaa said in a sweet voice, "I had heard a lot of stories about your cruel and ruthless nature, so I decided to judge you for myself. Presenting myself in an old, helpless woman, I had come to test you." Walking toward the king, she continued, "Unfortunately whatever I had heard about you has been found to be true. In fact, you are much more brutal, heartless, and inhuman than I had anticipated."

"Stop right there," Veersen, coming to his senses, roared. "Don't you dare accuse me, standing in my own court." Springing from his seat, he screamed, "You should be killed immediately."

"Veersen, I know you are eager to kill me, but before that, wouldn't you like to hear the news you and your Special Forces are dying for?" The Princess's sentence instantly stilled the king. Staring at him, she further said, "I know the whereabouts of Shivani." The princess's words blew away the anger from Veersen's face. In its place, newly born hope began reflecting. Watching that drastic change, the princess smiled. "And you were going to kill me."

"Stop saying any unnecessary words. Just speak about Shivani. Tell me, where is that scared cat hiding now?" He momentarily glanced at Kaalkoot, whose face was quite serious. Rubbing his hands on the armrest of his chair, he was looking at the princess.

"I will tell you all about..."

"Hey, princess, if you give this information to me, I will honor you with an exorbitant prize." Veersen was speaking excitedly.

"Oh, I see," the princess whispered sarcastically.

"I want to capture Shivani before she runs away again."

"Please be patient, Maharaaj." The princess smiled. "This time she won't run away. In fact, she has sent me to you."

"Did Shivani send you here? Do you know her well? Why did she send you?"

"Maharaaj Veersen, please ask one question at a time." The princess was enjoying the sight of fumbled Veersen. "I know Shivani very well. In spite of your efforts to kill her, she survived and got rescued from the forest Raat-Raan. Now, she has become a great warrior and is ready to attack you at any moment." After a moment's pause, she continued, "Although I may not be able to give any specific details about her location, she is currently very close to your capital."

"Wait a minute!" Staring at the princess with distrust, suddenly Veersen asked, "Why should I trust you? You are deceptive. You can present yourself in different forms."

"Whether to trust me or not, it is up to you, Maharaaj." The princess continued. "Shivani is planning to attack you, but before doing that, she sent me to you as a messenger of peace."

"A messenger of peace?" Wrenching his face, Veersen scoffed.

"Yes. Though she is capable of killing you at this very moment, she wants to offer you one last chance to plead guilty to all your crimes and ask her forgiveness."

"And may I know my crimes...please?"

Ignoring the sarcastic tone of his speech, the princess said, "You have been trying to kill her since the time she wasn't even born. Although she escaped safely, her parents were killed in the fatal attack. This is your first crime. Second, you have captured, lashed, and imprisoned Gurudev. His unconscious body is still pinned to the ground. After having entered your capital, I have gathered enough information to prove the authenticity of this accusation. Third, with the help of your beloved magician, you have been indulging in voo-dooism. You have been seeking help from the dark powers. Fourth," Nodding her head with displeasure, she said, "I am sorry, Maharaaj, but it is painful to recall your crimes. You are oppressing and harassing the poor, innocent people of your kingdom. I, myself, have witnessed their sufferings. You are abusing your powers."

"Am I?" Veersen was still sarcastic. "Oh! And to save my life from Shivani's wrath, what should I do?"

"Stop getting help from the dark powers, release Gurudev respectfully, and do the penance by dethroning yourself. Go in exile forever. You…"

"Hey, you witch." Dashing onto the princess, Veersen screamed with unbearable anger, "You should have been killed far earlier!"

Veersen was about to hit the princess with his sword, but just then, prince Amar darted forth and grabbed his hand. "Maharaaj, please come to your senses." Staring right into the eyes of Veersen, he said in a determined voice, "You can't kill a messenger. It is not ethical." But instead of discouraging Veersen, the sentence simply catapulted his anger further. Screaming wildly, he tried to free his hand from the prince's grip, but the grip was too tight.

"Prince Amar." Unable to witness the fight between a son and a father over her, the princess said calmly, "Thank you very much for your help. But I don't want to bother you anymore. I am leaving right now." Then, turning to Veersen, she added, "I did my best trying to convince you and save your life. Unfortunately I didn't succeed." Whispering softly she added, "But it was all anticipated. Veersen, now no one will be able to save you from Shivani. I will convey your message instantly and correctly to Shivani."

With his hand still being grabbed by the prince, Veersen shouted at the guards, "Why are you all just watching? Arrest her at once. Don't let her leave…" His sentence was left unfinished as Princess Aryaa vanished before everyone's sight as if she had dissolved into the air.

CHAPTER TWENTY-TWO

THE SIEGE

Sitting on a chair, Prince Amar was vacantly gazing out through the glass wall built all around the floating palace. It was one of his favorite seats in the palace. Peering through the wall, he would always enjoy looking at the gorgeous lake, veiled behind the misty fountains. The encircling blue lake, trimmed by the luscious, green trees, would mesmerize him for a long time. He would listen to the blissful concert of tweeting birds paired with melodious tapping sounds of the fountain droplets.

Although sitting on his favorite seat that day, the prince wasn't happy watching outside. It was difficult for him to bear the sight of scores of heavily armed guards standing all around his palace. Their presence was annoying him. But at the same time, it was making him realize his state of helplessness. After glancing for one last time at the guards patrolling his residence, he sighed heavily and hauled himself away.

Prince Amar was under house arrest, as per King Veersen's orders. All his activities were restricted. He was neither allowed to leave the palace nor communicate with anyone outside the palace, even with his own mother. The reason was quite obvious. A day earlier, the prince had challenged and obstructed Maharaaj Veersen in the royal court.

The prince stared at the door. One of the maids was standing with his breakfast. Signaling with his hands, he denied the breakfast. After the maid returned back, he walked to the nearby golden swing. The swing was sculptured in the shape of a half-opened shell. It was covered with soft, peach-colored fabric trimmed with bright pearls. On either side, the fish-shaped armrests were flanking the swing. Their scales were studded with bright-colored stones. After the prince dropped down on the swing, it slipped into a slow, dull sway. Letting his body fall against the back rest, he slammed his hands on the armrests in frustration.

His listless body was moving back and forth with the swing. His eyes were looking up at the ceiling, but instead of appreciating its intricate artwork, they were lost in despair. Suddenly something sparked in his mind. Instantly he jolted up from the swing and lurched toward his bed. After groping blindly under the pillow, his face dazzled with a pleasant smile. Gingerly taking it out from under the pillow, he looked at the thing. It was a bangle—a beautiful, delicate bangle, engraved with shimmering diamonds. It was Princess Aryaa's bangle. Her mysterious appearance and even more mysterious disappearance had been haunting the prince. Just like a lightning bolt, she had dazzled the court momentarily. Since her disappearance, the prince had lost his rest. Although the mesmerizing beauty disappeared, her bangle was left with him after her hand slipped off of his astonished grip. It was the only solace to his restless mind.

"So...pretty you are!" Caressing the bangle over his cheeks, the prince whispered, "But your owner is much prettier." The prince whispered with his dreamy eyes focused on the bangle. To him, each diamond was reflecting the pretty face of the goddess of beauty. The spark of her memory was sufficient to enlighten his depressed mind.

"I miss you so much. Where have you been hiding after stealing away my heart?" the prince muttered softly and sat on the bed. Suddenly he sensed footsteps outside his chamber. He fumbled for a moment but after swiftly slipping the bangle inside his shirt pocket, he stood up. As he turned to the door, he was baffled to see his mother, Maharaani Lalita-Devi, entering the chamber. Reeling with worry, she hustled inside.

The prince greeted her. "Namaskaar Mother."

"Namaskaar. Bless you my son." putting her hand on his head, she said softly, "Please have a seat."

Prince Amar was trying to read her mind. She had put herself in great danger by visiting him. He was quite worried for that.

Settling down in a chair, she whispered, "Thank you, my son." Her beautiful face was shrouded with worry. Her gracefully arched eyebrows; pretty, sharp nose; cute chin; slightly raised cheeks; and huge, dark eyes were all reflecting her concern about her son, Prince Amar. She looked at him. He had picked up many of her features. In addition, the prince had inherited her noble and kind personality. She was confident that, just like her, Prince Amar would be able to draw respect from the entire kingdom. With that thought she felt very proud of him and got a little relaxed. But it lasted simply for a few moments until she heard the guards talking amongst themselves. Her husband's cruel and inhumane attitude had devastated that soft-natured woman. In spite of trying hard, she couldn't succeed in changing Veersen's behavior. She was helplessly watching the kingdom suffer from injustice and atrocities. Recently, witnessing the escalating conflicts between husband and son had uprooted her.

"Mother, I am sure that you are aware of the royal orders. No one, absolutely no one, is allowed to visit me as per the Maharaaj's orders." Taking a deep breath, the prince added, "And that includes you too, Mother." The prince was fully aware of his mother's desperate situation. She had been wedged badly between husband and son. Staring at her sad, anxious face, a wave of guilt washed over him. Turning his eyes away, he added, "Mother, I think, you are risking yourself by coming here."

"Prince Amar, I am well aware of it." The queen answered calmly. "But I couldn't hold myself back. Son, I am a helpless mother." She whispered in disdain, "I was desperate to see you. Also..."

"Also what, Mother?"

"Also I wanted to share extremely important news with you. Just a while ago..." With her eyes at the door, in a soft whisper, the queen continued cautiously, "I overheard Maharaaj Veersen talking to Kaalkoot."

Listening to the name "Kaalkoot" immediately brought a frown to the Prince's forehead, though he continued listening. The queen said further, "Kaalkoot is going to perform a special ritual for the Maharaaj."

"Why? Is Maharaaj going to war?"

"I don't think so. Also, this seems to be a quite different ritual than the previous ones, performed before every war."

"Different? In what way?"

"This ritual will be a long one and will be performed at Kalkoot's far away mansion near the mountains. According to Kalkoot, after this ceremony, Maharaaj will be granted with immortality."

"Immortality?" The prince shuddered. "Immortality to a demon?"

"Yes, my son. For this ritual, Kaalkoot is taking Maharaaj to his own mansion. He wants to get it done as fast as possible...before Shivani's attack. According to Kaalkoot's predictions, Shivani is the only person from whom Maharaaj has the greatest threat, and she will be attacking at any time." After a pause, she added, "The army has already started the preparation. All the borders are sealed."

After a long pause, Prince Amar asked, "Mother, do you believe in this immortality ritual and all of Kaalkoot's predictions?"

"Son, previously I didn't believe, but after having watched Kaalkoot over the past few years, I have started believing in him now. Rather than ignoring, I would like to take his words seriously. He is a great but dangerous magician." She trembled at her own whisper. "Since I heard this news, a weird feeling has dawned upon me, and I came running here."

"Mother, I will help you as much possible."

"Prince, I love Maharaaj as my husband, but I hate his monstrous attitude. Because of that reason...I don't want him to be immortal." Staring at her son's face, she said, "Look at you. You are a living example of his cold-hearted nature. If he can harass his own child, the crown prince of Suvarna Raaj, it is easy for anyone to imagine his brutal attitude toward the commoners." The queen's voice was full of anguish, "Just think of the miserable and grim future for this world if, by chance, this beast becomes immortal."

Walking near his mother, the prince placed his hand gently on her shoulders. His assuring touch calmed her down. She rested her head on his hand. For the prince, it was painful to watch his beloved mother's anguish. Honestly, he didn't believe in the ritual of immortality, although he was very much aware of Kaalkoot's miraculous powers. He couldn't ignore the critical role played by the special powers endowed to his father through Kaalkoot's ritual. Such rituals appeared to make him victorious in every battle. Also, he was aware of Kaalkoot's faithfulness and loyalty toward Maharaaj Veersen. Maharaaj had literally picked him up from the road and gifted him a respectable position in society. There was no doubt, if needed; he would readily sacrifice his own life to save Maharaaj's life.

The prince whispered after thinking for a while, "So while the army keeps Shivani busy fighting at the capital, Maharaaj will go to Kaalkoot's mansion and get endowed with immortality."

"I guess so," the queen whispered hopelessly. "And with you being under the siege, no one can avert the ceremony."

"Mother." With borrowed hope, the prince spoke, "Please relax. I promise you, I will try my best. First, I will try escaping from this palace as early as possible." He looked all around, ensuring that no one else was listening. He asked, "When do you think Kaalkoot will be starting the ritual?"

"This evening."

"This evening?" he exclaimed with disbelief. Glancing at the sun, lowering down to the horizon, he sighed heavily. "We have to act quickly. I know Kaalkoot's mansion. Isn't it near the Giri Mountains?"

"Yes, my son. Kaalkoot said that the ritual is quite long, intense, and at any cost can't be interrupted. Even a little bit of disruption will ruin it. That's why the whole surroundings of the Giri Mountains will be guarded by tens and thousands of special battalions."

"Oh, I see." The prince was lost in serious thoughts.

Sitting under the trees of Prajakta, Shivani was holding the tiny flowers in her hands. With her eyes blissfully closed, she was moving her cheeks over them, enjoying the fleeting touch of their softness. From time to time, she was pulling their heavenly fragrance inside. Before heading to the capital, she wanted to spend some time under the Prajakta trees, her parents' memorial. Ever since the princess returned from the court of King Veersen, the war was decided.

Suddenly she heard Princess Aryaa calling her name. Her voice was quite desperate, quite frantic.

"What's the matter, princess?" Shivani asked, springing up.

"Shivani, Shivani!" After having run fast, the princess was trying to catch her breath. "It's really urgent. We have to act quickly, now."

"What is urgent?" the puzzled Shivani asked, staring at the princess's panicked face.

"Instead of going to the capital, you should race to Kaalkoot's mansion, right at this moment. Veersen won't be in the capital. Kaalkoot is taking him to his mansion." Grabbing Shivani's hand tightly, the Princess was spilling the information. "At his mansion, Kaalkoot is going to perform the ritual of immortality for Veersen. He is planning to finish that long, intense ceremony before your attack. That ceremony is going to endow Veersen with immortality. Shivani, please believe me. You must interrupt this ritual or else all our efforts will go in vain, and that beast will be invincible."

"Princess..." Shaking her head in disbelief, Shivani said, "Princess, how can that be true? Is it possible for anyone to be immortal?"

"I don't know," the princess said, "but I don't want to waste any time in having a discussion over that. First attack and kill Veersen, and later we will discuss the authenticity of 'immortality' ceremony. 'The immortal Veersen,' the very term sounds alarming to me."

"You are right, princess." Shivani said after thinking for a moment. "When is the ritual starting?"

"*This evening!*" the princess answered, stressing upon each word.

"What?" Shivani glanced at the sun and shook her head in desperation. But then suddenly swirling toward Princess Aryaa, she asked, "Princess, how and when did you learn all this?"

Shivani's question turned the princess bashful. That further perplexed Shivani. Avoiding looking at Shivani, the princess stretched both her hands in front of Shivani.

"Why are you holding your hands in front of me?"

"Don't you see my diamond bangle is missing from my right hand?"

"Oh, yes. But what's the connection of that with the news?" Shivani was unable to connect the dots between the coy princess, the missing bangle, and the unbelievable news about Veersen's ritual.

"OK, I will explain all to you, now." The reddened Princess whispered coyly, "My missing bangle is there...with the prince."

"With the prince?" Shivani suddenly screamed excitedly. "But how did it happen?"

"Oh, that day, the prince was holding my hand, and..." The princess hid her face with both her hands and left the sentence incomplete.

"Oh, now I understand!" Shivani answered, naughtily staring at the princess.

"Shivani!" With great difficulty, the princess started speaking again, "So the other bangle is with him now. Because of that bangle, I can hear him. I get to learn the things happening around him."

"And can he too listen to you?"

"Unfortunately, no," the princess sighed.

"Oh," Shivani whispered mischievously. "So...you were spying on him!"

"Shivani," Ignoring Shivani's teasing tone, the princess said, "The prince himself is in trouble. Veersen has put him in a siege, at his own palace."

"Why would the king do that?" Shivani was surprised. "The prince is his own son."

"I have already told you, Shivani. Prince Amar is totally opposite of Veersen. He is very nice. He did put himself in danger to protect me, and this siege is the repercussion of that event. I would say the prince is a unique blend of the best virtues of humans." The princess continued enthusiastically, "He is a compassionate, gentle, kind, and brave person. His voice is so polite that when he speaks, it feels like stardust. Anyone can easily trust him. I was highly impressed by his courage to challenge against the injustice and cruelty. He is the lone, bright star dazzling in the darkness. He is the jewel of the jewels." For quite a while Princess Aryaa was talking about Prince Amar. She had forgotten Shivani standing by. She had even forgotten herself.

Shivani was silently watching her friend. Then softly, she asked, "Princess, how does Prince Amar look?"

"Oh, Shivani." Staring at the trees with her dreamy eyes, the princess exclaimed, "Prince Amar is very handsome. I think he is the most handsome man I have ever seen in my…" After realizing Shivani's eyes were twinkling with naughtiness, she left the sentence incomplete and turned her bashful face away.

"Oh, I see." Picking up the white bunny in her hands, Shivani said, "Oh, that's why you were busy caressing your bangle ever since you returned back from the court."

"Shivani…" To stop being teased, the princess changed the topic. "So, Shivani, what have you decided? What are your plans now?"

"Princess, I think I will have to head to Kaalkoot's mansion." Shivani suddenly got serious. "But where is it?"

"It is by the side of Giri Mountains, to the left of the capital."

"Oh, I see! But you need to go to the prince and help him. "

"Shivani, you just read my mind!" Princess Aryaa said excitedly.

"Princess, we must thank your bangle." Tucking her bow on her shoulder, Shivani said, "It was good that it stayed with the prince, right Princess Aryaa?" Shivani ran away from there before the princess could realize the teasing in Shivani's sentence.

CHAPTER -TWENTY THREE

THE DEADLY DASH

Fighting back her tears, Shivani waved good-bye to all her friends one more time. Although her feet were dragging her body away, her mind was still lingering back with them. Also, because of the previous experience, she was extremely worried about their safety. She was unwilling to leave them alone, but there was no other option. She kept walking forward. After having walked for a while, a fantastic idea flashed in her mind.

Swirling back, she looked at her neighborhood. Then, taking her bow out, she shot an arrow up into the sky. It was a Seema Arrow, used for guarding the borders of a desired place. As the arrow zoomed up into the sky, it flashed a blinding spark all over her neighborhood, including the hut, the river, the trees, Jwala's den, the mango forest, the Prajakta trees, the lotus lake, and so on. That created a protective shell invisible to others. Glancing at the amazing work done by her special arrow, Shivani smiled with satisfaction. Now, although her friends could walk in and out through the shell, the enemy would not be able to do so. Her neighborhood was protected from intruders from air, water, or ground. She was confident anyone trying to do so would be instantly burned to ashes.

Soon after crossing over the wide, rugged terrain, the ranges of the Giri Mountains became visible to Shivani. Stalling momentarily, she glanced at the huge, brown landscape stretched ahead of her. The absence of even a speck of greenery in that vast landscape was quite obvious. At the far end of the brown landscape was an enormous edifice—the mansion of Kalkoot, and also his workplace. Here all his "special" rituals would take place. To reward his services, a few years ago Veersen had presented Kalkoot with this beautiful mansion. Later Kalkoot had it modified to his liking.

While watching and judging the site in front of her, Shivani began stepping toward the mansion vigilantly. Although Kaalkoot's mansion looked quite grand, an eerie feeling dawned on her at the first sight of it. Built in shiny, black material, it had numerous tall domes of varying heights. The glimpse of black mansion against the brown landscape was quite a sight. As her eyes glided down on the ground from the tallest of the domes, her grip instantly tightened over her bow. Scores of soldiers were seen surrounding the main entrance to the tallest dome.

To avoid being spotted by anyone, Shivani began crawling forward along the brown, deserted ground. She moved as close as possible to the main entrance. A little away from it was a huge boulder. Lurching forward, she hid behind it. Being on a higher ground, it was easy for her to keep a close watch on the soldiers.

Numerous divisions of heavily armed soldiers, led by their horse riding leaders, were marching. As ordered, each division was briskly taking its designated spot. In a short time, the armed knights, in multiple concentric layers, shielded the whole mansion, especially the main entrance. With her eyes squinted, Shivani was watching their each and every action very carefully. At the same time, her mind was busy planning a strategy for the attack. Just then, something glared in her faraway sight.

A beautiful golden chariot, led by five horses, was seen racing gracefully toward the main entrance. Although open at the top, its back was bounded by a lofty board. A spacious and elegant golden umbrella was seen hoisted up from the backboard, swaying along with the movement of the chariot. Atop the umbrella was Veersen's royal army's flag, flaring up. It was easy to guess the owner of that majestic chariot. "And that person under the umbrella must be Veersen." As she whispered, her whole body tightened like a rock. "I thought he would already be inside the mansion with Kaalkoot. I wonder, what is he doing out here?" Her eyes were glued to the target, Veersen.

Standing under the umbrella, King Veersen was talking to the chief of the army, riding on a horse beside the chariot. Before heading inside the mansion for the ritual, Veersen had come out to view the security of the area. Glancing at the tons of heavily armed soldiers, arranged cleverly all around the mansion, he nodded satisfactorily. Then turning to Senapati, the chief, he said, "Senapati, I honestly feel these many soldiers are unnecessary to guard the mansion from a little, puny girl."

"Maharaaj." Senapati's face was quite serious. He remembered the attack by Shivani in the forest of Raat-Raan. It was a frightening experience for him. He had admired his luck many times for keeping him alive through the deadly shooting. Touching the wound on his right shoulder, caused by one of Shivani's grazing arrows, he trembled. "Please don't underestimate that girl. I, myself, have experienced her archery. With great accuracy and strength, the streams of arrows zoom out from her bow in all directions. It is difficult to save yourself from their unforgiving wrath. Her archery is marvelous and deadly for the enemy. She is a prodigious archer."

"Senapati," Veersen screamed with anger. "Senapati, you are insulting me. How dare you call that tiny, naïve girl a prodigious archer in front of me? I could kill you for this contempt. I am the best archer in the world."

"Maharaaj, I am very sorry. I...I really didn't mean that. Please forgive me." Senapati was pleading pathetically. "You are the most supreme warrior in the world, in the universe." That calmed down Veersen a little bit.

Just then, a man walked out of the mansion. "Maharaaj Veersen." Paying his respects to Veersen, he said politely, "Honorable Kaalkoot is waiting inside for Maharaaj."

"Senapati," Veersen thundered with his still, angry voice, "I am going in now. Once I'm inside, absolutely no one should be allowed to enter. Do you understand?"

"Yes, Maharaaj." Senapati nodded. Just then a deafening sound was heard. The bow twang, arising from Shivani's bow, instantly tore through the air. It echoed the dreadful warning of death to her enemy. The sound simply dumbfounded all with surprise and panic, including King Veersen. He glanced at his chief, quivering with fear.

"Maharaaj." With an ashen face, he looked at Veersen and stuttered, "It is...her. It's...Shivani's bow twang! I can recognize it... even in my sleep. She must...be here...somewhere!"

"Shut up, you chicken," Veersen roared lividly. "Don't get scared like a coward." From inside the chariot, Veersen lurched toward him. Grabbing his neck, he thundered again, "Order the knights to search for her and shoot her at once. Attack her."

As the chief ordered, the baffled knights began fumbling to hold on to their weapons. They frantically began searching for Shivani. Watching their confusion, Shivani smiled and appeared out from behind the huge boulder.

"That is Shivani," the chief whispered with his frightened eyes. "I am pretty sure, Maharaaj." As Veersen looked in the direction and spotted her, he screamed at the top of his lungs, "Shoot her! Shoot her! Shoot her!"

At once Shivani disappeared behind the thick veil of arrows and spears darting toward her from the soldiers. The sight made Veersen laugh exuberantly, but that lasted for only a few moments.

Shivani's single arrow destroyed all their weapons instantly. Now, it was Shivani's turn. She began shooting at them. The speed of her arrows was simply dizzying. It was hard to notice her pulling the arrow from the quiver, aiming, and shooting toward the enemy. All the phases seemed to be blended together, creating an impression of never-ending streams of arrows radiating out from her bow. It looked as though she was an erupting volcano, exploding out from all directions and hitting the enemy precisely. The arrows were coming too quickly to be anticipated. No one knew from which direction they would be hit. The panicked soldiers began running helter-skelter.

Veersen himself was dazed, too. He couldn't believe his eyes. Forgetting to shout at his falling soldiers, with his eyes glued on Shivani, he stood at the spot like a statue. He had never seen such excellent archery before.

"Didn't I tell you, Maharaaj? She is the real deal," the chief exclaimed without his knowledge. That further triggered Veersen's frustration.

"Hey, you moron! Shame on you for standing here as a freak." Veersen furiously slapped him, and roared, "Run forth! Kill her or get killed. Don't even come back. You are not eligible to head my army."

Watching the chief kicking his horse and getting lost in the sea of soldiers, Veersen turned to the warriors around him and ordered them to intensify the attack further. With all their might, they began fighting fiercely. But their efforts seemed to be unsuccessful. Shivani was invincible to them. In addition to defending herself, she was fatally attacking them. A single arrow from her bow would be transformed into multiple arrows, hitting multiple targets at the very same time. Veersen's elite army was swept over by a wave of panicked screams, shouts, moans, and screeches. Forgetting Veersen's wrath, soon the soldiers began running away, saving themselves from the mayhem.

Watching the plight of his renowned army, for the first time in his life, Veersen became alarmed. Kaalkoot's sentence flashed in his mind, "*Shivani will be your death!*" After quivering momentarily, he pushed away all the fear. With borrowed hope, he twanged his bow and invited a very powerful Divya-astra—Parvata-astra!

The arrow from his bow, after surging high up in the sky, was transformed into a massive boulder and began falling over Shivani. Glancing at that, the panicked soldiers stalled in their spots. Marveling at their king's majestic weapon, they were waiting for their enemy to be crushed soon. But that didn't happen. Instead, the boulder was smashed into tiny pieces by another powerful Divya-astra—

Vajra-astra—a giant mace, risen from Shivani's bow. It destroyed Veersen's hope along with the boulder.

The angry, frustrated Veersen shot another Divya-astra, creating millions of poisonous insects. Their swarms instantly rushed toward Shivani. But within a few moments, they all got blown away as Shivani shot Vayavya-astra—the weapon-generating, powerful whirlwind. Frustrated by another defeat, Veersen shot Agneya-astra—fire-emitting arrow. As the bellowing flames of fire engulfed Shivani, Veersen couldn't contain his joy. But it didn't last long.

The Parjanya-astra shot from Shivani's bow produced drenching rains. In a flash, they completely wiped out the fiery flames. The rains pouring down from her Divya astra not only extinguished the fire but engulfed the entire region in heavy rains, making the soldiers run.

The plight of those poor soldiers disturbed Shivani. They shouldn't be penalized for the mistakes of their devil king, she thought. Her fight was with the king. Unfortunately she couldn't attack the king without first getting rid of his soldiers, vigilantly guarding him. A wave of guilt washed over her. Just then she remembered a fantastic weapon that would keep the soldiers safe.

The overjoyed Shivani closed her eyes and chanted the mantra. At once a wonderful arrow appeared on her bow. It was dazzling with a bluish hue. After shooting it high up into the sky, she kept staring at the weapon with excitement. It was Mohini-astra, a hypnotizing weapon. After having reached its desired height, it flashed brightly and began emitting its enchanting rays. Instantly the entire region, except for Veersen, was enveloped in a mysterious yet pleasant shine. Soon the soldiers closed their dreamy eyes, dropped their weapons, and fell under the spell of sweet, irresistible sleep. Even the horses couldn't resist the spell and started dozing too.

Watching his army falling under the spell of Mohini-astra, Veersen began trembling. He tried chanting different mantras but failed repeatedly to invite Divya-astra. Shivani smiled at his desperate acts. "Veersen, Divya-astra never arrives on trembling bows."

Her sentence ignited Veeren's pride. He chanted another mantra with determination and successfully obtained one Divya-astra. But before the arrow got a chance to soar up into the sky, it was destroyed on the bow by another arrow swooping down from Shivani's bow. The startled Veersen attempted again. Unfortunately for him, Shivani was too quick to let him succeed. Before he could shoot, Shivani's arrow again destroyed his weapon sitting on the bow. That wasn't enough. This time, his powerful bow was also broken into pieces. The dazed Veersen staggered back. Fear began creeping upon him.

He spun around. The utterly silent landscape had surrounded him from all the sides. Just then, another arrow whooshed in, and before he realized it, his prestigious golden, jewel-studded umbrella fell to the ground, along with the famous flag of King Veersen. Glued to the spot, he watched it helplessly. Yet another fresh bout of arrows raced toward him. Those arrows, grazing close to his body, plunged into the huge golden backboard of his chariot. The arrows were shot in such a way that they, without hurting Veersen, pinned his whole body to the backboard. The speechless and motionless Veersen was confined inside his own chariot.

Now, the arrogant, brutal, cruel King Veersen was experiencing the feelings of fright, helplessness, hopelessness, and desperation for the first time in his life. Kaalkoot's sentence kept booming in his mind, *"Shivani is destined to kill you, Veersen."* The horror bolted inside his mind.

"I have fought so many wars before, but never ever got injured even once. May be this young girl is my real death. That's why Kaalkoot's protective shell isn't helping me now. This is it. This is the end of me." He quivered. With his eyes closed, the fidgety Veersen was waiting for another arrow to zoom in, killing him. It was a long, torturous wait during which nothing happened, surprisingly. There was a strange silence around him, except for his thumping heart. As he opened his weary eyes, he became frozen with fear.

Swinging her bow playfully, Shivani was climbing onto his chariot. Jammed with multiple arrows, he was watching his death approaching him. This was the girl whom he had tried killing several times, even before her birth. This was the girl whom he had chased desperately without any success. In spite of his dire efforts, he could never find her. Each time, she got away safely.

"Why aren't you...killing me?" he asked nervously, avoiding looking at Shivani, standing in front of him. "I...I guess you are... enjoying my plight, aren't you?"

"Wrong," Shivani replied very firmly. Staring straight into the eyes of Veersen, she said calmly, "Veersen, I am different from you. I don't enjoy harassing people."

"Then...then why are you just standing here? Please kill me." For the first time in his life, Veersen was pleading helplessly.

"Veersen," Shivani said, smiling at him, "Don't worry. I am going to kill you and free the world from you. But before that, I want to have a closer look at you. I want to see the terrific monster, rampaging on the earth. I want to see the face of my parents' murderer and my Gurudev's jailer." Her face was gleaming with great resolve.

"Veersen, now you understand what fear is. My poor parents would have quivered the same way you are quivering right now. As per your orders, your soldiers hunted them brutally. My helpless Gurudev would have looked at you just the way you are looking at me. You ruthlessly ordered him to be lashed." Her quiet face was transformed into a raging expression. "You...you are a heartless devil. You are not allowed to live on this earth. Let me send you to your destination—hell!"

Shivani pulled out Shree-chakra, tied to her back. Just then, a gigantic black cloud appeared out of nowhere and blinded her completely. It lasted only for a moment. As she opened her eyes again and looked in front of her, she was stunned. With widened eyes and dropped jaw, she kept watching the empty place in front of her where just a moment ago, Veersen was pinned to the chariot. He was gone. He had vanished completely. She swiveled her head around. There was no sign of that mysterious cloud anywhere. Everything looked the same. In the clear sky, the sun was setting. All around her were the scores of Veersen's soldiers, still sleeping calmly under the spell of Mohini-astra. Throughout the entire region, she was the only one standing, dazed.

CHAPTER TWENTY-FOUR

A FLIGHT TO RESCUE

From far away, Princess Aryaa saw the gorgeous palace floating on Lake Pushkar. But the throngs of armed soldiers patrolling had tainted its beauty. "It's impossible for anyone to enter the palace, except for me..." The princess smiled. "Because I am awesome, out of this world...literally." In a flash, she transformed herself into a tiny size. As a pretty butterfly came zooming in, the princess swiftly jumped onto it. Riding her magnificent flying vehicle, she soared high up in the sky and began heading toward the palace. Soon they landed softly on a flower arranged in a vase beside Prince Amar's bed. While the butterfly was enjoying the juicy flower, the princess got down and began searching for the prince. After a while, she saw him, but his pitiful sight made her very sad.

His eyes gazing ahead vacantly, Prince Amar was sitting on the swing with a wilted face. His repeated attempts to escape from the siege were unsuccessful. In addition, his love, Princess Aryaa, after electrifying him momentarily had vanished forever. His world was trampled in darkness. For a while, he sat in despair on his swing. Then he slipped his hand into his pocket. The lovely touch of the bangle sparked his face instantly with excitement. He gingerly took out the diamond bangle and caressed it over his cheeks.

"Oh, my love!" Staring at it, he whispered, "You are the only comfort to this broken heart. To me, your shine is like the shine of the moon that enlightens the darkness around me." Getting up from the swing, he walked to the bed. "You remind me of the enchanting beauty whose fleeting appearance sparked my life forever." His grip over the bangle tightened. "I desperately yearn for that lovely enchantress. I...I wish she could be here, right now." Holding the bangle close to his heart, the prince leaned back on the bed.

Princess Aryaa couldn't watch the heartbroken prince anymore. At once she emerged in her original form and spoke softly, "Prince, your wish is my command." Looking at her, the stunned prince jolted back instantly and stood frozen. Coming closer to him, the princess whispered, "Prince I too have been longing to see you."

The dramatic appearance of his dream girl dazzled the prince's face. But still he had not come to his senses. He kept staring at her speechlessly as if it were the most unreal, unimaginable, but very pretty dream that he wanted to last forever. He wanted to speak to her but lost all his words. Instead, he shook his head to bring himself out of the mesmerizing dream. Luckily for him, it wasn't a dream but the splendid reality.

'Please, you…me…why…how…when…sit!" The baffled prince was unable to make any meaningful sentence. Looking at the funny sight of him, the princess couldn't resist. Laughing freely, she said, "Prince! Please do not worry about me. I am fine here, standing near you." Glancing at the bangle in his hand, she asked, "But can I have my bangle back, please?"

The prince continued to stare, mesmerized.

"The one you have been holding in your hand?"

"Oh, I see." By then the prince had regained control of his senses. Looking straight into her eyes, he said, "No…never. I don't want to give it back to you." Now it was the prince's turn to tease. "Instead, I would like to slip this pretty bangle on its owner's pretty wrist myself." Still staring at her, he asked, "Would you mind if…I do that?"

Glued to her spot, bursting with a radiant blush, the princess couldn't speak a word. How could she deny the fascinating, delicate demand of her love? Lowering her eyes coyly, she moved her hand forward, toward the prince, and braced herself for the electrifying touch of her love.

Captivated by the heavenly beauty, the prince kept watching Princess Aryaa's face for a long time. To the west, the red sun was setting behind the green wall of trees encircling Lake Pushkar. Its glorious red hue spread all across the chamber, further enhancing the beauty of his bashful love. Under the spell of romance, the prince moved his hand forward. Holding her hand, he slipped the bangle slowly onto Princess Aryaa's hand. The fleeting touch of love wrapped both of them in the swirls of a magical world. They were being showered with pleasant stardust. The two, gliding over a soft feather, were flying into the wonderful world of love. That world was just for the two of them. Holding each other's hands, forgetting the real world around them, the two were standing in front of each other for quite some time.

As footsteps were heard outside the chamber, the prince and the princess got knocked out of their dreamy world. The prince was frantically trying to hide the princess behind a secret door, but he was surprised when the princess resisted. Smiling at him, she said, "Prince, I have a better idea." At once, the two of them were transformed into miniature forms. Glancing at the armed guards storming into the chamber, the tiny pair, riding their butterfly, flew out of the window and disappeared, leaving the stunned palace behind.

Nearing the hills near Lake Pushkar, Princess Aryaa asked, "Prince Amar, are you sure Gurudev will be here?"

"Yes, I am pretty sure. Yesterday, my loyal servant obtained this information for me." With his eyes observing a cave in the hills, the prince said, "I can see the swarm of soldiers surrounding it. Definitely this is the place!"

Dodging the vigilant eyes of the guards near the cave, the butterfly and its royal riders swooped down inside the dark cave and landed in a groove near the roof. From there the two began spying on the people below. But as soon as the princess looked down, she whispered in dismay. The frail, bruised, motionless body of Gurudev was lying on the ground. All his limbs were anchored to the surrounding boulders with thick iron chains. There were numerous armed soldiers standing around him.

"Oh! No!" She put her trembling hand over the prince's hand. Her face was frightful. "I wonder if...if he is still...alive," she whispered in a muffled voice.

"Shhhhhh..." The prince swiftly placed his hand over her mouth. Speaking under his breath, he added, "According to my mother Gurudev is alive but in a trance. She never shared this secret with Maharaaj Veersen for ... she didn't want to. Maharaaj and his men still think Gurudev is unconscious." Looking at Gurudev, he continued, "Although hard to believe, I trust my mother. She says no one can break Gurudev's trance without his permission."

"Really?" Princess Aryaa was lost in some serious thought. After a while, she said, "I think I know a way to communicate with him and bring him back."

"How?"

"According to my Guru, a person in deep trance can be reached and awakened only by following the same path...the path of meditation." Looking at the perplexed prince, she asked, "Can I try?"

"Please...please go ahead and do whatever you can to bring him back to the real world." There was urgency in the prince's voice.

The princess sat down in lotus position and began meditating. Soon she was absorbed deep into herself. And surprisingly, within a few moments, Gurudev woke up. Though his body looked devastated, his mind was extremely energetic. During his long trance, he was able to regain all his powers, previously endowed to Shivani. The stunned prince couldn't believe his eyes. He thanked the princess, who also came out of her trance. But it was nothing compared to the event he watched next. Gurudev sat up smiling and touched a spot in between his eyebrows on his forehead with his right hand. At once there was an amazing transformation in his body. His previously bruised, wrinkled body was transformed into a healthy one, glowing with its uniquely spiritual hue.

The magical sight even mesmerized the princess. "Amazing! Magnificent! Prince, do you see? This is the power of meditation!"

As Gurudev got up, all the iron chains pinning his limbs were instantly broken. The dumbfounded prince was watching the unimaginable events with a stunned face, as if he was watching a series of magical spectacles. But he wasn't the only one. The surrounding guards, too, were dazed. Leaving them frozen in surprise, Princess Aryaa and Prince Amar, after returning to their original forms, walked near Gurudev.

"Gurudev, I am Prince Amar." Bowing down in front of him, the prince added, "And this is Princess..."

"Princess Aryaa." Gurudev completed Prince Amar's sentence. Watching his surprised face, he smiled and continued. "Princess Aryaa and I just had a talk." He placed his right hand on their heads and said, "Bless you, my children." Then in a serious tone, he added, "As per Princess Aryaa's information, I just came to know Shivani has gone to Kalkoot's mansion at Mount Giri. If that is true, she is in grave danger." While talking to them, a past event flashed in his mind.

Soon after Shivani's arrival to his Aashrum, he was compelled to make Shivani's horoscope. The reason was clear. Around the period of Shivani's birth, he had witnessed many dramatic events happening, such as her miraculous rescue by a wild tigress, a guardian cobra, and her unique vermilion birthmark on her forehead. Looking at the excellent planetary positions at her birth, he became overjoyed. It was the greatest astrological chart he had ever seen, indicating an exclusively successful and long life ahead. But there was an exception.

During her life, there was an ominous period, which could be life-threatening to her.

As the memory flashed in his mind, Gurudev shook his head in despair. That dangerous period was clearly coinciding with the current circumstances. Instantly he exclaimed, "I must go now. I must reach Shivani, at once."

Sensing the extreme urgency in his voice, the princess offered her help. In the blink of an eye, the three tiny forms flew out of the cave, leaving the baffled soldiers behind.

CHAPTER TWENTY-FIVE

VENTURING INTO THE DEATH

Still wondering about the sudden disappearance of Veersen, Shivani climbed off the chariot. Her surroundings were totally devoid of any movement or sound. The recently happened sunset was further adding eeriness to the region. A little away from her spot, Kaalkoot's black mansion was brightly illuminated against the increasing darkness. She looked at it.

"Definitely that spooky mansion has some connection with Veersen's disappearance." Thinking to herself, Shivani began walking toward the mansion. After a while she reached the main entrance. The guards at the door were still sleeping under the spell of her Mohini-astra, just like the others. She lingered momentarily and then peered through the half-open door. Similar to the outside, there wasn't any sign of life visible inside. Gazing one more time at the darkened sky, she entered the mansion with her grip tightened around her bow.

The mansion indeed was very beautiful. There were multiple chambers designed with sumptuous furniture; fancy, rich draperies; majestic floor rugs; gorgeous chandeliers; magnificent sconces; and vibrant paintings on the walls. Although Shivani was dazed by the extravagance, the subtle existence of darkness cautioned her. With a brave face, she kept walking. But even after having walked through all the chambers on all of the four floors of the mansion, she couldn't find any living being residing there. During the whole walk through, she was neither welcomed nor prevented by anyone.

"This is definitely strange...very strange," she whispered nervously, returning to the main entrance. Then all of a sudden she had a wonderful idea, and her eyes sparked with excitement. "I will use my special weapon—a Margadarshak arrow—a guide arrow, to find Veersen's location." With enthusiasm, she held her bow in front of her. As she finished chanting the mantra, a red, glowing stick shaped like an arrow appeared on her bow. After being shot, the red stick soared up to the lofty ceiling and then slowly began gliding down. Shivani's expectant eyes were following the guide arrow. After having circled a couple of times at the main entrance, the guide arrow began advancing toward the upper levels of the mansion.

Walking up the elegant stairs, Shivani was following the guide arrow. On the third floor, the Margadarshak arrow entered a chamber. It was the most luxurious suite of the mansion, at least Shivani thought so. After entering, the guide arrow kept circling over and over again in the chamber and dashing against the walls. The perplexed Shivani was following every single movement of the arrow.

After a while, the red arrow halted at a painting hung on one of the walls.

A beautiful garden filled with colorful flowerbeds was displayed in the painting. The painting was so huge that it covered the whole wall. There were tiny birds hovering over the flowerbeds. The guide arrow, after tapping on various birds, now settled on the eye of one of the birds and started flashing. The excited Shivani raced to the wall. She groped around the spot to find out if there was a secret key or a hole, but she didn't have any luck. Then she gently pressed over the guide arrow itself and in a flash, the entire wall began sliding aside, revealing a hidden passage.

Gasping in surprise, Shivani watched the secret way appearing before her eyes. Soon the wall stopped gliding, and silence once again reined over the mansion. The only sound was of Shivani's thumping heart. Coming closer to the edge of the secret passage, she peeked inside cautiously. It was pitch black. While she was still staring into the dark passage suspiciously, the guide arrow had already entered. After taking a deep breath, she too dashed inside and resumed following the arrow.

After having crossed a narrow hallway, Shivani reached a relatively open place. In the red glow of the guide arrow, she observed the area. The roughly circular area was bounded on all sides by tall, dark walls. In the center of the circular space was a pond, filled with murky-looking water.

"It smells extremely bad in here," Shivani scoffed with frown lines on her forehead. Just then, she realized the guide arrow was flashing and twirling over the center of the pond. She looked at it for a moment and instantly shot an arrow at the center. In the blink of an eye, a structure began emerging from the pond.

"Oh, my goodness." To suppress her scream, Shivani put her hand over the wide open mouth and kept staring at the now fully emerged statue.

"To me…it looks like a statue of a crocodile, standing upright," she exclaimed with her eyes stretched as wide as possible. The two green, glowing eyes on the crocodile statue were scanning the entire space. Soon the crocodile began opening its mouth. Eventually the lower jaw of the crocodile reached the edge of the pond, just a few steps away from the point where Shivani was standing. Watching that, Shivani reflexively jerked back in caution. But the guide arrow had no dilemma. As soon as the crocodile's jaw opened completely, the red, glowing stick darted inside.

Glancing around and merely imagining being inside the mouth of that spooky-looking crocodile, Shivani momentarily quivered, but steadying her grip on the bow, she stepped inside onto a circular staircase. At that very moment, the crocodile closed its mouth completely and the staircase began moving down speedily. Wrapped up in the jet black darkness, Shivani had no choice but to keep standing, braced for the next challenge. Each and every nerve in her body was tightened, and her heart was racing frantically.

Just then, her red guide arrow sparkled from a corner. A subtle smile flashed on her face. She instantly felt secure in its company. It reminded her of Veersen and her goal. As she closed her eyes, Gurudev's advice boomed from the recesses of her mind.

"Shivani, stay focused on your goal. It will give you courage. In the darkness, your goal will be your Guru. It will become your strength and pull you out of uncertainty and hurdles. It will guide you to success; remember this."

Gurudev's words at once eased her scared mind, and she regained control of her senses as well as the situation. Staring at the red arrow, she stood with determination in the moving darkness. As the staircase stopped moving she, along with her guide arrow stepped out cautiously.

The spot dimly lit with green light where Shivani landed was several feet underground. She looked ahead. It was a huge, cavernous place. Suddenly a whiff of a stale, stinky smell whipped the air. Wrenching her face in disgust, she swiveled her head around. There was nothing or no one in sight except for a subtle ghostly feeling. Shrugging the fear once again, Shivani focused her eyes on the red, glowing stick. Flickering with enthusiasm, it was swiftly moving forward, sneaking through the net of tunnels with confidence, as if it had been there several times before and knew each and every turn. Trusting it, Shivani, too, was vigilantly venturing into unknown territory.

"Without this arrow, I wouldn't have found this place." Admiring her smart choice of using the Margadarshak arrow, she praised herself. That helped to enlighten her thumping heart.

Suddenly a whisper from the back froze her at once. She looked around. There was no one. As she resumed her course again, the same sound was heard, but now it was in multiples. "There is definitely someone around me whispering. I am sure, without any doubt." As she spun around swiftly, the whispers stopped. Staring with a brave face, she observed again, but there was no one around. Just then someone laughed on her right side. Holding her breath, she jerked in that direction. Nothing was there except the darkness. "I think the darkness is alive here."

The perplexed Shivani decided to ignore the whispers and resumed her path because she didn't want to lose sight of the guide arrow. Surprisingly, the whispers and suppressed laughter also started accompanying her. Shrugging her shoulders, she muttered, "As long as they stay away from me, I won't mind." With each step, the cacophony was increasing. Braving them, Shivani kept pursuing the stick. Then suddenly, a pair of human feet—just the feet, without a body—walked across her path. While still glued to her spot in fear, she witnessed another stunning sight. Wearing a wild grin, a human skull glided by her side. That was followed by riotous laughter from the invisible crowd around her.

The scared Shivani controlled herself from screaming. Wiping her sweaty face, she closed her eyes and remembered Gurudev. The next moment, pushing away all the fear and holding tightly to her mind, she started walking again. Undeterred by multiple human limbs walking along with her and frequently crossing in front, she kept coursing toward her goal.

As she was moving deeper and deeper inside, the green light intensified, and likewise, the obnoxious smell. "They seem to have a common source, probably," she muttered to herself. After having walked a little further, now she could hear some faint words being mumbled. Even amidst the whispers from the invisible crowd around her, she could easily appreciate the mumbling sound.

Shivani kept walking behind her guide arrow. As they took a left turn in a tunnel, the mumbles suddenly got stronger. Just then a gigantic spider fell down in the path ahead. The body of the spider was double the size of a human head. With its long, thread-like legs slouched all across the path, it stared at Shivani. As the frightened Shivani jumped back, she almost bumped into the floating skull. Cutting the surroundings with its frightening laughter, the skull swooped down and landed over the spider scuttling ahead. Her face grimaced in sheer disgust, and Shivani watched the pair disappear inside one of the numerous tunnels.

"I need to be more vigilant here," Shivani cautioned herself, letting out her long-held breath. She held her bow in front of her with an arrow, sitting ready to dart at the mere hint of any danger. Pivoting her head cautiously from time to time, she continued going forth. With time, her invisible companions grew in number. It was evident from the increasing chatter now, including not only whispers but sighs, laughter, clapping, shrieks, and much more. But by then, Shivani had become desensitized to them. Instead of any real danger, they were just nuisance to her.

Soon she reached a spot where the tunnel ended in a massive space. It was the point where the murmuring, the green light, and the putrid smell were all strong—maybe the strongest because it was their home. Their common source was there. Just then, one surprising thing happened. As soon as she stepped into that space her guide arrow disappeared. "So this is it. This is the place where Veersen is hiding, I am pretty sure."

Standing at the end of the tunnel, she looked ahead. The space was filled with green smoke, completely obliterating the view ahead. She paid attention to the mumbling words, but in spite of listening carefully, the words didn't make any sense to her. "Surely some kind of weird activity is going on behind the smoke, probably Veersen's immortality ritual." Shivani lurched forward in excitement with her vigilant arrow still sitting on her bow.

At that moment a screech came from behind. As she turned in its direction, something fell on her, knocking her to the ground with a thud. It was a gigantic dark cloud. Before even she realized, her faithful arrow zoomed toward the dark cloud. But unfortunately, it went through and through without any success.

Now, the dark cloud began exerting its enormous weight on her. She felt as if thousands of elephants were standing on her chest. Pinned to the ground, the immobilized Shivani stared helplessly at her bow, landed a little away from her. She was trying hard to stretch her hand up to it but couldn't. Her whole body felt paralyzed. With all her limbs splayed lifelessly, she lay on the ground and kept staring at the ghostly cloud squeezing her life out of her body. Ironically the most powerful Shree-chakra was still tied to her back, where it was poking her. There was no way to use it. Soon it started getting difficult for her to breathe.

"Maybe just a few...more...moments," she thought while gazing at the dark and ominous cloud, blinding her sight. "I can't wait for this pain and the suffering to end."

Fortunately her time hadn't come yet. Suddenly the enormous weight was lifted off her body just the way it had fallen on her. It was getting easier for her to breathe. Also, she was able to move her limbs. At once she rolled onto her side. Bracing her trembling body, she looked up. To her extreme astonishment, the dark cloud was disappearing, as if it were being sucked by yet another mysterious force. Catching her breath, the stunned Shivani got up. As she gazed through the dark cloud, fading rapidly, she couldn't believe her eyes. An arrow, hovering in midair, was absorbing and eliminating her enemy.

But that wasn't enough of a surprise to her. After a moment of shock, she jumped in exuberance and shot herself past the arrow, "Gurudev, Gurudev." The overjoyed Shivani fell down at Gurudev's feet. With streams of joy rolling down his cheeks, Gurudev put his hand over her head. "Shivani." Helping her get up, he smiled with satisfaction. "Bless you, my child. You are safe now."

Gurudev surely had arrived with impeccable timing. A few moments of delay would have been fatal for Shivani. His powerful Divya-astra had effectively consumed the ghost, saving her life. It was the same Divya-astra Gurudev wanted to teach Shivani to protect her from the ghostly powers of Kaalkoot. Unfortunately that plan got curtailed by Shivani's unexpected strife with Veersen's army, forcing her to run away from her home. Turning to Princess Aryaa, Gurudev whispered softly, "I can't thank you enough for all your help. I owe you for saving my daughter."

CHAPTER TWENTY-SIX

THE MYSTERIES UNFOLDED

Seeing Princess Aryaa and Prince Amar flanking Gurudev on either side, Shivani was further surprised. Although Princess Aryaa's arrival made her happy, she was surely worried for her safety.

"Why in the world have you come here?" Shivani whispered in a voice full of concern. She glanced at Prince Amar, whom she was meeting for the first time.

As Shivani was about to tease the princess, Gurudev's cautious words alerted her. In the lowest possible voice he said, "Never ever forget…this is the citadel of the most evil spirits."

Huddled together in a small corner, the four of them were scanning the space ahead through the bursts of green smoke. Straight ahead of them was a huge stone wall that stretched vertically from the ground, covered with dirt to the lofty ceiling above. Into that wall was built a gigantic human skull.

The very sight of the monstrous skull was enough to make anyone quiver with fright. Its huge eye sockets were oblong shaped. Each socket was roughly about the size of a small pond. An intense beam of ominous green light was radiating out from those sockets. A triangular socket for the nose, also illuminated by the green light, further added to the horror. Beneath that was a humongous opening for the mouth. The jet black color of the circular-shaped mouth was hinting at its endless bottom. In front of the skull was a semicircular platform erected on tall pillars. Encircling the skull completely, the platform was attached to the stone walls on either side of the skull. In between the skull and the platform was a deep, moat-like pit filled with numerous bones and rotting carcasses.

"So that's where the nasty smell is coming from," Shivani exclaimed softly, pinching her nose and wrenching her face. She stole a quick glance at Gurudev. He was engrossed, studying the view in front of him. Without turning his eyes away from the bones, he muttered, "It is possible that these bones and the carcasses are the human remains of...maybe of..."

Gurudev's sentence was left incomplete as his sight caught a glimpse of a person sitting on the platform with his back toward them. Facing the monstrous skull ahead, he was mumbling continuously. The words coming from his mouth sounded incoherent. From time to time, he was sprinkling some red fluid over the skull.

"It is blood, surely." As Gurudev spoke under his breath, the remaining three stared in disgust. All around the person sitting on the platform were numerous bones, with flesh still attached to them.

Without pausing in his incomprehensible speech even for a second, he was feeding the skull by throwing the bones into its dark mouth.

"Definitely, without any doubt, it is Kaalkoot. I am pretty sure." Prince Amar spoke speedily, tightening his fists. Staring ahead at the person, he continued. "I never liked him. I hate him."

While they all watched the view with a dazed stare, the skull began transforming. Its bony frame became covered with muscles, followed by skin. Big, hairy ears popped out from either side of its face. A huge, ugly nose projected forward from its socket with the nostrils flaring out rhythmically. The green eye sockets were filled with eye balls, but without eyelids. From the top of its head, the hair in the form of worms crept up. Huge, blood-red lips surrounded the mouth, which once was a dark pit in the bare skull. The lips were partially hiding the two bloody fangs, jutting forward from inside the mouth. But the most dreadful sight was a gigantic tongue, slathered with fresh, red blood, wiggling out frequently.

Shivani, unable to watch the horrifying event, gave a brisk jerk to her head. She swiveled her eyes around. Gurudev, the prince, and the princess all looked stunned, witnessing the unbelievably terrifying and grotesque scene.

"Hmmm!" Gurudev's desperate sigh instantly drew everyone's attention. "To me, the whole situation feels to be much more ghastly than previously imagined." His remarks confounded them further.

"What else could be more ghastly than this?" the prince asked, turning to Gurudev. "I mean...the skull, changing into a devil face, and Kalkoot sitting in front of it? It is absolutely..."

"Prince." Gurudev's voice was extremely serious. "Can't you see? There is one more person sitting on the platform besides Kaalkoot."

Not only the prince but Shivani and the princess too were compelled to gaze in that direction.

After carefully observing through the green fumes to the left of Kaalkoot, a person, almost completely hidden behind a tall pile of bones, was seen sitting. Gurudev's eyes were reading the prince's face. "Do you recognize him?"

"Oh, my! He is Veersen! I…I can't believe…!" Shivani blurted with widened eyes, and everyone's eyes were instantly focused on the man. She whispered, "But I am not surprised by this find. I was expecting him to be somewhere here because my guide arrow disappeared…right at this place."

As Shivani glanced at the prince, he turned his eyes down. Staring at him, Shivani said in a consoling tone, "Prince, don't feel bad. It's not your fault." Then turning to Gurudev, she added, "Gurudev, perhaps…you know it already. Kalkoot is performing a special ritual for Veersen. It's for endowing immortality to King Veersen!"

"Shivani." With a grave face, Gurudev whispered, "I feel something different is happening here." Nodding his head in dismay, he added, "Watch Veersen carefully. He has been sitting as if he were a puppet…as if he were under some evil spell." While the rest were still stunned, he continued after a pause. "Witnessing the whole scenario, I am bracing myself for the worst of my fears. It might unravel the most chilling fact…which I had suspected many years ago!"

"And what would that chilling fact be?" the Prince blurted out. Just then, a deafening roar boomed through the space. It was coming from a mammoth sized wild beast, emerging out of the mouth of the devil face in the stone wall. The beast was the guardian of the special ritual. Breathing furiously through his huge nostrils, it was staring at Gurudev and his team. After emerging completely, the beast at once charged at the enemies of the ritual—Gurudev and his team.

After having fumbled momentarily, the prince shot an arrow toward the beast, but it was at once swallowed inside its huge mouth. With a fresh bout of roars, the beast continued racing toward them. Its two sharp, long horns projecting from its head were directed toward its enemy. Undeterred, Gurudev, as well as his disciple, Shivani, continued chanting for a powerful Divya-astra that would enable them to kill the beast. Unfortunately, the beast was too fast. Before either of them could obtain the Divya-astra, the enormous beast pounced on them, knocking Gurudev down and hurling Shivani away.

As Gurudev fell down, the ground around him at once caved in, burying him completely several feet under. The thick, dark clouds of dirt engulfed the whole space, blinding everyone. Tumbling inside the huge dust ball, Shivani was frantically searching for her missing bow. In spite of calling repeatedly for Gurudev and the others, she couldn't hear any response. She started coughing violently due to the irritating fumes rising from the beast's nostrils. The beast was roaring victoriously. Unable to bear those roars, Shivani clasped her hands over her ears.

Just then, her bow happened to sparkle through the darkness. The next moment, a crescent-shaped arrow appeared and dazzled toward the beast. In a flash, it beheaded the massive beast, letting its headless body fall to the ground with a big thud. Soon the body of the beast vanished completely, along with its dark, thick dust clouds, revealing the clear view of the devil face once again.

The ceremony was still going on undisturbed, as though the participants were unaware of the whole episode of beastly strife.

Shaking her head in disbelief, Shivani got up. Her eyes were desperately searching for her friends.

After being hit by the beast, Gurudev had hunkered down, trying to save himself from the falling debris. As the landslide stopped, he hauled himself up with difficulty. Wiping the dust off, he slowly opened his eyes. It was dark everywhere. After groping around on the walls, he found that the place where he stood was a small pit, bounded on all sides by the dirt. He tried to listen carefully but couldn't hear anything except for his own breathing, as if he was buried along with the utter silence. While wondering about his teammates, he began gently tapping the walls all around him. When there was a response to his taps on the left side wall, he was startled and jerked toward it reflexively. After a few moments, that wall tumbled down and his underground pit was flooded with light.

Peeking through the collapsed wall was Princess Aryaa. She too was stunned to discover Gurudev staring from the opposite side. When the beast attacked them, they both got buried, but in their separate pits. Unlike Gurudev's, the princess's pit was partly open upwards, letting the green light to percolate through.

"I wonder if Shivani and Prince Amar also got buried somewhere around us," the princess whispered. "We should keep tapping the walls..."

"Princess!" Gurudev interrupted, staring at the fresh bout of dirt falling from the hole in the towering roof. "We must rush and climb out of this pit before getting trapped again." As the two gazed up, their serious faces suddenly began reflecting sheer joy. It was Shivani, peeking down happily through the hole. In a flash, multiple arrows swooped down toward them. The arrows were shot in such a way that a ladder was formed that stretched from the front of Gurudev up to the roof of the pit. Glancing at it contently Gurudev, along with the princess, walked up the ladder. After rejoicing for a few moments, they all began worrying for the prince. He was still absent from their sight.

"I think Prince Amar, being on my side of the beast, got hurled away similarly," Shivani said, her eyes scanning the tunnel where she previously was wrapped up inside the dirt ball. As she turned to Gurudev for his suggestions, his face alarmed her. Holding his breath, he was rooted to his spot with widened eyes focused on the devil face.

Over the site of Kalkoot's ceremony, a big swarm of ghostly shadows had risen. Screaming happily and impatiently, they were whirring over him. Kaalkoot was now mumbling in an obvious haste. Then he turned to Veersen and signaled him to come. At once Veersen sprang up from his position and began walking to Kalkoot. With his face devoid of emotions and his eyes hooked onto Kaalkoot, Veersen was slowly stepping forward.

But after halting a few steps away from Kaalkoot, he again sat down on the platform facing the devil face. Now the devil's long, blood-red tongue was squirming just a little away from Veersen's seat. Needless to say, Veersen was unaware of it. After hurling a few more bones into the devil's mouth, Kaalkoot pulled a sword out of his bag. Its sharp edge sparkled momentarily amidst the green fumes. Soon the sword settled down on the platform in front of Veersen.

"Oh, my goodness." Her face reflecting a mix of fear and disgust, Shivani screamed without her knowledge. She was too engrossed in dealing with her emotions to notice the princess walking away from them in search of the prince. Clenching her jittery fingers into a fist, Shivani looked toward Gurudev. But before Gurudev could say anything, her scream, although quite subtle, had pulled someone else's attention toward her.

The devil face had turned its two huge eyes, fuming with rage, toward her. The next moment, two intense beams of green light sparkled and converged together, creating a humongous reptile. With its forked tongue flickering in and out rapidly, it began approaching the spot where Shivani, along with Gurudev, was standing. "Gurudev," Shivani called to him softly, but there was no answer. As she turned to him, the sight stunned her at once. Gurudev was frozen at his spot after been splashed by the green light from the devil's eyes. It was the most ominous light from which no one had ever escaped except for Shivani. The powerful Shree-chakra, still tied to her back, was able to save her.

For a moment, Shivani, unaware of the Shree-chakra's effect, looked at the reptile slithering toward her. The next moment, a powerful, star-shaped Divya-astra surged from her bow toward the reptile, but then a surprising thing happened. Soon after touching the reptile's body, the Divya astra disappeared, leaving Shivani dazed. But without any delay, another powerful Divya-astra zoomed from her bow toward the slithering reptile. It too vanished in the blink of an eye.

Keeping up her hopes, Shivani kept shooting Divya-astras; each one more powerful than the previous one, toward the reptile, but there was no success. The reptile, emerged from the evil eyes, was too powerful to be destroyed by any weapon. The helpless Shivani simply kept watching the reptile advancing forth. Now, a wave of frustration, hopelessness, and resignation washed over her.

She was reluctant to use the Shree-chakra because it was reserved for its special purpose—to kill Veersen. But as a last resort, she decided to use it on the reptile. At that very moment, she got wrapped up within the deadly embrace of the reptile's coils, and they began squeezing her. Shivani was trying hard to rescue herself from the powerful squeeze, but its strength was unparalleled.

Now, the reptile, with its head very close to Shivani, was staring at her. Unable to stand the sight of its ugly, green eyes Shivani closed her own eyes tightly. Still, she could easily feel its hot breath heating up her body. Soon, her whole body was so hot that she felt as if she was standing in fire. But it wasn't the reptile that was responsible for the heat. It was the vermilion-colored birthmark on her forehead, which was glowing and generating intense heat. Her body was covered with sweat. Gasping for her breath, she reflexively opened her eyes and noticed that the reptile, with its spellbound eyes, was staring at her forehead.

The vermilion birthmark on Shivani's forehead was glowing more and more intensely every second. Its vermilion glare against the dark green background had surely captivated the reptile. Its forked tongue was curiously flickering toward it. Eventually it licked the mysterious glowing spot. At that very moment, the underground, ghastly space witnessed the most shocking event. The touch of Shivani's birthmark instantly transformed the green reptile into a garland of flowers radiating green light. With extreme disbelief Shivani kept staring at the green garland, landed around her neck. Each flower of the garland was uniquely shaped as a miniature green reptile.

Still confounded by the whole episode, Shivani suddenly remembered the frozen Gurudev and instantly shot toward the site. She had run just a few steps when she saw Gurudev walking toward her. The unique birthmark on her forehead was able to break the evil spell and revive Gurudev.

"I am happy to see you safe, Shivani."

"I am happy to see you safe too, Gurudev." Shivani spoke with surging exuberance.

Gurudev and Shivani, wondering about the princess and the still-absent Prince Amar, walked back toward the devil face. Now, in front of them on the platform, was Kalkoot standing up. The pile of bones lying near him was almost gone. After feeding the last bone to the devil, he walked to Veersen.

"Shivani," Gurudev whispered, without turning his eyes away from Veersen, "Believe it or not, Kaalkoot is going to sacrifice Veersen to the devil face."

"Sacrifice!" Shivani whispered fearfully. "But Gurudev, why would he do that?"

"He wants to become immortal," Gurudev answered very quietly.

"So this whole ceremony of immortality is for Kaalkoot and not for Veersen?" Shivani was trying hard to keep calm and not reveal her shock.

"Yes, Shivani!" Gurudev's voice was very serious. While talking to Shivani, his eyes were scanning every action of Kaalkoot. He was muttering very softly as if talking to himself. "Long, long ago, I had read about this ceremony, the ceremony of immortality. According to the book, in the past, some humans, with the help of monstrous aliens, tried to perform such ceremonies. The person seeking immortality has to sacrifice about five hundred kings' heads to the devil face. And..." Gurudev lowered his voice. "The ritual must be completed by sacrificing an emperor's head. As far as I remember, till now, Kaalkoot has helped Veersen defeat about five hundred kings. After defeating them, they all were presented to Kaalkoot."

"Why?"

"Because Kalkoot had requested it. It was an understanding between Veersen and Kalkoot. Kalkoot would help Veersen to win the war and, in return, would get the defeated king as a gift. But no one, not even Veersen, knows what happened to all the defeated kings after been gifted to Kalkoot." After a quick pause, Gurudev continued. "I am sure they all, five hundred kings, died here. And recently I came to know that Veersen has been announced as an emperor."

Shivani looked at Gurudev's face. Although unbelievable, the mind-boggling puzzle pieces could be easily connected to each other. Squinting toward Kaalkoot, Shivani whispered, "Now I know why Kaalkoot was helping Veersen to win the wars. That way he could obtain his trust as well as the sacrifices for his ceremony. His loyalty was a disguise. Also, it is easy to understand the motive behind Kaalkoot's extreme interest in making Veersen an emperor. It is the last and most crucial requirement for his immortality ritual. Veersen was too stupid to recognize this all!" Shivani nodded her head in disbelief. "He couldn't read Kaalkoot's mind and walked himself into a trap."

With a whole different perspective Shivani looked at Veersen, whose back was toward her. The one presumed to be a 'predator' had been revealed as a 'prey'. The shrewd Kaalkoot was able to deceive the world by portraying Veersen as a predator.

"Shivani." Gurudev's voice startled the engrossed Shivani. "Our immediate action is to prevent Kaalkoot from killing Veersen and offering his head to the devil mouth. Otherwise we will have to face the immortal Kaalkoot."

Shivani conceded promptly.

Suddenly an eerie laugh from Kaalkoot boomed throughout the space. Gazing at the overjoyed ghosts above his head, he raised his hand with the sword and stood very close to Veersen. After glancing momentarily at Gurudev and Shivani for the very first time, he screamed, "Welcome, my friends." Sarcastically, he asked, "Hadn't you come to interrupt my ritual? Ha, ha, ha! Soon you will be watching your defeat and witnessing my triumph...my triumph over mortality. My friends, you have arrived at the right moment. You will watch me become immortal!"

With a swift, forceful blow, he instantly beheaded Veersen. Glancing at the head of the emperor, Veersen, falling speedily toward the desperately wiggling, blood-red tongue of the devil, the ecstatic Kaalkoot let out one more horrifying laugh. After an arduous ceremony, his long-dreamed desire of becoming immortal was getting fulfilled.

"Oh...no!" Gurudev cried with the utmost despair, gazing at the falling head of Veersen, Just when he slouched down in dismay, an arrow shimmered among the dark shadows. Swooping down momentarily, it soared up again toward the lofty ceiling after piercing through Veersen's head and carrying it along. Before anyone realized it, Veersen's head, instead of falling into the devil's mouth, landed on the ground away from the devil. It all happened in a flash. The bloodthirsty tongue of the devil went inside the mouth, never to come out again. The ceremony of immortality was interrupted forever.

Standing a little away, Shivani glanced at Veersen's head, tumbling in the dirt, and smiled with pride and satisfaction. Her arrow had accomplished its mission precisely. After coming to his senses, Gurudev couldn't contain his joy. But before he could reach Shivani to congratulate her, the space was shattered by the angry screams of the frustrated and livid Kaalkoot. His ritual of immortality, planned with the utmost care, was ruined in a moment. His lifetime goal was devastated in a flash.

Maddened with anger he picked up a dagger, lying nearby. After casting a spell, he hurled the dagger toward Shivani. Before she realized it, the dagger had already reached her. But the moment it touched her body, the dagger fell to the ground. That stunned not only Shivani but Kaalkoot too. His deadly spell had become ineffective, which had never happened before. While the dazed Kaalkoot kept staring at Shivani, Prince Amar, raising his sword and screaming with revenge, suddenly darted toward him.

After being attacked by the beast, Prince Amar, similar to Gurudev and Princess Aryaa, was buried underground. He was desperately trying to escape from his underground pocket and eventually became successful. After climbing up to the surface, he realized that he was separated far, far away from the rest of his teammates. His desperate calls went unanswered. Tracking the faint mumbles of Kaalkoot, and of course the green light, he began heading back toward the platform.

After struggling through the puzzling maze of tunnels, he eventually succeeded in reaching the main area where the ritual was going on. Completely ignorant of Kaalkoot's intentions of sacrificing Veersen, he reached the spot just in time to witness the brutal beheading of his father King Veersen by Kaalkoot. Instantly his young blood started gushing with anger at the fraudulent Kaalkoot. Raising his sword, he impulsively raced to Kaalkoot.

For the frustrated Kaalkoot, the prince presented himself as an easy target. He wiggled his fingers to create a massive fireball and threw it at the prince. The fireball dashed into the prince, inflicting a fatal blow. Kaalkoot began screaming happily. Before Shivani or Gurudev could interrupt the deadly attack, the prince was hit by the fireball and fell to the ground lifelessly.

"Shivani." Ignoring the victorious laughter of Kaalkoot, Gurudev turned to Shivani and suggested, "I will take care of the prince. You should go after Kaalkoot. Kill him before he can escape." Gurudev's voice was full of urgency.

Racing forth, he instantly lifted up the prince and walked away toward a distant tunnel. Kaalkoot's hysterical laughter was echoing throughout every tunnel in that dark place.

CHAPTER TWENTY-SEVEN

THE MISSION ACCOMPLISHED

Shivani was walking toward Kaalkoot, who was standing on the semicircular platform. Watching her face, gleaming with confidence, his laughter quickly evaporated. This was the girl whom he had been trying to kill for many years. Ever since he had heard from his deity—the devil face—that Shivani, although then unborn, would be a threat to his life, he had been preoccupied with plans to kill her. Protecting himself from any suspicion, the shrewd Kalkoot was able to convince Veersen that the unborn child of Himraaj and Saritaa-Devi would be ominous for Veersen's life as well as for his kingdom and must be killed. That led to Veersen's decision to pursue and kill Himraaj and Saritaa-Devi in Raat-Raan.

Unfortunately for Kaalkoot, Saritaa-Devi survived long enough to give birth to Shivani. While her parents died, Shivani, the chosen one, was saved by mysterious forces of Mother Nature. Since then, no matter how hard Kaalkoot tried to kill Shivani, he failed repeatedly. Now, the same girl was walking toward him. Many years ago, that was the scene he had envisioned in his dream, and to his despair, it had become alive.

The nervous Kalkoot tried a few more tricks to save himself from the wrath of Shivani but failed again and again. The undeterred Shivani kept moving closer and closer to him. Watching that, the panicked Kaalkoot hustled toward his deity, the devil face, and stood as close to it as possible. But he didn't know that his deity itself was now scared of Shivani, walking with the powerful Shree-chakra and wearing the green reptile garland. It had never ever seen anyone endure the green reptile's attack and survive. Its green eyes were hooked on the green garland in Shivani's neck. It knew, with the presence of that unique garland around her neck, Shivani was now invincible.

After having reached near the platform, Shivani glanced at the moat around it and paused to think about ways to cross over it. Just then a strange thing happened. The green garland from her neck glided off and transformed into a beautiful bridge spanning the moat. Astonished by the event, Shivani nodded in disbelief and walked over the bridge. As soon as she crossed the moat and reached the platform, the bridge vanished. Once again the green garland began glowing around Shivani's neck. Caressing the garland momentarily, Shivani resumed her course toward the target.

Gurudev carried the prince into one of the tunnels. In spite of his efforts, he couldn't revive him. Kaalkoot's fireball was quite powerful. Watching Prince Amar's blue face, Gurudev sadly dropped down beside the prince's body. Suddenly, he was startled by a whimpering sound coming from his left side. To his surprise he saw Princess Aryaa, standing with tears pouring endlessly from her eyes.

Consumed with worry about Prince Amar's safety, Princess Aryaa had walked away from the spot where Shivani and Gurudev stood. She searched for the prince in every possible tunnel but couldn't find him. Not only that, she herself became entangled in the complex maze of tunnels, preventing her from going back to Shivani and Gurudev. There were no sounds around her except for the echoes of her own desperate calls to her friends.

To worsen things further, her magical powers had stopped working. The last time she was able to use them was when she had flown in with Gurudev and Prince Amar to rescue Shivani from the ghostly embrace. May be that particular event stole her magical abilities, she thought. Just when she was about to give up her search, she entered a tunnel lit by the green light. Although very dim, the light helped her trace her way back. As soon as she saw Prince Amar, all safe and sound, standing at the end of the tunnel, Princess Aryaa couldn't contain her joy. The overjoyed princess dashed toward the prince, but she was a bit late. After witnessing his father's beheading, the enraged Prince Amar had already launched himself from the end of the tunnel toward Kaalkoot. Glued to her spot in terror, the princess watched the fireball hit the prince.

Now, hiding her face with her hands, the princess was sobbing hard. She couldn't even glance at the lifeless face of her love. Suddenly, something flashed in her memory, and instantly she sprang up from her spot. Without wiping her tears, she lurched toward the prince's body. As the perplexed Gurudev stood watching, the princess snatched her necklace from around her neck. Holding the pendant close to the Prince's mouth, she uncapped the pendant. The moment a drop of holy water from the planet Shreelok landed on prince Amar's lips, his face started displaying the glow of life. Within a few moments, he stood up, smiling at the princess and Gurudev. Watching her love being reborn, the princess couldn't hold back her tears of joy. The sight of Gurudev rushing forth and gathering him in a tight embrace faded behind the veil of her joyful tears. She kept thanking her mother, Maharaani Ushadevi, again and again for the pendant.

Shivani was standing on the semicircular platform directly in front of the devil face. The devil, with its green eyes, was looking at Shivani helplessly. The fear in those eyes could easily be read by anyone. Standing beside the face was Kaalkoot, quivering pathetically. He was scared and helpless, bracing for his final moment. The sweat from his face was sparkling in the green light. Shivani smiled at the dismal sight of the evil. Without turning her sight away from the devil face and Kalkoot, she untied the Shree-chakra from her back and wore it on her right index finger. At that very moment, she remembered the words spoken by her internal energy.

"The presence of Shree-chakra is essential in order to defeat Veersen, but it may not be actually used to kill him. Instead it will be used to achieve something far greater."

Standing in front of the Devil face and glancing at the Shree-chakra on her finger, Shivani now could relate to the meaning of those words. Soon the Shree-chakra started spinning around. The sparkling light from the jewels flooded the entire space. The ghostly shadows, till then happily residing in their safe haven, were alarmed by the sacred reflections of the Shree-chakra. Stumbling in a great commotion, they all started screeching horridly and ran toward their shelter—the devil face. Kaalkoot, panicked further by the screeches of his loyal ghosts, glimpsed at Shivani, wearing the Shree-chakra. Unable to watch her coming closer and closer, he shut his eyes. Just when Shivani was about to shoot the Shree-chakra, she picked up some movement on her left side. After swiveling her eyes momentarily in that direction, she smiled. There was Gurudev, walking out of the tunnel along with the princess and the prince. Seeing them all alive and well, she felt a wave of fervor surging inside her.

"Shivani, swipe the Shree-chakra in such a way that it cuts through the eyes of the devil face and Kaalkoot's body in one single blow," Gurudev ordered her.

Shivani conceded promptly, balancing the chakra over her finger. After shuffling and aiming it correctly, she shot the Shree-chakra.

With a deafening sound, a blinding light, and at a dizzying speed, the Shree-chakra at once pierced through the green, evil eyes of the devil face and Kaalkoot's body in one shot. After dazzling one more blinding flash, it darted toward the lofty ceiling. Cutting through it, the divine Shree-chakra soared toward its destination—Shreelok. It had successfully completed its mission. The evil was destroyed. Justice was done.

The astonished Shivani, along with Gurudev, Princess Aryaa, and the prince, kept staring at the ceiling for a long time; even after the

Shree-chakra vanished from their sight. For quite some time, they all stayed at their spots, engulfed by the stunned silence. Eventually Gurudev broke it. With a choked voice, he exclaimed, "Well done, my child! Congratulations!"

"Dhanyawaad, Gurudev." Her face gleaming with pride and satisfaction, Shivani jumped down from the platform and touched Gurudev's feet. "Gurudev, your blessings helped me achieve this victory." But her words didn't yet register with Gurudev. He was busy remembering his dream about the sand particle transforming into the bright, huge, glorious pearl in his hands. He could relate Shivani's face, glowing with victory, to the gorgeous pearl conquering the dark ocean.

"Oh my goodness!" Princess Aryaa's panicked words instantly jolted Gurudev out of his triumphant dream. As he glanced around, the fiery flames were seen leaping across the whole area. The extreme heat generated by the spinning Shree-chakra had erupted the fire.

"Gurudev, we should leave at once," the alarmed prince whispered.

"Yes, Prince Amar." Watching the billowing flames, Gurudev added, "Let the sacred fire purify this place. Let the fire god, Agnidev, incinerate the evil from this place."

As they all were walking away, Gurudev suddenly stopped. There in a corner, was the lifeless head of Veersen, slathered in dirt and blood. Throwing a pitiful glance at it, he muttered, "In the whole world, Veersen trusted one and only one person. That person was Kaalkoot. Ironically the very same person led him to this dire state."

Sighing softly, he picked up Veersen's head gingerly. At once, Prince Amar blurted out, "Gurudev, please drop the head of that cruel monster." He was bursting out with anger. "He has received the proper punishment for his spiteful and bestial deeds. I...I have no sympathy for him at all."

"Prince." The calm voice of Gurudev echoed through the flames. "I totally agree with you, prince. Veersen was merciless to me, to you, to Shivani, to Princess Aryaa, and to the rest of the world. He was an enemy to the whole humanity. But his death has wiped out the past. Remember, animosity ends with death." Having said so, Gurudev walked toward the nearby fire carrying Veersen's head in his hands and placed it in the flames.

The prince wasn't yet satisfied fully. Avoiding looking at Gurudev, he turned his unhappy face away. As Gurudev put his hand over the prince's shoulder, smiling at him, he said humbly, "Prince Amar, please learn to forgive, no matter how difficult you may find it."

Leaving the fire to conquer the underground malevolence, they all came up into the light. No one spoke. As they glanced up, the darkness of the sky was fading away. The light colored blue sky was announcing the end of the evil night. That lightened up everyone's faces. Finally lifting up the veil of vicious darkness, the auspicious dawn was now arising. Beyond the horizon, the sun's rays were anxiously waiting to witness the evil-free world.

Shivani happily closed her eyes. Drawing the fresh, pleasant, cold air into her lungs, she took a deep breath. Just then someone pounced on her and knocked her to the ground. It was Jwala—her mama tiger.

"Jwala!" She screamed excitedly. Jwala was licking Shivani's face, hands, legs, and her whole body. Shivani sat up with difficulty and began caressing Jwala's back. Just then Naagraaj slithered up her legs. "Oh, Naagraaj, you too!" Picking him up, she whispered, "How in the world did you come here? How did you find me?"

Flickering his tongue out, Naagraaj was staring at the birthmark on Shivani's forehead, glowing brightly.

Kissing Naagraaj's head, she said, "I missed you so much." But that wasn't enough. Soon she realized that Jwala and Naagraaj were not the only ones reaching for her. With her eyes widened in surprise and disbelief, she glanced around to see her animal friends, anxiously waiting for their turns. Soon she was knocked down again by her overjoyed friends. From a distance, Gurudev was watching the scene with misty eyes.

"Surely Jwala and Naagraaj led them all here," he whispered to himself. Long ago, he became aware of the special bond between Shivani, Naagraaj, and Jwala. The glow from Shivani's vermilion birthmark had always helped Naagraaj and Jwala to sense the dangers around her and the necessity for their help. Not only that, but it would also lead them to her location, precisely. This had been going on since Shivani's birth. Of course Shivani wasn't aware of it. Wiping his eyes, Gurudev walked to the animals. After looking at him, they all gathered around him. Now, it was his turn to get pounced upon.

"Princess Aryaa, you have obliged all of us by saving the life of our crown prince, Amar, and helping Shivani. How can we ever repay these obligations?" Gurudev whispered emotionally, going near Princess Aryaa.

"Gurudev, please don't make me feel embarrassed." The princess spoke in a very sweet voice. "I really don't deserve this much praise."

"Your humility is admirable." Blessing her, Gurudev said, "Your parents are very lucky to have you as their daughter. They must be missing you." Then turning to the prince, he said, "Prince Amar, we need to get ready for Princess Aryaa's grand farewell. You, being the new king of Suvarna-Raaj, need to make the necessary arrangements."

"Yes...no...G...Gurudev!" The prince was fumbling pretty badly. He wanted to say something, but wasn't able to find the proper words. "I mean, no problem...at all! Why not? May be she..." His hesitant face and incoherent speech puzzled Gurudev.

After exchanging glances with him, the princess came forward. Smiling at Gurudev, she said, "Gurudev, thank you, so much for thinking about my farewell. But there is really...no hurry. I...I can stay a little longer."

"No...no!" Gurudev was serious. "I am aware of your promise. You promised your parents that you would return home soon after Shivani's mission. We should never, ever break our promises."

"Gurudev." The princess too began struggling to find the words. "I...I can go, or stay here. I mean, why not? Should I...go or not?"

Gurudev was looking at the prince and the princess turn by turn. Nothing was making any sense to him. Their bewildered speeches perplexed him. Just then, a riotous laughter startled all of them. It was Shivani. She was enjoying the drama of irrelevant and complicated conversation. Bursting out with uncontrollable laughter, she was glancing mischievously at the bashful faces of the prince and the princess, as well as the puzzled face of Gurudev.

"What's the matter, Shivani?" Gurudev asked. "These two are all confounded, and you are laughing! I...I am unable to understand anything...anything at all!" Gurudev, renowned for his knowledge and wisdom, was frustrated with the whole scenario. He was looking for Shivani's help to understand the situation.

After controlling her laughter, Shivani stole a quick, naughty glance at the princess and said, "Gurudev, I think Princess Aryaa doesn't want to leave our earth. She is in love with the earth!"

"Princess," Gurudev said in a soothing and consoling voice, "My child, you need to return home now. I can sense the anxiety of your parents. In the future, you can visit us anytime you want to." His sentence made the prince more baffled and the princess more bashful.

Witnessing that, Shivani let out a renewed bout of riotous laughter. Then, taking a deep breath, she said, "Let me put it straight. Gurudev, instead of a farewell ceremony, we need to arrange a different ceremony for the princess."

"What?"

"A wedding ceremony! The wedding of Princess Aryaa with Prince Amar!"

"But you didn't tell me...I...I was not aware. No one ... told me...never...why ... you!"

"Oh, no. Not you too, Gurudev!" Shivani kept her hand on her head. "Now, you too have started speaking like them." And she began laughing. Soon everyone joined her.

CHAPTER TWENTY-EIGHT

THE CELESTIAL CELEBRATION

The joy was embracing the entire kingdom of Suvarna-Raaj. The evil empire was demolished. The ceremonies for the coronation as well as the wedding of the new king were ongoing. The energetic skies were swarmed with birds gliding across. Apart from singing their sweet melodies, they were hustling to spread the exciting news to the world. The breeze was also helping to permeate the joyfulness to the neighboring kingdoms. Shining in the azure blue skies, the sun was enjoying the glimpse of happiness bursting on the earth.

In the cheerful kingdom of Suvarna-Raaj, each and every house was embellished with festive decorations. Panels of colorful flowers and fabric flared on the entrances of houses. The ground in the front yard was sprinkled with auspicious saffron-water, imparting its special fragrance to the air. Various designs made with colorful sand—Rangoli—were displayed on it. The frenzied people, clad in their best dresses and wearing expensive jewelry, were streaming through the streets, dancing and singing merrily. The ecstatic crowd of old, young, rich, poor, women, and men was celebrating the victory of the good over the bad and the divine over the evil. They were fervently welcoming their promising and noble future.

The capital of Suvarna-Raaj, Suvarna-nagari, being the site for all the celebrations, was embellished as a beautiful bride. Its already broad and clean roads were adorned at various spots with tall, graceful arches. Raaj- path, the main road leading to the palace, was going to host the victorious parade and hence was blossoming with festivity. The lofty arches erected at numerous places were dazzling with golden ornaments and precious stones. Flanking on either side of Raaj-path were vibrantly colored silk valances flaring all along its course. The path itself was decorated with Rangoli and colorful petals. The throngs of richly dressed people were lining Raaj- path. They were busy listening to the various announcements made by the drummers from time to time. Also, they were anxiously waiting to watch the victory procession.

The royal palace, the heart of all the excitement, was bursting with unprecedented bustle. It was rushing to gear up for the heavenly celebration. No one had time to relax or sit or talk. Everyone was trying their best to host the unique ceremony. The lavish ornaments were glowing from every chamber, hallway, and garden, all accentuating the original stateliness of the Golden Palace.

A semicircular garden on the eastern side of the palace was going to host the royal wedding. On its luscious green lawn, sitar concerts were being played. Their melodious tunes were filling the entire space. Nearby, a huge canopy resting on graceful gold columns was built. It was encased on all sides by translucent, golden sheers. The ceiling was filled with garlands of white flowers of Nishigandha. The gold columns were wrapped in red velvet, studded with diamonds. The gorgeous, red roses, blossoming in their decorative vases, were displayed at various spots. The exotic fragrance of Nishigandha flowers and the roses had swept the whole palace with romantic and mesmerizing waves.

The charming girls, dressed in pretty saris, were standing at the entrance, busy receiving the guests. Each guest was being sprinkled with perfumed water, presented with a rose, and led to their designated chair. Then the guests were served a variety of tasty appetizers and drinks. No wonder, after having been received in such a majestic manner, the guests from Shreelok were thrilled.

As the trumpets blared, sheer excitement erupted from every corner of the palace. The honorable guests focused all their attention on the small dais in front of them. Amidst the blur of frenzy, Prince Amar and Princess Aryaa arrived. The cheerful cries hailing them boomed from all directions. Surrounded by relatives and priests, Prince Amar did namaskaar to everyone and accepted their greetings. He was clad in the traditional ceremonial dress. Wearing gold chest armor, bracelets, and many other royal jewelry pieces, he was definitely looking handsome and charming. On his left side was the bride, Princess Aryaa, covered from head to toe with shimmering jewelry. Her face was glowing with the unique blend of happiness and bashfulness.

She was wearing a green sari with hints of gold. Her long, silky hair was braided loosely with a gold ribbon. All along the braids were the fragrant flowers of lavender, tucked in with diamond pins, twinkling through her hair. Hanging from her neck were countless gold necklaces of varying lengths, designs, and precious stones. Her hands were full of bangles, which tinkled delicately. The armlets, engraved with rubies, were resting on her arms while a graceful, gold waistband was glistening on her waist. Dangling from the waistband were more gold chains, tipped with rubies. The tiny gold bells on her anklets were swaying with her every move, making a melodious sound. The attendees were captivated by the sight of the divine beauty clad in the heavenly attire.

As the wedding started, the bridegroom and the bride stood in front of each other, holding a rose garland in their hands. Separating them from each other was a soft fabric panel, held on either side by the priests. Standing behind Prince Amar was his cousin sister, holding a beautiful urn filled with holy water and topped with a coconut.

Holding a similar urn behind the princess was Shivani, the adopted sister of the princess. She was clad in a rich, silky sky-blue-colored sari. For Shivani, it was the first time in her life wearing such a soft, luxurious, fine dress. In addition to that, she wore magnificent jewelry all made of pearls. As per Princess Aryaa's request, those pearls and the dress were imported from the planet Shreelok.

A little away from them, Maharaani Lalita-Devi, Prince Amar's mother, was standing along with other members of the royal family. She was glancing adoringly at her charming son and beautiful soon-to-be daughter-in-law. Princess Aryaa's parents were also admiring the pretty couple.

Soon the priests began chanting eight auspicious mantras—Mangal-ashtak. Those mantras were the blessings to the new couple, wishing them a long, happy married life. From time to time, they were sprinkling the couple with the perfumed water and flower petals. After finishing the chanting of mantras, the fabric panel separating the couple was removed. Amidst loud clapping and blaring trumpets, the couple adorned each other with rose garlands held in their hands during the chanting. Then after holding each other's hands, they circled seven times around the fire. In the presence of the sacred fire, the priests, and relatives, the newlywed couple exchanged their wedding vows and sat on their throne. The throne was the wedding gift from the princess's parents. Depicting two peacocks with their fanned-out trains joined in the center, it was definitely a majestic site.

Wiping her misty eyes, Maharaani Ushadevi whispered to her husband, "Wasn't I telling you that something good would result from our daughter's visit to earth?"

"Yes, I surely remember that." Smiling at her, Maharaaj Aditya-Raaj added, "But that wasn't your sentence. It was mine."

"You are wrong. It was my sentence. I remember it correctly."

"No...no...no! You never said that. That was me."

As the wedding ended, the grand procession began from the capital. Coursing along Raaj-path, the procession was heading toward the royal court, where the coronation ceremony was going to take place. Hundreds of decorated horses with their riders, musicians, singers, dancers, and acrobats were seen participating in the procession. They were cheered by the thousands of people lining Raaj-path.

Keeping some distance from a herd of horsemen was Guru Yogidev, standing in an open chariot. His return to the capital was definitely reassuring to all the subjects of Suvarna-Raaj. His arrival marked the beginning of a golden era. The overjoyed citizens were cheerfully welcoming him.

Following Gurudev was an ornately decorated chariot being led by five beautiful horses. In that chariot was everyone's hero—Shivani. By then, her thrilling life story and the adventurous triumph over the dark powers were well known to the world. Being that she was their savior, the people were dying to get a glimpse of her. With their eyes full of respect and admiration, the crowd was watching her pass by.

A little behind from Shivani was the royal couple, sitting in a beautiful palanquin called Ambaaree, mounted atop the stately adorned elephant. A graceful umbrella covering the palanquin was swaying gently with the majestic gait of the elephant. Throngs of people were flanking Raaj- path. They were jostling desperately to get a glimpse of the royal pair and shower the flower petals over them. The slogans hailing the new couple were reverberating throughout the entire region. The new king and queen, sitting in the Ambaaree, were accepting the greetings from their beloved citizens.

The dancers, singers, and acrobats participating in the procession were busy entertaining the huge audience gathered on either side of *Raaj- path*. The royal elephant was followed by many more chariots carrying the relatives and family members of the royal couple. The royal procession had frozen all the attendees gathered along *Raaj- path* in sheer awe. They kept staring at the site, even after the majestic procession concluded.

At the royal court, the new king and queen arrived amidst their relatives and priests, chanting mantras. Walking along the lavish red carpet, the royal couple was led to the dais holding their thrones. The whole court was full of honorable invitees, including the courtiers, the representatives from various countries, and relatives of the royal couple. As soon as the couple entered, they all stood and welcomed the future king and queen.

Prince Amar and Princess Aryaa accepted their greetings and walked up to the dais. But instead of heading straight to their thrones, the two halted in front of them. Facing the audience, the prince said, "My beloved friends, I am really overwhelmed by the love and respect displayed by all of you. We both are thankful for that. Today, after being ruled by evil for decades, we are free from its dark clutches. Once again, the sunlight is sparkling on our kingdom, famous for its glorious past." Glancing around, he added, "By now, I assume that all of you are aware of the person whose daunting efforts led to this victory."

Suddenly everyone's eyes turned to Shivani, who was standing among the invitees and enjoying the festival. She had never expected to be the center of attention. She turned her perplexed face to the royal couple, who were smiling at her. She was further puzzled as the prince walked toward her. Holding her hand, he brought Shivani forth to the dais.

"My dear friends, this is Shivani—the real hero!" A loud applause boomed throughout the building. Shivani was further bewildered and embarrassed.

As the applause ebbed away, Princess Aryaa started speaking. "My friends, Shivani is really a great character. I am not saying this because she is my best friend. During her long ordeal, she has displayed the wonderful blend of bravery as well as strength of a warrior. In addition, she has a just and mature mind of a great leader. I was very fortunate to witness these amazing qualities in her. This young girl is an epitome of virtue."

"I totally agree with the princess," Prince Amar added. "Hence, today I am announcing Shivani as the ruler of Suvarna-Raaj. She is the real owner of the throne. The noble legacy of this throne of Maharaaj Dharmasen—my grandfather—will be further accentuated by Shivani's rule."

The unexpected announcement stunned the whole court, but they soon conceded in unison with the prince's decision. Soon the thunderous applause and the shouts hailing Shivani as well as the royal pair echoed from every corner.

But Shivani was completely astounded by that announcement. Throughout the whole mission, she had never, ever expected or dreamed about ruling the kingdom of Suvarna-Raaj. All she wanted was to demolish the tyrant Veersen and free the subjects. With a startled face, she glanced around for a while. Then she began speaking. "Honorable attendees, first of all, I would like to admire the prince and the princess for their extreme generosity. Offering such a huge kingdom to others is not an easy thing. Suvarna-Raaj is their true ancestral right. I am extremely thankful to them." After a quick pause, she continued. "But. . .but I can't accept this offer."

Once again the royal court was stunned into silence. The prince, quickly overcome with emotion, blurted, "Shivani, you have won the battle and thus earned this throne. Now it is your right. How can I offer your own prize to you? This kingdom is yours now."

"Prince." Smiling at him, Shivani said, "I have only accomplished my duty as a citizen of this kingdom. Suvarna-Raaj was, is, and will remain yours." Leaving the puzzled prince staring at her, she placed his hand in the princess's hand and announced, "The new king and queen may proceed to the throne now. All eyes, including mine, are waiting to get a glimpse of the royal couple seated on the throne."

Standing among the priests, Gurudev was witnessing the unprecedented incident with disbelief. Slowly walking to the front, he blessed the prince and Shivani. His humble voice started reverberating. "My fellow citizens, I think we are surely stepping into a golden age. Until now, we all have been witnessing and hearing about the fights over the throne. But today is a special day for us to witness the most exclusive fight. This fight is over offering the throne to the opponent."

Clearing his choked voice, Gurudev added, "I respect these two noble persons of Suvarna-Raaj. I hope all of us will be able to imbibe this unselfish heritage into our minds." The grand ovation kept echoing throughout the court for a long time. As per the advice of Gurudev, eventually the prince and the princess started walking toward the throne to become the king and queen of Suvarna-Raaj.

Amidst the auspicious chants, the coronation ceremony began. The holy waters collected in huge golden urns from the seven rivers and the three oceans were being sprinkled onto the heads of the new king and queen. The thrilled audience was watching the grand event with their dreamy eyes. Standing with everyone there was Gurudev, enjoying the ceremony. Needless to say, he was the most content person on Earth.

As he glanced around, Shivani's absence was quickly picked up by his eyes. With a puzzled face, he walked out of the court and began looking for her. Finally he found her. Along with all her animal friends, Shivani was sitting in the garden outside the banquet hall, enjoying the grand feast. The enormous joy was spilling over there and spreading over the entire kingdom.

CHAPTER TWENTY-NINE

THE GOLDEN ENCOUNTER

Christina closed the book but kept staring at it for a while. Her mind was still thinking about Shivani. As she put the book down and glanced at the clock, she was stunned. "I have been reading for almost the whole night!" she whispered. Throwing herself back on her bed, she gazed at Shivani's profile on the front of the book. Her tiny figure held an elegant bow with an arrow, ready to take to the skies. It was the first time she had looked at the picture. The young girl on the cover, probably of her age, fascinated Christina in many ways. With her mind lost in Shivani's world, Christina closed her eyes and soon fell asleep with *The Book* lying in her lap.

Christina was fast asleep for a while and then suddenly jolted out of bed after hearing a sound outside her room. Raising her head, she glanced around, but there was no one else. It was still quiet everywhere.

"That's weird," she muttered to herself, slouching back into bed. But it happened again. This time she could clearly hear footsteps outside her room. With her heart racing, she sprang up in the bed. The footsteps stopped at her door, and she heard a gentle knock.

"Yes?" Christina answered, still sitting in her bed, bracing her thumping heart. As the door opened slowly, Christina froze in disbelief. After a while, she got up but kept staring, completely speechless. "Who...what...are ...you ...mean?" Christina was struggling to form a sentence. "Are you...?"

A naughty, riotous laughter echoed throughout the room, and the girl standing at the door entered.

"Yes, Christina. You have guessed correctly. I am Shivani."

Christina jerked her body briskly, as if trying to wake from a deep sleep. The girl walked a few steps into the room, and then suddenly stalled. There were the broken pieces of Christina's crystal unicorn, spread all over the room. The girl sat down on the floor and began picking up the pieces carefully. Soon, a small pile of the broken crystal sat near her. With Christina still watching her perplexed, the girl caressed the broken glass pieces with her hands, and Christina's most treasured crystal unicorn began to dazzle once again, in pristine condition.

Looking at the pretty unicorn, now glistening in the moonlight entering through the window, Christina jumped up from the bed. "Marvelous! Fantastic! Fabulous!" she shouted, picking it up in her hands. "How did you do that? How could...you? You are a magician! You are...amazing and wonderful!"

Watching Christina, the girl started laughing freely. Christina smiled back. "Who are you? Please tell me the truth."

"I have already told you," the girl said. "I am Shivani."

"Really?"

"Really! Believe me." The girl walked toward a corner where earlier, Christina had hurled away her necklace with the lotus pendant. Picking it up, she came near Christina. Placing it back around Christina's neck, the girl whispered, looking at the shining lotus pendant, "It looks great here. Please keep wearing it." Sitting on a nearby chair, she asked, "How are you, my friend?"

"Friend? Am I your friend?"

"Yes, Christina. You are my friend. In fact, whoever reads my book becomes my friend." Looking at Christina's perplexed face, she added, "The book that you just read is my life story. It is true."

"Your life's...true...story? Really?" With raised eyebrows, Christina asked again in a whisper, "Are you real? Have you ever lived before?"

"Absolutely, yes. Once upon a time, I used to live on the earth... far, far away from here, in a land now known as India."

"So where do you live, now? And how did you get here?"

"Christina." The girl got up from her seat and, still speaking, began cleaning up the room. "Believe it or not, I have been blessed with a special gift. Whenever someone on the earth thinks about me or remembers me, I can instantly appear in front of that person." She paused from her tidying to survey Christina's reaction.

Her eyebrows furrowed in disbelief and confusion, Christina asked, "Why do you do that? I...I mean...why do you appear in front of that person?"

The girl shrugged her shoulders. "To help that person." With a meaningful glance, she added, "So, at present, I am here to help you, my friend."

"To help me?" Christina's voice was filled with bitterness. "No... no one in this world, or from any other world, can help me. Shivani, you can't understand what I have been through."

"Christina," the girl whispered with a heartfelt sigh, "This is a misunderstanding. I know everything about you."

"Do you?" Shaking her head in disbelief, Christina asked, "How could you know?"

"That I will tell you later. But after reading my story, I am sure by now you have become well aware of my own hardships and my arduous life."

"Compared to my hardships, yours are nothing, Shivani!" Christina blurted angrily. She refused to look at the girl, instead staring at the wall across from her. "You were blessed with a wonderful teacher like Gurudev, who helped you learn the magic of archery. You had wonderful friends like Jwala and Naagraaj. They had amazing abilities, and they were able to help you when you needed them. You could travel to the planet Shreelok and obtain the divine Shree-chakra. You were victorious. You were...the hero," she ended in a sigh.

Staring straight into the girl's eyes, Christina added, "Shivani, after being blessed with all those supernatural and fantastic powers, your life was definitely much easier and comfortable than mine." Scoffing, she said with derision, "What do I have here? I don't have your treasures. I am not as lucky as you. My...my life is much harder than yours." Letting herself fall back onto the bed, she added, "No one, absolutely no one can help me."

Still cleaning up the room, the girl was quietly listening to Christina's arguments. As Christina paused, the girl looked up at her and asked, "Are you done? Can I have my turn now?" Putting all the loose papers neatly in a pile, the girl continued after getting a silent nod from Christina. "Christina, while cleaning your room, I have come across many wonderful gadgets like this television set, the air conditioner, the heater, the light bulbs, the music box, this comfortable bed, pretty dresses made of soft fabric, pretty shoes, and so many more things." Playing with the light switch, the girl suddenly exclaimed, "Wow! With just a flick of one finger, you can erase the darkness. This sure looks magical to me." Caressing Christina's soft comforter, the girl said, "When you compared your life with mine, you conveniently forgot about these wonderful things that I didn't have."

Christina's face suddenly turned guilty. She avoided looking at the girl. The girl continued. "Don't feel bad. You are not the only one doing that. The majority of people behave this way. This is human nature. We get jealous of a person for having the things we do not. That jealousy makes us forget the wonderful treasure we are blessed with but the other person lacking. Am I correct?"

Gazing out the window into the darkness, Shivani whispered, "It's unfortunate for you to deal with the sudden loss of your father." Sighing subtly, she continued. "But do you remember the story of the lucky stone from *The Book*?" Glancing at the crystal unicorn in Christina's hands, she added, "Christina, until your father's death, you were fortunate enough to be living with him and experiencing his fatherly love. His tragic death has definitely torn your life, but you should still consider yourself lucky for still having your mother, loving and caring for you. Unlike yours, my whole life, right after my birth, was devoid of a single touch from either of my parents. I was deprived of parental affection. I spent many years of my life sleeping on a grass bed and wearing dresses made from tree barks. While living in the wild, I made friends with the creatures around. They became my friends and family.

"Now let me tell you about my extraordinary skills in archery. I didn't get them as gift, but I earned them by working hard...very, very hard." The girl began speaking animatedly. "Definitely, my Gurudev was a wonderful teacher. But that's true with your teachers, too! Teachers always try to make the best of their students. Just like me, if you work hard and have faith in your Guru, you will be able to bask in success."

Slowly walking toward Christina, the girl put her hand over Christina's and said in a soothing voice, "My dear, your worst enemy is your self-pitying attitude. By playing you as victim, you end up with nothing but frustration and sadness. This frustrated mind then starts seeking targets to ease its pain." Sitting next to Christina, the girl added, "...and the easiest target for your frustrated mind is ...simply you. Then 'self-blaming' begins. You start calling yourself weak, failure, unlucky, and so on. This vicious downward spiral of self-pity, frustration, inactivity, and defeat continues on and on. Am I right, Christina?"

Without looking at the girl, Christina nodded her head slightly.

The girl brought Christina's chin up to face her. "My friend, sometimes in our lives, tragic incidents happen. They...just happen. We have no control over them. They take us down into the darkness." After a quick pause, she whispered, holding the picture of

Christina's father, "At those times, you can do one thing and one thing only. Take control of yourself. Get away from the dungeon and start walking toward the brightness."

There was silence while Shivani's words reverberated around the room. In a remorseful voice, Christina broke the quiet. "Shivani, you...you are quite right. I...I guess I am not strong enough to haul myself up from this...this corner where I have been hiding since the accident." Her voice began cracking. "I am not as brave as you, Shivani." Christina broke down in tears.

"Christina." Shaking her head in despair, the girl said, "You are a very forgetful person, aren't you?"

Christina raised her puzzled face.

A mischievous sparkle reflected in the girl's eyes, and she asked, "What did I just tell you now? Don't blame yourself for every single thing. Please don't become your own enemy." Looking straight into Christina's eyes, the girl said in a serious voice, "Listen, my friend. Here is some advice for you. Always look at the world and at yourself with a positive attitude. Focus your attention on the wonderful things around you. Concentrate on the stuff you 'can' do rather than you 'can't'." Then with a naughty twinkle, she asked, "Now can you wiggle your nose like this?'"

Christina jerked her head up to the girl. Looking at her funny face, Christina smiled.

The girl asked again, "Do you want to be like the grumpy man from the story?"

"No, of course not!" Christina blurted, flashing a pleasant smile, her first smile after many, many months. Breathing easier, she felt as if an enormous weight had been lifted off of her chest. She gazed around her room. It looked neat and tidy and clean. She got up and

327

stood by the door, surveying her room as if it were new. "Shivani, thank you...for showing me a different perspective of life. From this angle, my life looks different, quite comfortable and wonderful, too."

At once, the girl embraced Christina lovingly.

"I am so happy to see you smiling like this, C!"

"C?" Christina was startled. That was her nickname her father had given her. "You called me C. How do you know my nickname?"

"Your father told me. 'C' is a very special girl,' he said."

"My father...told you this? Do you know my father?" Christina gasped in disbelief.

"Yes! I know your father." The girl, glancing once again at Christina's father's picture, said, "Christina, he is quite happy where he is right now. His only grief is your sad face. So stop being sad and start smiling. Don't keep holding on to grief. Leave it as early as possible, and start forging ahead in your life."

Christina was staring past the girl at her father's picture now, her mouth agape slightly.

Reaching for Christina's hand, Shivani asked, "C, can you promise me this?"

"I promise, Shivani."

"Excellent. Now, I will leave. Bye-bye!" Shivani said as she started walking toward the door.

Christina jolted immediately and ran in front of her. "Are you leaving? Why? Can you stay a little longer?"

"I would love to, but I have a few more friends to visit." Placing 'The Book: Legend of Shivani' in Christina's hands, the girl said, "They, too, are thinking about me and remembering me."

Shivani opened the door into a bright light and dissolved, leaving behind ephemeral gold twinkles. Christina stared at the spot where the girl had sat. Looking back at the door, she thought Shivani had forgotten something in her haste. Hurrying to the spot, Christina bent down and picked up a small, delicate Prajakta blossom. The tiny flower had just bloomed, and the soft, curvy petals were fully open, proudly magnifying its glory. Her face breaking into a soft smile, she cupped the flower and lay back down on her bed, still staring at the door. But soon she fell asleep. It was a pleasant sleep, full of bliss.

Christina woke up but lay for a while in her bed. Squinting at the sunlight entering the room through the closed curtains, she was still thinking about the dream. "It was a silly dream." She whispered, smiling. Walking to the window, she moved the curtains aside. Soon her whole room was flooded with splendid, golden rays of sunshine. Her mind still in the dream, she sat down on her bed. Her eyes, swiveling over her room, suddenly paused. The sight left her astonished. Her previously messy, cluttered room was now clean and neatly organized, just the way she saw Shivani cleaning in her dream.

"It can't be real." Christina shook her head in disbelief. She looked at her table and instantly sprang up. There on the table was the crystal unicorn, dazzling joyfully in the sunshine. Stunned, she began walking toward it.

"It was definitely broken last night. I...I still...surely remember." Grabbing the unicorn at once, she muttered, "But then...Shivani came and joined it...piece by piece." Kissing the unicorn, she looked at her dad's picture. His face was radiant with a beautiful smile. "Unbelievable!" Taking a deep breath, still holding the unicorn, she sat down on a nearby chair. Her eyes were inspecting the unicorn minutely. It was glowing in pristine condition. "Did I break it in my dream? Or did I break it in real life and it magically got fixed by Shivani?" Christina kept thinking. She looked around and whispered, "And my room too! It looks very clean and organized, just the way Shivani cleaned it in the dream. Maybe that wasn't a dream at all, and she really came here. Did she really come here?" Christina's mind was spinning with a jumble of thoughts.

"Christina...honey!" She heard her mother calling from the kitchen. "Are you awake now?"

"Yes, Mother!"

"Please come down. Breakfast is ready."

"Coming, Mom." Christina excitedly bounded down the stairs, almost knocking her mother over when she entered the kitchen.

"Good morning, Mom! Good morning, Aunt Sheila." Flashing a nice smile, Christina entered the kitchen.

Her bright smile stunned her mom as well as her Aunt Sheila. They exchanged looks and then kept looking at her without saying anything, as if they were looking at her for the first time. This was a different Christina standing in front of them. Ann didn't want to take her eyes off her daughter's radiant face. After regaining some control over her surprise, Aunt Sheila replied, "Good morning, my child. How are you?"

"Great." Christina replied, pouring milk into her cup.

"You look quite energetic today," Sheila said. "I bet you had a good sleep last night."

"You are right. I really had a nice sleep. Not only that, but I had a lovely dream too."

"Oh, I see!" Sheila said after taking a sip of her tea.

"And Aunt Sheila, remember the book that you gave me yesterday? I liked it a lot. Last night I read the whole book! It is quite entertaining and interesting."

"You read the whole book?"

"Yes! I loved it."

"Oh, I see! That's why you got up so late today."

Christina glanced at her Aunt Sheila's naughty face and smiled. It reminded her of Shivani's naughty face. Just then, Christina walked to the window and peeked through it.

"Oh! It's Liz!" A girl her age was playing basketball in the back. Seeing her classmate excited Christina to no end. Swirling around, Christina grabbed her mother. "Mom, can I go out and play with her?"

Until then, Ann had been speechlessly scrutinizing Christina. It was the old, jumpy, bubbly girl she used to know. Pulling herself together, she answered, "Yes, honey. But would you first finish your breakfast?"

"Oh, yes! Of course," Christina said.

After Christina left, the two sisters sat side by side looking out the window. For a while, neither of them said a word. Then, with a choked voice, Ann broke the silence. "Sheila I...I think I got my Christina back."

"I think so, too!" Wiping the corners of her eyes, Sheila whispered in a crackly voice, "Ann, can I tell you something?"

"Of course!"

"While I was in India, I came across a strange report about *The Book: Legend of Shivani*. It said that after reading this book, many children with behavioral problems have shown dramatic improvement."

"I...I don't believe in that, Sheila."

"Even I didn't believe in it until now. I dismissed the report as ridiculous and didn't give it a second thought." Looking into Ann's eyes, Sheila whispered, "Ann, you know me very well. I never buy these silly rumors. I had forgotten all about it until now." Watching Ann's serious face, she continued. "This morning, we both witnessed a dramatic change in Christina's behavior."

Rising up from her seat, Sheila went to the window. Christina was giggling happily with her friend. With a smile on her face, Sheila closed her eyes contently. Turning to Ann, Sheila said, "Ann, last night, after seeing Christina, I couldn't sleep at all. She wasn't my happy, exuberant, bouncy Christina that I saw last time. She was a heartbroken, grief-stricken zombie! But this morning, the same girl appeared—a joyful girl." After a quick pause, she asked, "Do you have any explanation for the sudden transformation of a grief-stricken girl into an energetic, bouncy girl overnight?"

Ann was shaking her head.

Sipping her tea again, Sheila said, "And...the moment she told me about reading *The Book: Legend of Shivani*, I was compelled to connect her magical transformation with the report. It sounds unreal, but..."

"Sheila," Ann interrupted. Her voice was heavy. "Whatever the reason may be...I don't care. I am surprised and very happy right now. If the legend of Shivani is true, then..." She cleared her voice and looked through the window again, to a part of her life she had been missing for the past few months. "...then I am really thankful

to Shivani for bringing my daughter back to me and...back to life."
Ann let the tears roll down her cheeks. Those tears washed away a
mother's worries and made her ready to witness her child's radiance.
Christina's laughter from outside poured through the window.

GLOSSARY OF INDIAN WORDS

Name	Sanskrit Meaning and Reference in the Book
Shivani	(**Shee-vaa-nee**) Wife of Lord Shiva; main character in the book
Aditya-Raaj (Aa-dee-tya-raaj)	Aditya = Sun, Raaj = King; King of alien planet Shreelok
Aryaa (Aa-r-yaa)	A woman of Aryan origin; name of the princess of alien planet-Shreelok
Apsara (Up-su-raa)	Beautiful woman; dancers of Sangeet arena on planet Shreelok
Amar (u-mu-r)	One who never dies; name of the prince and son of King Veersen
Aashrum (Aa-sh-r-m)	A hut for a sage; Shivani's neighborhood

Agni-baan (Ugnee-baan) Agni = fire, baan = arrow; a weapon, a fiery arrow acting as a space shuttle

Aagneya-astra (Aa-gne-yaa-stra) Agneya = fiery, astra = weapon; a kind of Divya-astra

Ambaree (Um-baa-ree) Elegant seat/ throne on the back of elephant

Dev (dev) Dev = god; a respectful address to a man

Devi (de-vee) Devi = goddess; a respectful address to a woman

Dharmasen (dhu-r-m-say-n) Dharma = religion, justice; one who follows justice; Veersen's father

Dhanyavaad (dhu-nya-waad) Thank you

Divya-astra (dee-vyaa-ustra) Divya = divine, heavenly, astra = weapon; divine weapons in archery, used by Shivani

Dhawal (Dhu- wu-l) White ; one of Shivani's white-rabbit friends

Dhoomrastra (dhoo-mraa-astra) Dhoomra = smoke, astra = weapon; a kind of Divya-astra

Dhoti (Dhoa-tee) Dhoti = traditional men's garment; used by the priest on planet Shreelok

Gurudev (goo-roo-dev) Guru = teacher, dev = god; Shivani's teacher

Guru (goo-roo) Teacher ; a title of Yogidev

Giri (gee-ree) Mountain; a mountain in Suvarna-raaj

Himraaj (heem-raaj) Heem = snow, raaj = king; Shivani's father

Jwala (Jwaa-laa) Jwala = flame; tigress's name, Shivani's foster mother

Kalkoot (kaal-koot) Kaal = death; name of King Veersen's magician

Krurvarmaa(koo-r-wur-maa) Kroor = cruel; King Veersen's army officer

Lalitadevi (lu-lee-taa-de-vee) Lalita = woman, devi = goddess; King Veersen's wife

Mayur (mu-yoo-r) — Peacock; Shivani's peacock friend

Mahatejaa (mu-haa-tay-jaa) — Maha = great, tejaa = awe; name of the river

Mahaatmaa (mu-haa-t-maa) — Maha = great, aatmaa = soul; a title given to Guru Yogidev or Gurudev

Mahaaraaj (muhaa-raaj) — Maha = great, raaj = king; a word to address a king

Mahaaraani (muhaa-raa-nee) — Maha = great, raani = queen; a word to address a queen

Madhur — (mu-dhoo-r) Sweet; Shivani's kokil friend

Madhuban (Mu-dhoo-bun) — Madhu = sweet, ban = garden, park; King Veersen's recreational park

Mahameru (mu-haa-mey-roo) — Maha = great, meru = mountain; a mountain on planet Shreelok

Mangal-ashtak (Mung-ul-ush-tuk) — mangal= auspicious, ashtak= eight, eight auspicious mantras to be recited during an Indian wedding.

Margadarshak (maa-r-g-du-r-shuk) Guide; a guide arrow used by Shivani

Megh-land (Mey-gh-land) Megh = clouds; a fun land on planet Shreelok

Namaste (nu-mu-stey) Respectful greetings

Namaskaar (nu-mu-s-kaar) Respectful greetings

Naagraaj (naag-raaj) Naag = snake, raaj = king; Shivani's cobra friend

Naath (naa-th) Naath = sir, master; a way to address husband

Nishigandha (Nee-shee-gun-dhaa) nishi=night, gandha=scent; flowers used at princess Aryaa's wedding

Pradhaan-mantri (pru-dhaan-mun-tree) Pradhaan = chief, mantri = minister; chief of royal court of planet Shreelok

Pratismruti (pru-tee-smroo-tee) Prati = similar to, smruti = mind; a mantra to travel with speed of mind

Prajaktaa (praa-j-k-taa)	a kind of flower; flowering tree that rose from Shivani's parents' ashes
Parvataastra (pur-vu-taa-stra)	Parvat = mountain, astra = weapon; a kind of Divya-astra
Pirulok (pee-troo-loak)	Pitru = dead forefathers, lok = world; a planet where Shivani's parents lived after death
Pushkar (poo-sh-kur)	Pushkar = flower; prince Amar's floating palace
Ravaa (Raa-vaa)	Parrot; Shivani's parrot friend
Rangoli (Ru-n-goa-lee)	Designs made with colored sand; used at the coronation ceremony In Suvarna-raaj
Raaj-path (Raaj-puth)	Raaj = royal, path = road; royal road of Suvarna-raaj
Raag (Raa-g)	Raag= melodic mode used in Indian classical music; Sung by princess Aryaa
RaajGuru (Raaj-goo-roo)	Raaj = royal, Guru = teacher; royal teacher of king Aaditya-raaj

Raat-Raan (Raat-raa-n)	Raat = night, raan = forest; forest where Shivani was born
Samraat (Su-mraa-t)	A title for emperor
Sanjeevan (Sun-jee-wun)	Rising from dead; a classical ragaa sung by princess Aryaa
Sangeet-arena (Su-n-geet)	Sangit = music; an amphitheater on planet Shreelok
Saptak (Su-p-tuk)	Saptak = seven; series of seven musical notes
Saritaadevi (Su-ree-taa-de-vee)	Sarita = river, devi = goddess; Shivani's mother
Saavdhaan (Saa-v-dhaa-n)	saavdhaan = Attention; a call to warn the enemy
Seema (See-maa)	seema= Border; an arrow used by Shivani to protect her friends
Senapati (Sey-naa-pu-tee)	Sena = army, pati = chief; the chief of Veersen's army
Shreelok (Shree-loak)	Shree = auspicious, prosperous; lok= world; an alien planet with advanced civilization

Shree-chakra (Shree-chu-kra)   Shree = same as above, chakra= a circular object / weapon; Divine weapon

Shreeyans (Shree-yuns)   Residents of planet Shreelok

Shubha-prabhaat (Shoo-bh-pru-bhaa-t)   Shubha = auspicious, great; prabhaat = morning; a way to say good morning

Shubhra (Shoo-bhr-a)   shubhra= White; a name of one of Shivani's white rabbit friends

Sunetraa (Soo-ney-traa)   Su = beautiful, golden, netraa = eyes; Shivani's deer friends

Suvarna-Raaj (Soo-vur-na-raaj)   Suvarna = golden, raaj = kingdom, rule; Veersen's kingdom

Suvarna-nagari (Soo-vur-n-nu-gu-ree)   Suvarna = golden, nagari = city; King Veersen's capital

Surya-namaskaar (Soo-r-y-nu-mu-s-kaar)   Surya-sun, namaskaar = respectful salutation; a kind of yoga exercise

342

Tilak (Tee-lu-k)	A circular dot worn on the fore-head by Indians
Ushadevi (Oo-shaa-de-vee)	Usha = dawn, devi = goddess; Queen of planet Shreelok and wife of Aaditya raaj
Vimaan(Vee-maa-n)	A flying machine or aeroplane; eagle-shaped flying machines of planet Shreelok
Yogidev (Yo-gee-dev)	Yogee = one who has conquered all his emotions; dev = god; Shivani's teacher

ABOUT THE AUTHOR

Dr. Varsha Gogte-Deopujari was born in India. After earning her MD degree in ob-gyn, she practiced as a doctor for a few years in India. In 1995 she, along with her family migrated to the United States. At home, while taking care of her young children, she began writing short stories and stage plays. That opened a new field of fantasy and imagination for her. A few of her stories have earned awards.

Stories about ancient India heard from her parents and grandmother, the books read on Indian mythology as well as inventions happened in ancient India, classes taken on meditation, and the events witnessed regarding 'life and death' while working in critical care units in hospitals all played important role in Dr. Varsha's novel, *The Book: Legend of Shivani.*

Currently she is residing in Virginia with her family. She works as a respiratory care practitioner at Inova Fairfax Hospital, Falls Church, Virginia.